I0604821

NO QUESTIONS / NO LIES

BY

JOHN B. WREN

ISBN: 978-0-9889371-9-2
No Questions / No Lies Copyright © 2024 All rights reserved.
No part of this book may be reproduced in any form without
permission.
This book is a work of fiction, the characters and events cited herein
are a fabrication and not intended to reflect any real person, place or
event. Any error or misrepresentation of fact is my fault alone.

DEDICATION

For Tanya

ACKNOWLEDGMENT

I acknowledge the counsel of editor and proofer, Tanya Besmehn. The patience of family, the access to friends—both new and old. I thank them for their help, their input, their criticism, and their praise. Without them, this book would not be.

*　　*　　*

1

Ian McLarry spent 12 years as a street cop in Pittsburgh. He took the department's test for detective and passed with a respectable grade, but still came in a few slots below the list of accepted candidates. Disappointed but not discouraged, he looked around the country for other opportunities as a detective and found a dozen openings in as many states.

While discussing several of those opportunities at a family gathering, his cousin, Colin said, "Ian, you did a few years in the corps, and we used to talk about the possibility of a Special Operations Group assignment. You're still in the reserves, you should think about a return to active duty and take a shot at that SOG."

"That's a thought," said Ian.

"Listen, I have an op tuning up this week, maybe gonna take a few weeks," said Colin. "When I get back and have some time, we should get together down at Quantico, maybe kick around the SOG thing. Ya never know 'til you've tried."

"True," returned Ian, "I'll think about it."

*   *   *

Ian considered all his options, including a return to active duty, sent out a few letters with his resume, and waited for replies. In less than a month, he had visited two of the communities that had responded to his inquiries and while keeping the idea of a return to active duty in mind, he decided to accept a position as detective in Vaneksburg, a small town in Northern Virginia where major crime was all but a bad dream.

"It ain't Pittsburgh," Ian said to Colin in a phone conversation, "but it's a step up from the streets. I get to do more of the thinking and a little less of the lifting."

"I hear you cousin," said Colin, "but I'll try to keep the door open if you change your mind."

"Thanks, Colin. How about getting together soon for dinner and a few pints?"

"Sounds good to me," returned Colin, "but I'll be going dark for a while soon. I'll give you a call when the dust settles, and we can meet up."

Keeping Colin's offer in mind and having very little to do in the small Virginia town, Ian searched for things to challenge him. "Cold cases, there must be some cold cases to review and maybe do some good," he wondered aloud. Ned Bowen, Vaneksburg's Chief of Police guided him to the basement and the old case files. "Cold cases are in row four," said Ned, "if you find one to check out, we'll talk about it."

His search turned up a 19-year-old case, the murder of a 14-year-old boy that was never solved. The resulting investigation led Ian to a fifteenth-year high school reunion and a revenge plot that ended with a bombing and a single prime suspect. That individual had died, was never arrested, and never charged. All evidence collected was circumstantial. There were no witnesses, no other suspects under consideration, and thus both cases were closed, and the community returned to its normal peaceful, quiet self.

Ian was now in his second year on the job, and the *quiet* was again taking a break.

*   *   *

Vaneksburg Police Department, Vaneksburg, VA

Ian pulled the aging Crown Vic into the parking spot labeled *Detective*. He eased himself out into a gentle misting rain, balancing a paper cup with a green mermaid in one hand and a bag containing a bagel in the other. He nudged the car door closed with his knee, tasted his coffee, and briskly walked into the Vaneksburg Police Station. Shaking a few drops of rain from his hair, he noticed the clock on the wall behind the middle-aged receptionist indicated it was almost 9:45. He winked at the woman, "Good morning, Monica."

Monica tilted her head, raised an eyebrow, and replied, "Detective, Chief wants to see you immediately."

"Oh," Ian hesitated, then turned to Monica again, "immediately?"

"Yep," she smiled, "that means now."

"I'll just ..."

"Now, detective," smiled Monica. "He's in a bad mood, and he's seen coffee cups and brown bags before."

Ian nodded and went straight to Ned Bowen's office. He raised his mermaid in a mock salute as he walked through the door, "Mornin' Chief, you're looking for me?"

Ned Bowen took off his wire-framed glasses and gestured toward a chair, his delivery gruff, "Ian, we have a situation on the east side of town. A man was murdered right outside his home."

"Murdered?" said Ian with a touch of surprise.

"Yeah," Ned blustered, "two bullets to the back of his head. That ain't no suicide, and it ain't no damn accident. It's a damn murder."

Ian was tempted to say that would be his guess too, but noting the edge to Bowen's voice, he instead asked, "Did you know the victim, Chief?"

"Yes and no," replied Ned. He took a deep breath and continued, "We've met a few times, but I never had any real conversation with him and don't know much about him except what I read in the newspapers."

"Ah, a big fish," said Ian between sips of his coffee.

"Yeah, and this is our little pond," returned Ned. "He was in the import/export business, and he was suspected of dealing on the shadier side from time to time so, I expect the feds or ATF to be all over this one.

"Feds and ATF, what's their interest?'

"Recently, our victim has been the subject of a number of inquiries regarding the movement of firearms and a drug outfit in Texas or Mexico. His firm has offices in several U.S. cities with the main office in the District. He has a condo in Arlington and a home out here with a wife, two kids, land, horses, dogs, cats, the whole nine yards."

"And somebody killed him here on our turf?"

"Yeah," returned the chief, "I got a file started, not much here, just some of the basics, name, and address. You get to fill in the blanks." He handed the folder to Ian.

"Is the victim still at the scene?" asked Ian.

"It's rainin', and the techies were there long enough to photo the victim and the immediate area, do a search for a weapon and interview some of the neighbors. They're still there controlling the scene and looking for anything interesting."

"The body, is it still at the scene?"

"Bill Aikins is on the scene, waiting for you. He said he was waiting for you to determine when to transport the body," replied Chief Bowen, "he leaned back in his chair, "The state medical examiner will determine where he wants the body, most likely Manassas but for now, our victim can be held in the Vaneksburg Hospital morgue."

Ian looked at the name listed in the file, *Millington, James Denton.* "Okay Chief, I'm on it." He started toward the door and added, "I have two other ..."

Ned cut him off, "Everything else goes in the backseat—including your personal life. We need answers ASAP, and like I said, the feds or ATF will be in on this." Ned picked up his glasses, "You remember the feds, Ian. Those fellas you were ready to kill a year ago when they got in your way?"

"Understood Chief, I'll play nice."

"I don't care about nice. I care about answers," grumbled Ned. "If you ruffle a few feathers or step on some toes, I don't care, as long as we get answers, but don't break any bones, understand?"

Ian got the message, went to his desk and called Bill Aikins. "Bill, what's the situation?"

"We have the vic covered with a tarp, waiting for direction."

"You've had the scene photo'd and searched thoroughly," said Ian, "so I'll check with the ME's office, ask if we should keep him at the scene or transport him to the Vaneksburg Hospital Morgue."

"The rain is getting heavier," said Bill, "I think the hospital morgue is the best thing to do."

"I'll get back to ya in a few minutes."

Ian called the state medical examiner's office in Manassas.

"We have a load of work stacked up," said the ME. "I'd appreciate it if you could do a photo shoot and video everything and search the area for trace, anything interesting. I'll call you when we have a crew ready to come get the victim, hopefully by tomorrow."

"You sure our guys can handle the scene?" asked Ian.

"Yes, as you may remember we have worked with your guys before. They did a damn good job at that barn bombing a year or so ago."

Ian called Bill at the scene, "You can let the ambulance pick him up. The M.E. will try to get to us tomorrow."

"We'll have him there in less than an hour."

Ian looked in the chief's office, "Things are moving forward, chief."

"Come on in and bring me up to speed," said Ned.

Ian briefed the chief and hurried out to the reception area, "Monica, I'm on my way to the hospital, then I'll run over to the Millington house, somewhere east of town," he glanced at the half-open file, "Barnstable Drive. Thank God for GPS." He closed the file and shrugged, "I'll be back here this afternoon." As he continued toward the door, he took a final gulp of coffee and dropped the mermaid in the trash.

The trip to the hospital only took a few minutes; he pulled into the parking lot a few seconds before 11:00 a.m.

*   *   *

Vaneksburg Hospital, Vaneksburg, VA

Vaneksburg Hospital was fairly new, only in operation a few years, and had a number of trendy features; large, tinted windows, electronic signage, an internet café, a gift shop, a coffee bar and a few bold architectural features at the main entrance. The morgue was accessed at the rear of the building to the left of the loading docks and maintenance shops. Ian parked in a slot designated for police and wandered into the office. He saw a familiar face and tapped on the glass door.

A tall, athletic man in a white lab coat waved him in, "Hey Ian, good morning." The two men shook hands, "I think I know what brings you here today," said Dr. Jeff Marshall.

"Good morning, Jeff," Ian opened the file folder and said, "Millington, James D."

"Yeah, I just checked him in, ran a quick external exam and found him an open locker. I guess we have him until the M.E. comes to get him. They'll want to do the autopsy, so I just noted a few basic bits," said Jeff as he led Ian down a hall to the autopsy lab. "In here," he said. He went to the adjacent refrigerated room and opened a locker drawer, pulled out the tray and Ian saw Mr. Millington covered with a white sheet.

"Height; 6'-0" even. Weight; 187 pounds. Age; 50ish," said Jeff, looking at a clipboard.

Ian entered the same information on his form, "Cause of death?"

"Most likely the bullet wound in the back of his head. Entry wound here," he said as he turned the victim's head, "but no exit, so bullet not recovered yet. The apparent trajectory and powder burns indicate an upward path angle of about 20 degrees and close, like within three or four feet."

"Probable height of the shooter?" asked Ian.

Jeff continued, "We'll let the M.E. run all the calcs, but I think it'll come in around 5'8" to 5'10". Second bullet wound also in the back of the head, again entry and no exit, bullet not recovered yet." He looked at Ian, "I think Mr. Millington was down, and the second shot entered at an angle of about 45 degrees."

"Anything else?"

"Yeah, no defensive wounds or bruising that I could see. Like he turned his back and boom, he was down."

"Time of death?" quizzed Ian.

"I have it figured about 6:45 this morning, plus or minus a nickel or a dime," replied Jeff.

"Early," said Ian.

"Yeah, he was wearing clothes appropriate for a run. Tee-shirt, baseball cap, shorts, running shoes," said Jeff as he pulled back the sheet.

"Had he had his run or was he getting started?" asked Ian.

Jeff raised his eyebrows, "Based on the time of day, I think he was in the process of loosening up but again, that's the M.E.'s call."

"Which was the kill shot?" asked Ian.

"I'm sure it was the first and the second was insurance," said Jeff, "but, again, we'll let the Medical Examiner list the official numbers and cause."

"Professional?" mumbled Ian, "Or somebody who watches TV?"

"Yeah, who knows?" said Jeff, as he held the sheet.

Ian scanned the body, and Jeff said, "His hat, watch, ring, sunglasses and a twenty-dollar bill he had have been bagged and tagged. That kinda' rules out robbery."

"A twenty-dollar bill?" quizzed Ian.

"Yeah, and sunglasses," returned Jeff. "Like he was prepared to make a stop at a coffee shop if the rain got to be too much and he'd finish his run when the sun came out."

"Anything else?" Ian asked.

"Nope, that's it. Unless he had something else that the shooter may have taken."

"Okay, Jeff. When will the state kids come get our friend here?"

Jeff looked at a clock on the wall, "The sooner, the better, we were notified before Millington was brought in, it may be a day or two."

"They'll take him to Manassas," said Ian. "Thanks, I'll probably be back with more questions later."

"Any time," said Jeff as he covered the body and slid the tray back into the refrigerator. "I'm here all day."

*   *   *

2

Barnstable Road, Vaneksburg, VA

Ian got back in his Crown Vic and entered the Barnstable address in his GPS. The drive would take about twenty minutes in the morning rush hour with traffic heading east toward the Nation's Capital. As he started to drive out of the hospital grounds, his phone buzzed.

"Good morning, Cousin," said Colin, "I have a few days off so, how about dinner at the Auld Shebeen tonight?"

"Sounds good to me," returned Ian, "I can be there by eight."

"That works," said Colin.

"I'm in traffic, Cousin, see you this evening."

His GPS took him to a neighborhood set in gently rolling terrain, with a wealth of tall, old oak and sycamore trees bordering the winding roads. He drove past a series of mansions on lots that were in the five to ten-acre range.

Millington's house was set atop a rise, nearly two hundred feet back from the street. The property lines were identifiable with polite fencing, trees, flowerbeds, and bushes. A football field could have been laid out between the houses on both sides, all one hundred yards plus the end zones.

Bill Aikins held a large green and white umbrella and stood at the end of the driveway, next to a grove of bushes and four short pylons wrapped in yellow crime scene tape that surrounded a blue tarp on the ground. Two parked squad cars ensured no outside access to the scene. "Good morning, Ian," said Bill, "where do you want to start?"

"I got a few things from the hospital," said Ian as he ducked under Bill's umbrella, "name, height, weight, eyes, hair, the basics." He quickly scanned the neighborhood, "Nice house, big lot, what did this guy do?"

"The name of his company is Millington Imports & Exports," said Bill, "looks like he was doing alright. What else can I tell you?"

"You tell me what you know, Bill, then I'll have questions."

"Okay, first, you know Millington's body has been taken to Vaneksburg Hospital. It was raining, and we didn't want to lose any trace, so after the techies had their time on scene, and he was transported, we covered the space where he was with a tarp. We have four more cars blocking the street at the next intersections. The Doc may look at him and have more for us to do here. The CSI guy got way more photos than we need of the scene, and we taped it off. We've checked the bushes and walked the area from here to across the street and at least 50 feet in every direction and we're expanding that perimeter to 75 feet, still looking around but, haven't found a weapon or any brass, so it's my guess the perp kept the gun and picked up his brass or used a revolver. The man's wife found him. She's up in the house, pretty shook up. They have two kids, high school age, they're up there too. We haven't pestered them, that's your job, but we started a scan of the neighbors." Bill looked around and continued, "Of course, these houses are hundreds of feet apart, trees are everywhere. Nobody saw or heard anything. Mrs. Millington was sitting in their kitchen when her husband left for his run. She thought she heard something like a firecracker, wasn't sure, then heard it again. She looked out the kitchen window," he stepped to the side of a stand of bushes and gestured toward the house, "that's just over 180 feet away. She didn't see anything and decided to walk out and check. Found her husband right there," said Bill, pointing at the four short orange pylons spread about eight feet apart in a rectangle and the tarp on the wet pavement. "Didn't see anyone, didn't see a car, bike, nothing."

"So, did you ask how long between hearing the shots and getting down here to see her husband?" asked Ian.

"Yeah, I was just about to do that," said Bill. "I wondered what a good answer might be, so I walked up to the house, stood on the porch, and hit the timer on my cellphone. Imagined I was in the kitchen, made like I heard something and looked out the window. Then I woulda stepped outside, paused on the front porch with a cup of coffee in one hand and an umbrella in the other, come down the steps, and walk over to the drive, then down to where I coulda seen him on the ground."

Ian made a few notes and looked at Bill, "Okay, then what?"

"Then I figured she probably went straight to him without looking around, knelt, dropped the umbrella and coffee mug, and tried to make him do something, anything. Probably went right into shock when she realized she was looking at two holes in his head."

Ian made another note, "Okay, then?"

"That's probably when she screamed, and the kid heard her. He comes outside and runs down the drive, about halfway. She sees him and tells him to call 911. My little calc has it about 90 seconds since the shots were fired, and she's still not looking for the perp. She's probably hoping her husband is going to be all right."

"With two holes in his head?" mumbled Ian.

"Yeah," said Bill. "She's probably never seen anything like that before. By the time I got here, it had sunk in."

"How long did it take you to get here?" asked Ian.

"I was up near 66, on my way into the station when the call came in. I answered it at 6:55 and got here within six minutes. EMT was right on my heels coming down Barnstable. We noted the time of arrival as 7:01am."

Ian looked at Bill, "So, the perp has 90 seconds to get outta' sight." He looked up and down the street, turned to Bill, "Start your timer again and stop when I'm outta sight."

Bill started his timer and nodded. Ian stood over the outline of the victim and mimed firing two shots. He paused for a second, turned toward the nearest natural cover and began to walk at a slightly hurried pace. When he was out of Bill's line of sight, Bill hit the stop on his phone. He whistled to Ian.

"I got 74 seconds, Ian."

Ian looked around and stopped cold, "He was prepping for an early morning run, right?"

"Yeah, it looks that way," said Bill.

"So, someone else already in mid-jog, passing by, wouldn't raise an eyebrow?" pondered Ian.

Bill looked about the winding road in both directions. "Perp coulda' had a car just down the road, waited for Millington to come out for his morning run, jog up behind him, two shots and hardly break stride."

Ian wiped the gathering mist off his forehead, "Time to talk with the family. Are they up in the house?"

"Yeah, I got them separated,' said Bill, "wife is in the living room, girl in the family room and boy on the back deck."

They walked up the driveway to the house, entered and found Julia Millington sitting quietly on a wing chair in her living room. Her eyes were red and damp, her nose a bright shade of pink and her hands wrung a tea towel. She stared at the floor, then noticed the two policemen standing in front of her. She looked up at Bill, then at Ian.

"This is Detective McLarry," began Bill. "He's in charge of this investigation."

"Are you able to tell me what happened here this morning?" asked Ian.

Julia moved to the edge of her chair, "I'll tell you what I know," she replied, "what I saw." She looked frightened as she began, "Jim had just left for his morning run."

"Just?" quizzed Ian.

"Yes, he wasn't out there more than two or three minutes," she replied.

"Did he run every day at the same time?" asked Ian.

"Almost every day," said Julia. "He had time for a longer run today because he had a lunch meeting in town at 12:30 and nothing else this morning."

"Who was he meeting for lunch?" asked Ian.

"His name is Bernard Temple," said Julia, "he's also in the import/export business. They have been talking about a merger of their firms."

"Any idea where they were going to have lunch?" asked Ian.

"I think the usually met at Garner's, in the District."

"Okay so, what happened next?"

"He couldn't have been out there more than a few minutes when I heard a noise." She paused and looked toward the window, "It wasn't that loud, then I heard it again and it seemed louder," she lowered her head. "I don't know, maybe the first one was louder." She looked confused and tears welled in her eyes again, "I'm not sure."

"That's okay, Mrs. Millington," said Ian. "What did you do when you heard the noises?"

"I, I looked out the window, the kitchen window. I didn't see Jim or anyone else." She looked worried and continued, "I went out the front door and stood on the porch. I looked up and down the street and still didn't see Jim. I thought he must have already started his run, but I wasn't sure, so I walked down the steps and looked down the street. I didn't see him, and I went farther down to look the other way. He could have gone either way and then I saw his feet, he was laying on the ground." She stopped and looked at Ian, she started to cry again and hung her head.

Ian sat down in a chair next to Julia, "We can stop and pick this up later."

"No, no," said Julia, "we should do it all now." She sat quietly for a moment and turned toward the window, "Is it still raining?"

"Yes," said Ian, "a little, it's slowing down and will probably stop soon."

She nodded, "If he had waited, just a few more minutes, maybe," she wiped a tear away and looked at Ian. "I was saying, he was laying in the street, well, more on the side of the street behind those bushes," she said as she pointed out the front window.

Ian looked and made a note in his book, "Then what did you do?"

"I don't remember exactly, but I tried to help him, I couldn't, he was gone."

"Who else was there?" Ian waited for a reaction.

Julia slowly shook her head, "Nobody, then Jimmy came down the drive and saw his dad. He said something, and I told him to call 911, get us help." She looked down again and quietly sobbed.

Ian looked at Bill, "Where are the kids?"

"Ben's keeping an eye on 'em. Jimmy is on the back deck and Elaine is in the family room, I'll go get 'em."

Ian shook his head, "No, you stay with Mrs. Millington, I'll go to the kids."

Bill pointed toward the front hall and indicated Ian should turn right, "The deck is straight ahead, and the family room is off to the left."

*   *   *

Millington House, Vaneksburg, VA

Ian turned right and saw Ben, "I got this. You go help outside." He stepped into the family room and saw Elaine sitting at the end of a sofa, wiping tears away from her eyes. "Elaine, my name is Ian McLarry, I'm a detective with the Vaneksburg Police. I'd like to ask you a few questions."

Elaine took a deep breath and responded, "Okay."

"Tell me what you remember about this morning."

"I don't know. I didn't hear any shots," said Elaine, "I heard Mom scream, and Jimmy came in the house and grabbed the phone." She looked confused and continued, "He called 911, and I heard him tell the operator that Dad was hurt and there was a lot of blood."

"Then what?"

"I don't know, I went down to Mom and saw Dad. He wasn't moving and I saw the blood on the street, a lot of blood," she said as she began to cry again.

Ian stood and walked out to the back deck where he found Jimmy sitting under an umbrella, staring out across the yard and open fields beyond. He had a stunned look, and Ian joined him at the table below the umbrella. "I'm Detective McLarry." He sat down, "I know this is a difficult time, but I have to ask you some questions."

Jimmy turned toward Ian with a blank stare.

"Can you tell me what you heard and saw this morning?" asked Ian.

"Yeah, sure," said Jimmy, "where do I begin?"

"First, relax. There are no wrong answers here. Let's go in the house and walk through your morning."

Jimmy stood up, and Ian followed him into the house. Jimmy paused by the front door and looked at Ian, "I got up, took a shower, got dressed, and came down the stairs." He thought for a moment, "Dad was by the door and said I should take the SUV to school. He was going to take his morning run and work from home until he had to go into town for a lunch meeting. Then he went outside, and I went into the kitchen." He looked at Ian, "You're a detective?"

"Yeah, I've been with the Vaneksburg PD for a few years now."

"You said your name is McLarry?"

"Yes," he answered.

Jimmy looked into Ian's eyes, "You were you in on that barn bombing a year ago." Then he turned toward the door without waiting for a reaction. "I was going to eat something and get my phone off the charger when I heard Mom scream so, I ran out to see what was going on." He opened the door and stepped out on the front porch. "I couldn't see her, so I went down the driveway. I looked across the street, at the Randall's, and saw someone in the house or behind it on the deck. You can see through the big front window, right through to the deck and into the back yard if the drapes are open."

Ian was writing in his notebook, "Randall?"

"Yeah, but they're not home. They're on vacation," said Jimmy. "I thought maybe the Randalls had come home." He paused and looked at Ian, "Then I saw Mom, she was kneeling next to Dad. I saw the blood, and Mom told me to call 911. I didn't have my phone with me, so I ran back up to the house and called 911. Elaine said something and ran outside. I followed her with the phone, but everything we did was too late. Dad was already dead." He looked to Ian, "Why would anyone want to kill my dad?"

Ian put his hand on Jimmy's shoulder and said, "I don't know, Jimmy, but I'm going to find out."

Jimmy's eyes began to tear up. He shook his head, paused, and looked at Ian again, "It wasn't the Randalls'. They always park their SUV in the driveway, and it's not there." He turned and walked back up to the house.

Bill approached Ian, "Chief Bowen called, asked if we need anything."

"Yeah," said Ian, "call him back and tell him we could use a couple more uniforms. The press will swarm this place." He looked at Bill, "The boy, Jimmy, said he saw someone through the window across the street, and nobody should be there. Family's on vacation. You and I are gonna walk over and ring the bell, get a closer look. Get Ben and anyone else not doing anything, I want a little backup on this."

"I already asked for more people. We have the street blocked off with our cars," said Bill. "Dave is taping off as much turf as he can. So, I'm ready to go with you. We knocked on their door earlier, nobody answered." Bill paused and added, "The kid never said anything about them being on vacation or seeing somebody through the windows."

"Okay," said Ian, "second time knocking, much better with the backup in case someone is there, and we'll check the back of the house as well."

$*$ $*$ $*$

Barnstable Road, Vaneksburg, VA

Two more squad cars arrived, and they blocked off the street. Bill briefed the additional uniformed officers and joined Ian heading to the Randall house. They went to the front door; rang the doorbell and there was no answer. Ian tested the door…locked. There wasn't any obvious activity inside, so Ian told two officers to stay at the front as he and the others walked across the front lawn, heading for the rear. As they passed the large front window, Ian looked through the dark interior and saw the top of an umbrella through the back window of the house.

Access to the rear was easy, no fence, no bushes, nothing blocking their way. They crossed the lawn and went up a set of three stairs to the back deck. Ian knocked on the door and announced their presence. There was no response, and he tested the door…again locked.

He turned his attention to the furniture on the deck. There were two tables, each with an umbrella and four chairs. One of the umbrellas had been raised, and a chair pulled away from the table but still under the umbrella. Ian took out his cellphone and photographed the deck, both tables, and the chairs. Then he noticed the seat of the chair moved away from the table was dry. The other three chairs at that table were damp. He touched the arms on the chair, dry. The other three chairs, wet. Standing behind the dry chair, Ian could see through a pair of sliding glass doors and the large front window to Millington's front door across the street. He photographed the chairs close-up and told Bill, "Let's get the techs over here and have them scour the deck and these chairs and the table. Perp may have sat here waiting for his opportunity to do his thing."

Ian looked through the window again. The drapes covering both the sliding glass doors and the large front window were open enough to allow a partial view of the Millington house. He squatted behind the chair, and his line of sight through the house centered on Millington's front door. He imagined seeing Jim Millington stepping out of his house, walking down to the street, and loosening up as he might have. Millington would have been visible as he stepped outside and again when he reached the street where he stretched.

"Perfect," he mumbled.

Ian looked to the right and the left, trees and bushes gave this deck privacy from adjacent neighbors. To the rear, the land rolled away down to a stream and fields of corn beyond. He stood on the deck thinking until the techs arrived. "Check the table, chairs and the way around the house to the street."

The techs nodded and set to work. Ian re-crossed the street and joined Bill in Millington's driveway. "One possible scenario is, our perp sat and watched the front door, knowing Millington is a runner and would be doing a few miles every morning. He comes out, starts to loosen up and 'El Perpo' goes around the house, comes up behind Millington and pops him twice, then circles back around the house and waits for the right time to walk away."

Bill nodded, "That's a maybe. He could have continued straight back through Randall's property, across the creek, through the cornfields and to the access road back there."

"Access road?" said Ian.

"Yeah," replied Bill. "I don't know what shape it's in, but there was an old dirt road back there that goes out to the highway."

"How far back?' asked Ian.

Bill scratched his chin, "Could be a half mile, maybe more."

One of the CSI techs approached and said, "We have a track through the damp grass, walking around the house and back here, then across the back lawn toward the cornfield."

Ian looked back toward the Randall house, "Into the cornfield?"

"Yes," returned the tech.

"Shoe size or stride?" asked Ian.

"Nothing definite," returned the tech, "I've photographed 'em around front and I'm ready to do the track to the cornfield. Looks like he left tracks both ways, but he shuffled his feet, so the tracks are messy."

Bill looked at Ian, "We'll take my car."

Bill and Ian drove back out Barnstable to Halton, turned right and a half mile down Bill turned right again on an unmarked, old dirt road. Less than a mile on the road he stopped and pointed, "The Randall place should be there, on the other side of the cornfield." They got out of the car and walked the last hundred feet to an opening in the cornfield that led toward the Randall house.

"It looks like he parked here," said Ian. "Went through the cornfield, across the stream and up to Randall's deck. Whoever this guy is, he knows the area, knew where to park, where to cut through, where to hide and wait."

They surveyed the ground and found tire tracks that could have been from that morning. "I think this character made his hit, hurried behind the Randall house, took a quick look through the windows and hightailed it through the corn field, came right back here, and drove away." He thought for a second and looked at Bill, "When you arrived at the scene, you passed the intersection at Barnstable and Halton. Did you see any other cars on Halton or Barnstable?"

Bill shook his head, "I don't recall seeing anybody, but I wasn't looking for anyone at that point."

*   *   *

Ian was back in his office finishing his report on the days activity when he noticed the time, "Seven-fifteen," he muttered as he closed the file and headed out the door.

He arrived at the restaurant a few minutes after eight and met Colin in the library, "Colin, good to see you. How have you been?"

"Busy," returned Colin, "and I hear you have a new case to occupy your time."

"Yeah, a murder," said Ian with a questioning look.

"We hear all kinds of news at Langley," said Colin.

"Do you have an interest in this murder?" quizzed Ian.

"You know the answer to that," said Colin, "ask me no questions …"

"And you'll tell me no lies," said Ian, finishing the line.

*   *   *

3

The eighth-floor offices of Temple Enterprise were busy from 9:00 a.m. through the remainder of most days. Bernard Temple usually arrived before his employees, started the coffee, and quietly read the newspaper in his office as the day ramped up.

It was 9:05 when Myra tapped on his door and entered with her notebook in hand. "Good morning, Mr. Temple," she said as she sat in a chair across from Bernie. "You have a light schedule today, a 9:45 meeting with Mr. Bardain; 12:30 lunch at Garner's with Mr. Millington, then the afternoon is open until 4:00 when you have a meeting at the Fulton Road warehouse and a conference call with the LA office." She closed her notebook, "Is there anything else I may have missed?"

Bernie folded his Wall Street Journal neatly, thinking, and replied, "Nothing comes to mind, Myra. Thank you."

Myra stood and turned to leave, "I'll be at my desk if you need anything."

Bernie's phone chirped a few minutes before his scheduled 9:45 meeting time. He lifted the phone and said, "Yes, Myra."

"Sir, Mr. Franklin is on line three."

"Thank you, I'll take it." He pushed the blinking button on his phone, "Hello, Franklin."

"The project is complete," stated the mechanical voice, "all the doors in question have been checked and secured. The final payment is due in one month."

"Thank you, Franklin," said Bernie. "Is there anything else to be done?"

"No," said Franklin, and the connection was broken.

Bernie stood, picked up a remote control, and turned on his television. He scrolled the stations until he reached a local news program, lowered the volume, and sat at his desk looking more at the television than the papers on his desk.

*   *   *

Less than an hour later, Myra tapped on Bernie's door and entered, noticing the phone back in its saddle, she spoke, "Mr. Bardain is here. Would you prefer the conference room, or shall I bring him here?"

"The conference room," replied Bernie. "Oh, Myra, please schedule a final project payment to Sandway Security at the end of the month."

Myra opened her tablet and made a note, "Yes, sir."

Bernie glanced at the television and Myra moved to the side giving him a better view of the screen.

She spoke, "George Klemper called, asking if you want him present for the LA conference call this afternoon."

"Yes, it would be good for George to join me at the warehouse. Be sure I have the offer letter for him, before I leave," said Bernie. "Is Bardain in the lobby?"

"Yes, he is."

"Good, I'll go see him, I want this to be a short meeting." He picked up his notebook, glanced out the window, said "It's a beautiful day," and walked out of his office.

Myra looked out the window toward the Washington Monument, then turned toward the door. She stopped, picked up the TV remote, watched the end of a report of a shooting in Vaneksburg and turned off the television.

*   *   *

Vaneksburg Police Department, Vaneksburg, VA

"You learn anything?" asked Ned Bowen as Ian walked to his desk.

"A few things Chief," he replied.

"Come on in and brief me," said Bowen. "I got off the phone a few minutes ago with the local press guys. Pretty soon the networks and papers from downtown will be out here, and I need an update."

They sat down in Ned's office. Ian began, "Millington, James Denton," he droned on giving Chief Bowen everything he had discovered thus far.

"Across the street, sitting on the neighbor's deck, and you couldn't see him from any other neighbor's house?" puzzled Ned.

"Right, the techies are looking for trace on the deck, around the house, and across the front and back yards," said Ian. "Millington had a lunch appointment in the District with a Bernard Temple."

"Temple, I know that name. What do you know about him?" asked Chief Bowen.

"Very little but I'll know better by day's end," replied Ian. "I plan to show up at Garner's Restaurant."

"In the District?" quizzed Ned.

"Yeah, I'll keep it above board. Remember my cousin, Lake is an MPD detective, I'm gonna ask him to join me for lunch with this Temple character."

"Okay Ian, keep me in the loop. It's gonna get touchy soon, and like I said, I want to be ready when I speak to the press."

*   *   *

Metropolitan Police Department, Washington, DC

Mike Farley was sitting in his office when Detective Lake McLarry stepped in and asked "Mike, did you hear about the shooting out in Vaneksburg?"

"Yeah, and we may get involved," replied Farley.

"Really? I just got a call from my cousin, Ian. He's on it out there and has some questions about one of our favorite people."

"Oh yeah," said Mike as he leaned back in his chair. "Like who?"

"Like Bernie Temple," said Lake.

"Come in," said Mike, "sit down and talk to me."

"The victim, James Millington has a lunch appointment with Temple today," said Lake as he looked at his notes, "Garner's Restaurant at 12:30."

"Millington, I know the name, he's a player in the import/export business, like Bernie," said Mike, "and he's into some bad stuff, again, like Bernie. Does Temple know about the shooting?"

"I don't know," said Lake. "No names have been released by Vaneksburg PD, so, he may not know anything yet."

"And your cousin has the case?" asked Mike.

"Yeah, Cousin Ian," returned Lake.

"I remember him," said Mike. "How's he doing?"

"He's good," said Lake, "he's on his way in. We'll go to Garner's, see if Bernie shows up. If he doesn't, we'll go to his office on K Street."

"Nickel says Bernie will be there," said Mike. "He's smart enough to be dumb when he should be." Mike paused then continued, "Cousin Ian, eh. I was impressed with him when we met back then. A little rough around the edges, but a good cop. Any chance he'd make the jump to the big city, see what big time cop work is like, maybe come join us here?"

Lake chuckled, "Big city? He did twelve years on the streets of Pittsburgh. He's been there and done that. He may be happier away from big city troubles."

"Yeah, well, ask him anyway," said Mike. "Ben Morrison is going to retire soon, and we'll have an open spot."

"Okay, I'll ask, but you know we have a lot of talent in our own ranks," returned Lake.

"I know, I know," said Mike, "but I liked workin' with him."

*   *   *

'M' Street, Washington, DC

Lake met Ian outside his office, and they drove over to Garner's Restaurant on K Street.

"Never been here," said Ian. "It looks too steep for my wallet."

"Mine too," chimed in Lake. "I probably couldn't afford a water in this joint."

"So, we're just visiting, no time to eat," said Ian with a grin.

"We'll find Bernie, talk a little, maybe order a glass of water to share," said Lake. "Maybe we flash our badges, and the water will be free."

"Is there anything special I should know about this guy?" asked Ian.

"What we know and what we think are worlds apart. We know this guy is into some nasty stuff, but we've never been able to pin anything on him."

"I know he's import/export but what kinda stuff do you think he's into?" asked Ian.

"He runs an import/export outfit and we're sure he has handled weapons, drugs, anything that will turn a big profit. He does it blended in with legitimate goods and the feds have never found anything in any of his stateside facilities. Our interest is in the disappearance of three people over the last twenty years."

"Have any of them ever been found?" asked Ian.

"One, a guy named Paul Weston. He wasn't in our jurisdiction. California boy. Loosely connected to Temple and he goes missing. He turned up a year later in a hole in the desert somewhere between LA and Vegas. They were competitors and the consensus is, Weston was in Bernie's way. Then he disappeared, and Bernie had one less competitor."

"Nice guy."

"Yeah, I was surprised when I first met him," said Lake. "Easy to talk to, very cooperative throughout the investigation into Weston's death, but never anything tying him to the murder."

"Standard stuff, means, motive, opportunity?" mused Ian.

"Yeah, Bernie was in Europe when the guy went missing and seemed genuinely surprised when he heard what happened to him."

"How did he get it?" asked Ian.

"Two in the head. Kinda' like your friend out in Vaneksburg," said Lake.

"And Bernie was in Europe?" asked Ian.

"Yeah, but he has minions," returned Lake. "A whole crew of questionable characters. The feds talked to a bunch of 'em. Got nothing. They couldn't shake anything loose, and it went cold."

Ian scratched his head, "So, we have our new victim about to sit for lunch with Bernard and he gets a similar send off."

"We have the feds do the ballistics and let their database look for matches. But I'd be surprised if there is one," said Lake. "Even if it is the same hitter, a pro, a cheap handgun, like a 22 gets tossed into the ocean, or dropped into a well."

*   *   *

Garners Restaurant, Washington, DC

They went into the Garner's, and Lake spotted Bernie sitting alone. Lake looked at the maître d, "We'll join Mr. Temple for a few minutes," he said as he flashed his badge.

"Yes, of course. Will you be staying for lunch?" asked the man in a tux.

"Not today, thanks," said Lake, and he led Ian across the floor to Bernie's table. "Bernie Temple, may we join you for a minute and a few questions?"

"Detective McLarry," said Bernie, "I haven't seen you in a while. What brings you to me?" Bernie appeared slightly confused, glanced at his watch, and added, "I have an appointment, and it seems my guest is running a few minutes late." He looked back at Lake. "If this will take some time, we could meet back at my office in an hour or two."

"Bernie, this is detective Ian McLarry from Vaneksburg," said Lake.

His eyes darted to Lake, then back at Ian, "McLarry, are you two related?"

"Cousins," returned Ian.

Ian sat and looked at Bernie, "When did you last speak to Mr. Millington?"

Bernie thought for a second and replied, "Tuesday, I believe in the morning. What's this all about? Is Jim alright?"

"Tuesday is the last time you spoke to Mr. Millington?"

"Yes," said Bernie. "We confirmed today's lunch meeting."

"Mr. Millington was attacked this morning. He's in Vaneksburg Hospital."

Bernie looked appropriately shocked, "Is it serious?"

"What is the nature of your meeting with Mr. Millington today," asked Ian.

Bernie looked puzzled, "We recently began talks about a merger of our companies. Today was to be a continuation of that discussion."

Ian leaned in, "Do you know of anyone who might wish to harm Mr. Millington?"

"Harm Jim? No, I mean, we're in a tough business, and this merger would make us a much bigger and tougher competitor for some of the smaller firms, but no, I can't see anyone resorting to hurting either of us for that."

"How will this affect your merger?" asked Ian.

"Well, I'll have to discuss it with Jim. Hopefully, it won't hurt the negotiations at all," said Bernie. He looked at both Detectives, "Just how serious are his injuries?"

"Mr. Millington was shot twice at close range. He has succumbed to his wounds," said Ian.

Bernie looked stunned, "You said he was in Vaneksburg Hospital."

"Yes," returned Ian, "in the morgue."

Temple acted as anyone would with the shocking news, "My God, he's dead?"

"Yes, Bernie," said Ian. "Anything you can tell us about Mr. Millington's business and your relationship would be helpful."

"I'm at a complete loss, Detective," said Bernie as his cellphone announced a call. He looked at the screen, "My office, please excuse me," he said as he answered his phone. He listened for a moment and said, "Yes, cancel the session this afternoon. I'll be back in the office shortly." He pocketed his phone, looked at the two Detectives, "What can I tell you, Jim is…was a good man. This is tragic."

Bernie appeared shocked, confused, and not very helpful. The two detectives left him to his lunch minus Millington.

"If he knew, he's a good actor. If not, he acted as you'd expect," said Lake.

"Yeah," said Ian, "If he's involved in any way, the keyword is *act*."

*   *   *

4

George Klemper was a college dropout, an army veteran, and a jack of few trades. He was best at running errands for people of questionable character and thus, had been brought in for questioning on several occasions, but never arrested. A few times he was let off because he unknowingly provided information used to capture and reel in a larger fish. On other occasions the questioning did not result in any charges and George remained clean. The MPD quietly considered him a valuable source of information, even though he never knowingly gave up anything. Each time he was picked up over the years, he was released after questioning. It was assumed by his employers that he never talked and his relationships in the dark world were maintained.

George read the newspapers religiously and could carry on an intelligent conversation with many people about as many topics. He also dressed for each occasion and was able to fit in boardrooms or barrooms with ease. Bernie found George to be a useful tool, able to perform numerous simple tasks and was considering offering him a permanent position with his firm.

*   *   *

The ATF had been watching Millington's office since the murder of Jim Millington and recognized George as a courier who had transported numerous items for Millington as well as other firms over the last several years.

"What's he up to?" mused Special Agent Craig Robins.

"Who knows, let's call it in," replied Bob Leonard.

As George was leaving Millington's offices, Bob Leonard was advised to keep Klemper in sight, "We have to follow him, could be nothing, then again, who knows?" said Leonard.

George hailed a cab near L and 21st Streets. He was dropped off at the front of Union Station, and Robins looked at Leonard, "You stay on him I'll park the car."

Leonard maintained his distance and when his phone chirped, he said, "He's at the ticket counter. Come on down."

Robins stepped off the escalator and listened to his phone again.

"Track five, I'll call it in," said Leonard after George had bought his Amtrak ticket. He was finishing his report when Robins arrived. "We're going to New York," Leonard told Robins. "We can have lunch on the way up and check-in with the New York office."

They tracked George's progress to an office building in Manhattan where The Millington Company occupied space on the sixth floor.

"We'll wait until he comes out and probably stay on him all the way back to DC," said Robins.

George was in the building for less than an hour, and when he exited, Robins and Leonard followed. "I'll call it in," said Robins. A moment later, he answered a call and said, "We'll pick him up and take him to the office."

"Federal Plaza?" asked Leonard.

"Yeah, I'll get a cab," said Robins.

Bob Leonard walked up to George, "Mister Klemper, would you accompany us to our office for a brief conversation?" he asked as he opened his badge wallet, "Just a few questions."

"Am I under arrest?" asked George.

"No sir," replied Leonard, "we just have a few questions for you."

George was accustomed to police questioning sessions. He knew this recent transport for Millington was nothing even slightly shady, so he gladly agreed to accompany the two agents.

They sat him in a conference room and plied him with coffee. He honestly answered all their questions, repeating that he was just delivering a document package that needed to be reviewed and signed as soon as possible. "I suppose the unexpected demise of Mr. Millington has caused a degree of reorganization, and each branch office will be similarly visited with documentation requiring signatures and return to the main office," explained George in his finest executive tone. "I am to return to the Washington office with this package today, so I hope this will be a quick session."

"What is the nature of these documents?" asked Robins.

"I'm afraid I'm not privy to the specific content," replied George. "The firm employs many people, and the continued operation of business is imperative," he added. "Goods must be delivered, salaries must be paid, and life goes on. I've met Mr. Millington several times, he is, or was, a good man, and I enjoyed working for him. A good fellow. But as I said, life goes on."

"What do you do for Millington?" asked Leonard.

"This is what I do, gentlemen," George reiterated. "I carry sensitive documents to various locations around the country and sometimes abroad, when necessary," he boasted. "I was a bonded courier for years, and now I specialize in documents. Firms like Millington's trust me and depend on me to take proper care of their materials."

They continued to quiz him for half an hour about other such trips and the deliveries he had made over the last year and others he may be making in the future.

"Not enough to hold this bozo any longer," stated Robins. "We're gonna have to let him walk."

"Ya know, Craig, since he also does runs for our friend, Bernie Temple back in DC, and since we have him in our house, we might ask him a few more questions," said Leonard. "They've both been using him more frequently lately, and any info we can pick up could prove useful."

"Anything's worth a shot," replied Robins.

They asked George specifically about working with Temple Enterprise, including activity at the Fulton Road warehouse. George had nothing to offer, he actually knew less than they thought, and since he couldn't shed any new light into their dark corners, they ended the interview and offered to give him a ride to Penn Station. George declined the offer of a free ride and walked three blocks from Federal Plaza before hailing a cab. He caught the Acela Express back to Washington and went straight to Millington's Office.

Robins and Leonard caught the next train home. "So, what did we get from our friend, George?" posed Leonard. "He mentioned something about possibly going to other offices within the Millington organization, but nothing about Temple."

Robins leaned back in his seat, closed his eyes, and summed up the interview, "We took a shot and got nothing, so, maybe we're asking the wrong questions."

Leonard watched the lights outside as the train made its way south and Robins fell asleep.

When the train pulled into Union Station, Robins woke, and the two men walked to the escalators leading to the parking garage. "We'll put all we gained today on the table tomorrow and see what happens next," said Leonard.

*   *   *

ATF Field office, Washington, DC

Several people piled into the conference room, including Leonard and Robins. At the head of the table, Special Agent Al Grandison, opened the conversation, "This Friday, we'll conduct a search of Temple Enterprise's warehouse in Virginia."

"The Fulton Road address," added another agent.

Grandison nodded and continued, "Everything we've learned from our sources point to a series of shipments from Germany, labeled 'machine parts,' that will contain various weapons parts as well. We don't know which shipments or what weapons parts there may be, but we have it from several different sources, and there is a shipment coming in this week that fits the bill."

"We're gonna need a search warrant," said Robins.

Grandison grinned, "It's in the works. We should have everything ready to go on Thursday or Friday morning at the latest."

"Will the shipment still be there on Thursday?" asked Leonard.

"The way we understand it, the shipment is opened, the illegal parts are removed, and other bits are added to keep the weight the same," said Grandison. "Then the weapons are repackaged and shipped out to their final stateside destination. What happens beyond that, we don't yet know."

"So, they remove metal and add metal," said Robins. "Not like drugs that a dog could sniff out. How do we know which parts are machine and which are weapons?"

"We'll have a couple of weapons techs with us," said Grandison. "They'll look at everything, and we'll depend on their judgement on any questionable items."

Robins nodded and Leonard inquired, "Thursday, early or late?"

"If it gets past noon, we'll put it off 'til the morning," responded Grandison.

*   *   *

Fulton Road Warehouse, Springfield, VA

Bernie wanted to clear his schedule to allow for Jim Millington's funeral on Thursday, so he arrived early at the Fulton Road warehouse to discuss a shipment with his warehouse manager, Dave Saunders. As they were talking, George approached.

"Bernie, I have to tell you, I carried a package of documents to New York for Millington, yesterday and a couple of feds followed me. They took me to Federal Plaza and questioned me for the better part of an hour." He smiled, "The package was just some sensitive contract documents that needed to be signed and returned to Millington's DC office quickly. It was nothing the feds should have been interested in, but they questioned me anyway."

Bernie wondered why George was telling him about Millington's business and waited for the other shoe to drop.

"Then, when they finished asking me about things at Millington's, they started in on Temple Enterprise," he said. "I told them nothing of any consequence, and I was finally let go after a while." George waited for a reaction from Bernie and added, "I thought you should know."

Bernie thought about the shipment of "machine parts," the Millington murder, and wondered if George knew anything of consequence. He looked at George, "I wonder why they questioned you,

George." He paused, "Well, no worries, nothing to tell, nothing to fret over," he smiled.

"George, I have a package I was going to deliver myself to a very important client in Cleveland. Jim's funeral has changed everything, and I'd like you to deliver for me."

George liked being given important tasks, "Of course, Mr. Temple. What is the package?"

"It's several paper items, copies of wills, and a family heirloom which we brought over from London for a Mr. Corydon." Bernie touched George's arm, "I want Mr. Corydon to know we'll give him and his shipments special attention. I think you're best suited to convey that message since I can't be there." Bernie walked George toward the door, "Go to the office and see Myra. She'll have the package and make all the travel arrangements. You'll go up tomorrow morning and be back in time for dinner."

Bernie watched George walk out, then turned to Dave, "The feds may know something. I want the shipment out as soon as possible. Can it move today?"

"We have a truck scheduled tomorrow to LA," said Dave. "I'll check, maybe we could switch loads."

"When is the next load due?" asked Bernie.

Dave scanned through a few pages on his monitor, "Next Tuesday," he continued to look at the monitor. "We could redirect that load to KC on Tuesday, move it to LA on Thursday then, assemble everything there."

Bernie thought for a moment, "Yes, let's plan on that. Meanwhile, I'm going to find an offsite location in LA where we can assemble all the parts and repackage them away from our warehouse." He looked at Dave, "Make it happen. The sooner, the better. Tell the driver to leave tonight. Just get it out of here."

Dave nodded and reached for his cellphone, "I'll check on the truck now."

*   *   *

George flew up the following morning, his nose in a book for most of the flight. Upon arrival, he headed to Shaker Square to hand off the package, grabbed lunch with his contact and caught a flight back to Washington.

Just another day in the life of a glorified courier.

*   *   *

5

Fulton Road Warehouse, Springfield, VA

The FBI arrived with the search warrant for the Fulton Road warehouse at 7:30 Friday morning. Dave Saunders met them at the main gate and instructed his people to cooperate fully with the agents and he immediately called Bernie, "We're being visited again, and they have a search warrant."

"Can you tell me what it is you're looking for, perhaps we can move this process along," Dave asked Bob Leonard.

Leonard pointed at the warrant and said, "Machine parts, we're looking for parts that came out of Germany."

Dave shrugged and said, "There have been several recent shipments from Germany and, I believe, several more due in here this week or next. I'll check the schedule." He casually scanned the monitor and turned to Bob, "The next shipment is currently being offloaded in Baltimore, and as soon as it has cleared customs, it will be delivered here. The clearing process sometimes gets bogged down, so we allow an extra day or two in our scheduling." He again checked the terminal, "We have the shipment scheduled to leave for California on Friday the 19th, but that date is not cast in concrete, we can change as conditions change."

"When was the last shipment from Germany?" asked Leonard.

"We have four containers that came in the other day."

"Let's look at them," said Leonard.

"Sure," returned Dave, "they're in our secured area." He led Leonard and several of the FBI team through a door with a number lock. He logged into another terminal and scanned a few screens, then punched a few numbers into his cellphone. "Nate, bring a lift truck to secured. We have to move a few crates."

Leonard was looking impatient and asked where the containers were.

Dave walked down an aisle and pointed toward the top of a stack, "There, no problem, Nate will be here in a minute."

Nate arrived with the forklift and moved four crates down from their stored locations, set them in an open area. Dave instructed his workers to open them. As several of the items were removed from the crates, Dave made a point of looking at each one and telling the Federal Agents, "Please be careful, these parts have been machined to a very close tolerance, and even a little ding or scratch could send it to the recycle bin." He watched closely and as each piece was exposed and cleared by the agents. Dave had his people set them aside, "If you are finished with these pieces, I'd like my people to rewrap them and reload the containers."

The search went on for several hours, and as pieces were cleared, the warehouse team had rewrapped and repackaged them in new crates. Dave filled out an incident report and asked Bob to review and sign it. "I have to do this with every search of our warehouse, even if the authorities just walk through and don't open anything."

Leonard signed the paper and left with his team, disappointed but satisfied the weapons were not in the warehouse. "Back to surveillance and quizzing their people."

Dave smiled as he watched the agents leave, then went back to his office. He lifted the phone, "Let me speak to Mr. Temple."

"We may be visited again next week," said Dave. "They might want to see the next shipment."

Bernie said, "No problems, then. Correct?"

"Correct," returned Dave.

*   *   *

Fulton Road Warehouse, Springfield, VA

Even though the FBI came up empty, the search was too close for comfort, and Bernie wanted to know exactly what had been discussed at George Klemper's FBI interview. Thus, George was asked to join in on the Tuesday afternoon conference call with the LA office and stay for a second meeting with Bernie.

Bernie knew that information had to come from within his organization to justify a search warrant. George fit the profile, and with no other possibilities, Bernie assumed George had said something in his interview to result in the warrant. During the second session, Bernie got very little from George. It was a calm conversation, and George seemed as surprised as everyone else that a raid had been conducted.

After the meeting, George left the warehouse, Dave resumed his duties, and Bernie prepared to drive back to his K Street office with Myra.

"If you don't mind, Myra," said Bernie, "I have a few items to leave with my boat that have been in my trunk for weeks. It will be a quick stop."

"Not at all, Mr. Temple," she replied, "I rather like boats."

As the drive to the yacht progressed, Bernie continued to think about George's FBI interview. "I'm not satisfied with the answers George provided," he said to Myra. "I'm sure he has talked to the authorities, and he is now a liability. Would you please contact Franklin and tell him we have a small task for him? I want to know exactly what George relayed to the authorities."

"Certainly, Mr. Temple. Shall I adjust the monthly payment at the same time?"

"Let's wait until he sends the next invoice then we'll respond accordingly," replied Bernie.

Myra made a quick note in her steno pad and calmly looked out the window, "I'll take care of it, Mr. Temple."

*　　*　　*

Yacht Club, Alexandria, VA

The ride to the Yacht Club took them east to Route One and north toward Reagan National. Bernie parked the car, popped open the trunk, and retrieved two duffle bags, "Diving belts, these things weigh a ton," he said. "Each belt can hold forty pounds of weights, and I have four of them."

They walked to the boat and went aboard. "This is remarkable," said Myra. "It's so big. You must need a crew."

"No, not really," said Bernie, "I'll show you." He led her to the internal bridge, "I can easily handle this thing all by myself. Everything is automated, even the steering. Once out of the restricted zones and on open water, I can set a course, go to the galley, fix dinner, and this thing will stay on course."

As Bernie led Myra through the rest of his yacht, she paused several times and asked a question. At one point, she noticed a wrapper for a protein bar lying on the deck. She picked it up, and as they continued their walk through the boat, she rolled the wrapper and tied it in a knot, then as they walked through the galley, she left the wrapper in an empty trash bag. When they finished the nickel tour, Bernie checked his watch and said, "We have to get going." They returned to the car, left the parking lot, drove over the Memorial Bridge and into the District.

*   *   *

Temple Enterprise Office, Washington, DC

"I received a call from Mr. Franklin," Myra said. "He stated that he is in Oregon on another contract and won't be available for two weeks."

Bernie spun in his chair towards the window, "Have Dave Saunders meet me in Rosslyn at the coffee shop in an hour." He turned and looked at Myra, "Franklin may not want this little project, so we'll handle it internally."

"What project?" Myra asked.

"We're going to find out exactly what George Klemper divulged to the feds."

"I see," said Myra.

*   *   *

Ian, driving home received a text message, *'hey cousin, how about getting together tonight for a few pints?'*

"Colin…" muttered Ian, "I wonder what he's up to." He wrote a quick response to Colin, *'see you at 8:00 p.m. at the Auld Shebeen.'*

The first question from Colin was, "So, how's your investigation into this Millington character's murder going?"

Ian hesitated, looked at Colin and replied, "Are you curious or are you working?"

"Equal parts," said Colin, "let's leave it there for now."

*   *   *

6

Capitol Crescent Trail, Washington, DC

Detective Lake McLarry was taking an early break with a large coffee, a bagel with cream cheese and a walk along the Capital Crescent Trail near the Key Bridge. His phone disturbed the late morning solitude, bringing him to the world of reality and murder. He looked at the display on his phone, "Yeah, what's up Kat?"

Kat Murano had worked a few cases with Lake, this would be their sixth. "The water guys pulled a body from the river near the Torpedo Factory dock this morning. We got a date in an hour at the ME's office. Wanna' pick me up?"

Lake strained his neck looking south toward the Kennedy Center as he listened to Kat. "That would be around a bend or two in the river," he muttered, "I'm a mile or so up-river on the DC side." He relaxed, "Yeah, I'll swing by and get you. Give me twenty."

"Okay, Lake. I'll be out front."

Lake walked back to his car, tossed the remains of the bagel and empty coffee cup in the trash, and pointed his car towards M Street.

The two detectives arrived at the M.E.'s office about 11:30 a.m.

*   *   *

As the Medical Examiner was dictating his findings, one of the crime scene techs, Freddy Knolls, wheeled in another victim.

"Hey Doc, busy day, I gotcha' another customer. This guy was shot three times, very messy," said Freddy as he approached the aging ME. "I'll start a new folder, download the pictures from the scene and do some prelim input for ya', Doc."

"Thanks, Freddy. I'm just getting started with Mr. Klemper here."

Freddy was very bright, capable, and motivated to learn. He looked at George Klemper for a minute or two, then said, "Looks like a box cutter, a baseball bat, and a gun. What ya' think, Doc? What happened to this guy?"

"Very good, Freddy. I believe the bruising is from something thinner than a bat. Probably a broomstick. I believe this man was tortured, then executed," said Dr. Colburn. "Not a nice way to go."

"Then pitched in the river," added Freddy.

"They pulled him out near the Torpedo Factory."

Freddy looked at the body, then at Dr. Colburn, "Was he floating?"

"I believe he was, Freddy."

"I saw Detective McLarry down the hall. Is this his case?" asked Freddy.

"Yes, would you please ask the detective to come in, and I'll give him a preliminary rundown."

"Sure, Doc," said Freddy as he hurried through the doors to the vending area.

Lake was getting a taste of his fourth cup of coffee when Freddy approached. "Hey, Detective, the Doc is ready to do a preliminary run-through for you. C'mon in." Freddy saw Kat, "Good morning, Detective Murano, always a pleasure to see you."

McLarry and Murano followed Freddy into the lab area. Lake set his coffee down on an empty stainless-steel autopsy table and accepted a thin file folder from Dr. Colburn. He perused the file, looked at Dr. Colburn, and said, "Geez Doc, how long did they work on this guy before they shot him?" He handed the file to Kat.

"I'm not certain yet. It coulda' been a coupla' hours, maybe three." Dr. Colburn pulled the trauma forms from the victim's file. "These findings are all preliminary. It may take a week or more to get tox reports and some other lab work done, but these," he pointed at the form, "these cuts are the most interesting. None are very deep. These were meant to hurt, not kill. The same with the bruising, someone inflicted a lot of pain on our Mr. Klemper before they shot him."

Lake took the form and put it back in the file, "Do we have a time of death, Doc?"

"Not yet. I can estimate he was in the water for a few hours. He didn't drown. He was probably killed within a four or five-hour window before going in the water."

"Any personal belongings?" asked Kat.

"Yes, all bagged and tagged." Dr. Colburn looked at Freddy, "Could you help the detectives, Freddy?"

Always ready to get more involved in a case, Freddy eagerly led the two detectives to an adjacent room where several plastic bags were spread out on a table. "There you are, Detective," he pointed at the first bag, "The man's wallet. Everything was photographed and labeled in separate bags." He lifted a small bag with a driver's license and handed it to Lake. "George Klemper, Virginia license," he picked up another bag, "three business cards, looks like he worked for or with Temple Enterprise, import/export guys down on K Street, eighty-seven cents in his pocket, two fives and a single in his wallet, coupla' credit cards, keys and that's it."

Lake looked at Kat, "Temple, what a surprise." He walked back into the autopsy room, "thanks Doc, Kat and I will get on this one right away." He walked out of the lab. Dr. Colburn turned to Freddy, "Our new victim was shot three times?"

Freddy looked at the clipboard and replied, "Yeah, and the scene was a mess. An alley, trash everywhere. Not a robbery, guy was still wearin' his bling, cheap stuff, left green stains around his neck, and he still had money in his wallet." He pushed a gurney next to the autopsy table holding Mr. Klemper and helped Dr. Colburn transfer the victim.

*   *   *

Metropolitan Police Department, Washington, DC

"What do you know about Temple Enterprise?" Lake asked Kat.

"Only what I've heard you and your cousin talking about, the Millington murder," she replied. "I'll run Klemper through the system, see what pops up."

Lake checked his file drawer and pulled out a folder labeled *Millington, James, D.*

Kat leaned toward Lake, "I have Klemper's sheet. Seems harmless enough, a few interviews, but no charges filed, or time served. Looks like he was a delivery boy for several people, including Temple and Millington."

Lake asked, "Others as well?"

Kat scanned the monitor, "Yeah, various firms have used him as a courier. He's been picked up and questioned several times by us and recently by the feds in New York as he was leaving Millington's office in Manhattan."

"Is there a name and a number to call in New York?" asked Lake.

Kat looked at the monitor again, "Nope, not New York, Agent Bob Leonard is here in DC."

"Anything else, like why he got picked up?" asked Lake.

"Nope," said Kat.

"I'll give Leonard a call, see what he has to say," said Lake.

Lake called Bob Leonard and invited him to join in a conversation that afternoon. He then went into Mike Farley's office, "Mike, are you open this afternoon for a brainstorming session with the feds, Ian, and us?"

"Do we have something?" asked Mike.

"Nothing solid, just a lot of motion and commotion. We need a direction, a target. Something or someone to apply pressure to Bernie Temple."

"Temple, eh. This afternoon, I'm open at 3:00," said Mike.

*   *   *

7

Ian walked into the conference room, joining Lake, Kat and Mike Farley. "What's the occasion?" he asked.

"Ian, we may have a connection between one of our new cases and your Millington case," replied Mike.

Ian sat down, "Don't keep me guessing, my case has run up a blind alley. I can use anything you have."

Lake put a file on the table, "We have a victim, pulled out of the river early this morning. His name is George Klemper."

Ian scanned the table, "What's the connection?"

"Don't know specifically yet," returned Lake, "but your case, the Millington murder and our victim, Klemper both have a connection with Bernie Temple."

"How did Klemper meet his end?" asked Ian.

"He was tortured, shot and dumped in the river," said Lake.

Bob Leonard tapped on the glass door and entered the room, "Afternoon, all." He looked at Ian, "How've you been, Detective?"

Ian nodded, "Alive." He stayed at the far end of the room.

The others introduced themselves and shook hands. Lake opened the meeting.

"We have two murders, James D. Millington in Vaneksburg, Virginia on September fifth and George Klemper found floating in the Potomac on September nineteenth. We're not sure where Klemper was murdered, but he was floating in our river." He looked at Ian, "Tell us about Millington."

Ian began, "Millington, James D. Shot in front of his home in Vaneksburg on the fifth at approximately 6:45 a.m. Two .22 caliber gunshots to the back of his head. First shot killed him, the second was insurance. The victim was preparing for his morning jog when the hit occurred. The shooter knew the area and used a neighbor's house across the street to lie in wait. We think the perp sat on the neighbor's back deck where he had a view of Millington's front door and street. The shooter came up behind him, shot twice, then retreated through the neighbor's backyard, across a cornfield, and to his car parked on an old dirt road." He looked about the room, "This was a well-planned hit. The perp knew Millington's morning ritual and had scoped out the area."

"Witnesses?" puzzled Leonard, "Or security camera footage?"

"So far, none," returned Ian.

Mike looked puzzled, "You said the perp sat on the back deck and could see the front door."

"Yeah," said Ian, "there's a large window on the front of Randall's house and sliding glass doors on the back. You can see right through if the drapes on both are opened."

"So, who set the drapes?" asked Kat.

"Good question," replied Ian. "We talked to the Randalls, and they can't remember where the drapes were positioned when they left, but they are pretty sure they closed the front set before leaving."

"Any signs of B&E?" asked Mike.

"Nope," returned Ian. "No scratches at the doors, no unlocked windows, no dog doors."

"What about spare keys?" asked Bob Leonard.

"Yes," said Ian. "There is a spare in the tool shed. They kept it in a flowerpot with a second pot on top, on a shelf. Not a bad place to keep a spare, it was undisturbed."

"So, does the perp find it, let himself in the house, adjust the drapes and then return it to its hiding place?" asked Mike.

" We don't know if the perp moved the drapes, said Ian. "If he did, he'd need access to the house. A key would have been the cleanest way in and out."

"Any other keys?" asked Mike.

"The Randall's each have one," said Ian. "Their kids no longer living in the house both have keys, as well as their maid service," said Ian. "We've talked to each of them. No missing keys and no one has borrowed a key. I think it's a dead end."

"A pick?" said Lake.

"That makes more sense," said Ian, "and that's what I'm going with." He wrote a note on the whiteboard, 'KEY / PICK.'

"That's a lot of detail on two families for a hitter to gather," said Leonard. "You don't spend one day watching the neighborhood and come away with a calculated line of sight, and access to the Randall's house, knowing the Randall's are out of town, knowing Jim Millington does a morning run. This guy took his time and planned this hit out, right down to the dirt road and his getaway car. Makes me wonder if there was some inside assistance."

"Agreed," said Ian. "If we assume someone close to the victim was involved, we could explain some of the bits. The daily exercise routine, the dirt access road, the line of sight, and maybe even the key." He scanned the room, "I don't get the sense that anyone in his family or any of his neighbors had motive, at least none that I see today."

"His business," said Leonard. "We think the strongest possibility is business-related. He apparently was a very 'hands on' type and his company is now in a bit of disarray. His competitors are probably making moves to soak up his clients."

"Millington had a lunch appointment with Bernie Temple scheduled that day," said Lake. "Ian and I met Bernie at the restaurant. He seemed appropriately surprised to hear about Millington."

Ian continued, "Apparently, they had been discussing a buy-out of Millington's firm or merger of the two. Bernie implied the negotiations were in the early stages, and this incident was not advantageous to him."

"So, where does that leave us?" asked Mike.

"As of today, there are no firm suspects, no fingers pointing directly at anybody, no smoking gun, nothing," said Ian, "but this Temple character has my attention."

Lake stood, "Okay, now let's talk about our second victim, George Klemper. This morning a body was recovered from the river near the

Torpedo Factory on the Virginia side. The victim, George Klemper, had been severely beaten, cut multiple times, and finally shot before being dumped in the river probably with some kind of weights to hold him down. Sloppy job, whatever was holding him down didn't hold, and George floated. The M.E. said the cuts and bruises indicate this man was tortured for as much as three hours before being shot. As of this meeting, there are no other clues and no suspects."

"No suspects, no definitive clues," said Mike Farley, "but we have a possible connection." He looked at Lake, "Continue."

"Bernie Temple," said Lake.

"George Klemper had ties to both Millington and Temple," added Kat. "They're both import/export outfits, and George often acted as a courier for both of them. He carried smaller items like jewelry and documents. Used to be bonded when he ran for a larger company, but now, he was operating alone."

Leonard interjected, "We followed Klemper to New York on a Monday. He delivered some papers for Millington and we invited him into our office in New York for a brief, casual conversation. We asked him about Temple's operation, but he didn't have anything for us."

"As far as we know, his last trip was for Bernie Temple to Cleveland, Ohio a few days later," said Lake, "up and back the same day."

"Then he's murdered less than two weeks after that," added Kat.

"When you talked to George in New York," Ian said looking at Leonard, "you said he didn't give you anything?"

"I hate to admit it, but that's it, nothing. He couldn't give us anything on the shipment we were looking for," said Leonard.

"So, George talks to you," said Ian, "then you raid Bernie's warehouse, and a few days later, George is floating in the Potomac."

Leonard nodded and quietly said, "Yeah."

Kat opened a file and put the M.E.'s trauma report of George's wounds on the table, "This poor guy was tortured. Somebody wanted information out of him or just wanted to punish the guy."

"What could he have known or done?" asked Ian.

"It's not what he knew," said Leonard. "More than likely it's what someone thought he might have known and could have passed on to us in his 'casual conversation' in New York."

"What exactly were you looking for from George?" asked Ian.

"Temple Enterprise has been moving weapons around the world and the country. Every time we hear of a shipment, we gather as much intel as we can and go for a warrant to search the suspected shipments. This last one is a new handheld, rapid-fire weapon that supposedly makes the Uzi look tame. We were informed that the weapons were mixed in with machine parts from Germany. Probably disassembled and looking like part of some machine."

"So, perhaps Bernie Temple thinks his minion, George, told us enough to get a warrant, and we raid the warehouse," said Leonard. "But we didn't find anything."

"It's not what you did or didn't find," said Ian, "it's the fact that you searched in the first place."

"Okay," said Mike. "These two murders have threads going back to Bernie Temple but appear to be unrelated."

"Maybe," said Lake. "So, we'll take the lead on Klemper, and Ian has point on Millington. Related or not, they're close."

"Okay," said Mike. "Now, what about the same hitter doing both?"

"Millington was a professional hit. Klemper was messy. I don't think the same hitman did both," said Leonard.

Ian looked at Leonard, "Yeah, but we still have those threads to Bernie."

"And that makes me look at Bernie even closer," said Lake.

Ian nodded, "We're on the same page."

There was a moment of silence, then Mike Farley stood and said, "We're all on the same page." He looked at Lake, "You gonna talk to Temple?"

"Oh yeah," returned Lake, "soon."

Mike looked at Ian, "You goin' with him?"

"Any reason I shouldn't?" asked Ian.

"Every reason you should," said Mike.

*   *   *

The Auld Shebeen, Fairfax, Virginia

Colin and Ian sat in the library, talking. "So, how's the detective slot working for you?"

"It ain't the streets of Pittsburgh, but so far, thrilling enough for me," replied Ian.

"So tell me about this murder investigation," said Colin.

"I think it'll end up with the feds due to the interstate and international implications," said Ian.

"Well, I find it interesting on several levels," said Colin. "Maybe we can talk more about it when I get back from my next op."

"When will that be?" asked Ian.

"Can't say much," said Colin, "everything is up in the air, we're trying to find the right window of opportunity to move forward."

*   *   *

Later that night Colin checked the family website and learned of his cousin Jessica's death from an overdose of a designer drug. He called Jake on a secure line, "Jake, since we have a little downtime, I'd like to take a look into this drug thing that killed Jessica."

"I didn't know Jess all that well, but I was thinking about doing the same thing," returned Jake. "She apparently was with a friend, a Declan Carson when they somehow got the drugs. She's just out of high school and he was a student, first year at university. Now they're both dead."

"I'll start with that," said Colin, "and see where it takes me."

"Keep me in the loop," said Jake.

"You're on," said Colin. "I may get answers that I don't like and want to do something … something quiet."

"Okay, just remember, we're on family time, not the agency's," said Jake, "so don't make too much noise."

*   *   *

A few weeks later Colin was back in Jakes office. "It looks like we have a connection between the source of the drugs that killed our cousin and a possible buyer of the weapons coming from Europe."

"And who's in the middle of this? None other than our friend, Bernie Temple."

"I'd like to get into this right away, but you had another dark project for me?" said Colin with a question.

"Yeah, and this one will require your team fully prepped," said Jake. "Once again this is on the quiet side, and you can get back to Temple when you return."

"Is it tied to Temple?"

"No, this is a stand-alone project your team is perfect for. The Temple thing is growing some greater interest due in part to the drug problem we touched on recently."

*   *   *

8

Temple Enterprise, Washington, DC

The fourth Monday in September was cool in the morning and rose to the 70's in the afternoon. "A perfect day to hike around the links," said Lake as he and Ian approached Temple's offices on K Street.

"When I was a caddy, we call it cow pasture pool," said Ian. "I never got the thrill of it, walking around, chasing a little white ball. Saw too many guys lose it because he couldn't hit the damn thing 300 yards."

Lake laughed, "So, what's your game? Football?"

"I played a little, but hockey is my sport," returned Ian.

As they entered the building, Lake checked the directory and found the elevators. They got off on the eighth floor and went through a pair of glass doors labeled *Temple Enterprise* into a large reception area. The walls were decorated with paintings of cities around the world. Pricey vases and statuettes adorned the tables and shelves, each worthy of placement in a museum. There was a plush leather seating area for guests and a large rosewood desk with a computer monitor, a keyboard, a notepad, several file folders, a protein bar, and the wrapper for a second bar, tied in a knot. The person seated at the desk was a tall, slim, young woman in a Brooks Brothers suit. She stood as the two detectives entered, recognizing Lake, she said, "Good afternoon, may I help you?"

Lake opened his wallet, displaying his shield, "We would like to speak to someone about one of your employees," he looked at the nameplate on the desk that read, 'Myra Wallace,' "Ms. Wallace."

She smiled and said, "I will tell Mr. Temple that you are here, gentlemen. May I tell him your names?"

"Detective McLarry, MPD," responded Lake.

Ian opened his badge wallet, "Detective McLarry, Vaneksburg PD.

"May I ask which of our employees this involves?"

Lake thought for a second, "Yes, George Klemper."

Myra nodded and said, "Please have a seat, and I'll let Mr. Temple know you are here." She extended her hand toward the leather seating, turned, walked down a corridor, and disappeared.

Ian looked at Lake, "Not bad, eh cousin?"

"What, the room or the dame?" said Lake.

Ian shook his head and raised an eyebrow, "Yeah."

They waited a few minutes, and Myra returned, "Mr. Temple was not expecting you. He will finish his current business in a few minutes then see you. Do you know how long this will take? I can reschedule his next appointment."

"Not long," replied Ian. "Fifteen, maybe twenty minutes."

The wait was shorter than they expected and Myra led them down a corridor to Temple's office. As they walked, Lake filled his eyes with Myra's hips moving in front of him, and he never noticed the camera at the ceiling. Ian looked up and saw the dark glass bubble.

Bernie observed the detectives on his monitor. He grinned at Lake's eyes on Myra, and then he saw Ian and wondered if Ian knew he was being watched. He clicked back to a view of the company lobby as Myra led the two detectives into his office.

"Welcome, Detectives," said Bernie, "please come in and sit," Temple gestured toward a seating area to the right of his desk. Similar to the reception area, Bernie's office was decorated with expensive statues and paintings.

Myra handed Bernie a folder, "Mr. Klemper's personnel file."

"Thank you, Myra," he said to the woman and turned back toward the detectives. "How may I be of help to you this morning?"

Lake said, "George Klemper, he is one of your employees?"

Temple paused for a second, "Yes, he's one of our part-time people."

Ian asked, "When is the last time you saw Mr. Klemper?"

Temple paused, "Well, let me think, I saw him last Tuesday at the warehouse." He paused, looked at each detective, "Is he in some trouble?

Is he hurt? I know he has some history with the police, but he is a good man."

Lake asked, "Is he in good standing with you and your people?"

Temple looked surprised, "As far as I know, yes. He does part-time work with us, he has been very reliable, and we've been using him so much that I want him on full time. What is your interest in him? If he needs a lawyer, I can certainly arrange that."

Lake continued, "No, he is not in trouble. He's dead."

Again, Temple looked surprised, hesitated for a moment, then said, "Dead, oh my, I'm sorry to hear that," he paused, then continued, "I don't know his family. I don't know if he had anybody." He paused again, "How did he die? He seemed to be in reasonable health when I last saw him."

Ian posed the next question, "Do you know anyone who may have wanted to hurt him?"

Temple answered quickly, "No, he's not a confrontational person, he's a good worker, gets along very well with clients and the others on our staff."

Lake leaned forward, "The FBI obtained a search warrant a few weeks ago to enter one of your warehouses and look around. Do you recall that?"

"Yes, of course, I do," replied Temple with a smile. "We are in the import/export business. There was a suspicion that some form of contraband may have been included in a shipment from Germany. We are constantly watched and inspected. It's part of doing business."

"Then why was a warrant necessary?" asked Ian.

"You would have to ask the FBI, Detective. But once again, we have nothing to hide."

"So, the search was not a problem for you?" asked Ian.

"No, not really," returned Bernie, "oh, I try to have one of our legal team and our security team present when you search. As I said, keeps it all above board."

Lake said, "We thought you might have assumed Mr. Klemper's interview with the FBI might have inspired the search."

"Yes, I recall George telling me he had a conversation with the FBI while he was in New York. I don't know what he may have said to them that would have inspired a search of our warehouse." returned Bernie. "There's nothing to hide or keep secret unless you might be referring to our secured storage or confidential transport of documents." Bernie looked thoughtful, "George did carry confidential papers for various clients, but never anything illegal."

"He was carrying documents for the Millington firm when he traveled to New York," said Ian. "Were you aware that he was working for Millington at the time?"

"Well, I didn't know until I saw him the following day at the warehouse, but that's what he has done for years. It's also why I wanted to put him on fulltime, we had so much more for him to do." Bernie seemed to drift away, "Dead, oh wow."

"We still come back to the same question," said Lake. "Someone killed George, and your company surrounds enough events to make you suspicious to us and the FBI."

Temple looked at Lake, "The FBI? Detective, why would I be on their radar? Do you think I have something to hide, or worse, something to do with George's death?"

"It is a logical assumption," replied Lake. "George is interviewed by the feds, your warehouse is searched, and George is pulled from the river, dead."

Temple sat up straight, "The river, he was in the river?"

"Yes, he was found near the Torpedo Factory."

"Oh my God, that's terrible," said Temple. "Did he fall in and drown?"

"No," said Ian. "He was murdered and then thrown in."

"Yeah," said Lake. "So, who would have killed the guy? And for what?"

"I have no idea, really, I just don't know," responded Temple. "What could he have possibly done or known that would merit someone murdering him? I have no idea."

Lake leaned back in his chair, "You do see why we came to you?"

"Am I a suspect, detective?"

"You are the most logical suspect."

"I see, I suppose you're right, I am a logical suspect, but I have nothing to hide." Bernie paused, "Poor George."

*   *   *

Fulton Road Warehouse, Springfield, VA

After the meeting, Bernie called Dave at the warehouse, "We need to talk, I'll be there as soon as I can."

Thirty-five minutes later, Bernie drove into the warehouse yard and saw Dave supervising the unloading of a truck. Bernie approached, and Dave could see his boss was not happy. His voice carried a hint of anger as they began their conversation.

"George Klemper is dead," said Bernie as he nodded toward the open yard. The two men walked away from the buildings and stopped between two trailers. "He was pulled from the river this morning."

Dave looked confused, "He was floating?"

"Apparently," returned Bernie.

"He should have stayed down, four concrete blocks."

"The blocks stayed down, the body did not … obviously, you need a lesson in knots," said Bernie. "It was a very messy job, and there are no excuses." He looked around, then continued, "He was floating near the Torpedo Factory, and now the DC Police, the feds, and a detective from Vaneksburg are all on my case."

"Vaneksburg?" said Dave.

"Yeah, Jim Millington lived in Vaneksburg."

"I had nothing to do with Millington," said Dave.

"I know, Dave," said Bernie as they walked back toward the building. "Another shipment is due in here in a few days, and the client is sending a couple of people to check it out before we send it on. The search by the feds has them a little edgy."

*   *   *

9

Metropolitan Police Department, Washington, DC

Lake wanted to know more about Temple's operation. He had a confidential informant he knew had done some part-time labor at Temple's Fulton Road warehouse. The CI's name was Jason Barrett, a small-time hustler, trying to make a fast buck any way he could. If he had a girl, he would have been a pimp. If he could score a stash, he would be a dealer. But Jason was a loser. He tried begging on a street corner and made enough to eat on a semi-regular basis. His home was in an abandoned office building in Southwest, DC, his neighbors were pigeons, rats, and bats.

"Kat, let's take a ride," said Lake. "I want to check in with one of my CI's. He may have something for us." They drove over to McPherson Square. "There he is," said Lake, "walking down 15th Street. Let's go talk to him."

Jason had a bandage around his ankle, and as he neared the square, a limp began to appear. He sat on a low stone wall, held an old coffee can, and began to smile at the people passing by. "Thank you, sir. God bless you, ma'am."

Jason saw Lake approaching, "Aw, geez Detective, you got some kinda rotten timing."

Lake sat down next to Jason and said, "I think we should have a little talk."

"C'mon, man, I'm tryin' to make a buck here," said Jason. His plea resulted in a ten-dollar bill appearing in Lake's hand.

"A buck a minute, Jason. Let's step over to the bench."

They walked to the middle of the square and sat on a park bench, "So, what does the city's super cop want from me today?"

"You know a lot of people on the streets, my friend. And I just want to talk to one of them."

"Yeah, who's that?"

"I don't know yet. That's what I want you to figure out."

"Hey, you're the cop, you should do the figurin'."

Lake pulled the ten farther away, "Let me tell you what I need, maybe it's worth more than a buck a minute. You've heard of Temple Enterprise, import/export?"

"Yeah, sure, you know I have. Now and then, they have a cleanup of their yard in Virginia, and we try to show up, free food and a twenty when we're finished."

"That's a good deal."

"Yeah, especially when you're hungry and broke."

"So, what I need is a little dirt on Bernie Temple, whatever you can gather without being obvious."

"The warehouse is in Virginia, you're a D.C. cop," said Jason.

"Yeah, and I don't fit in over there, which is why I'd like you to keep your ears open."

"Yeah, look around. I know a guy, works over there on a regular gig. Sweepin' and stuff, ya' know. He lets me know when they need a crew, and we get the food, and the bucks."

"Who's your friend?" asked Lake.

"You ain't gonna put him in jail or nothin', are ya?"

"No, just a little conversation, that's all," said Kat.

"Okay, his name is Ross, he stays at someplace in Virginia, down near Fullerton. Near the warehouse."

"What's Ross' last name?" asked Kat.

"I dunno, but I got a number to call him at."

"Can you get him over here?" asked Lake.

"Yeah, they finish around three in the afternoon. If there's a copula' bucks in it, he'd probably come over tonight."

"If the info is good, there's fifty in it. You can split it any way you want."

Jason took a flip phone out of his pocket and punched in a series of numbers.

*   *   *

McPherson Square, Washington, DC

Ross met Jason on the square near the stairs to the Metro, just after 6:00 p.m. The two of them sat on a bench, waiting in the center of the square. Lake and Kat arrived and found them talking, laughing, and smoking funny cigarettes. Jason saw Lake walking across the square and elbowed his friend as he dumped the last of his joint, "Fifty bucks, man, fifty."

Ross sat up straight, trying to look as respectable as possible. Lake looked at Jason and said, "What have we here?"

"We just sittin' here waitin' on you and your friend," he said, looking at Kat. "This here is Ross," he continued, putting his hand on Ross' shoulder. "We go back a few years. He works at the warehouse we talked about." Jason paused, hoping to see the fifty bucks, and watched Lake's hands.

Lake looked around at the other people in the square, then back at Ross. "So, Ross, you work for Bernie Temple?"

Ross fidgeted, grinned, and said, "Yeah, kinda part-time, ya know. Sometimes I get a whole week in, and the money is okay, usually I get maybe three days a week in, ya know."

Kat stepped a little closer, "Ross, what's your last name?"

Ross looked confused, "Ross, that's my name, Andy Ross."

Lake looked at Jason, Jason rolled his eyes, he didn't know.

Kat made a note in her notebook, "And what does Andy Ross do for Temple Enterprise?"

"I sweep mostly in the yard. They bust up a lotta crates, and I clean up the mess, ya know."

Lake walked behind the bench, leaned on the back and said, "Ross, you know what I would like to hear, I'd like to hear about anything going on at the warehouse that shouldn't be going on, ya know?"

"Yeah," said Jason, "like when they roughed up that guy a few weeks back."

Ross nodded his head, "Yeah."

Lake came around in front of the two, "Whatta ya mean, roughed up?"

Ross looked concerned, "Ya know, he done somethin' stupid or maybe told somebody somethin' he shouldn't of…"

"And this guy?" started Kat.

"Jimmy, I dunno his whole name, he works inside. I dunno what he does, but I think he does it better now, cause now he looks happy, and they don't yell at him no more, ya know."

"So, Jimmy didn't get killed, he's alive and still working for Temple?" asked Kat.

"Yeah, I seen him this mornin', he was talkin' to some other guys."

Lake thought for a moment, "Do they rough guys up a lot, like every day?"

Both Ross and Jason shook their heads, "Naw, just sometimes, not a lot," said Jason, "not when I'm there." he looked at Ross.

"Yeah, not a lot, ya know."

Kat asked Ross, "How long have you worked at the warehouse?"

"Coupla' years, maybe four or five, ya know," replied Ross.

Lake looked at Kat and asked Ross, "Do you know a guy named George Klemper?"

Ross looked worried again, paused, then said, "George, yeah, he's a nice guy." He hesitated, "But I think he pissed off the boss, ya know. And now he's gone."

"Gone?" said Kat.

"Yeah, I ain't seen him in a couple of weeks. I guess he got fired, ya know," said Ross.

"Why do you think he pissed off the boss?" asked Lake.

"They were yellin' at him, and the boss was there that day. He was maybe yellin' too, ya know."

"Did you see anybody hit him?" asked Kat.

"Like rough him up some?" added Lake.

"No, I heard them yellin', and I went over to the other side to sweep up. Where I couldn't hear nuthin', ya know."

"And you never saw him again?" said Kat.

"George? No. Never seen him again," he replied, looking lost.

Lake thought for a minute, "Listen Andy ..."

"Ross, everybody calls me Ross."

"Yeah, Ross, I think it best we don't talk about this to anybody. We wouldn't want to get those guys pissed off at you, now, would we?"

"No, no way man," he replied with a smile.

"So, we don't talk about this, right?" persisted Kat.

"Yeah, I mean, no, we don't talk to nobody, nobody, ya know."

*   *   *

Temple Enterprise, Washington, DC

Myra informed Bernie that two gentlemen from California had arrived at National Airport and would be at the warehouse by 10:30 a.m. They were there to inspect a shipment from Germany prior to it being sent on to Los Angeles.

"Thanks, Myra, I may drive over a little early and meet these two before our afternoon meeting." He went back into his office and called Dave.

"Our client in California is sending a couple of people to check out this latest shipment. I believe there are six crates of 'machine parts,' and they should all be here today. We should keep them in secure storage until our visitors arrive and check them out."

"Okay, do we know who they are?" asked Dave.

Bernie looked at his cellphone, pushed a few buttons, and replied, "Yeah, it looks like Clint Marsh and Tomas Relatto."

Dave laughed and said, "I know those two, not the sharpest sticks in the pile, but if all they have to do is look at the shipment and verify the contents, I guess they can handle it."

Bernie put up his hands, "That's who the California people said Ricardo picked to look, they were probably hanging around with nothing else to do, so they were sent here."

"They're better at breaking legs and heads than verifying shipment contents," said Dave. "Do we have any idea what's really in those crates?"

Bernie knew well the phones could be tapped. "It's listed as 'machine parts,' but who knows," he said facetiously, it may be something simple like dumbbells."

Yeah, thought Dave, *dumbbells with triggers.*

*   *   *

Fulton Road Warehouse, Springfield, VA

Bernie arrived and found Dave giving two men a tour of the yard. He joined them and introduced himself, "Good morning gentlemen, I'm Bernie Temple."

"Yeah," said the taller of the two, "I'm Clint Marsh, and this is Tomas Relatto."

Bernie looked at Dave, "Have you reviewed the shipment?"

"Four of the crates have been received, and I'm having Nate move them to the secured room. Two more crates have yet to arrive."

Bernie looked unhappy, "My apologies, I had hoped they would all be here by now. I wanted this shipment out of here today."

Ross was sweeping up broken pieces of pallet and nails as the four men walked into the secured area. He seemed invisible; nobody said anything to him or even looked in his direction as they passed. Ross ambled closer to the building, and he heard their voices but couldn't understand what was being said.

Then the large overhead door began to close, and Nate walked out of the building. He saw Ross and said, "Hey you, there's another mess in section 4. As soon as you finish here, take care of that one."

Ross nodded and continued his sweeping. After finishing his shift, he was walking toward the gate when Dave called out, "Anybody want a coupla' more hours tonight? I got a cleanup in secured storage."

Ross raised his hand, "Yeah, I'll do it."

Dave waved him back in and said, "This is a secured room, so somebody has to watch you as you sweep up, okay."

"Yeah, that's okay, ya know," replied Ross, "I'll clean up and get outta there, ya know."

Dave took Ross over to the building and in through a pass door to the secured area. He led Ross to the area where the crates had been opened and said, "There, clean up around those four crates and don't touch anything else." As Dave started to walk away, Tomas came in through the door. He looked at Tomas and said, "Squirrely here is gonna clean up the mess on the floor, and he's not to touch anything else, understand?"

"Yeah," returned Tomas. "What about when he's done?"

"Then you walk him over to the time clock, let him punch out, and watch him leave through the gate."

Tomas stared at Dave for a moment as he thought through Dave's words, "Yeah, okay."

*   *   *

10

Ross thought about the crates in the secured room as he walked home, "The cops want to know about that kinda stuff," he muttered to himself. "Fifty bucks, maybe more," he continued. "Yeah, I gotta call Jason." He looked at his cellphone and wondered how much money was on it. He punched in Jason's number and waited.

"Hey, Ross, what's up?" answered Jason.

"We gotta talk, man," said Ross. "I think I got somethin' else for the cops."

"Ross, we don't wanna give them junk. Only good info," said Jason.

"Yeah, yeah," said Ross. "Well, this is maybe good stuff, ya know, so, maybe it's fifty bucks for us, ya know."

"Yeah," returned Jason, "fifty bucks. I'll give the man a call. You come meet me at the Square."

"Yeah, the Square," said Ross.

"McPherson," said Jason.

"I know, McPherson Square. I'll be there in an hour."

*   *   *

Tomas joined Dave and Clint in Dave's office. The three sat talking about the next two crates due in to complete the shipment.

"We gotta look at all of 'em," said Tomas. Then they can be sent to LA."

"Do you want to open each crate?" asked Dave.

"Yeah," replied Clint. "That's what we were told to do."

"Yeah," added Tomas, "but get somebody else to clean up after. That squirrely guy is a little too nosey. He kept getting' too close and tryin' to look in the open crates. He even asked me twice what was in 'em.''

Dave wondered if maybe Ross had been passing on information to the feds. Maybe it wasn't George, maybe it was Ross. He would keep an eye on him tomorrow. If necessary, the river may be his resting place along with six concrete blocks and a better job of tying the knots.

*   *   *

McPherson Square, Washington, DC

Ross got off the train at McPherson Square and walked up to street level. He saw Jason sitting on the low stone wall with his cardboard sign and tin cup and joined him., "They got something in the secret room, ya know. I don't know what it is, but they don't let nobody near it, ya know.''

Jason looked at his friend, "Ross, don't go doin' nothin' that's gonna get you in trouble with them.''

"No, it's no trouble," said Ross. "They come got me and I was sweepin' in there after they opened the crates and I heard 'em say there was more comin' tomorrow, ya know.''

"Don't go doin' nothin'," repeated Jason. "I'll give super cop the call in the morning and see what he says.''

"I thought you was gonna call him today and we'd see him tonight, ya know.''

"Yeah, well he already went home when I called today, and I figured we should talk first, so I didn't push it. I'll call him in the mornin'.''

The two men sat on the stone wall talking about everything from baseball to women and what they'd do with fifty bucks.

*   *   *

Fulton Road Warehouse, Springfield, VA

Ross walked into the foreman's office. "Ya need any sweepin' today," he asked.

The man looked up, saw Ross, and pointed to the time clock, "Go ahead, punch in and start on Section 2 today. I think there was a spill so take a shovel and a wheelbarrow."

"Yeah, okay," said Ross. He went to the time clock, punched in, and went to work in Section 2.

A truck entered the yard at 10:15 that morning, and Dave directed it toward the storage building. Ross was finishing up in Section 2 and pushing his wheelbarrow half full of debris when Dave spotted him.

"Hey partner, you helped clean up late yesterday, right?" said Dave.

"Yeah, inside that building there, ya know," said Ross pointing at the storage building.

"Well, we're gonna need help again this afternoon, so after you dump that load, come on over."

Ross felt a little chill. He was going to score that fifty bucks. He did as he was told and returned to the storage building. The door was locked when he arrived, and he wasn't sure what to do, so he sat on a bench outside the door in view of the office window. After a few minutes, Dave came out and asked him to come in.

"We have to be careful with some of the things we move around, some of this stuff is very valuable, and people depend on us to handle it the right way. You understand that, right?"

"Oh yeah," replied Ross. "Special stuff, special treatment, ya know."

Dave rolled his eyes and led Ross across the building to the secured room where the crates were being opened. "These guys are going to be busy here for a few hours, so, I'd like you to come back here around three o'clock and clean up, they'll be done by then."

"Yeah, okay," said Ross. "I'll go back to the foreman's office and see if there's anything else for me to do."

"Listen, partner, if there's nothing else to do, you come back here and wait outside the office, and don't punch out," said Dave. "If anybody asks, you're waiting for me, understand?"

"Yeah, yeah," returned Ross.

*   *   *

Fulton Road Warehouse, Springfield, VA

Ross sat on the bench, waiting as he had been told. He was dreaming of finding some secret that the police would deem worth of more than fifty bucks when Dave broke the silence.

"Hey, partner, there you are. Come on in, and we can get started cleaning up." He led Ross through the door to the secured area, to the several open crates and said, "Look, partner, I have to call the main office, but I can trust you to not look in those crates or touch anything else but the mess on the floor, right?"

"Oh, yeah," said Ross, "I'm just here to clean up, ya know."

Dave said, "That's my man. I'll be back in a few minutes." He went to a stair and went up to the second level.

Ross started to sweep up the splinters and nails on the floor when he noticed a light turn off in the second-floor office window. He paused, noticing the window, and wondered if they were watching him. He moved closer to the crates, still sweeping, but kept his head down and resisted the temptation to look under the tarp loosely covering the crates. He kept sweeping and eventually moved his pile of debris away from the crates and started to shovel it into a container.

Dave stood in the office with Tomas and Clint, watching through the darkened window. "He's not looking at the crates," said Dave.

"Yeah, but we took all the stuff outta them two crates," said Tomas. "There ain't nothin' there for him to see but them gears."

Clint looked at Dave, smiled, and said to Tomas, "That's the whole thing, he was told not to look, and he didn't." He looked back at Dave, grinned, and said, "Tomas' strength is in other areas."

Dave went back to the main floor and found Ross dumping the trash into a larger container. "Hey partner, you finished already?"

"Yeah," said Ross, "there wasn't so much mess, ya know. I think I got it all."

Dave took a quick look around, "It looks great, you go ahead and punch out, and we'll see you tomorrow."

*   *   *

Ross was not a spy, not a trained investigator, not as clever and as quick as one should be to do what he planned on doing. He had been watched, he thought he might have been, but he wasn't sure. He thought he might be able to come back later, sneak into the building, look under the tarp, and have something for Jason and his friend, the cop.

He wandered over to the foreman's office. "I finished the clean-up in 2 and the mess in the building, ya know. You got anything else for me?"

"Yeah," returned the foreman. "Section 5 needs a little attention. You want, it's yours?"

"Yeah, sure," said Ross. "Big mess or just a push broom?"

"You push it to a pile, and I'll have a truck stop there with a shovel to pick it up."

Section 5 was at the far end of the property, remote. Ross opened his phone and called Jason. "Two big crates. I dunno what's in 'em, but they got 'em locked in a special room and said they ain't to be looked at, ya know."

Jason heard his friend and knew he was playing a dangerous game. If these guys knew he was snooping around, it could get him roughed up, get him killed. "Ross, I think we should stay away from these guys and be happy with the money we make sweepin'."

"But they have somethin' there, somethin' illegal, maybe if I looked inside the crates, I could tell ya what it was, ya know."

Jason was worried for his friend, "No Ross, don't mess with that stuff. Just come on over to the square tonight, and we'll talk to McLarry. I'll call him and tell him we'll meet him there around 7:00."

"Okay," said Ross, "I'll be there."

Ross closed his flip phone and looked toward the warehouse. He didn't see anybody, and he thought this might be his chance. He set his broom next to an outdoor storage crate went toward the building, "I'll tell 'em I gotta take a leak if they see me," he muttered to himself. The main overhead door was open, and Ross went inside. He didn't see anyone and walked over to the secured room door. He could see through the window in the door to the open area where the crates were, then, he heard a noise. He ducked behind a stack of crates and watched. Dave walked over to the secure room pass door, opened it and went inside. Then a lift truck approached the door, stopped, and Nate hit the horn. Dave peered out the pass door, waved at Nate, and went back inside. A second or two later, the overhead door began to open. Nate moved the lift truck and its load into the room, positioned it where Dave pointed, and drove out of the room.

Dave looked up at Nate, "Get the other crate with the same label and bring it over."

"Okay, Dave. You wanna lock it up 'til I get back?"

"Naw, I'll just stand here and wait for ya."

Nate went out to a waiting truck to get the other crate. Dave stood waiting at the door when his phone rang, "Yeah, I got one more to put away then I'll be done. Maybe ten minutes. Okay, okay, I'll be right up."

As he was about to close the door, the lift truck came into view, Dave waved the truck into the room and said, "I gotta run upstairs, the boss needs something, lock up when you pull out."

"Okay, Dave." He pulled into the room, and Dave disappeared up the stairs.

Ross watched. Then as the lift truck pulled out and Nate hopped off to power the overhead door down, Ross hurried into the room when the driver's back was turned and hid behind another crate. The door closed, and Nate pushed several keys on the door lock, opened the pass door, walked out, and pulled the door closed.

*   *   *

It was almost 6:00 p.m., and the workday was over, people were leaving, the watchman had punched in and started his rounds. Ross was inside the room, light filtered in through screened openings at the top of the walls allowing Ross to see where he was going. He found the crates that were 'special.' The tarp covering one of the crates was loosely tied in place. He forced it back and made more noise than he wanted. He paused, listened, heard nothing, and pulled again. Again, noise, he paused, listened—nothing. He finally had it open enough to see inside. Odd-looking packages wrapped in brown paper. He reached in and felt one. It was hard and heavy, like steel. He tried to lift it, and it fell from his hand with a loud clank.

"Oh crap, somebody coulda heard that," he muttered. "I better get outta here."

The nightwatchman was passing the secured door when Ross dropped the steel gear. He started to call the foreman's office when he saw the two California thugs approach holding nightsticks.

"Is there a problem," asked Clint.

"Yeah," said the watchman. "This room is closed, lights are out, and I heard a noise, a loud sound like a hammer hitting a piece of steel.

Dave came down the stairs, "What's the problem?"

"Dunno' Dave," said the watchman, "I heard a noise from inside the locked room. I was about to call it in, and then these two showed up. Is that okay?"

Dave nodded, "Yeah Bart, you did right. You continue on your rounds, and we'll check it out. Probably just a mouse."

Bart turned and walked away, continuing his rounds. He mumbled as he turned the corner, "Yeah, sure, or a really big rat, but it wasn't no damn mouse."

Dave cautioned the other two, "If someone is in there, I want to talk to him, understand, don't shoot him, hold him for me. Understand?"

They both nodded and showed him their nightsticks. "Don't have guns," said Clint.

Dave unlocked the pass door, and the three men walked in. Ross was hiding behind a pile of crates. Stealth was not his forte. They heard him almost immediately. Dave stood at the door, Clint went to the left of the stacks, and Tomas went right, coming up behind Ross.

The two thugs converged on Ross as he tried to run. Tomas was close enough to slow him down with his nightstick. He tried for Ross' shoulder, but poor aim and a slight stumble had Tomas connecting with Ross' head. "I got 'em," said Tomas.

Ross lay on the floor, face down. Clint came around a stack. "Roust the little squirrel," he said to Tomas. "Dave wants to talk to him."

Tomas prodded Ross with his nightstick, "Okay guy, get up," he paused, "come on, get your ass up."

Ross didn't move. Ross was dead.

Dave came around the crates and asked, "You hit him?" looking at Tomas. "I told you I wanted to talk to him."

Clint glared at Tomas, "I think you killed him."

"Hey, I didn't hit 'em that hard," said Tomas. "I didn't mean to kill 'em."

Dave looked at the two thugs and walked away. He paced back and forth for a minute and returned, "Okay, let's move him outta here. I wanna dump his body somewhere away from here. Far away from here. He knelt next to Ross and searched his pockets. He found Ross' cellphone, opened it, and checked the most recent calls. There was only one that day, less than an hour ago. He pushed the redial and waited.

Jason answered, "Ross, where are you?" He waited and heard nothing. "Are you flyin'?" He heard nothing. "I'm gonna wait another hour, and you better get here."

Dave did his best Ross imitation, "Where?"

"The square. Get on the damn train and get off at the square."

Dave thought for a minute, "M... phers..."

"Damn it, Ross, you're out of it. The cops ain't gonna believe you if yer stoned."

Dave thought again, "Yeah, comin'," and he closed the phone. He looked at the two thugs, then down at Ross.

"Let's clean this mess up."

*   *   *

Fulton Road Warehouse, Springfield, VA

Tomas bent over and moved Ross' head, "No mess, there's no blood. Hell, I said I didn't hit 'em that hard." He looked at Ross, then up at Dave, "Okay Dave, how are we gonna take care of this?"

"I have an idea," said Dave, "you two stay here and don't let anybody in the building."

Both thugs nodded and moved to the door. Dave said, "I'll get the van." He went out to a parking area as he called Bernie, letting him know what had happened. He returned in less than two minutes and backed the van into the warehouse. He pulled a box out of the van.

"Here, put on some of these latex gloves and best to double up, they tend to rip. Now help me get this guy in the van."

They lifted Ross as Dave said, "Keep him in the same position, face down."

*　　*　　*

11

Dave and the thug tag team drove to McPherson Square with Ross' body in the back of the van. He spotted Jason as he turned on to 15th Street, pulled over to the curb, and said to the two thugs, "You two wait here, I gotta get this guy in the van, and then we'll get outta here." He handed his gun to Tomas, hopped out of the van, walked up behind Jason, and surprised him, "Jason, Ross asked me to come and get you. He's been hurt."

"Ross? Is he okay?" Jason stood and looked panicky. "Is he hurt bad?"

Dave was ready, "He was in the warehouse, behind a large crate when Nate tried to move it with a forklift, and Ross' leg got caught on something. The ambulance took him to the emergency room. Doctor said he'd be okay, but he's gonna hurt for a while. We gotta go."

Jason was confused. He saw Dave's hands and asked, "Why you wearin' rubber gloves?"

As Dave had been talking, he was also moving Jason closer to the van. "They gave them to me in the hospital. There are more in the van for you too." The van side door opened, Dave rushed Jason in and closed the door.

Across the square, Lake and Kat had just arrived to meet with the two informants.

"Lake, that's Jason, being pushed into that van," said Kat as she got out of the car and closed the door. She started to run across the square. Lake put the car back into gear and drove around to block the van. He hit the com control and reported his location and direction. He was not in time to prevent the van from crossing K Street. Dave drove across L Street and turned into Burns Alley. Lake made his way through traffic and pulled in the same alley. The van had gone in about ninety feet and stopped. The front passenger door opened, Tomas jumped out and began to move a dumpster out of the way. Lake requested backup and drew his weapon as he got out of the car. Lake approached the van on the right. He saw Tomas pushing the dumpster and shouted, "Stop! Police!"

Burns Alley, Washington, DC

Kat was running across the square, heading for the alley.

Tomas still had Dave's gun when he jumped out of the van to move the dumpster. He turned with the gun in his hand, looked at the van, saw Lake running up behind it, and fired at Lake, hitting him in the right shoulder. Lake spun to his right, against the wall, staggered forward, passing the van's sliding door. He was wide-eyed, not focusing, trying to raise his gun, and he started to slide down the wall near the front of the van.

Jason stared through the window in the side door in disbelief as Dave looked out the opened passenger door and saw Lake slide to the ground. Tomas approached Lake with the gun partially raised, and Jason covered his head with his hoodie, trying to hide.

As Lake looked up at Tomas, his gun fell. He tried to speak, but words didn't form, and the world was blurring.

Tomas stopped less than five feet away from Lake, brought the gun up, and fired again, twice, putting two slugs into Lake's vest. He cursed as he fired and didn't see Kat coming down the alley.

As the second bullet ripped into Lake's body armor, Kat was approaching the rear of the van. She screamed at the shooter and fired. The bullet hit Tomas high in his chest, slowing him down. She was about to fire again when Clint pushed the van's side door open, leapt out, and grabbed her.

Tomas was stunned by Kat's shot. He walked slowly up to Lake, looked at Kat, then back at Lake, and fired, hitting Lake in the forehead. He stepped toward Kat, then as he looked her in the eye, he tried to raise his arm. He was unsteady and feeling her bullet in him. His arm came up, shaking. He squeezed the trigger, sending a bullet through her cheek exiting near her ear. The slug then struck Clint in his chest. He let Kat fall to the ground as he staggered back against the wall.

Dave came around the front of the van, "What the hell?"

Tomas was angry. Kat was on the ground with her left arm raised over her head. He pointed his gun at her. As he squeezed the trigger, he yelled "Bitch…" and sent a bullet into her chest below her raised arm. Tomas was shaking uncontrollably as he tried to aim at Kat again; his arm dropped to his side.

"Get in the damn van," yelled Dave. He surveyed the scene; two cops were down and probably dead. The two thugs were wounded and bleeding. He looked at Tomas and said, "Give me that gun," as he forcefully took it from him.

Both thugs were wounded. Both would live, but not comfortably for a week or two. Both needed medical attention. Dave looked around the alley at the mess they made. "Get in the van," he ordered Clint, "and don't bleed on anything." He quickly looked around again, "Tell Tomas to keep the squirrel covered up," he said nodding toward Jason.

Dave slowly walked over to Lake, leaned over and touched his neck. Lake was dead. He looked at Kat from ten feet away and took a deep breath. Looking around the alley he had an idea. He eyed Clint, "Come here, we have work to do," he said as he put a finger to his lips, "Shhhh," again, nodding toward Jason.

They walked to the rear of the van and removed Ross' body. "We'll put him over there," he quietly said to Clint, "near the cop." They carried Ross' body out and laid him on the ground in front of Lake. "Get that nightstick Tomas used on him," he said. He wiped down the grip, and wrapped Lake's hand around it, and rubbed it in Ross' hair where Tomas had hit him, then let it drop next to Ross' body.

Dave took Lake's gun, his badge, and his wallet. Then he looked at Kat, blood puddling below her arm, and took her gun, badge, and purse. He threw the guns, badges, purse, and wallet in the van and said to Clint, "Let's get the hell outta here."

The van slowly pulled ahead in the alley. Dave stopped, got out, and pushed the dumpster back close to where it was when they pulled in the alley. He drove to the end of the alley and out onto M Street heading west, then drove cautiously, not wanting to draw any attention. He stopped at a signal, turned to the thugs, and said, "Find out where the squirrel lives!"

*   *   *

Burns Alley, Washington, DC

An MPD patrol car arrived as the van exited the alley to M Street at the far end. The two officers radioed in their location, then exited their vehicle and moved around Lake's car. The van had already turned into traffic, over two hundred feet away, and the two officers didn't see it. There was no activity in the alley. As they passed Lake's car, they could see three bodies on the ground. They approached cautiously.

"It's a woman," said the first officer as he touched Kat's neck. "She's alive, bleeding from her face," he paused, looking closer, "hey, it's Murano, and she doesn't look good. She's bleeding like hell." He opened his mic, "Officer down, need an ambulance, NOW!" He pulled her coattail into a ball, placed it over the wound, and applied pressure. "Where's the damn EMT?"

The other officer reached Lake; he felt his stomach churn as he saw a slow trickle of blood from the wound in Lake's head. He felt for a pulse, "It's Lake McLarry, he's …" he paused, "he's dead." He quickly moved to Ross. "I got another one," he felt Ross' neck, "he's dead too."

The EMTs arrived and were directed to Kat. "She still has a pulse," said the officer as the EMT moved to check Kat's vitals.

"I got her," said the EMT. He turned and yelled, "Bring the board. We gotta' move this one now!"

A team of crime scene techs arrived within minutes of the ambulance. Freddy Knolls saw Kat and froze. She was a friend, a good friend. He was shocked back to reality when one of his team asked if he was alright.

"Yeah, Sal, I'm okay," he replied. "I know her," he paused, "is she…?"

The EMT said, "It ain't good Freddy, we gotta get her to the hospital. Fast."

"Her name is Detective Kat Murano," said Freddy, as he took as many pictures of her as he could without getting in the way. He turned quickly to the other officer, "How's Lake?" he asked as he moved toward the officer standing next to Lake.

"You know these two, Freddy?" asked one of the officers.

"Yeah," he replied as he tried to look past the officer.

Freddy looked at the officer, "Is he dead?"

"Sorry, Freddy, yeah, he's gone."

Sal asked Freddy if he was too close to this one, "I can take it from here," he said. "You don't have to do this."

Freddy stood still for a moment, then looked at his partner, "No, Sal, I want this one," and he moved closer to Lake. He knelt and touched Lake's shoulder, "Lake…" He quietly thought through a prayer, stood, and began to photograph the site, then he moved back toward Kat and photo'd everything around her as the EMTs finished getting her on a stretcher.

"Freddy, we gotta move her now," said one of the EMTs.

He stood aside, once again in a state of shock. He watched as Kat was loaded into the ambulance, the flashing lights came on, the siren wailed, and Freddy was again brought back to reality with the thought, *Lake, I gotta do Lake.*

"Okay, Freddy," said Sal, "this one took at least four, one in the right shoulder, two in his vest, and one through his forehead."

Freddy looked at the body half propped against the wall, a blood trail across his left eye and cheek, "Lake..."

"You don't have to do this one, Freddy," said Sal again.

"Yeah, I do," he replied. He stared at Lake for a minute, then said, "Okay, Lake, let's figure this out," he lifted his camera and went to work.

*   *   *

12

It took less than a minute for Jason to spit out his address, and Dave drove the van to an old boarded-up building in Southwest, DC, "Is this the place?"

Jason sat up, squinted as he looked out through the front window, "Yeah, this is it." He looked at the two thugs, "What happened back there?"

"These two guys got in some trouble with the cops," said Dave.

"Yeah, I saw you shoot McLarry," Jason said, looking at Tomas.

"He was gonna shoot me," said Tomas.

"Yeah, then you shot the lady cop," said Jason, "this ain't good."

"I think I got it covered," said Dave. "We have to lie low for a day or two, then everything will smooth out."

"Ross, what about Ross?" asked Jason.

"He's being taken care of at the hospital," said Dave. "Does anybody else know you live here?"

"Naw, just Ross," returned Jason. "He stays down near the warehouse so he can get to work easy. Can I call him, make sure he's okay?"

"Not yet, let's get settled in and take care of our friends here. What about the cops?" quizzed Dave, "Do they know about this place?"

"I used to stay a couple a miles from here, they knew about that place but not this one."

Dave drove behind the building, parking the van out of view of the street. He saw an entry to the building and prodded Jason, "Is this where you can get inside?"

Jason strained to see out the window and answered, "Yeah, we can get in there." He got out of the van, looked around the area cautiously, and started toward the open doorway.

Dave helped Tomas out of the van, and Clint stumbled out next to him. They made their way into the first level of the building. Jason went to a dark corner, fumbled through a few boxes, producing an old flashlight, then led them to a stairway and up to the third level. They walked halfway down a corridor to a closed door. They walked in. There was a mattress in a corner with several blankets lumped in the middle, a cooler, an old suitcase zipped closed, several small crates forming a table and chair, and a camping lantern. There was no electricity and no running water.

"Do you drink that stuff?" asked Tomas, looking at three buckets of water near the doorway.

"No way," returned Jason. "Those are for the toilets."

Dave grimaced at the response and ushered the two thugs to sit on the crates. "What do you do for light?" he asked.

"I got a couple 'a more flashlights and two lanterns," answered Jason. "I can cover up the windows a little, but I don't use the lantern if I don't have to. The cops drive by, and if they see a light, they might come in to take a look."

Dave looked around the room, the lay-in ceiling was completely gone, and all four of the walls went to the floor above. The windows were all intact but not operable, and the door looked solid. He nodded in approval, then told the two thugs he would look at their wounds.

"Hey, Jason," said Dave, "let's cover the windows then you can get comfortable on the mattress and check out the guy's wallet and lady's purse. See if there's any cash or credit cards."

Tomas had picked up one of the guns and was about to check the magazine. Dave walked over to him, "Le'me have the gun."

"What for?" groused Tomas.

"Just gimme the damn gun," said Dave.

Clint looked at his partner and had an idea where this was going, "Give it t'him."

Dave took the gun with a rag he found on the floor, wiped it down, removed the magazine and walked over to Jason, handed it to him, and asked, "You know how to use one of these?"

"Yeah, I shot a gun a coupla' times before," replied Jason, accepting the gun and moving it from hand to hand.

Dave handed him the magazine, "Well, load up, partner."

Jason felt safe as he took the weapon and the magazine. He fumbled with the two and looked up at Dave quizzically.

Dave watched and said, "Oh, yeah," and handed Jason a box of ammunition. "That magazine is kinda old and half empty, but these bullets should go in easy, give it a try."

Jason accepted the box of bullets and dumped a few on the blanket. His hands shook slightly as he turned the magazine over a few times. He picked up a bullet and lined it up to push into the magazine. "I haven't done this in a long time," he said as the first bullet was successfully loaded. "There, I got it." He picked up another bullet.

Dave watched as Jason loaded the magazine, constantly dropping and restarting a few of the bullets. He struggled with the last one and grinned with satisfaction as it finally went in. Dave nodded and said, "Almost, partner, now just turn the mag over so the bullets will go out the front and slide 'er home."

Jason smiled as the magazine clicked home. He looked up at Dave and started to pull back the slide.

"Not yet, buddy," said Dave, "let's wait 'til we're ready to shoot something. We don't want it to go off accidental like." He looked out the window and back at Jason, "Let's lay low for the night. We'll get a good start in the morning."

Jason lay the gun down next to him. He picked up Kat's purse and examined the contents.

Dave went over to Clint, "I'm gonna step outside and call around, find a doc to patch you two up. Stay here and let the squirrel play with the cop's stuff. Let him get his prints all over everything." He walked to the door, "Play nice, kids."

Out of earshot of the three, Dave called Bernie. "We have a complete mess," he began as he relayed the day's events and described his plan to point suspicion in a different direction."

Bernie was not pleased, "Damn it, man, I'm getting enough heat over the Millington thing. I was prepared for that. Then you couldn't tie a knot, and the thing didn't stay down. That changed the dynamic, and I'm just getting back on an even keel. Now, there are three, soon to be four more problems, and that will change everything again." Bernie paused, "Make sure this plan of yours works, no connections to us."

"I got it handled. Everything is coming together," said Dave. "I just have to get these two items back to California, like they were never here."

Bernie was still concerned, but the plan as Dave laid it out seemed to be workable. "Call me in the morning with an update," replied Bernie.

*   *   *

Vaneksburg Tavern, Vaneksburg, VA

Ian McLarry had stopped for dinner at the Vaneksburg Tavern with friends and was walking to his car when his cellphone chirped. The name on the screen was Farley, MPD. "Mike, what's up?"

"Ian," Mike hesitated, "where are you?"

"Just leaving the tavern, on my way home," he replied. Then it hit him. This was one of those dreaded calls. "Mike, what's happened?"

"Ian, it's Lake..." Mike paused, "he's been shot."

Ian felt a cold chill run up his spine, he stood tall, drew a deep breath, "Mike, is he..."

Mike Farley was a twenty-plus-year veteran of the MPD. He had dealt with death many times and had often been the bearer of the news to a victim's family, but this was different. This was one of his team, a fellow officer, a long-time friend, and he was talking to another friend, "Ian, he's gone."

Ian hesitated a moment and said, "I'm on my way in now."

"Ian, you're too close to this," said Mike.

"I'll be there within the hour," said Ian. "Has anyone told Shelly yet?"

"The boss is on his way down here now," said Mike. "I'm going to meet him there as soon as I locate Lake's cousin, Dan Carney."

"I want to know what happened, and then I'll go see Shelly and Marty." Ian thought for a second, "Who's leading the investigation?"

"Stan Reed," said Mike. "He's at the site now and will probably be back in the office when you get here."

"Okay," said Ian. "Is there anything else I should know?"

"Yeah, Murano. She was hit as well."

"Is she ...?"

"She's in the hospital, hanging on. Maybe when I get back, you'll tell me more." Mike took a deep breath, "Ian, this is the District, you're Virginia."

"Mike, there's no way you or anybody else will keep me out of this," said Ian. "I'll respect the boundaries, and I won't screw up any legal issues." There was a second of silence, then, "I'll see you when you get back."

Ian held his phone and looked up at the night sky. "Talk to me, cousin, talk to me." He bowed his head for a minute, then raised the phone and called Ned Bowen, "Chief, I'm gonna need a little time." He rattled off what he knew thus far, got in his car, and he steered the Crown Vic east on Route 66.

*   *   *

Burns Alley, Washington, DC

Stan Reed first went to the site of the shootings, the alley. He arrived as two med techs from the M.E.'s office were preparing to remove the bodies. Freddy Knolls was busy with his camera, looking at the ground near the dumpster. He photographed several angles of the paved surface and moved to his left about four feet and did the same thing. Stan approached Freddy, "Whataya got, Freddy?"

"Hey detective, I'm not sure what I have here could be nothing. But I'm gonna shoot it anyway." He took several more photos and looked at

Stan Reed, "It's okay to move the two bodies. I've already surveyed the whole alley, videoed and lasered it, got a boatload of stills covered everything and some stuff twice."

"What else do we have?"

"I found five shell casings, look like 9mm, bagged and tagged, a nightstick could have been used on the victim next to Lake. His pocket contents include a busted cellphone, one of those throwaway types, a small package of weed with papers, a lighter, a metro ticket, seventy-two cents in change, and a wallet."

"What's in the wallet?"

"I haven't checked it yet. I want a little better light for that."

"Okay, Freddy, if you're finished …"

"No, I haven't found Lake and Kats stuff yet. They each had a weapon, IDs, wallet, purse … stuff. I got a lot more work here."

"Okay, when you're done, we'll make sure the site is secure. Its yours until you're finished. We can take it back inside and start puttin' the pieces together."

"Okay, detective, and I'll want some more time out here in daylight to look around again."

"Look for what?"

"As I said, we haven't recovered their guns or badges yet. Checked the car and their pockets, their wallets are also gone. So, who knows what else may turn up in the morning. It's dark, the floodlights are doing their bit, and the team will be here all night but a place like this can look very different in the daytime. I don't know what I'll find, but I'll be back in the morning and I'm gonna find out."

Stan felt empty. This case was not close to home, it was home, it was two detectives out of his office, one killed, and the other, a friend, was in surgery. He knew she probably wouldn't make it, and he felt very inadequate. He looked at Freddy, "I'm gonna review their notebooks and see what they were workin' on." He called Mike Farley, "Hey boss, could you push a few buttons and get video from cameras in the area."

Freddy was collecting blood samples around the scene. He paused, stared at the ground for a second, then turned toward Stan, "Hey, any word on Kat Murano, how's she doin'?"

"Dunno, Freddy. I talked to one of the guys at the hospital a few minutes ago, no news yet. I'll let you know when I hear something."

Freddy looked back at the pavement again, then paused, "Yeah, and let me know if they recovered the slug from Kat."

"Will do, Freddy, will do."

*　　　*　　　*

Washington Hospital Center, Washington, DC

Dan Carney made his way to the hospital around 9:00 p.m. Kat was still in surgery when he arrived. He entered the surgical waiting area and saw Kat's father talking to Frank Tollar, the first officer she rode with nine years ago. He approached the two men, "Frank, Mr. Murano, any word yet?"

Frank shook his head, "A nurse came out a few minutes ago and told us the surgery was going well, but it will be a while before they can say anything definite."

Dan looked at Kat's father, "She's as tough as they come. I'm sure she'll get through this."

"I know, Dan. But she's my daughter, and I won't relax 'til she's back on her feet and arguing with me."

Dan's cellphone chirped. He answered, listened then bowed his head.

*　　　*　　　*

Stan Reed went from the scene to the hospital. He walked into the surgical waiting area. Dan Carney and three other officers were there. The room was quiet, the mood somber. Stan approached the three officers, "Are you guys here for Detective Murano?"

"Yeah, detective," replied one of the men, "you've heard about Lake McLarry?"

"Yeah, I know he didn't make it," said Stan.

Dan bowed his head, "Has anyone told Shelly? Lake's wife."

Stan looked at Dan, "That'll be the Chief of Detectives and possibly the boss."

"I want to be there," said Dan. "Lake is my cousin, and I'm close to the family."

"They're probably on their way now, may have already been there," Stan said as he stepped closer to Dan, "you go ahead, I'll clear it with your sergeant."

"Thanks, Stan," and Dan looked at one of the other officers, "call me when you hear about Kat." He walked out the door and found his cruiser. "Dispatch, 6120, I'm 10-7B, at Lake McLarry's house."

*   *   *

Telling someone that a person close to them has been killed is not an easy task. Telling a wife her husband will never come home again or a boy his father is gone forever can be the most difficult thing a person can do.

Shelly had prepared herself several times over the years to be ready for that knock on her door. Ready, but not ready. No one can hold that prepared posture for long. When it happens, it happens at an inconvenient time. A time between periods of being ready, a time when the man and woman are closer than ever, a time when the little boy has question after question, and now dad cannot answer those questions.

Dan arrived as the chiefs were leaving.

"She needs her family and friends now," the chief told Dan. "Take time off if needed and stay close." Dan walked to the door and saw young Marty holding onto his mother.

*   *   *

Metropolitan Police Department, Washington, DC

Stan Reed had gone back to his office to begin his review of Lake and Kat's notes. As he was reading through a notebook, Ian walked up to him, "Good evening, Stan." Mike Farley saw him and joined the conversation, "Let's go into the conference room. I want to talk to both of you."

They sat at the large table, and Mike began, "I know everybody in this entire building would like to be in on this investigation. That can't be. We have to keep this thing perfectly clean, no snafus. I also know that I have no control over Ian, so I've contacted Ned Bowen in Vaneksburg and our chief." He looked at Ian, "You've been assigned to me for the next few weeks, maybe longer. You have an open investigation into the Millington killing, which may tie into a few things we have going on here. You will play by our rules, and I am your boss."

Ian didn't hesitate, "No problem, Mike. I know you have a great team here, and I don't want to get in the way. I'm just not good at sitting on the bench. I want to be involved."

Mike sat up straight, "Stan is leading this investigation, and you will follow his lead, agreed?"

"Agreed," returned Ian.

"You can work your case here or your own shop, but when it comes to this case, you're on Stan's team, and he drives the bus. Okay, let's take it from the top," said Mike as he looked at Stan.

*　　*　　*

Washington Hospital Center, Washington, DC

Three hours after Dan left, Doctor Burton came out and approached Roberto Murano, "She's out of surgery and in recovery." He looked at the several officers, turned and said to Mr. Murano, "The bullet hit a rib, did a lot of damage but stopped short of hitting the heart. Your daughter is in remarkable shape, and we have every reason to think she will make a full recovery. It will take time, and someone will have to wait on her for a few weeks."

As they were talking, another doctor joined them. When there was a pause in the conversation, she said. "Mr. Murano, I'm Janice Montoya. I'll be taking care of Katrena's facial wound after Dr. Burton has fully addressed her chest injury."

"Thank you," said Roberto.

"There will be a small scar," said Dr. Montoya, "but I can recommend an excellent plastic surgeon, and she will make it disappear."

"One step at a time," said Roberto, "she will want to take one step at a time." He smiled, looked at the doctor, and said, "She's gonna be okay."

Dr. Burton added, "She's going to be out for a while. You may as well go home, get some rest and come back in the morning.

"Thanks, Doc," said one of the officers in the waiting room, "we'll stay right here. An officer will be here until she can walk out the front door."

"Don't you have work to do?" asked the doctor.

"Yeah," replied one of the officers, "we'll be coming in here after our shifts are over. The three of us are all off duty."

The three officers moved several chairs in a circle around a low table and sat down to wait. A nurse came down the hall from the ICU. "Gentlemen, there's a coffee machine and several vending machines down the hall, and the restrooms are there," she said, pointing back from where she had come.

The night passed, and Kat did not wake up. Her condition was upgraded, but she remained in the ICU. A second shift of three officers came in to wait with Roberto. They were all awake through the night. Nobody slept.

In the morning, the Doctor checked Kat's condition and allowed Roberto to go into the ICU to see her.

The tubes, wires, monitors, drip lines, and all the beeps and chirps of the equipment monitoring, medicating, and feeding Kat combined with the bandages and restraints holding her in place were overwhelming to Roberto. He felt weakened when he saw her, and the doctor held onto him as they stepped closer to her bed.

A nurse smiled and said, "She's resting very comfortably now. Probably won't wake today, but the doctors were pleased with the surgery, and we're going to take good care of her."

"Can I touch her hand?" asked Roberto.

"Don't move her, just touch gently," replied the nurse.

*   *   *

13

Freddy was back at the scene in the morning. He approached one of the officers on site, "Have you guys have been here all night?'

"Yeah," returned the officer, "the day shift is due in here any time now."

"Has anything new been found?"

"Yeah, a shell casing was found over there," said the officer , pointing at a yellow numbered marker near the dumpster."

"The light is different in the daytime, in some ways much better," said Freddy. "Now, what else did I miss last night?" As he searched the ground, a door to one of the office buildings opened, and a man stood looking out behind several rows of yellow tape.

"Hey, what's going on out here?"

"Stay behind the tape, sir," said one of the officers. "This is an active crime scene, and we will be out here for a while."

"Crime scene, like on TV? What happened here?" He was holding a clear plastic bag full of trash. "And where am I supposed to put my trash?"

Freddy looked around the alley, "Where do you usually put it?"

The man leaned against the yellow tape, "There," he replied, nodding toward the dumpster. "Why's it in the middle of the alley?"

"Where is it usually?" asked Freddy.

"Well, sometimes it gets left out there by the pickup guys, too damn lazy to put it back where it belongs. Should be turned and up against that wall."

"You mean rotated this way?" asked Freddy, pointing.

"Yeah, that way," said the man, "against the wall."

Freddy backed up and photographed the spot where the dumpster should be. He walked over to the dumpster and looked inside again, it was near empty, just a few scraps of trash left after it had been emptied. "When do they empty this dumpster?"

"Hell, if I know. Sometime yesterday, I think. Not sure." He looked anxious, "Can I dump this stuff?" he nodded toward the two bags in his hands.

"Pretty soon, after we finish in the alley here, I'll knock on your door."

"Yeah, sure," he said as he backed up and kicked the door closed.

Freddy looked at the marks on the pavement again. The dumpster had obviously been moved several times recently. It had been rotated, probably so the trash truck could lift it and dump the contents into the hopper. Then it appeared it had been pushed straight back toward the wall and then again, pushed out away from the wall. He roughly measured the clearance left if the dumpster was moved in that direction and a car could get by, then it was pushed back. Why? Probably to make it appear no vehicle had been able to pass through the alley. "Interesting, very interesting," he mumbled.

*   *   *

The surgery had removed one bullet from Kat's chest. The bullet that had gone through her cheek was missing.

Freddy stood in the alley, trying to figure where Kat had been standing when she was shot. The bullet in her chest entered below her arm on the right side. The powder burns indicated the shooter was close, within two feet, maybe closer. The shot to her cheek entered and exited near the same height, and there were no powder burns.

"The shooter was more than ten feet away," mumbled Freddy.

He stood where Kat had fallen, faced the dumpster, and thought, *why would I be against this wall? If I was going around something like another car and the perp moved the dumpster to unblock the alley, Kat could have come up around the car, he shoots her, then moved his car and pushed the dumpster back again.*

Freddy studied the scene, imagining a car stopped in front of the dumpster.

"A man pushing the dumpster out of his way," he mumbled aloud, "an empty dumpster is not hard to move."

He paced the alley, stood where the man moving the dumpster would have stood, and looked back where Ross, Lake, and Kat were found. He called over two patrol officers and said, "You stand there," pointing where Lake would have been standing. "You stand behind him," indicating where Kat was shot. It didn't work. The two should have been on opposite sides of the parked car. *Why were they on the same side?* He opened his laptop and reviewed the video of the scene from the previous day. *One door open on their car, driver's side, Kat may have been on foot, Lake drove into the alley, saw the parked car, saw the man moving the dumpster. Why would he hit the other guy on the head?*

Freddy paused and looked around the scene again. He walked back to the location of Lake's car and stood, looking at the dumpster. It still didn't make sense.

He was leaning up against another dumpster, letting his mind drift when Stan and Ian entered the alley.

"Gentlemen, glad you're here," said Freddy.

"Whatcha got, Freddy?" asked Stan.

Freddy walked the two detectives through the few possible scenarios as he saw them. "Lake didn't carry a damn stick. That's something uniforms have on their belt, Lake had a gun, stick woulda been in his way," said Stan. He looked around the immediate area, "Yeah, so where's his gun?"

"Haven't found his gun or hers," said Freddy. "Both their badges are missing as well."

Stan and Ian ran their own scenarios through their heads as they wandered the scene and asked Freddy questions.

"So, Freddy, the scratches on the pavement show the dumpster had been moved," said Ian. "Could that have happened a few days ago?"

"The trash truck was here yesterday afternoon," returned Freddy. "Some of these scratches are fresh with tire marks across one set and not the other."

Ian grinned and looked at Freddy, "Just like it was moved to allow a car to pass through and moved back."

"Yep," said Freddy, "just like that, and it wasn't a small car."

Ian looked quizzically at Freddy, "Full size?"

"More like a pickup, based on the tire sizes and spread."

*   *   *

Abandoned Building, Washington, DC

Morning had come with the sounds of a city waking up, traffic raising an increasing hum of engines and tires rumbling over the nearby highway. Dave walked out of the abandoned building to the van and turned on the radio. He tuned to an all-news station and listened as a reporter finished a traffic report with a cautionary statement, "The police have blocked off a part of M street and Burns Alley..."

Clint tapped on the window, "Dave, open up. We gotta do something pretty quick. This bullet is hurtin' like hell."

"Get back inside," grumbled Dave. "If anybody sees you, we're fried."

Clint was angry and pounded his fist on the van's side, then walked back inside the building.

Dave followed after hearing about the police activity near McPherson Square and hearing that there were no leads as yet. "We may just get out of this okay," he muttered to himself as he returned to the third-floor room. He found Clint sitting on a crate, Tomas on the floor leaning against a wall, and Jason studying a credit card. "Okay guys, here's what we're gonna do. First, Jason and I are gonna get a little practice in with his new 9mm, then, we can go out and get you two some help." He looked at Jason and said, "Let's take a walk, buddy, see what the rest of this place looks like. You lead, partner. Show me someplace we can fire a few rounds and not draw attention."

A gun in his hand, 'partner' this and 'buddy' that, Jason felt reassured. "Sure, we can go into the basement."

They went down a few flights of stairs, and Jason said, "Down lower it gets dark, and ya can't see anything. This should be pretty good here."

"Okay, let's find a target, see how good you are." He spotted an old grey electrical box about twenty feet away. "Try that box over there," he pointed, and said, "Now pull the slide and load the first round."

Jason tried to look like a TV cop, held the gun with both hands and pointed, then squeezed. The sound was deafening in the enclosed space and the two thugs heard it four levels above. Jason fired four more rounds and paused.

Dave seemed to be counting, and Jason said, "Whatcha doin?"

Dave replied, "Counting, gotta see how good you are, partner." He had counted seven or eight shots at the alley, but he wasn't sure. Safe would be eight or nine, and he decided on eight. He walked over to the grey electrical box and was surprised by what he saw. Two indentations were nearly centered on the panel. "Hey, not bad, you nailed the thing twice." He walked back next to Jason, "Now, try two, like real fast at the target, you know, boom, then another boom right away."

"Yeah, okay," said Jason, and he assumed the pose firing twice as quickly as he could.

As Jason was firing, Dave noticed the floor was covered in dust, and his footprints were visible halfway to the electrical box. The floor where they stood was clear, as were the stairs. He thought for a minute, mumbled to himself, and said, "Can you see my footprints in the dirt over there?"

"Yeah," returned Jason.

"Sometimes you don't want anybody to know you were there, so you look for old footprints and walk in the same places." He watched Jason soak up all he was saying. Give it a try, walk over to the electrical box and back here, stepping in my footprints."

To Jason, this was a game. Like playtime for a couple of little kids, but to Dave, this was serious. Jason walked in Dave's footprints and returned as he was told. "Like that?" he asked.

"Yeah, perfect. Now you run over there and back, and I'll try to step in your prints."

Again, Jason was playing. He ran over to the box, shuffled around, and ran back.

"Ha, that's the way, partner," said Dave. "Now I have to match your footprints." He looked as if he was ready to run in Jason's footprints when he said, "Hold on, my phone is vibratin'."

Dave put his phone to his ear and said, "Hello." He looked at Jason and said, "Okay." Then turned to Jason, "We gotta go."

Jason looked disappointed, and Dave said, "But first, I want you to try one more thing. This time hold the gun down at your side, and when I say 'go,' you put another round in the box, okay?"

Jason was enjoying this, "Just one, or should I empty the clip into the suckka?"

Dave found it amusing, laughed but didn't want him to empty the clip, and said, "No, just one shot, you may need the rest for another bad guy."

"Okay," Jason posed, waited, and when Dave said "go," he raised the gun and put another round in the grey box.

Dave was again stunned. This guy could shoot. "Okay partner, I feel a little safer that you're with me. You're pretty good at this."

"Can we practice some more?"

"Yeah, we should do this every day, so tomorrow, we'll do it again." It was coming together, "let's get back upstairs."

Dave didn't run through the dust, and Jason didn't give it another thought.

*   *   *

14

CIA Headquarters, Langley, VA

The news of Lake's death traveled through the family, through the Clann. A phone rang in an office in Langley, Virginia. Jake Brennan was not in his office, and a message left a return number in Ireland. "I'll be on a flight to Dulles tomorrow afternoon and arrive in the evening at 7:38 your time," said the deep voice. "Select a pub somewhere convenient, and we'll meet for a pint or two and plan out the next few days."

Within ten minutes of the call, Jake listened to the message, and his phone rang again. This time it was answered. "Jake Brennan."

"Jake, Lucas," said the caller. "Have you heard about Lake?"

"Yeah, I have," he responded, "and himself is flying in tomorrow evening, 7:40 at Dulles. I was about to call Ian and suggest we gather somewhere out in Fairfax."

"Would you mind if I joined you?" asked Lucas.

"You were next on my list. How about the Auld Shebeen in Fairfax City at 8:30?"

"I know it well," returned Lucas. "I'll be there."

Jake thought for a second, then dialed another number, "Ian, the Auld Shebeen tomorrow evening, around 8:30. Himself will be in town."

*   *   *

Abandoned Building, Washington, DC

On the third floor, back in Jason's space, Dave went over to the two thugs and looked at their wounds. "Not bad, not good either. I'll get you to a doc, but you two should be alright getting back to LA." He looked around the room, "I'm gonna take our friend for a little walk, get you two something to eat, maybe some water. Keep a low profile, and we'll be back." He looked at Jason, "Hey man, it's gettin' warm outside. You wanna' lose that jacket?"

Jason was feeling warm, "Yeah, good idea." He took off his jacket and started toward the door.

Dave smiled at him, "Hey partner, never leave your weapon behind," he said, pointing at the gun laying on the mattress.

"Oh, yeah," responded Jason. He turned around to retrieve the gun.

"You gonna let him carry that gun?' asked Tomas.

"Yeah, it makes him feel secure, hell we ain't gonna shoot anybody with the damn thing." He started out the door, "Play nice. We'll be back."

Clint looked at Tomas and said, "I know what he's doin'. Don't worry. They'll both be back in a little bit."

*   *   *

Parking Lot, Washington, DC

Dave and Jason drove to a parking lot next to a gas station. He looked around and spotted the security camera, pointing at the gas station pump area and not in his direction. He asked Jason to go inside and get something for the two thugs to eat and some water, "Make that enough for four, partner." He looked at the gun in Jason's hand, "Put that in your belt and pull your shirt over it so it won't be seen." Jason did as Dave told him, then went inside. Dave called Bernie, "I think I have it under control, but the two items sent here need to be repaired, they're both broken."

Bernie replied, "That's a shame. How extensive is the damage?"

"Both are dented and scratched, some leakage, probably repairable, but non-functional in their present condition," said Dave.

Bernie thought for a second, "I'll check on a repair schedule and cost. I'll call you in a few minutes."

"Okay," said Dave, "if we ship 'em back to the factory, maybe they can be fully repaired or recycled." He hung up.

*   *   *

Temple Enterprise, Washington, DC

Bernie Temple sat at his desk, thinking. Myra entered his office and noticed his obvious discomfort, "Mr. Temple, is everything alright?"

"Myra, I think a little episode at the warehouse may turn into a problem. One which I would like to avoid. Perhaps we could use our friend, Franklin to recommend a solution and handle the details." He looked at Myra, "Would you please contact him?"

"Are there any specifics I should relate to him?"

"Tell him we have four items broken, two may be salvaged, one has been scrapped, and the other will be scrapped. Let him know Dave is trying to handle it, but he may not have all the proper tools or skill set for this."

Myra paused, her look of concern changed to one of business, pure business. "Yes, sir, but if Franklin is not available immediately…"

Bernie frowned, "I understand. Let's check anyway. Right off it is his advice that I require, not necessarily action."

Myra went back to her desk, brought up the company website on her computer, and colored the little square red.

*   *   *

Parking Lot, Washington, DC

Dave looked around for Jason, wondering what he was doing. As he was watching the door, Jason came out with a bag in his hand. Dave could see the gun sticking out of his pants from thirty feet away. He smiled, "Perfect," he muttered. His cellphone buzzed. It was Bernie.

As Jason got in the van, Dave said, "I need some juice man, do you have a connection around here?"

Jason thought for a second, "Yeah, down the block a little ways."

Dave appeared concerned and said, "Listen, we got some problems, and our friends need a little help. If we could score a few ounces of good stuff, it would get us over the hump." He turned to Jason and knew he was dreaming about a fix. "Here, take these," he handed Jason three credit cards, "see if there's any money we could use. Try the numbers 6826 and 7345 in the machine, and then get the best stuff you can for this," he handed Jason the money from Lake's and Kat's wallets and added a one-hundred-dollar bill.

Jason was now shaking. He needed a boost and said, "Yeah, I'll be right back." Then he walked away from the van, around the corner, and another two blocks to an ATM. He tried one of the credit cards, punched in 6826. It didn't work. He tried the second number to no avail. Then he tried the other cards with the two numbers. None worked. "I need a different damn number, but what number?" he punched in a few random numbers and was rejected again. He took the cards and left the ATM, walked another block to the spot he had used in the past to make a connection. He waited.

Soon a young kid about ten approached him. "You lookin' for sumpin?"

Jason answered, "Happiness, pure happiness."

"Yeah, go on in that door," said the boy, pointing at a door across the street.

Jason went in, and two men came out of the shadows, "What you after, there slick?"

Jason took the money out of his pocket. "I told the kid outside, happiness, pure happiness. I need the best stuff you got."

"How much happiness you lookin' for?"

Jason fanned out the money, "Whatever this will buy me."

"You get more if we cut it for you."

"True that," he replied. "But pure is what I need."

"Is this for you, or you buyin' for another?"

"Yeah," replied Jason, "and he said, pure, pure."

One of the two men took the money and disappeared. He returned in less than a minute. "Don't got none of that stuff here, dude. You best try somewhere else."

"What about my money?" he asked.

"Cost of asking dumb questions," the man replied, "and don't forget that little envelope you left on the banister downstairs."

Jason went down the stairs, saw the envelope, picked it up, and went out the door. He squeezed it with his fingers. It was a powdery substance. He grinned and went back to the van. Dave looked at the envelope and smiled, "Hold on to that, we gotta' get back."

"Yeah, okay, hey, why you still wearin' those gloves?"

Dave laughed, "Makes me feel like a doctor."

Jason wasn't listening to Dave, he was looking at the envelope, already feeling the high.

*   *   *

Temple Enterprise, Washington, DC

Myra walked back into Bernie's office, closed the door and sat in a guest chair, "Franklin will be in Las Vegas tomorrow. He will address your situation there."

Bernie leaned forward, obviously perturbed, "The two clowns are going to LA, not Vegas."

"Yes sir," said Myra. "Tell them to change their tickets to Vegas and meet a…" she looked at her notebook, "a Mr. Pallman. He will take care of them." She looked around and said, "He will transport them to a hospital where they will be checked and treated," she smiled, "treated."

Bernie leaned back in his chair, and smiled, "Treated."

*   *   *

Abandoned Building, Washington, DC

Jason was sitting on the bed with all the things taken from Lake and Kat. Two police badges, two 9mm pistols, an empty purse, credit cards, cash, Lake's wallet, and the 9mm used to shoot Lake and Kat.

"Hey partner," said Dave, "I talked to the boss, and he said you could have a job inside starting next week. How's that?"

Jason was confused, "What about Ross?"

"Oh, Ross will be out for a while. Looks like he was hurt worse than we thought. But, hey, let's celebrate your new job."

Dave asked Jason to prep a needle, "Enough for all of us."

Jason lit a candle and set to work. Finished, he held a full syringe and looked at Dave, "You wanna go first?"

"Hey partner, this party is for you. You take the first hit."

Jason smirked and tied off his arm, "Yeah, I'll take the first bump." He injected some, then leaned back. He closed his eyes and felt the rush.

Dave told the two thugs to re-bandage their wounds and get ready to move out.

Jason was in orbit somewhere near Pluto. Dave picked up the syringe, reloaded it, held it out to Jason, and said, "Hey partner, let's have another hit."

Jason's eyes were not focusing on anything, and he smiled but didn't say anything. Dave waited another minute and said, "Hey, come on partner, take your fair share, that was just a little hit, come on now. I'll help you." He tied off Jason's arm, leaned over, and inserted the needle in the same spot as his first injection.

"Hey, you ain't doin' that right," said Tomas.

Dave let the needle droop partially in Jason's arm and leaned back. "Yeah, I know." Then, he reached in and depressed the plunger about halfway and waited. Jason didn't move; he wouldn't move again. Dave let the needle fall slack on the pillow below Jason's arm, looked at Tomas, grinned, and looked back at Jason, "Careful there partner, that's some high-class stuff."

*   *   *

Dave left the needle in Jason's arm, picked up a blanket, collected several small items, including the ammunition box, and most of the remaining bullets, then looked at the two thugs, "Okay you two, let's get outta' here."

They left Lake's and Kat's possessions on the mattress with Jason and walked out of the building. Back in the van, they removed their latex gloves, checked for anything that was Jason's or Ross', and drove away.

Dave had a connection with access to a man who could perform minor repairs. He referred to him as The Doc and assured the two California thugs he was especially good with gunshot wounds. "Two tours in 'Nam, so he's an expert on pluggin' holes in guys." Dave turned onto 395 and headed to Virginia. As they crossed the bridge over the Potomac, Dave noted the traffic was light. He slowed as he turned into the right-hand lane, lowered his window, and lobbed Ross' cellphone over the top of the van into the river. They drove to an apartment building in Virginia near Fort Belvoir on Route One and went up to the third floor.

*   *   *

Apartment Building, Valley View, VA

Angus McDowell, The Doc, ordered the two men into a large bedroom with an adjoining bathroom. "Strip down and shower up lads," he looked at Tomas, "you first."

Tomas did as he was told, and The Doc pointed at a table with a white sheet, "Up there, head to my left, and don't move. I'm going to give you a shot that may sting, and you'll go to sleep."

He administered the anesthetic and proceeded to secure Tomas with three straps across his body. Tomas drifted into outer space, and The Doc began to inspect the wound. "Very lucky man," said McDowell. "The bullet struck his ribs," he probed and found the slug had drifted down and toward the stomach but did not hit any vital organs. "Unbelievable. Usually, this would have gone right through, ripping havoc on at least one organ." He retracted his probe and looked at the wound, the trajectory, and the depth of his probe. "Much better if I go in from the other side and get it out."

Dave glanced at Clint, noticed he was not listening, and quietly asked McDowell, "Could you leave it in him?"

McDowell thought for a second, "Better for him if I take it out. Leave it there, and it would go septic, then you'd have to scrap the man."

Dave seemed to consider the advice and continued, "Can he travel as is?"

"Not far, not long," returned McDowell.

"How about a flight to California?" asked Dave.

"No, not with the slug in him," said McDowell. "He'd be in pain, serious pain, and might be dead by the time they touched down." He looked closely at Tomas' side and said, "I'll get the lead out of him, stitch 'em up, give 'em a healthy dose of painkiller, and he could fly, but he'd have to take it real easy for the next week or so and he'll need regular painkillers and antibiotics to make a complete recovery."

"Make 'em both good to travel. I want these guys in LA by tomorrow night," said Dave.

"Yeah, sure," returned McDowell. "Let me get at it."

Bullets removed from both men, their wounds stitched and bandaged, McDowell gave Dave a bottle with twenty pills, "They should each take two every four hours. I'll give you more in the morning for their trip. When they get to their next stop, they should give the bottle to the medic who will pick up the treatment."

"Okay," said Dave. "When can we leave?"

"Let 'em sleep through the night. I'll see they are fed in the morning, and they'll be good enough to travel," said the Doc.

Dave called Bernie to report. "They can travel," he said, "but will need further treatment at the other end."

Bernie said, "We have a slight change in plans. Send the two packages to Vegas tomorrow. They'll be picked up by a Mr. Pallman for their ride to the hospital, where they will be checked out and probably kept overnight. They'll return to California when they are ready to work again."

Dave said, "Okay, anything else?"

"No," said Bernie, "then we can get back to business."

Dave hung up, looked at the two thugs, and quietly said, "You may have to spend a week in Vegas before returning to LA."

"They're both out cold," said McDowell, "can't hear a word, but I don't think they'll mind."

Dave grinned, "Yeah, a week maybe, in Vegas. No problem."

*   *   *

Metropolitan Police Department, Washington, DC

An officer poked his head in Sergeant Mike Farley's office, "We got a report of a shooting in an abandoned office building."

Farley looked up, "And?"

"And they found a guy OD'd on something."

Farley, angered by this interruption, "Yeah, and?"

"Dead guy had Lake and Kat's badges."

Farley looked stunned, "What else?"

The officer replied, "Info still comin' in. When they saw the badges, they called us."

Farley was on his feet and moving, "Get a car, get the CSI guys, hell, get the goddam Marines and get me there NOW!"

*   *   *

Abandoned Building, Washington, DC

The old, abandoned office building was crawling with police. Freddy arrived about the same time as Farley and began a visual scan of the third-floor room. When three other CSIs arrived with the equipment, the scene was scanned with a laser and video camera. The team then began to photo close-ups of specific items, the badges, the guns, two spare ammunition clips, the needle, the spoon, and anything that looked interesting. The review went on for an hour.

Freddy spotted a few drops of blood near the crates. He photographed then swabbed the blood. There were several more drops on each side of the table, and he noted the spatter patterns. "Bleeder was sitting here for a while," he muttered. "Then he walked out the door."

An officer called out to Farley, "Hey Sarge, we have a shooting gallery in the basement. That may have been where the report of gunshots came from."

Farley asked, "When did the report come in?"

"We got the call from central this morning," replied an officer, "Apparently, the witness said there was a shooting here, didn't say much else."

"Who's the witness?" groused Farley.

"John Anonymous," replied the officer.

"Man, woman, old, young, accent … anything?" asked Farley.

"What I got was a, 'See the man' call," answered the officer. "And when I got here, nobody was around."

Freddy finished his review of the room and was taken to the lower level. "Get me some lights," he said to Sal. The basement level was filthy. Rat tracks were obvious in the dirt and dust on the floor. He kept everybody out of the area and waited for the lights to be set up. "Footprints — three or four guys." He looked at the officer who found the evidence of a shooting, "Where did you walk?"

"Just in a few feet, like there," he pointed at a shell casing on the floor. "I saw the casing, wasn't sure how many there were, but I saw more than one, then I went up and got you."

"Anybody else come in here?" asked Freddy.

"No," replied the officer. "Carl stood here while I went up to get you guys."

Freddy looked at Carl with a quizzical expression.

"Nope, I stayed right here," said Carl, "and nobody else has been in there either."

"Okay," said Freddy. "Let's get the lights on."

As Freddy began shooting the scene, Stan and Ian arrived. "Gentlemen, good to see you," said Freddy. "Would you two like to begin on the third floor?"

"You lead, Freddy," returned Stan. He looked at Ian, "Have you two met?"

*   *   *

15

Dave met with The Doc, and they talked about bandages, painkillers, and travel. It was agreed the two thugs could fly to Vegas and be taken to another 'Doc' to receive further treatment.

The Doc checked the bandages one last time and handed them each a small bottle of pills, "Take one every two hours and don't move about if you don't have to. The stitches should remain in for a week, maybe more depending on how you're healing, so no heavy lifting or running around 'til you're cleared by your doctor."

Tomas and Clint had a decent night's sleep, been given a heavy dose of meds, and were ready to travel. Dave gave them each a preprinted ticket, hustled them into his van, and drove out to Chantilly. The two were dropped off at Dulles. Dave reminded them to act normal. "No aches, no pains. Smile and be nice. Remember, a Mr. Pallman will pick you up at McCarran and take you to the treatment center."

The two wounded thugs cleared security without incident and made their way to the gate. A final phone call to Dave from Clint told him they had boarded the aircraft and were in their seats, waiting for takeoff.

Dave left the airport, drove out to the toll road, went a few miles to Fairfax County Parkway, and turned south. As he drove back to the warehouse, he called the airline and confirmed the flight had departed on time. "One more call to Bernie," he muttered to himself as he pushed another button on his cellphone. "Bernie, I've sent the two damaged parts back for repair. I'll be back at the warehouse in less than an hour."

Bernie listened to Dave and breathed a sigh of relief, "When should they arrive in Vegas?"

"Not sure," returned Dave, "but certainly by 6:00 tonight our time. I'll check online when I get to the warehouse."

"That's alright. I'm sure I'll receive a call from my friend if they aren't on time."

*   *   *

Apartment Building, Las Vegas, NV

Will Garnos closed the laptop, put it under his arm, and walked into the adjoining room, "Hey Rich, we got a go on that job for Franklin."

Rich Pallman hit the television mute button and sat up straight, "Okay," said Rich, "so what are we doin?"

"Gotta pick up a couple of dudes at McCarran and take 'em out to a 'hospital' near Mesquite," said Will.

Rich grinned, "You mean those holes we dug in the desert."

"Yeah," said Will. "But first we gotta fix a coupla special water bottles for 'em," he laughed.

Rich laughed, "Franklin's special red soda."

"We're to tell them it's a pain killer and antibiotic," said Will.

As they mixed the drinks, Will added, "We should take the laptop in case he tries to get hold of us."

"Yeah, good idea," returned Rich, "and maybe we get home in time to catch the end of tonight's game."

"Who's playin'?" quizzed Will.

"Padres at San Francisco," returned Rich, "starts around 7:00. Maybe we see the whole game."

*   *   *

McCarran Airport, Las Vegas, NV

The flight was on time at McCarran International. Tomas and Clint walked out of the secure area and spotted Rich holding a sign that read "Marsh/Relatto." The three men walked out to the passenger pickup area when Rich noticed Tomas was not looking well and said, "Did the Doc give you meds for the pain?"

Clint showed Rich the bottle, "Used the last of 'em on the plane. We could use more."

Rich grinned, "Gotcha covered, Doc on this end gave us some stuff for you both. It's in the van."

They waited a few minutes then a dark blue minivan with tinted windows pulled up. The side door opened, and Rich said, "This is our ride. Hop in."

"I ain't hoppin' nowhere," said Tomas as he staggered into the van and sat behind the driver.

Clint was more mobile and managed to enter the van without any obvious discomfort. "Buckle up, gentlemen," said the driver as he pushed a button, and the door slid closed. "I'm Will, I'll be your driver, and you've already met Rich. We're gonna take you to our private hospital where they'll fix you up."

"Where is this place?" asked Tomas as the van began to move.

"The other side of Mesquite, just off 15. We should be there soon," replied Will.

"How soon? This damn thing is starting to hurt like hell," said Tomas.

"About 20 minutes," said Will.

*　　*　　*

Route 15, Las Vegas, NV

Rich, sitting in the front passenger seat, turned and handed Tomas a bottle of red liquid, "Here, Doc says it's a pain killer and an antibiotic. He said you should drink the whole thing."

Tomas drank near half the bottle. He sat for a few minutes staring out the window, relaxed, and fell asleep. Rich looked at Clint, "How are you doin', any pain?"

"Not that bad. I'll wait 'til the Doc checks me out."

Rich shook his head, tapped the bottle in Clint's hand, "Doc said you should be hydrated, and if it hurts, it'll take the edge off."

Clint took the bottle, held it, and looked out the window watching the desert pass by. After a few minutes, he took the cap off and tasted the liquid. "What is this stuff?"

Will looked in his rear-view mirror. He grinned as Rich said, "No idea, I know it's mostly water, but I don't know what the meds are. Doc says he's used it before, and it works."

Clint took another drink, then again and again. Soon he had drunk the entire bottle. "Juss red water," he mumbled as he fell asleep.

*　　*　　*

Desert, Northwest, AZ

The private hospital, in fact, did not exist. The car with the four men pulled off 15 in Mesquite and drove several miles into the desert. Neither Clint nor Tomas were aware of this change in plans—they were dead.

There was nothing visible in any direction except dunes, dirt, and those scruffy weeds that somehow survive in the desert. Will drove the van into a swale, not visible from the dirt road. There were two holes, over four feet deep, with dirt piled next to them. Will and Rich removed their coats and dragged the two bodies to the graves.

"We should check their wallets," said Rich. "No sense throwin' away good money."

Will removed Tomas' wallet and took out four twenty-dollar bills, a five and two singles. "Bingo, eighty-seven bucks." He then checked the pockets for change, "Every penny counts."

Rich did the same to Clint and netted fifty-three dollars and three quarters. Then they rolled the two bodies into the holes and shoveled the dirt over them.

Back in their van, Will said, "I need a hot shower."

"Yeah, me too," said Rich, "then we should go to dinner and catch the game."

They arrived back at their apartment, and the computer indicated a message was received. "Probably Franklin," said Will.

The message was simple, direct, "Is the project complete? Before you go out and celebrate, be sure to have the van cleaned, both inside and out."

Tomas and Clint had violated a rule, *don't bleed*. Their blood could be traced. They could be identified. They were liabilities. They were now in a place where no one will ever find them and no longer a liability.

*   *   *

16

Dulles International Airport, Chantilly, VA

Jake Brennan parked the black suburban in short-term parking near the International gate and walked into the lower level of the terminal. He checked his watch, noted he had at least a half-hour wait, and found a source of coffee. He waited less than fifteen minutes when his phone chirped, and a woman's voice with a pleasant brogue said, "Mr. Brennan, we've just now landed. Where should we meet you?"

"I'm at the exit from customs," returned Jake, "I'll recognize himself when you come through." He pocketed his phone and wondered who the young woman was. "I guess I'll find out in a few minutes," he muttered to himself.

Customs took twenty minutes then the trio exited the tunnel. "Jake," said the old man, "good to see you again."

"Aaron, you're looking as well as ever," returned Jake.

"You're a great liar. Jake," as he extended his hand. "This is Kate Dixon, my right arm. She handles all sorts of details, so anything you need, she speaks for me." He turned toward his other companion and continued, "This is Jack Gannon, my grandson. He helps me get around."

"I've got a car outside," said Jake, "so, if you have everything, we can be on our way."

"You'll forgive me just a minute," said Kate. "There's a convenience just there. I'll be right back."

Jake watched as she hurried across the open mall. Aaron said, "It just occurred to me, Jake. She looks so much like your Kate."

"She does that," said Jake. "Maybe thirty years ago. Now, She could pass as our daughter."

Aaron smiled, "Are we going to stop for a pint or two?"

"We are," said Jake, "and Lucas will be joining us as well."

Jack looked slightly puzzled, "Lucas?"

Aaron smiled, "Yes, Lucas. Your kind of man." He looked at Jake, "I believe I heard he has retired. Is that possible?"

Both Aaron and Jake laughed, "Thirty years in the Marine Corps, now he drives a camper around the country visiting relatives," said Jake. "He just happened to be a few miles south when the news broke about Lake."

Kate came back, and the four walked out to the parking area. She took a deep breath, looked up at the sky, "When does the sun quit the sky here?"

"After six and before seven," returned Jake, "In another month, it'll be around six."

"Where are we off to?" asked Kate.

"The Auld Shebeen," answered Jake.

"To be sure," she returned, "is it down a dark alley? Do you have to use a password to get in?"

"Ian should be there as well," said Jake."

"Dan McLarry's boy?" asked Aaron.

"Yes," returned Jake, "you've not seen him in a few years."

"In '91, we gathered for the Shelton girl. I saw him then. He was a slight boy."

"Was," said Jake, "he's had time to grow."

*   *   *

The Auld Shebeen, Fairfax, VA

Lucas and Ian were sitting at the fireplace in the library, a small room immediately to the right as you entered the pub. Both stood as Jake brought the three travelers in, "Aaron, good to see you."

Jake extended his hand to Ian, "Ian."

"Is this wee Ian McLarry?" asked Aaron.

"Yes, sir," responded Ian, "I've heard stories about you from my father."

"Ah, a good man, Daniel, a good man. I was sad to hear of his passing." Aaron marveled at the size of the boy he met over twenty years past. "Ian, this is my grandson, Jack Gannon, and this little lady is Kate Dixon, my personal assistant. She tells me what to do and when."

Jack smiled and added, "Probably the only person in all of Ireland that could do that."

Kate was a little taken aback, "So, this is the skinny little boy you knew years ago. He looks more like that painting hanging in the great hall at Draighean Cnoc."

Aaron nodded in agreement, "A pint, and down to the business at hand."

They talked about Lake McLarry and what they collectively knew about the shooting in the alley. The conversation drifted to what they could do for Shelly and Lake's son, Marty.

"We're going to leave her a small sum of money that will ease the strains of raising a boy by herself. It's not much, but together with what she'll be getting from the MPD, it will be enough to smooth out some of the rougher edges they may encounter. Kate will take care of all the details at Shelly's bank."

Kate sat quietly and nodded slightly when Aaron mentioned her. As the evening wore on, she became more animated, and Jake asked how she came to be Aaron's assistant.

Aaron answered for her, "Her father and I were good friends. We were both active in the IRA in the sixties and seventies in the north. I took a bullet in my leg back then and he kept at it 'til he was killed in '94. After I was treated for this," he slapped his left leg, "I wasn't much good for the things we were planning to do, so, I brought Kate and her mam, Sheila to Draighean Cnoc. Sheila and my wife became very good friends, and when this little one was ready for university, we helped her out a bit. Now she's a daughter to me, a part of the family.

The evening passed with several pints and food. Jake convinced Ian to stay the night at his house in Fairfax rather than driving out to Vaneksburg, and they'd get a good start in the morning. Around 9:00 p.m., Jake drove the visitors to their hotel in the District.

Aaron was looking tired. Jake suggested they call it an evening. "Jet lag, it's almost 3:00 a.m. in Cork. Time you folks got some rest. Ian and I will come get you in the morning around 8:30."

Aaron looked at Jake, "Could you get me to the Wilson Building in Washington by half-past nine? I'd like to see an old friend."

"No problem," returned Jake, "how much time will you need?"

"No telling," said Aaron. "Probably less than an hour. My friend has a rather busy schedule."

"We'll take Jack and Kate on the nickel tour. When you're ready, just give us a beep on the phone."

Aaron looked at Jack, "You enjoy the city. I'll be just fine."

Jack smiled, "To be sure, grandfather. I'll have a look at this building in the morning and decide."

Aaron raised an eyebrow and smiled.

*   *   *

17

Hotel, Washington, DC

Jake and Ian arrived at the hotel and went straight to the dining room. Aaron, Jack, and Kate were finishing breakfast. Ian waved a waiter over. "I could use a large coffee," he looked at Jake.

"Make that two," said Jake.

As he sat down, Jake's phone chirped a familiar tune, "I have to take this." He stood and walked to a quiet corner and returned in less than a minute. "Ian, I got some feedback from some inquiries I made yesterday." He looked at Aaron, "I'll get you to the Wilson Building, then I have to see someone at my office." He turned to Ian, "I can drop you at my house, and you can pick up your car," he looked at Kate and Jack, "The nickel tour will have to wait."

Ian waved at the waiter, "Can we get those coffees to-go?"

On the ride to the Wilson Building, Jack said he was going to stay with Aaron.

Kate looked at Ian, "Well now, I'll stay with you, and you can tell me more about this city as we pass the Washington Monument and Mr. Lincoln's Memorial."

Jake dropped the two at his house and hurried off to his office.

"Well, young lady, are you ready to see the Washington Monument?" asked Ian.

Kate smiled and said, "Actually, I'd like to see Mr. Lincoln's Memorial."

"Easily done," said Ian, "they're actually quite close to each other. We'll see them both at the same time."

As they drove back into the District, Kate asked about the shooting in the alley. "He was very upset when he heard about Lake. He'll not show it to anyone, but I know the man, and he was hurt." She sat quietly as they drove in on Route 66. As they approached the river, Ian pointed out the Washington Monument and the Kennedy Center. Kate looked but remained quiet. They crossed the bridge and turned right to the Lincoln Memorial. Ian found a parking spot and they and got out to walk.

"It's beautiful, this memorial," said Kate. "The people must have liked Mr. Lincoln very much."

"The war was a terrible time in this country. When the shooting stopped, we still had a long way to go to heal. There are still hard feelings on both sides."

Kate looked up at Ian, "I know what you mean. We're going through the same thing in Ireland."

They walked up the steps to the statue of Lincoln. Kate walked the interior perimeter, reading all the panels. She turned to Ian, "Where is Gettysburg?"

"It's a ways up north, into Pennsylvania," replied Ian.

"I'd like to see that," said Kate as she walked back to read the Gettysburg address again.

Ian watched her, and his mind drifted to thoughts of a casual walk across the mall to the Washington Monument. As he was about to suggest they leave, his cellphone chirped. Aaron was ready to be picked up, "Kate, time to leave. Aaron is ready."

She turned as if coming out of a dream, shook her head, and said, "Yes, we should go."

The drive to the Wilson Building on Pennsylvania Avenue took a few minutes in light traffic. Aaron and Jack were standing at the curb and were quickly picked up then, Ian drove to the O'Leary Funeral Home in Northwest.

*   *   *

Funeral Home, Washington, DC

Shelly was in the reception area, still shaken but standing and greeting every visitor as they entered. Ian hugged Shelly and turned to introduce the visitors from Ireland. Shelly recognized the older gentleman and smiled, "Aaron McLarry, you've come a long way," she said as she embraced him.

He smiled, "He was a good man. My regret is that I've waited 'til now to come see him." He smiled and continued, "MacLaoghaire, m'name is MacLaoghaire."

Shelly returned the smile, "You're in America, and here we say, McLarry." She turned to Ian and looking at Kate and Jack said, "And who have you brought with you?"

Introductions done, Aaron went to the casket with Kate and knelt. He quietly offered a prayer and touched Lake's hand, then stood, stepped back, turned, and walked across the room with Shelly.

"I'd like to offer the condolences of those in the family in Ireland who could not travel this distance." He looked at Kate and nodded to her. Kate joined them, and they went into an adjacent room.

"Shelly, the family carries a small insurance policy for some of its members. Martin was included in the program. Now, it's not much, but it will help you out as Little Martin grows." He touched Kate's arm, "Kate will take care of the details and arrange for the money to be deposited in your bank. You use it as you see fit."

"Thank you," said Shelly.

Kate added, "Your son, Martin is he here?"

"He stepped out for a bit of air and should be back here soon," returned Shelly. "He's not one to sit about, and this has him hurt, confused, and angry. Very angry."

They returned to the viewing room as a young man came in from the parking lot with another man, a tall man with a very stern look. "There's Marty now," said Shelly as she waved him over.

Kate looked at Marty as he crossed the room. "A fine lookin' young man you've got there," she said to Shelly. "How old is he?"

"He'll be fourteen in two months," replied Shelly.

"More's the pity," said Kate. "I'm near old enough to be his mother."

Shelly looked at the tall man with Marty, she smiled and said, "Colin, it's been a long time," as she took his hand and squeezed.

"Too long," returned Colin, "far too long."

Ian approached with Aaron MacLaoghaire, he looked at Marty and said, "Marty, this is Aaron MacLaoghaire, from Ireland, and I see you've already met Colin."

Colin smiled, nodded and said, "My condolences," to Shelly as he released her hand and turned to Aaron, "when you have a minute or two …"

"Understood," returned Aaron as he turned toward Marty.

"I've heard your name, sir, from my dad," said Marty. "I thank you for coming here today."

Aaron took Marty's hand, "I wish I had come sooner, your father was a good man, and although we've only met a few times, he will be missed by me and others who knew him."

Marty lowered his head, then stood straight and looked at Jack. "Hi, I'm Marty McLarry."

"Jack Gannon," replied Aaron's grandson, "we're cousins, probably a few steps removed, but still family." He turned to Kate, "And this is Kate Dixon."

Kate smiled and took Marty's hand, "I'm sorry for your loss."

"Are you also a cousin?" asked Marty.

Kate raised an eyebrow, smiled, and replied, "Unofficially, sort of," she looked at Aaron.

Jack chuckled, "Kate's at a loss for words. Never thought I'd see the day."

Ian patted Marty on the shoulder, "A story for a time when we can sit and relax, but yes, she's family."

*   *   *

Saint Patrick's Church, Washington, DC

The procession from the funeral home to the church was lined with more than 100 cars following the hearse. The ceremony in the church was brief and the same at the gravesite.

"Martin would not have wanted all this fuss," said Shelly, "but there's no way we could have done any less."

Ian stood next to Marty as the final prayers were delivered, and he stayed with him as Marty took his mother's arm and walked her back to their limousine.

Mike Farley took Ian aside and told him there was to be a dinner held at a hotel's banquet hall at 3:00 that afternoon, "You should be ready to say a few words. Family should go first, then maybe the chief and a few others will say something. I'll probably get up there too."

Ian accompanied Shelly and Marty back to their home, where they had an hour of quiet time before they got ready for the dinner. Jake Brennan arrived with Lucas and the travelers at 2:45. "Ian, take Lucas and Marty in your car, and I'll bring the others," said Jake.

The dinner was a buffet with an open bar. The conversations plentiful. As the tables filled and the conversation slowed, Lucas stood and held a microphone, "Good afternoon, everybody."

The several speeches were brief and gracious. After Lucas, Shelly, Jake, and Ian spoke, Marty stood and accepted the mic from Ian, "I want to thank everybody for coming today. You all have said some very nice things about my dad, and that means a lot to me and my mom." He paused, and Ian saw Marty's eyes begin to water.

Ian put his arm around Marty's shoulders and said quietly, "I see your dad in you."

*   *   *

18

Aaron had suggested a lunch meeting at the Auld Shebeen in Fairfax to review recent events and plan out the coming days. Jake, Ian, Dan, and Lucas joined Aaron, and his companions, and Jim McLarry also joined in.

"It'll be a seven-hour flight from Dulles to Dublin and another two hours by train to Cork," said Kate, "that'll fill the day when we travel."

"When will we make this trip?" quizzed Jack.

"Well now, I know if we left today and were home by tomorrow, I'd hear it from himself that we could have taken an extra day or two and visited more of the family here in America," replied Kate. "So, there you are, Jack. We'll see who's close enough to visit in the next few days, and then we'll go home."

Aaron nodded in approval and added, "Cleveland, Cincinnati, Pittsburgh, Philadelphia, Boston, and Buffalo. I'd like to visit each one."

Kate opened a notepad and said, "I have a list of people across this country. I think we should pick two close cities and not do too much."

Aaron nodded again, "I'd like to see the Sheltons in Cleveland and perhaps Jim O'Leary in Boston."

"I'll make it happen," said Kate as she opened her cellphone and began to tap out a message.

Jake smiled and said, "I see why you brought her along."

"Tell me, Jake," said Aaron, "do you think we might hear from others across the Clann about this incident?"

"It's hard telling at this point, but I think we should leave the doors open and see what comes in," replied Jake.

"Ian, you have a direct link into the MPD," said Aaron, "and I think you should be our point of contact. Dan Carney is my suggestion as a backup." He paused as this sunk in, "I know the temptation to take charge and jump into the fray is present, but we should remember, we want the right people caught and brought to justice. Any freelancing that could screw up the official investigation would be bad, so, whether we learn something legally or not, we should transmit it to the authorities as an anonymous tip, and we, the family, have no idea from whence it came."

Jake grinned, "We've dealt with situations like that before," he glanced at Aaron, who returned his knowing grin. "We know how difficult it is, but we have to take a backseat. Let the process work."

Aaron said, "The word is out, the family is aware, and even though it is probably a local situation, the website is open across the country and beyond." He looked at Ian, "You're our contact so, be careful what you say and to whom. Again, we'll run any information we gather through you to the proper authorities. You've already established contact with the lead investigator, Detective Reed, so let him know we may be sending him something through you."

Ian nodded, "Okay," he paused, "how did you know who the lead investigator is?"

"Ian, what you don't know, you can't tell. I know what I know, and I'll share almost everything with you as it is significant."

"Understood," replied Ian, "I think."

Jake added, "Don't push anything. If there is something, it'll be put on your plate, and you just pass it along."

Ian nodded, "Again, understood."

Jim McLarry said, "Ian, I was a member of the CHPD when we were investigating the disappearance of our cousin, Annette Shelton. It was very difficult staying back and letting the process work. As it turned out, the information that came to me wasn't enough to nail the perp. He disappeared. His remains were found several years later. I still don't know what happened to him," said Jim as he looked around the room, "but I have some suspicions."

Both Aaron and Jake feigned innocence. Lucas remained as still as a rock and showed nothing. Jim looked at Ian, "Someday, we may learn more."

Then Lucas added, "Or not."

Kate returned to the group. She looked at Jim McLarry, "You'll be driving back to Cleveland this afternoon or tomorrow morning?"

"Tomorrow," replied Jim.

"Well then, would you be so kind as to give these two poor travelers a ride to Cleveland as well?" said Kate with a smile and a glance toward Jack and Aaron.

"My pleasure," said Jim.

"On Saturday morning, you two will fly to Boston, visit with James O'Leary, then Sunday you'll take the Amtrak train back here."

"And you, Kate," said Jack, "what about you?"

"I've got a little business to take care of with Shelly, and maybe I can get Mr. Detective McLarry to give me a proper tour of the Washington Monument."

Ian looked surprised and quickly said, "Sure, and maybe the Jefferson."

Aaron looked pleased with the schedule and added, "Then home on Monday?"

"Unless you'd like another day here in Washington," said Kate.

Aaron thought for a moment, "Tuesday will be soon enough."

Dan Carney stood, "Listen folks, Kat Murano is still in the hospital, and I want to check on her, so, can we plan on meeting again on Monday, here for dinner.?"

Kate looked at Dan, "Wish her a speedy recovery Danny Boy, we're all keeping her in our prayers. Dinner here on Monday is an excellent idea. I'll reserve a table for the lot of us."

*　　　*　　　*

19

Fulton Road Warehouse, Springfield, VA

Dave Saunders was back in the warehouse, business as usual. No problems, no worries. Bernie was making his weekly visit to the warehouse, and the two men walked around talking about various shipments. They finished their tour and made their way up the stairs to Dave's office, "Coffee, Mr. Temple?"

"Thanks, Dave, that would be nice," replied Bernie.

Dave pulled a couple of K-cups out of a drawer and started the process. "It's been almost a week since we shipped the broken parts back for evaluation. Is everything settled? Were the items repairable?"

"Oh, yes. Beyond repair, I'm afraid, but all settled," returned Bernie. He sipped his coffee and continued, "We don't need interference from outside, and I hope there are no other amateur spies or clumsy inspectors with whom we must contend."

The two men raised their coffee mugs in a toast, "All's well that ends well," said Dave.

Bernie smiled. He was feeling comfortable again. "Yes, Dave, you handled the situation very well."

Dave knew that meant something extra at the end of the month. *Yeah*, he thought, *all's well.*

*   *   *

Abandoned Building, Washington, DC

The investigation into the incident in the alley was tied to the shooting in the abandoned office building. It appeared as though Lake and Kat were shot by Jason Barrett. The weapons, badges, contents of Lake's wallet, and Kat's purse were scattered about the mattress where Jason was found. It all pointed to him. The attempts at the ATM using

Lake's and Kat's credit cards were made by Jason. He was identified by a gas station clerk as carrying a weapon when he bought several items. It was also obvious the drugs he used were most likely purchased in the same area as the ATMs and the gas station. The entire sequence was all very neat and obvious at first glance.

Freddy Knolls wasn't happy; he didn't buy the sequence. His conversations with Stan Reed and Ian left all three with a sour taste. "It's all too convenient," he said several times as he went over the collection of evidence with the detectives.

Ian came back to the scratches in the alley, "The dumpster, the truck, all this stuff he collected scattered about his happy little home. I'm with you Freddy. It don't add up."

Stan said, "The guys in the office want this to be the end. They want this little guy to be the answer. Everything points to him, and I'll admit, I'd like it to be him too." He kicked the corner of the mattress, "But, damn it, Freddy, you have a point. It's all too neat."

"Let's look at the truck," said Ian. "Where is the damn thing? If Barrett used a truck, where did he get it, and where is it now?"

"Stolen and dumped, maybe," said Stan.

"Or we have a second bad guy with a vehicle like a truck," said Freddy.

Ian paced the floor, looked out the window, and said, "Why would a second boggy leave this stuff here. Guns, drugs, credit cards. There has to be another player or two in this deal." He looked at Freddy, "Your guys dusted for prints, right?"

"Yeah, a few miscellaneous prints came up," said Freddy, "some were the other vic in the alley, Andrew Ross, and another guy identified as another doper, living on the street. A few others were partials that went nowhere, coulda been a year old, or more."

"We're looking for him now, this doper," said Stan. "No telling if we can find him, these guys often blend in with the scenery, sleeping under bridges or in the bushes."

Ian, still pacing, stopped and asked, "The 911 call, any trace on it?"

"I got the number, one of those throwaway phones. No telling who it was," said Stan.

"This Barrett character had a cellphone," said Ian. "We should see if the two ever connected."

Stan called into MPD and waited a few seconds, "Yeah, whoever called in the 911, has called this Barrett guy a number of times."

"So, who is the other caller?" posed Ian. "Maybe Barrett's connection, his dealer. Maybe the other prints you found, or somebody completely new." He thought for a minute and took his phone out, "What's the number of the 911 caller?"

"We already called it, not working," said Stan. "Like it's been turned off, battery pulled, or run over by a bulldozer."

Ian said, "We should track the pings on both phones over the last few weeks, see where these guys have been, and maybe we find the third man."

"I'll get on that," said Stan.

"Murano is still recovering and a little fuzzy on details, so what else do we have?" asked Ian.

Stan looked at Freddy, "Run through the positioning again, Freddy."

"It works, everything comes together," said Freddy. "And then again, it doesn't work."

"Okay, I can see how it works, now you tell me how it doesn't," said Ian.

Freddy reviewed all the evidence collected and got to the scratches on the pavement in the alley, "Why was the dumpster moved and moved back?"

Ian listened, "Keep going."

"Why was Kat on the same side of the alley as Lake?" continued Freddy.

"You're getting me hooked, Freddy. Is there more?"

"Yeah, Jason Barrett shot up more than once, now he shoots up and OD's, not just a little, but by a long shot, no pun intended."

Ian was making notes and looked at Freddy for more.

"Jason has no external wounds, he didn't have a nosebleed, and the doc says he was not spitting blood."

Dan looked puzzled, "Okay, and…?"

"Whose blood was in the office building, on the stairs, on the floor leading to Jason's apartment, and around the table?" Freddy paused as Ian made a note. "And why are there blood drops with directional spatter indicating the subject was not only coming in the building but also going out at some point?"

Ian's interest was growing, "Yeah, is there more?"

Freddy folded his arms across his chest, "Where did a guy like Jason get a pistol like the one he used to shoot both Lake and Kat?"

Ian mumbled, "Pistol," as he made another note.

Freddy continued, "That dumpster, it's not easy to move, but a big man could push it as the scratches indicate. I don't think Jason had the strength."

Ian made the note and looked at Freddy, "That's a lot of questions needing answers."

"Yeah, yeah it is," replied Freddy, "and I ain't done. I've got more to check and more to process."

Ian sat up straight, "Such as?"

"The lab work won't be back for a few more days at best, some will take longer, maybe even a couple of weeks."

"We're far from done, aren't we?" said Ian.

"I'd say."

*　　　*　　　*

20

Metropolitan Police Department, Washington, DC

The connection of George Klemper to both Bernie Temple and James Millington kept all three cases on the table for discussion. Mike Farley suggested a little crazy speculation. "Let's put Klemper, Millington, Ross, Barrett, and McLarry all together and find a common thread."

Stan said, "I've been reading Lake's notes, and he had a bead on this Barrett character, something about another guy, I assume Ross, was doing clean-up or some day-labor thing at Temple's warehouse and had some information to share with MPD."

"Yeah, I know Lake dropped a fifty on a couple of informants, and they were going after more info, more bucks."

"Do we know it was Barrett?" asked Ian.

"Not exactly," said Mike, "but that's who he'd been dealing with that week."

Stan added, "The camera at an ATM near Barrett's hangout recorded an individual attempting to withdraw money from both Lake's and Kat's accounts. The man using the ATM cards is easily identified as Jason Barrett. We checked the neighborhood. A store clerk positively identified Barrett as the guy who bought water and some trash food. He had a gun in his belt, and he was alone."

Farley said, "The guy didn't have the right pin numbers and didn't get anything out of either machine." He tossed three black and white printouts across his desk, "But that's our guy—Jason Barrett."

"Freddy's still looking at this as if someone else could be involved," said Stan.

"That's possible," returned Farley. "He painted a picture for me the other day, and I want him to keep looking. We could have this all wrong, but it really looks good for this Barrett character," said Farley.

"But not good enough to put it to bed?" said Stan.

Farley thought for a moment, "No, not yet. Let's see what Freddy comes up with. I can't tell you how many times I heard Lake say he wanted to be sure. Something like, 'We want the guy who did the deed, not just somebody who looks good for it,' or something like that."

As Stan was taking another sip of his coffee, his phone chirped. He answered, "Hey Dan," then he paused and said, "we'll be there as soon as we can. Keep your cellphone handy, if she wakes and starts to mumble, record it." He stood as he said, "Dan Carney is with Kat. She seems to be ready to wake up." He looked at Mike, "If she can, she'll tell us what we need.

Mike added, "Yeah, she's a tough little lady, she might surprise us." He looked at the two detectives, "Well get moving, it's about time we started getting breaks."

*   *   *

Washington Hospital Center, Washington, DC

Stan and Ian arrived as a nurse was leaving the room, "She's been stirring," the nurse told Stan, "a little movement here and there this morning. She may wake up soon."

They went into the room and waited as the nurse completed a check of the patient. "Gentlemen, she's had a very rough time, so don't expect too much." She turned as she was leaving the room, "And *do not* push her to answer questions."

Dan greeted Stan and Ian, "She may not have any memory of the incident, or it could be all distorted. I don't expect too much from her."

Ian nodded, "Understood, Dan." He thought for a moment, "Let's not crowd her. Stan and I will step out of the room and be right there," he pointed at the chairs where three uniformed officers were keeping vigil.

Stan talked to the three officers, and Ian went to the coffee machine. As he tasted his brew, Kat's father exited the elevator and approached, "Good afternoon, Detective, how are you today?"

Ian smiled, "Better than yesterday, and Kat may make our day. She may be starting to come around."

Roberto's eyes widened; he turned to her room and hurried in.

A minute later, Dan stood in the doorway and waved Stan and Ian in.

"Yeah, she woke up for a few seconds, said something."

The nurse said, "Yes, she stirred and said something like she was calling to someone. Lake, does that make sense?"

Dan shook his head, "Yeah, that's her partner, Lake McLarry. He was shot and didn't make it."

The nurse sighed, "I'm sorry, I knew her partner was killed, but I thought his name was Martin."

Dan breathed deeply and exhaled, "Yeah, Lake was his middle name, and that's what we called him—Lake."

They continued talking quietly. Her father was standing next to her bed with her hand in his. He looked up at the three, smiled, and said to Dan, "She was awake a second ago."

Kat stirred again, she mumbled something, and the nurse patted her gently, "You're okay Detective, a little beat up, but we're taking care of you."

Kat was agitated, tried to sit up, and said, "Lake, Lake."

Dan stepped closer, "Kat, it's Dan. You're in the hospital. You're going to be okay."

Kat opened her eyes enough to see a large dark figure in front of her, "Dan, Dan, Lake's shot, hurt."

She closed her eyes and relaxed. The nurse said, "That's what she did earlier."

Dan moved closer, stood next to her father, and quietly looked at her.

As they were speaking, an older man of average height, and grey hair entered the room, "How's our friend doing this morning?" he asked the nurse.

"All signs are good, Doctor. She's responding to the reduction in meds, and she has stirred twice in the last fifteen minutes. Last time she showed concern for her partner, Detective McLarry."

The doctor made a note on Kat's chart and proceeded to check her breathing with his stethoscope. He looked into her eyes and felt her pulse, then looked at the monitors. "Okay, she's on track." He looked quizzically at the three men standing in her room, "I know Detective Murano's father, and these gentlemen are, who?"

Dan extended his hand, noticed the name tag read Dr. A.G. Blanton, "Officer Dan Carney and this is Detective Stan Reed, MPD, and Detective Ian McLarry, Vaneksburg PD," as he touched Ian's shoulder.

"McLarry, related to the other detective involved in this shooting?"

Ian offered his hand, "Yes sir, Lake was my cousin."

"I'm sorry for your loss, Detective, but pleased to say your colleague here will recover. She'll need time and some rehab, but she is very fortunate."

As they were talking, Kat stirred again, "Lake, help Lake."

The doctor immediately went back to Kat's side and spoke to her, "Detective, can you hear me?"

Kat responded, "Who are…?"

"My name is Dr. Anthony Blanton, and I'm going to help you," he touched her hand.

Kat turned her head toward Blanton and tried to focus, "You're fuzzy."

"You're doing fine, a little more time, and you'll feel like talking. Right now, you should rest," said Dr. Blanton.

Kat repeated, "Lake, he's been hurt," she blinked her eyes, trying to clear her vision.

"Yes, we have taken care of Detective McLarry. Now you relax, we'll talk more later."

Kat took a deep breath and turned toward Dan, "Dan, is that you?"

"Yeah Kat, I'm right here."

"Dan, did you get them?"

Dan looked at Kat, "Them, was there more than one?"

"Tomas, his name is Tomas," said Kat.

Kat took a deeper breath and blurted, "Tomas, he shot Lake, I shot him, other man grabbed me." She seemed to be lost.

Dan looked at Stan and Ian, "Tomas?"

Ian approached Kat, "Kat did you see their car?"

Kat blinked her eyes several times and said, "Van, white van." She slipped into sleep.

Dan looked at Stan, "A white van, Tomas, two men."

Stan had his cellphone out and was heading to the waiting area where the reception was better. He looked at Ian, "You wanna call this in?"

"Your case, Stan, you call."

*   *   *

21

The new information was on the Clann's website almost immediately, and Lucas got a call from Kevin Shelton, a cousin in California and a Detective with LAPD, "You're looking for two thug types, one named Tomas?"

"That's a big maybe. All we got is one guy's name, Tomas," said Lucas.

"Give this a try, Tomas Relatto and Clint Marsh. A pair of leg breakers that I've been keeping an eye on for a few months. They flew out of here last week, Monday. Heading to your area and expected to return here yesterday."

"You have them?" asked Lucas.

"Nope, they changed plans and flew into Vegas, now I gotta go find 'em again," said Kevin. "They're just the type that could have been brought in to do a little strong-arm stuff, and they're not above shooting first." He paused, "I'll send photos and data on both."

"That's great, Kevin. Can you send the info to Ian McLarry at MPD?"

"You got it," said Kevin.

"Who did these two work for?" asked Lucas.

"Not sure on this one. They've done a lot of freelance stuff, like 'Thugs R Us', leg breakin' neatly done."

"Thanks, Kevin, we'll check on this end."

*   *   *

Ian found Lucas at the bar, having an evening pint, "Lucas, I got your message. What's new?"

"Word went out on the website," said Lucas, "and we got a hit out of LA almost immediately."

"Tell me, what do we have?" asked Ian.

"Two possibles, a couple of guys being watched by LAPD," said Lucas. "The name Tomas caught Kevin Shelton's eye. He gave me a call. One Tomas Relatto and the other, Clint Marsh."

"So, what do we have on them?" asked Ian.

"All we know is these two characters were in the area, and this is their kind of action," said Lucas. "What we don't have is a direct connection. They were here, then they flew to Vegas instead of back to LA. So, you put their names on the table and see if MPD can do anything with that."

"Where do I say this info comes from?" asked Ian.

"California cousin," returned Lucas, "these two have been under casual observation for a few months because they have dipped their toes in the risky water, and LAPD wants to be able to grab 'em up when they do it again. Kevin will send sheets on both of them to you at MPD."

"But this? Coming in here to do a hit?" puzzled Ian.

"I'm more inclined to think they were here for something else, and the killing somehow developed out of a bad situation," said Lucas. "I don't think Lake was a target, probably a surprise to everybody."

"So, what do we do now?" asked Ian.

"Like I said, Ian, pass it along and sit tight, see what MPD makes of it."

"Maybe do a photo line-up for Kat?" said Ian. "If they look good, we go to Vegas and grab 'em up."

Lucas nodded, "Yeah, that's what I'd do, but Nevada ain't Virginia, so you go through the locals out there."

"Yeah, I know," said Ian, "but I'd really like to be there when they get cuffed."

Lucas took out his phone, "Give me a minute here," he said as he pushed a few numbers. "Jake, we have a lead, the two characters who probably hit Lake are in Nevada." He relayed everything he had learned and asked, "Who do we have in Vegas?"

"Greg Hanson," said Jake, "a private detective who had retired from the LAPD after twenty-five years on the job. Moved to Vegas, loved the city and the amenities it offered, and found a second career with a private security and investigative firm."

"Give Kevin a shout, suggest he forward the same info to Greg, and I'll call Greg, tell him where we are," said Jake.

Lucas called Kevin, Jake called Greg, and the ball kept rolling. "Now we wait," said Lucas. "See what pops. We may be going to Vegas."

*   *   *

The Strip, Las Vegas, NV

When Greg received the info from Kevin, he immediately contacted the airport authority security office. "We're looking for a couple of guys from LA," he told the security officer, "they flew to DC on Monday and were ticketed back to LA on Thursday originally, but they changed and flew into McCarran on Friday. They're persons of interest in a DC shooting."

"You got pics?" asked Art Stanton, the security officer. "I have eyes on all the doors and more. If they were here, we'll be able to track them at least out to the airport exits."

Greg took the photos and sheets on both men and drove out to McCarran International Airport, to review the security footage. Through a combination of cameras, it was determined they arrived on a flight from IAD, they had no luggage, were picked up by two other men in a blue mini-van then headed north on Paradise Road.

"The plates aren't very clear," said Greg. "Now to find a camera or two on the road maybe we get a better pic. Thanks Art."

Art grinned, "This ain't my first rodeo. Let me give you a few places to stop and check," he said as he made a few notes and handed it to Greg. "I'll call now and tell 'em you're comin'."

"Art, I can't thank you enough," said Greg as he hurried out the door and headed to the first address on his list. He stopped at all three locations, and the cameras did their bit, showing the blue van on Paradise and onto Tropicana. He extended his search up to Route 15, and two cameras showed the mini-van continuing north on 15. Greg drove up 15 looking for ATMs or convenience stores on or near off-ramps. He arrived in Mesquite and found another camera with a view of the off-ramp from 15 and very close to the calculated time, the same vehicle or one looking very much like it, passed a service station, this time heading east. Greg followed the road, looking for more video cameras, and after a day's search, determined the vehicle turned a few times, eventually heading south on Riverside Road. It appears the same vehicle returned a few hours later and took 15 back toward Las Vegas. A map of the area, an estimate of how far they could have traveled, and a circle drawn on the map left the question wide open where they had gone. The videos he reviewed were inconclusive, but he did not notice anyone in the rear seat of the vehicle on the return trip.

"Listen, Ian," said Greg, "I'm not positive that it's the same van. I've identified the two local guys from the airport, couple of thugs like your two. I'll send you sheets on both of them, and we can talk to them, but they may just clam up and give us nothing."

"I hear you," returned Ian, "and I'll talk it up here, see if there's any more strings we can pull. Thanks Greg."

Ian sat with Jake, Dan, and Lucas at a pub on M Street. He laid out what they had thus far learned and finished with, "These two lumps may just say nothing, lawyer up, and we're no further ahead." He drained his mug of beer and said, "Wait for the Vegas folks to check out their two characters and hope for something else to move this thing forward."

Jake said, "Well, that's it then. I've got to go. Lucas, can I give you a lift?"

Lucas accepted, and the two left the Pub. Jake's car was parked less than a block away. The two sat in the car for a few minutes, then Lucas got out and walked to his car down the block.

*   *   *

The Strip, Las Vegas, NV

Early the next morning, Lucas caught a flight to Las Vegas, getting him there in time for lunch with Greg. "I'd like to meet these two people," said Lucas, "we may come to an accord."

Greg said, "Okay, are you here, or is someone else?"

"You mean on my ticket? It says James Martinez, and I may have a friend or two join us. This afternoon, let's find Heckle and Jeckle, and I'll take it from there."

Greg looked at Lucas, "James?"

"Yep, the guy you're looking at is James. If anybody ever asks, name is James Martinez. Let's leave it at that."

*   *   *

The Strip, Las Vegas, NV

After lunch, Greg located the two men and called Lucas. They met at a casino on the strip. "They're in the restaurant. I'll show you." They went into the restaurant and sat in a booth, "Three tables over, that's them," said Greg. "Rich Pallman and Will Garnos, they come here every morning and have breakfast, then hit the strip, take in a few shows, place a few bets and try to pick up women." He looked at the two thugs and back at Lucas, "What happens now?"

"We'll follow them, maybe pick them up and invite them for tea," said Lucas. "Then we talk to them, find out where they took their friends, and then see what happens next."

"Okay, so there is someone else going to be involved in this party?" asked Greg.

"Ask me no questions and I'll tell you no lies," said Lucas. "You just pointed out the people we want to talk to so, that's it, and now, you're out of it. Remember, if it ever comes up, my name is James Martinez. Other than that, be completely honest, answer all questions honestly, and you'll have no trouble." Lucas finished his coffee, noted the two thugs were ready to leave, "I'll take it from here."

"Okay, Lucas, I mean James, but be careful, these are pretty rough dudes. They don't play around."

"Oh, I will," replied Lucas. He looked back at Greg, "They come here every day for breakfast? About what time?"

"Yeah, so far, for the last four days around 9:00 a.m., give or take a few minutes. Then again, they stop in for coffee once in a while, like now." They watched the two men as they finished their coffee and walked out of the casino. Lucas looked at Greg, "Okay, man, I got this. You stay clear, don't try to contact me or look around for these two. They may be busy with other things for a while." He stood and walked outside, keeping the two in sight, and followed them.

*   *   *

The Strip, Las Vegas, NV

A few days later, Lucas and Jake decided to take the next step. They had tracked the two thugs and nothing was happening. It was time to stir the pot.

"Are you ready?" asked Jake.

"As ever was," replied Lucas. He now sported a four-day beard, and his hair had been colored a dark brown. He wore dark-rimmed glasses and washed his mouth out with cheap whiskey.

"What did you eat this morning, Lucas?" asked Jake. "Your breath could kill plant life at ten paces."

Lucas smiled, "Nice touch, eh. And my name is James Martinez," he said with a slight Hispanic accent.

Jake grinned, "Okay, and you call me Adam, just Adam."

They stood outside the restaurant, waiting for the two to emerge. When they did, Lucas fell in behind them. Jake drove to the garage where the two had parked their minivan. He backed into a space near the thugs' van and waited. Lucas caught up with them as they reached their van. He had a key ring in his left hand and feigned a trip in front of their van. His left hand slid across the hood, leaving a large scratch in the finish.

Lucas stood up as the two men came around the van and were about to attack him. Jake pulled the car out of his parking space and moved toward Rich and Will.

Lucas didn't hesitate, spun to his left, and caught Will with a fist to his throat. Then a quick continued turn, he landed a punch to Riche's chest. Both men staggered, and Lucas pushed them up against the van. He looked around at the floor and spotted the keys that were in Will's hand. He picked up the keys, opened their van, and pushed both inside.

He took several pull ties out of his pocket. Bound, hand and foot, the two thugs were not problematic.

"I'll see you at the warehouse," said Jake, noticing the two securely bound. Just don't get pulled over. That," he said, nodding towards the two thugs, "might be hard to explain."

Jake drove out of the garage and on to 15, heading south. He drove for about twenty minutes and came to an abandoned industrial building. As he approached, a large overhead door rose and allowed his car to enter. A minute later, the van stood outside, and Lucas sounded the horn. The door rose, and the van entered.

*　　　*　　　*

Abandoned Warehouse, Las Vegas, NV

Inside the warehouse, there were three other men. The two guests were carried out of the van and tied with several ropes stretching them in a spread-eagle pose suspended about a foot off the floor.

Lucas looked at Jake and said, "Adam?"

Jake nodded, "James, our friends are ready to talk to us."

Stripped naked and suspended with arms and legs spread, the two thugs were slowly recovering from the punches. Lucas told one of the others to wrap something around their waists and added, "They'll probably dump everything they got before we get too deep into this." He looked at Jake, motioned him toward a table, opened a tool bag, dumped the contents on the table, and said, "Careful, Adam, these things are sharp, and I haven't cleaned them."

Jake smirked and quietly said to Lucas, "You're one sick bastard, my friend."

"Yeah, but I get answers," replied Lucas as he attached a mylar strip to the edge of the table.

Lucas went to Will, "Tell me, Will, when's the last time your nose was broken?"

Will was groggy but awake. He didn't know what to say or do.

Lucas walked up to him again, close. He breathed in Will's face letting him smell the garlic and whiskey on his breath, "You didn't answer the question, Will," and he punched Will's nose. "See, you didn't answer the question, so I helped. Now you have a broken nose, and I have my answer." Lucas smiled and continued, "I have another question. Are you ready?" He stepped closer to Will and said, "When is the last time you broke your right thumb?"

Will tried to say he'd never broken his thumb. Lucas shook his head, "No, no, no, now that's not right." He took Will's right hand and twisted his thumb 'til the sound of snapping bones and Will's screams made him smile. He walked around to the other hand and said, "Now, next question, When's the last time you broke this thumb?"

Will's eyes were full of tears. He wouldn't be able to take much more of this treatment. He tried to answer, but his face was a mass of blood, and his hand was in pure pain.

"Oh, okay," said Lucas, and he twisted Will's other thumb until the bones snapped.

He looked at Rich, "Your friend is not cooperating, and all I want is a simple answer to a simple question. Now, I know some of the details, but I need to know more, you understand?"

Rich wasn't sure what was coming, a broken nose, broken thumbs, what else, he didn't know. He watched as Lucas walked over to the table.

"I know what you're thinking. You want to know what else I can do to you two. Well, I have some tools, like this old skinning knife." He picked up a knife and held it up for Rich to see. "Wanna see how it works?" He slowly walked toward Rich.

Rich was trying to think of a way to get out of this mess. He looked at Will, then at Lucas holding the skinning knife. He could smell the alcohol on Lucas's breath and didn't want any part of this drunken Latino and his filthy knife. "What do you want? I'll tell ya anything you wanna hear."

"Like I said, Richey, I know some of it, so if I ask you a question and you lie to me, well then, I'll just start the skinning on you and get it out of your friend while he watches you bleed."

"Anything, I'll tell ya anything," cried Rich.

Lucas wiped the knife on a dirty rag, held the cold metal against Rich's ribs, grinned, and said, "What did you do on Tuesday?"

Rich knew if he talked about Tuesday, he'd be in trouble with his employer. *Talk to anyone about this, and I'll kill you,* he'd been told. But his employer wasn't here now; this sick man, James, was here holding a knife. Rich knew something of his employer; he would kill him and Will. He didn't know if this James character would actually skin him.

"Tuesday, nothin', we didn't do nothin'." He blurted, "Nothin'."

"Oh Richey, that's the wrong answer," said Lucas, "stand by 'cause this is really gonna hurt." Lucas smiled, put the knife's edge against Rich's leg, and started to cut, "See, you begin with a very shallow cut."

Rich screamed, "We went out to the airport, picked up some guys."

Lucas paused, "What guys?" He walked over to the table and stropped the knife on a mylar strip.

Rich's leg was bleeding. He imagined Lucas starting to remove his skin. Before Lucas was halfway back to Rich's leg, he continued, "Two guys from DC, Tomas, and Clint."

"Very good, Richey, Tomas, and Clint who?" asked Lucas.

Rich panicked. He didn't know their last names. "I dunno," he spat out, "we wasn't given no last names."

Lucas wanted to emphasize that he knew some of the details, "Okay, Richey, I'll let that one slide. See, those two guys worked for the same man we work for, and that man wants to know where his friends are. So, you're going to tell us what we want to know." He looked closely at his knife, "Clint Marsh and Tomas Relatto," he looked back at Rich, "but you probably already knew that."

"No, we didn't know those names, really," sputtered Rich.

Lucas grinned, "Like I said, I'll let that slide, but I know you know the answer to the next question." He again placed the cold metal against Rich's ribs and asked, "Where did you take them, Richey?"

Rich knew he had no choice, "We took 'em out near Mesquite."

"Yeah, out 15 to Riverside, then where?" asked Lucas as he put the knife back in the cut on Rich's leg.

"We went a little past Mesquite into the desert. We had a coupla' holes dug, and that's where we put 'em."

"Okay, Richey, so far so good," Lucas put the knife against Rich's ribs again, "and now, where are they?"

Rich shuddered, "They're still out there, buried."

"And why did you bury them out there?" asked Lucas.

Rich replied, "Because they was dead."

Lucas wagged his finger in Rich's face, "They weren't dead when you picked them up."

Rich thought for a second, "No, they wasn't, but they had something to drink, and they died so, we buried them?"

Lucas held the knife close to Rich's face, "Something to drink?"

"Oh, yeah, we was given a coupla' bottles of stuff and told to give it to them in the car after we got outta the airport."

"What stuff?"

"I dunno, stuff," Rich replied, "it looked like red soda, but we was told to not drink it."

"Did someone give the bottles to you?"

"No, we was told to buy a couple bottles of water and mix in some stuff."

"What stuff?" asked Lucas.

"I don't know. I wrote it down on paper and got it at a hardware store."

"Where's the paper?"

"I threw it away when I got the stuff," said Richey, "at the hardware store."

"Anything else?"

"Well, we made the water bottles and put 'em in the fridge, then kept 'em in a cooler in the van 'til we gave 'em to the guys."

"So, they drank it and died?"

"Naw, they fell asleep in the back seat of the van, and when we got out in the desert, they didn't wake up. They was dead. I thought we was gonna hafta shoot em, but, like I said, they was dead and so, then we buried them."

"So, when did you dig the graves, Richey?"

"We was out there the day before, cause we didn't want to spend too much time out there when we was buryin' 'em, so, we got the holes dug and all ready the day before. All we had to do was put 'em in and push the dirt in on 'em."

Lucas was constantly amazed at the callous nature of people who committed murder. It was a very matter-of-fact scenario. Thugs 1 and 2 are an impediment to someone, so thugs 3 and 4 are told to take them out in the desert and kill them, then bury them like so much trash.

"Efficient," said Lucas. "Okay, Richey, now for the next couple of questions, I want you to remember, I don't have a lot of time. If you don't tell me what I want, I'll make Will watch as I pull your skin off. That will inspire him to talk."

Rich squirmed and looked at Will, "No, I'll tell ya."

"See, Richey, that wasn't so difficult," Lucas paused, set the knife down on the table, then picked up a pair of wire cutters. "Now this is very important, Richey. Who told you to pick them up and take them out to the desert?"

"A guy we do jobs for sometimes," replied Rich.

Lucas picked up a piece of wood and cut off the end with the wire cutters, "Richey, come on, you know I want more than that." Lucas stood close to Rich and held his little finger in one hand and the wire cutters in the other hand. "Not just any guy, Richey, a specific guy," he said as he started to put the wire cutters around Rich's little finger, "So you should tell me his name."

"We call him Franklin," said Rich.

"Franklin who?" asked Lucas.

"Nothing, just Franklin," said Rich.

As Lucas began to tighten the cutters around Rich's finger, he asked, "How do you know this, Franklin?"

"We was lookin' for some work a couple a years ago, and this guy calls us on the phone. He said he was lookin' for guys to do some things here in Vegas, and so, we told him we was available for any kinda stuff."

"Yeah," said Lucas, "then what?"

"Then he tells us we should have an email account, like an AOL thing, like that," said Rich, "and then he says we should call the AOL thing 'RandW101' and then we should wait."

Lucas nodded, "Keep going."

"So, we get signed up with the AOL," continued Rich. "and then we just sit back, and we wait."

"And he writes to you," said Lucas, "and tells you to do things?"

"Yeah, and then like a week later, we get a package delivered from UPS," said Rich, "it's a cheap phone and a note. It says, 'put the battery in' and there's a message on the phone, says, 'Phone will ring at 8:00 p.m., and we should answer."

"Where's the phone now?"

"Coupla' months ago, he told us to pull the battery and smash up the phone, then toss it, and watch the emails."

"You get emails from Franklin?" asked Lucas.

"Yeah, on our AOL thing," replied Rich.

Lucas paced about, thinking, "How does he pay you?"

Rich was now very talkative, "It goes into a bank, and we have debit cards."

"How many times have you taken people out into the desert?" asked Lucas.

"Couple a times, maybe five," said Rich.

"Could you show us where those bodies are buried?"

"I don't remember too good," said Rich.

"Come on, Richey, try so I can find just one of 'em."

Rich looked at the wire cutters in Lucas' hand and said, "One of 'em was found. Some animal dug him up about a year ago."

"How do you know he was found?"

"It was in the papers. Some kids runnin' round saw where the bones was being chewed on. Then Franklin called us on the phone. He was really pissed. He said we should dig deeper holes and use a lot of rocks when we cover 'em up."

Lucas was almost finished, "What if you want to get hold of him?"

Rich looked puzzled, "Franklin? We didn't never have to do that, so I don't know. Like I said, he told us to smash up the phone."

Lucas and Jake moved away from the two and reviewed the information they had collected. "These two birds aren't bright enough to have planned this adventure," said Jake.

Lucas nodded, "They get orders from someone they've never met. They communicate through emails and don't ask questions."

"I assume the name 'Franklin' is bogus, maybe just for these two," said Jake. "They aren't bright enough to know anything and if they did talk, they could tell us everything they know and still couldn't pass along anything meaningful."

Lucas nodded again, "So Franklin, or whatever his name is, is shielded, and we can't draw a connection."

"Agreed, let's locate the two bodies from DC and notify the authorities. If they can find any of the others, we may be able to zero in on our friend, Franklin, then we get outta here," said Jake.

Lucas agreed, "First, let's pick up their computer. We'll use it to send an email to Ian with their location and whatever info we have."

"Right, and leave their computer to the feds," then he walked over to the two thugs, "Now, you're going to take us to your apartment, then out to the desert and show us where you buried our friends."

Will was in pain, his thumbs were swollen, and his bloody nose was shifted to the right. He didn't expect to be alive in the morning. This is what he did to others, beat them, torture them, and kill them. Now, he figured it was his turn.

Rich was not sure what was going to happen. As dumb as Will was, Rich was more so. He hoped for the best. After all, he still had his skin.

The two thugs were cut down, wrapped in blankets, and carried over to their minivan. "Hey, this is my van," protested Will through the mess on his face.

"Yeah, I'm gonna borrow it," said Lucas in his best fake accent.

Jake handed the keys to his car to one of the three men helping them and said, "Follow us."

The two thugs, their clothes, and personal belongings were put in the rear of the minivan. They were both given a bottle of water, and as thirsty as they were, neither took a drink.

*   *   *

Apartment Building, Las Vegas, NV

Lucas drove to Rich and Will's apartment, took the keys, and went in, returning in a few minutes with a laptop and a power cord that allowed the unit to be powered in a car. He also had a cord to connect their cellphone to their computer.

"Hey, how'd you know where we live," asked Will through his swollen face.

"We've been watching you," replied Lucas.

*   *   *

Desert, NW AZ

The van traveled back through Vegas and north to Mesquite. A turn onto Riverside and a ride past the buildings brought them to a desert. Lucas looked at the two and asked, "Okay, which way and how far?"

Rich sat up straight and said, "Straight ahead, about a mile, I think."

They crossed the Virgin River and turned on to Lime Kiln Canyon Road, then drove several more miles across the state line into Arizona and Lucas again asked, "How much farther?"

Will was not looking, and Rich said, "There, right Will?" he was pointing at tracks next to the rise. "Yeah, I'm sure that's it."

The van crested the rise, and the burial site was obvious. Jake pulled the van close to the disturbed earth and stopped. Everybody got out. Jake handed Rich a shovel. "Dig em up."

"Aw man, they gonna stink like hell, and I'm bleedin'," said Rich.

"Yeah, and you're alive, now dig," said Lucas.

"What about him?" asked Rich pointing at Will.

"I don't have time to deal with two broken thumbs trying to dig a hole."

*   *   *

22

Ian was having dinner with Kate at The Auld Shebeen. They talked about the family in Ireland and the family's Manor House, where Aaron, Jack, and Kate lived. The conversation drifted from the family in Ireland to America and the Provinces of Canada, and then to Australia.

"We've twelve horses, and himself insists on keeping a few head of cattle at Draighen Cnoc," said Kate. "It's a fine beautiful stone house with more rooms than we can live in. It is the home of the Clann, a bit more than a fair stretch of the leg outside of Cork and we do have many guests stopping by, some for a cup of tea, some for a bit longer. We've given shelter to some who were down on their luck 'til they could stand on their own again. I can say I've never known Aaron MacLaoghaire to hold the door closed to anyone in need."

"Tell me more of the history of the Manor," said Ian.

"Well now, the land was originally settled in 1023 by the man who brought the family together, Conall MacLaoghaire. He had six sons and two daughters along with a brother and sister, each of whom had children and the families moved to this little spit of land they found defensible. They built homes and a wall to keep out invaders. They opened the door to others and built a second wall a mile or so away. Today you can still see where the walls were. Most of the stones used in their construction remain, some were used in building the manor house when the Normans invaded. Long story short, the Clann has continued to grow over the last nine centuries, and even though the Normans came in with their army, the family has never left that land. In one way or another, the land we have called Draighean Cnoc since the days of Conall has been in or cared for by the family."

As Ian was about to add to the conversation, his cellphone beeped, "Excuse me while I check this message." He stared at his phone,

"RandW101, I don't recognize that one." He opened the email and read the first few lines, "I gotta' call Stan Reed, now."

"Does this mean you're back at work?" laughed Kate.

"It does," replied Ian, "and I'm probably going into MPD as soon as I can." He tapped the forward button and sent the email to Stan, then called him. "Stan, I just forwarded an email that came to me a few seconds ago. Basically, says the two jackwagons we were looking for turned up buried in the desert in NW Arizona, and the two characters that killed them are by now in custody with the Arizona State Police. And no, I don't know how they got my name and address. I'll be in the office in an hour."

"You've caught them. You should be happy about that," said Kate.

"Yes and no," returned Ian. "We have the two we were after, but they're dead. Hard to get info from a dead guy. We also have the two that killed them, and we have a name, Franklin. Could be a first name, last name, or an alias." He waved the waiter over, paid the bill, and said, "Do you mind if we stop at the office before I take you back to Shelly's house?"

"Not at all, tall man," she replied, "I'd love to see you catch these hooligans."

*   *   *

Metropolitan Police Department, Washington, DC

Ian and Kate walked into the reception area and met Mike and Stan. "Mike, Stan, you've met Kate Dixon. We were having dinner when that message came through." He looked at Kate, "Please wait out here while I check on a few things, then I'll get you home."

The three men went into the conference room, and Ian asked, "Mike, has anything else come through yet?"

Stan answered for Mike, "The information provided was thin so, I contacted the Arizona State Police, had a conversation with a man named Dennis Coyne in their office in Flagstaff, and forwarded the email to him. Dennis sent a helicopter out to the location cited in the email, and as promised, his search team found the two thugs, Richard Pallman and William Garnos, chained to a rock." He looked at Ian, "Two bodies,

Clint Marsh and Tomas Relatto, were laying on the ground only ten feet from those two, they were allowed to bake and smell through the late afternoon heat."

Mike said, "We have a follow-up call set for now so, pull up a chair, and let's see what else they've learned." He punched a few numbers into the conference room phone, and Dennis Coyne answered.

"Mike, I have a few more bits and pieces," said Dennis.

"Dennis, I have Stan Reed and Ian McLarry here with me," said Mike, "so, fire away, we're hungry for any info that'll move this investigation along."

"Okay, first, transporting the two victims across a state line is going to have other implications, meaning Will and Rich were in for an entirely new adventure with the feds."

"Copy that," said Mike. "Are they still in your house, or have the feds taken them?"

"Still in our custody," returned Dennis. "Tell me, how did you guys in DC find out about these two, or should I say four characters in my desert?"

Stan replied, "I have the email from two of them, Pallman and Garnos. No idea where they got the contact info for our man here or why they wrote to us, but we're investigating a shooting of two of our detectives here in the District that may involve the two dead men at your site."

"I heard about that. How are your detectives?" asked Dennis.

"We lost one, and the other is in for a long recovery, but she'll make it," responded Reed.

Dennis was silent for a moment, then he said, "I'm sorry to hear that, Stan. Did you know them?"

"Yeah, we worked out of the same office here in the First District. Lake McLarry was a good cop, a straight-up guy, and Kat Murano is also a good cop. She'll be walking out of that hospital one day, and I hope she comes back on the job. Tough little lady."

The conversation went quiet for a minute, then Stan said, "So, how are the two winners, are they in your jail?"

"Naw, we sent em to the hospital to get patched up. They're a little beat up. One guy has a pair of broken thumbs, two lovely shiners, and a busted nose. The other has a sizeable cut on his thigh, claims someone was going to skin him alive," said Dennis. "The guy, Rich Pallman, said the guy's name was James Martinez and the other was Adam something. He didn't get a last name, and he didn't get the names of the other three guys there."

"Do we have descriptions, prints, DNA, anything?" asked Stan.

"Martinez, James, six feet, plus or minus, two hundred pounds plus, long black hair, heavy tan, short beard and mean," said Dennis. "They said he smelled like a drunk, and had a slight Hispanic accent, he was wearing shades and latex gloves, so we have no DNA or prints yet. Still looking."

Stan chuckled, "Sounds like someone questioned these two and got information we couldn't get legally." He thought for a second and continued, "Drunk, Hispanic, shades, I'll bet he was neither a drunk nor Hispanic, and the shades, maybe to cover up blue eyes. This was too neatly done." He paused again, thinking, then, "I'm not pointing a finger at anybody, but the detective who was killed is related to cops all over this country. Family name is McLarry," he paused, "James Martinez and Adam X. Okay, we'll work with that for now, but the name may actually turn out to be McLarry."

"McLarry, yeah," said Dennis, "I know the name, we have a McLarry on the force here. If he's related, maybe he can answer a few questions."

Stan laughed, "I wouldn't bet on it. This family is very tight, and they know the ropes, good luck."

Mike looked around the table, "Any questions?"

Both Ian and Stan shook their heads, "Not right now," said Ian.

Dennis signed off, "Call any time. I hope we can be helpful in closing this one,"

Mike looked at the two detectives, "Franklin, we should start there."

Ian went back out to the reception area, "Okay, we can go."

Kate stood, "Well, can you tell me what's happening?"

Ian hesitated, "Some of it, but we won't pass anything specific on to Shelly until we have more solid info. She's got enough on her plate for now."

*   *   *

Metropolitan Police Department, Washington, DC

Dan and Ian were in the office talking to Stan Reed when Mike Farley waved them into his office. "The chief wants to see both of you. This cross-country business doesn't work. We have a case here, and we're working it, you and your family have got to stay out of it."

Ian leaned on Mike's desk, "Sarge, we don't control what our family does. We haven't stepped out of line, and we won't. If the family or friends of the family do something outside of our control and pass it along to me, I will pass it along to you and let the dirt settle where it may."

"Anything your cousins do could be writing a 'get outta jail ticket' for the bad guys," said Mike.

Ian added, "Mike, I know it was our family, but there's no way anybody could prove it. They picked up those characters and got some information out of them. Now you have more than you did before, and this party can continue."

Mike was angry. He felt a little slap in the face, with the implication his department couldn't have gotten the same information through proper procedure. "You tell them …"

Ian interrupted Mike, "Tell who? I have no idea who did this and if I ask, the answer will be the same from everybody, 'I don't know' end of story." He paused and looked back at Mike, "Take it for what it is, information from a confidential informant. We didn't ask for it, and you didn't pay for it, but there it is, a gift. Take it and make the most of it."

Mike scowled, "Well, we have complicated a murder case for our friends in Arizona, and now the feds are dragged into this mess. What else is your family gonna screw up?" As he was about to continue, his phone rang. He paused, listening, as he hung up, he looked at the two and said, "Chief wants you two—now!"

The chief of detectives was a nice enough man, but his sense of humor was not in evidence when Ian and Dan entered his office. The lecture matched the one they just received very closely, but with a larger sense of authority than Mike's. The chief seemed to be finished and the two hesitated, then started for the door. "By the way you two, I met one of your uncles the other day, Aaron MacLaoghaire, nice fellow. I told him my wife and I are planning a trip to London and Paris later this year, probably in September. He suggested a side trip to a place called Draighean Cnoc. Said the salmon fishing was worth the trip on its own." He shuffled a few more papers, "Do you think we'll have this wrapped up by then?"

Both men looked at the chief, then at each other, "I hope so," said Ian. Dan nodded in agreement. They were dismissed and walked out of the chief's office. They stopped in front of the elevators and looked at each other, "He knows the old man," said Dan.

"Yeah," responded Ian, "why do I feel like a kid just caught pocketing the loose candy in the candy store?"

"Salmon fishing?" said Dan.

*　　*　　*

23

As predicted, neither Rich nor Will knew anything worth the time and expense of questioning them further. They had given the two thugs something to drink, mixed per Franklin's instructions and were told when the two thugs died, they were to be buried in the desert.

Dan Leonard was notified of the killing of the two thugs in Arizona because of their connection to Temple Enterprise and the raid on the warehouse in Virginia. "Craig, we may be taking a side trip to Flagstaff," said Dan.

"Sounds nice, what's the attraction in the southwest?" inquired Craig Robins.

Leonard poured a cup of coffee and joined Robins at a breakroom table, "The Temple Enterprise warehouse in Virginia, these two characters were there a week ago, tying them to our investigation, and a cop killing in the district to which they may be connected as well."

"You're referring to McLarry? Lake McLarry?" asked Robins.

"Yeah, and he's related to …"

"Ian McLarry, the cop in the bombing thing about a year ago in Virginia," said Robins.

"You got it." Leonard sipped his coffee, "Looks like we get to see our old friend again. But this time, his interest is personal, not professional."

"He's a good cop, I wouldn't mind working with him again," said Craig.

"Yeah, I think we may be talking to him soon. This is a case of murder in Arizona and Nevada, apparently the two victims were alive when they arrived in Vegas, and dead when they were deposited in

Arizona. They could have both died in one state or the other or one in each, we may never know."

"Anywhere near the Navajo Reservation?" asked Craig.

"Close, but no, not really," said Dan. "The reservation starts a few miles east of where the bodies were found. Several security cameras at gas stations and ATMs along the way, verify the story these two guys from Vegas told." He looked at his notes, "Will Garnos and Rich Pallman. They said they picked up these two thugs, Relatto and Marsh, at McCarran International, transported them from there, up 15 to Mesquite, then across into Arizona about two miles and ten miles south, out into the desert. Somewhere along the way, Relatto and Marsh were each given a water bottle, they were told the doctor said they were supposed to keep well-hydrated, and they were supposed to drink the entire bottle. They drank and they both fell asleep. When the van got to the grave site, Relatto and Marsh were both dead. If they had gone a little farther east, or if they had come up through Flagstaff, we could've had another complication with the reservation police."

"Let's take a ride over to Virginia and visit with McLarry first, then we may want to go to Arizona," suggested Craig.

"Yeah, I'll give him a call and let him know we're coming," said Bob. He pulled out his cellphone, "I think I still have his number here," and he pushed the buttons. "Ian, this is Bob Leonard, I'd like to come out and visit with you this afternoon. Are you available?"

Ian was surprised at the call and replied, "Actually, I'm in the District on some personal business. Where are you?"

"You're here, that's good, we're at our building on Pennsylvania Avenue, where exactly are you?"

"Right now, in a car heading for the first district office on M Street, we should be there in about fifteen minutes."

"Great," said Dan. "I have another name at the first district to check out, a Dan Carney. I might be able to catch up with both of you at the same time if he's available."

"He will be," replied Ian, "we'll meet you in the reception area in twenty."

"We're on our way," said Dan.

*   *   *

Temple Enterprise Offices, Washington, DC

Bernie Temple was sitting in his office on K Street. He stood and paced in front of the large window that offered a view of the Washington Monument, muttering to himself. He leaned over his desk and pushed a button, "Myra, could you please come into my office?"

"Certainly, Mr. Temple," she replied as she picked up a steno pad and pen and walked quickly to the corner office.

"Myra, I'm concerned about the events of the last few days. I think Franklin may be able to resolve this situation, could you please contact him and ask for a meeting?"

"Yes, of course, sir. Is there something I may do to help?"

Bernie forced a smile, "No, no. This is something that will require his special talents. I really need to talk to him."

"I'll color the square red immediately, sir."

"Thanks, Myra."

"Then I will run out for a quick lunch."

Myra made the change on the website and walked out to the elevator.

Bernie was sitting at his desk when the phone rang again. He picked it up, "Hello."

The voice sounded mechanical, "Myra Wallace, please."

"She has stepped out for a minute or two, may I help you?"

"Yes, please tell her Franklin called and will call again in one hour."

"Franklin," said Bernie, "this is Bernard Temple, can we talk?"

There was a pause, "A limited conversation only. What is the subject?"

Bernie hesitated, "I'm very uncomfortable with the number of parties involved in this specific situation. There is far too much room for error."

"I understand," the voice replied, "I will verify several points and call you back at this number in two hours."

Bernie looked at his watch, "Three-fifteen, I'll be here."

"Send Ms. Wallace on an errand and have no one else in your office. I'll call at 3:15."

The line went quiet. Bernie looked at the phone and wondered if he was doing the right thing. "I've rarely spoken to him," he muttered to himself. He sat behind his desk again and thought, "I've used his services for six years," as he remembered a few instances where Franklin had solved a problem."

At 12:35 Myra hurried back into the office with a cup of coffee and a small brown bag. She went directly to Bernie's office, "I was in a line for the longest time," she said apologetically.

Bernie smiled and said, "Not a problem. Franklin called, and we talked." He looked at his hands and continued, "We have used his services for something over six years." He looked up at Myra, "Just after you started here."

Myra sighed, "Well, what do you think of him?" She sat in one of Bernie's guest chairs.

"I don't know. Mysterious, I guess. I mean his voice, it isn't natural," said Bernie as he leaned back in his chair.

Myra said, "Yes, I thought he may be using something to disguise his voice, like talking into a tin can or whatever spies do. Well, as long as you're comfortable working with him, I guess he'll continue to be our answer to those difficult situations." She smiled as if relieved of a burden. "He's all yours."

Bernie cleared his throat, sat up straight, looked at his watch , "It's almost 2:00PM, things are quiet here and we will have a big day tomorrow so why don't you take the rest of the afternoon and go check that art display you mentioned yesterday. Come in tomorrow rested and ready."

Myra looked at Bernie quizzically, "I would like that," she replied. She stood, "And I won't argue." She turned toward the door, stopped and looked back at Bernie, "Mr. Temple, have you had lunch?"

He looked at her, "No, I'll get something later."

She walked back to his desk, set her coffee and little brown bag in front of Bernie, "No you won't. I haven't touched this, so enjoy and I'll get something on my way to the art gallery."

Bernie was about to say something when he looked up and saw Myra turn and walk out of his office. He looked at her, noticing her figure and how she walked, "Six years," he muttered.

*   *   *

Temple Enterprise Offices, Washington, DC

The phone rang at precisely 3:15. Bernie answered, "This is Bernard Temple."

"Are you alone?" asked the mechanical voice.

"Yes, I am," replied Bernie as he fingered the record button.

"Ms. Wallace?" inquired the voice.

Bernie remembered her walking out of his office, the way he had never looked at her before.

"Bernard, are you there?"

Bernie came back to reality, pushed the record button and replied, "Yes, excuse me, I'm here and she has gone to the art gallery."

"Art gallery?" the voice paused, "Okay, I will review the situation and determine a course of action that will best benefit you. Please understand, when I advise you in this matter, there will be no alternatives. You must do as I say, or I will completely back away from any further involvement with you."

"I understand," returned Bernie. The line went dead.

*   *   *

24

State Police offices, Flagstaff, AZ

Arizona State Police and the FBI had questioned Rich and Will over the weekend, gaining very little information. The two knew nothing more than what had already been discussed and further questioning brought minor variations to the original story. Their connection to Franklin was never a face to face, each contact was through the electronic media, cellphone or email. Franklin had used them on four occasions prior to the Clint and Tomas murders. Three of their prior victims had been taken out into the desert and buried and one was left in a motel, south of Las Vegas. One of the desert graves was discovered by critters and found by a traveling family, taking a break.

The other three desert graves were still undiscovered and neither Rich nor Will could remember who they had buried nor exactly where. They gave the FBI general locations of the burial sites and two teams equipped with ground penetrating radar were dispatched to search those areas. The search went on through the weekend and two more sites were found.

The questioning of Rich and Will went on through the weekend, constantly switching subjects between their actions with Tomas and Clint then shifting gears to ask about Franklin or the other people buried in the desert.

The descriptions of the men who had tortured them were compared. Each had a different set of details to contribute and even though the final result was skewed by the disguises worn by Jake and Lucas, an identification of the two bore basic information they agreed on. The height and weight of the two prime figures was narrowed to their approximate dimensions, but other information including skin, hair and eye color were left in doubt. The voices and accents of both were defined as Hispanic and perhaps Russian. No description of the other three men, who remained primarily at a distance and in the shadows was possible.

"I seen two or three other guys near the big door, but they was like a hundred feet away," stated Rich.

Asked the same question, Will remembered the "Mexican guy that broke my nose and my thumbs," and he recalled another man coming closer a few times. He acknowledged there were some others in the building, but they were little more than shadows to him.

Rich and Will were now going to be charged with the murders of Tomas and Clint. The FBI was considering other charges including kidnapping, transporting victims and weapons across state lines. The door was also open to responding to any discovery of other victims which would be added to their list of problems.

They had provided their services to Franklin among others over the last several years and never asked questions. The people they deposited in the desert were picked up at the airport or a bus station. Two were in perfect health and had to be shot, one was willing to drink the water provided and one of the victims was found in his motel with a bullet in his head. Rich and Will were Franklin's Vegas clean up and disposal unit.

*   *   *

State Police offices, Flagstaff, AZ

Leonard and Robins were comparing notes and having a cup of coffee in a breakroom. "This Franklin character has a neat operation," said Leonard. "He lines up the victim and has these two do the deed, ditch the bodies and he stays out of the picture. This guy could be in Nome, Alaska or Paris, France and do his thing."

"I'm gonna call McLarry back in DC," said Robins, "he may have a few questions we haven't thought of." He punched a few numbers in his cellphone.

Ian answered immediately, "What can I do for you."

"We have these two characters, Pallman and Garnos. Do you have any questions we could put to them?"

Ian laughed, "Yeah, ask 'em if they know anything about Jim Millington."

Robins replied, "Seriously, these two aren't bright enough to do that piece of work."

"I know they didn't do Millington, I wonder if his name ever came up in conversation with Franklin."

"Yeah, what the hell," said Robins, "anything else?"

"Nope, but I'd be very happy if there was something tying Millington to this crew of clowns," said Ian. "Give it a shot, see what happens."

In their next session questioning Will Garnos, Robins said, "The name of the other guy you left in the desert, was it Walters, Connor, Millington, Garvin?"

As Robins recited the names, Leonard noted a flash of recognition at Millington's name. "Let's talk about Millington, you two went to his house, knocked on the door and stabbed him, right?"

Will was shaking his head through the question, "Naw, he couldn't make the trip to Vegas, so that one was canceled."

"Canceled?" said Leonard. "Who canceled that deal?"

"I don't know, we was told he was gonna come out in like July or August, but then he couldn't make it," said Will.

"How do you know he couldn't make it?" asked Robins.

"We was told," said Will.

Robins almost smiled as he asked Will, "Who told you?"

Will looked confused as if the answer was obvious, "Franklin."

Robins left the interview room and called Ian. "You asked a dumb question," said Robins, "and the dummy answered." He relayed the interview sequence and said, "Any more dumb questions."

Ian laughed and said, "I'll try to think up a few more." He ended the call and punched in a few new numbers, "Ned, we have a connection between Franklin and Millington. Weak, but a connection.

"Tell me, I could use a bit of good news," said Bowen.

Ian ran through the sequence and added, "We'll get a copy of the interview tape, and you know what this little bit of info does?"

"That makes it a connection to Temple," said Ned Bowen with a sigh of relief.

"It does," said Ian, "now to put a little meat on these bones."

*   *   *

The Auld Shebeen, Fairfax, VA

Kate reserved a table for nine and when Shelly and Marty arrived, the group was complete. "It's unfortunate that it takes something like this to bring us together," said Aaron. "I'm thinking that we should plan another trip to America this coming spring, before the intense heat of one of your summers."

Jack raised his glass and offered, "Here's to our family, our Clann. May we stand together forever."

Ian offered, "And to our cousins from the old sod, our doors are always open as you are always welcome."

When dinner was done and the hour grew late, Jake was prepared to take the visitors to their hotel. Hugs and handshakes completed; the group began walking to the parking garage. Aaron stopped outside the pub, took Ian's hand and said, "I think you should come to Ireland, there's so much you should know about our family and so many people you should meet."

"I'd like to visit, but it may not be in the budget for a while," said Ian.

"You find the time and Kate will see to it you have a ticket. The expense is not a problem, you should come, and you'll see why."

Ian looked at Kate, "As soon as we finish this case,

I could take some time, maybe months."

"When you're ready, I'll send a ticket." She smiled and took his hand, squeezed and said, "It was a pleasure meeting you, Ian MacLaoghaire." Then she climbed into the back seat of the Suburban.

Aaron again shook Ian's hand and said, "It'll never be too soon." He gave Shelly another hug and climbed into the front passenger seat.

Jake steered the black SUV out of the garage and pointed toward route 66.

Shelly and Marty followed Jake out of the garage and Dan said, "I'm going back to the hospital, check on Kat."

Ian slapped Dan on his shoulder, "We'll talk tomorrow." Then as Dan went to his car, Ian and Lucas went back into the pub.

"Another pint to clear my head," said Lucas, "and you can bring me up to date on your investigation."

As the first drink was finished, Ian said, "So, Lucas, when were you last in Vegas?"

Lucas was ready for the question and replied, "Oh, it's been a while, but I plan on getting back there soon. The shows, the food, the games and of course, the people. Some very interesting people."

"I know the two Vegas thugs decided to talk rather than lose their skin. So, tell me, cousin …"

Lucas put up his hand, "Ian, ask me no questions and I'll tell you no lies."

Ian knew the answer and didn't ask the question, "Jake went with you," he said.

Lucas looked at Ian with no expression, "Have another draft. What's done is done and you have the info those two would not have given up if they were not properly questioned."

Ian sat up straight, ordered another beer, and said, "I wonder how many people those two lugnuts have buried out there."

"Hard tellin'," said Lucas.

*　　*　　*

Metropolitan Police Department, Washington, DC

Stan Reed had finished his second cup of coffee and was heading for his third when Ian walked into the office, "Mornin', Stan."

"Ian, what's on the schedule today?"

"This new information could open a whole new can of worms and mess up both of our cases. Then again, maybe some of these findings will be tracible back to our friend Bernie."

"Where are you going with this thinking?" asked Stan.

"I don't think Bernie was running a Murder Business. More likely this character, Franklin is. He sends people out to Vegas and his minions do 'em and ditch 'em. We have no idea who Franklin is and neither do the two doing the deed."

"What do you want to do?" asked Stan.

"I wonder if Bernie knows who Franklin is?" Ian wondered aloud. "My case, out in Vaneksburg, was a clean, professional hit. It was well planned and well executed. It appears Jim Millington was in line for the same desert treatment as the Relatto and Marsh team but, for some reason, it fell through. So, this Franklin character has another hitter here, who is more like a technician. Someone who takes his time, plans the thing out and knows or learns the turf. He has a way in and a way out. He makes the hit at a time when few, if any people are about and leaves the scene by a route that is very unlikely to be in use."

"So, are you going to see Bernie again?" asked Stan.

"Oh, definitely," returned Ian, "but first, I'll talk to Julia Millington. If Jim was planning a trip, she may be able to add a few more details. Every bit and piece are important at this point." He stood and checked his watch. "I'm gonna run out to Vaneksburg and see the lady. Care to join me?"

*   *   *

Barnstable Road, Vaneksburg, VA

"Julia, this is Detective Reed from MPD," said Ian.

She invited them in and they went to the living room, "Can I offer you some tea?"

"No, but thanks," said Ian, "we just have a few questions, and you may be able to help us out."

"Anything I can do," she said.

"Did Jim ever go to Las Vegas?" asked Ian.

"We've been there several times. Jim and I would budget a few dollars and when that was gone, we'd come home."

"A few dollars?" said Stan.

"Yes, usually a thousand each," she said, "and occasionally we'd win a little something."

"When was the last trip to Vegas?" asked Ian.

"It was about two years ago," replied Julia. "Then in the summer, we were thinking about going again, but my dad was very ill and so I went to help my mom and we canceled our trip. We thought we might go in the spring, when the kids will be on break from school."

"Did anyone else know about your plans to go in the summer?" asked Ian.

"I told a few friends and Jim scheduled the time with his office, it was not a secret," said Julia.

"So, you were going to wait 'til spring before rescheduling," said Stan.

"Yes, well, my dad got better, and we thought about going in September, but Jim got very busy with work again and, well it just didn't happen."

"Was this a normally busy time of year?" asked Ian.

"No," replied Julia, "it was very unpredictable. Jim tried to be ready for both up and down times and we just went with the flow."

"Did he have to bring people in at different times and let them go at other times?" asked Ian.

"Sometimes, but …"

Ian noted a slight hesitation, "But what?"

"Well, he started talking to another firm about sharing work and keeping the people more fully employed."

"You mean like a merger or buying the other firm out?' asked Ian.

"I really don't know, he talked about things, and I listened, but I really didn't care that much. I mean, it's like baseball, I understand and I'm happy he and Jimmy liked baseball and I go to Jimmy's games in the summer, but I'm just not into the game. If Jim wasn't in the import business, I wouldn't give it any thought at all."

"I understand," said Ian. "Did he talk about any other people in the business?"

"Sometimes, but again, I didn't give it a lot of thought."

"Any names come to mind?" asked Stan.

"Mostly the people that worked for him and sometimes others," she said.

"We'd like to speak to other people who knew him professionally," said Ian. "Do you remember any names of people who might be able to point us in the right direction."

"There were several. Most recently a Mr. Temple and he were in conversation about cooperative solutions to that 'up and down' thing."

"All positive conversations?" asked Ian.

"Oh, there were concerns about different things, but again, not something I dwelled on," said Julia.

"Have you ever met Bernard Temple?" asked Ian.

"No, I met one of his people. A woman, I don't recall her name. She dropped off some papers for Jim a few months ago."

"A few months ago, like around the time your father took ill?" asked Ian.

Julia thought for a moment, "After he was getting better. I'm sure because I was home and not visiting Dad as much."

"You don't remember her name, but could you describe her?" asked Ian.

Julia thought for a moment, "Tall, slender, nicely dressed, brunette, very polite," she paused, "Myra, that was her name."

Ian was making notes when she said Myra, he looked at Julia, "Did this Myra stay long?"

"No, she said something about the papers, excused herself for interrupting my day and left."

"Do you recall what kind of car she was driving?"

"No," Julia thought again, "it was black, that's all I remember."

The conversation continued for a few more minutes and Ian stood, "Mrs. Millington, thank you. If anything comes to mind that you think may help us, never hesitate to call."

*   *   *

Metropolitan Police Ddepartment, Washington, DC

Stan tapped on Mike Farley's door, "Mike, I'm back."

"Is McLarry with you?" asked Farley.

"Yeah, he's getting a refill on his coffee," said Stan.

"Conference room, in five minutes. I want an update," said Mike.

"Okay, five."

Ian sat at the table with Stan when Mike walked in holding a notepad and a bottle of water.

"Okay guys," said Mike, "what's the latest?"

Stan started with the Las Vegas thugs recognizing Millington's name and ran through the conversation with Julia Millington.

Mike looked at Ian, "You want to add to that?"

"Yeah," said Ian. "I want to know what 'dumb and dumber' planned to do with Mrs. Millington, if the two of them had made that trip."

"Have you talked with our FBI friends today?" asked Mike.

"Not yet," returned Ian.

Mike raised an eyebrow, "That's why we have phones."

Ian glared at Mike, "As soon as we're finished here, I'll call."

"On that note, we're done for now," said Mike as he stood and went back to his office.

Ian leaned back in his chair punched a few numbers into his cell and listened. "Robins, this is McLarry, I have another dumb question."

Ten minutes later Ian walked into Mike's office, "Collateral damage. If she was with him, make the hole big enough for two."

Mike looked up, "Cold, was it this Franklin character?"

"Yeah, he's the only contact these two bozos have," said Ian with an icy look.

*   *   *

Metropolitan Police Department, Washington, DC

Ian went into the conference room and started to write on the white board. "Millington, September fifth," he mumbled as he wrote. "Klemper, September nineteenth, question mark, Ross, September twenty-fourth," he paused, took a deep breath and continued, "McLarry, September twenty-fourth, Barrett, September twenty-fifth, Relatto September twenty-sixth, Marsh, September twenty-sixth." He stepped back, looked at the board then, sat at the conference table and said, "Seven people, who's next?"

Mike walked in as Ian was looking at the list, "You think they're all connected?"

"Yeah Mike, I do," said Ian. "Everything comes back to Bernie Temple. Millington was in talks with Temple, and I think Bernie just wanted a bigger piece of the pie. Klemper was questioned and killed, just a few days after a raid on Bernie's Fulton Road Warehouse. Now, Millington was a straight up hit. He was targeted, the scene was scoped out and the perp had a well-planned escape route worked out. It was quick and clean."

"There was nothing clean or quick about Klemper," said Mike.

"I think George was done by someone other than Millington's hitter," said Ian. "It was sloppy, and he was pitched in the river, probably meant to sink out of sight. He had no family, they likely figured he wouldn't be missed, but he floated."

"A second killer?" puzzled Mike. "Could it have been the two from LA?"

"No, the info I have says they arrived after the Klemper killing," said Ian. "I'm not sure why they were here, but they probably did both Barrett and Ross. Ross worked at the warehouse and Barrett was his buddy. According to Lake's notes, he paid the two of them $50 for info on activity at the warehouse. So, killing them may have been intentional, but more likely, Ross saw something and ran to meet his buddy, Jason. The two California clowns caught up with them at the square at the same time Lake and Kat arrived. Then the gunfire exchange that left Lake and Ross dead, Kat wounded and maybe one of the thugs taking a bullet."

"Ross wasn't shot," said Mike. "His skull was caved in."

"Yeah, that still has me wondering," said Ian, "but the rest works for me."

Mike nodded, "When Kat comes around, we'll get more on what happened in the alley," he said and added, "Freddy also has a few scenarios mapped out, hopefully we put it all together soon."

They both looked at the white board, "But how do you tie Millington to Klemper and the warehouse?" asked Mike.

"Logic doesn't always rule the turf, Mike," said Ian. "Not everything necessarily fits the same puzzle, but all the puzzles touch Bernie. We may never know why he targeted Millington and Klemper, but he knows."

"Okay, Ian," said Mike. "So, what's next on your plate?"

"I think someone else was there at the alley. Someone who had access to a vehicle and probably drove the two Californians to the square," said Ian. "Bob Leonard told me there's a guy there, a Dave Saunders, he fits the profile. If there is something illegal going on, he'd know about it. If Barrett or Ross were a problem, he'd be the one who could direct the thugs to deal with them."

"Dave Saunders?" quizzed Mike.

"Yeah," said Ian, "he's in charge on the warehouse site, so he's prime on my list."

"You're going to see Saunders?"

"Yeah, I'd like to go tomorrow morning. Those two California wing nuts were working with or for somebody there and he's the logical center point.

"Okay, Ian. But first, contact the Fairfax police, let 'em know you're coming," said Mike. "They may want to join in on the party," he looked at the list again, "and take Stan with you."

*   *   *

Fulton Road Warehouse, VA

Ian called Fairfax County Police before he and Stan left the First District office. The Fairfax Police thanked him for the heads up but said they didn't need to be there if all that was going to happen was a Q&A session. They arrived at the Temple Enterprise Warehouse just after 8:40

a.m. and were told Dave was out in the yard directing the unloading of a truck. The guard at the gate called Dave's cell and told him there were two detectives there to see him.

"Point them toward the office," said Dave. "I'll meet them there in about five minutes."

They met just outside the overhead door to the secured storage building, "Detectives, what can I do for you?"

"We're looking into the murder of Andrew Ross," said Ian.

"Andy, yeah, he worked here on a part-time basis. Mostly did clean-up, sweeping and hauling the trash to the dumpsters."

"So, you knew him?" asked Ian.

"Oh, yeah. He was a nice guy, a little on the slow side, but a pretty good worker," said Dave.

"Was he in good standing here?" asked Stan.

"Yeah, as a matter of fact, I was gonna have him come in a little more often," said Dave. "If the guy could stay off the drugs, he was quite dependable."

"Did he have any friends here?" asked Ian.

"I really don't know. He has a buddy that he brings in when we have a big clean-up to do."

"Do you have a name on his buddy?" asked Stan.

Dave thought for a moment, "No, not right off. Another druggie as I recall." He shook his head and added, "A more hard-core druggie, we let Andy bring him along only if the guy was clean."

"And you can't remember his name?" asked Ian.

Dave feigned wonder and said, "I think it was Jason. We probably have his name on file in the office, do you want it?"

"Yeah, that'll be great, and an address if there is one."

Dave returned with two sheets of paper, "Here, I gotcha' these two guys. Ross and Barrett."

"Shifting gears, Dave," said Ian. "Are you acquainted with a Tomas Relatto?"

Dave was ready for the question, "Yeah, he and Clint Marsh were here to check out a few crates that were going to LA."

"So, where are they now?" asked Ian.

"I don't know, back in LA, I'd guess," said Dave. "Last I saw them they asked if they could borrow one of the vans to move something in DC. They work for one of our clients, so, I let 'em use a van. They brought it back, said thanks, and walked out the gate."

"Did they have a car?" asked Ian.

"I don't know," returned Dave. "Like I said, they walked out the gate and I had other things to do besides watching them."

"Did they know Andrew Ross?" asked Stan.

"Andy, I saw them talking to him a few times, but have no idea what it was about," said Dave.

"Your best guess," said Ian, "could it have been about the crates the two California men were here to check?"

"No, the crates were in our secured area and Andy was not cleared to be in there," said Dave.

"Could Relatto and Marsh have had a reason to suspect Andy had tampered with their crates?" asked Ian.

"Tampered?" said Dave. "I have no idea how he could have tampered with anything. He was a sweeper, worked out in the yard, not inside."

"Could they have had a reason to hurt Andy?" asked Ian.

"Hurt him, you mean did they kill him? Hell, I don't know." Dave was now feeling a little pressure and starting to get nervous. He looked at his watch, "Are we almost done here? I have another couple of trucks due in here about now and I gotta get them unloaded."

Ian felt he had enough for the time being and said, "Yeah, if anything else pops up, we'll give you a call." He and Stan left the Warehouse yard and drove back to MPD.

As the two detectives passed through the gate, Dave called Bernie and relayed the conversation. Bernie was sitting at his desk talking to Myra when Dave called, and she heard all that he had said.

"Relax," said Bernie, "they're just doing their job and we have nothing to be concerned about. Just keep business as normal and this will all pass."

*   *   *

Temple Enterprise Office, Washington, DC

Bernie looked at Myra, "Please color the little box red, Myra. Franklin is assessing our current situation and this development may affect his thinking."

Myra went back to her desk and modified the website. An hour later the phone rang and Myra listened then said, "Please hold." She buzzed Bernie and told him Franklin was on line two.

Bernie answered, "Franklin, thank you for calling. There has been an event this morning which may affect your analysis as we discussed." He relayed the conversation and Franklin said, "Okay Bernie, give me about two hours to finish what I am doing now, and I'll call you back. It is important that you are alone when I call, so send the girl out to lunch."

Bernie agreed and hung up.

*   *   *

Temple Enterprise Office, Washington, DC

As noon approached, Bernie called Myra into his office, "Myra, I'm going to need you to help with something this afternoon, so please go have lunch now and we'll get into it after 1:00 this afternoon."

She smiled and walked out of the office.

At 12: 09 the phone rang, and Bernie picked it up.

"Bernie, Franklin. I have considered everything you have told me, and I believe the best course of action is to reduce the number of leaks in your boat."

"As in—?" began Bernie.

The voice cut him off, "As in I will take care of these two problems. You will do as I say and there will be no negotiation, is that understood?"

"Yes," replied Bernie. "Two?"

"Yes Bernie, two. First you will authorize Ms. Wallace to approve the invoices for this month and next month."

Bernie thought for a moment, "Two? I'm afraid I am not aware of two."

"I have never met your warehouse manager."

Bernie saw how Dave could be a problem and understood the need to eliminate him, "Oh, yes. I should introduce you two."

"I will take care of that, Bernie. The other will be closer to the boat's bridge."

Bernie thought for a moment, Myra, she was the only one that fit the definition.

"Is that one necessary? I mean six years."

The voice interrupted, "Yes, Bernie, it is."

Bernie hesitated, then said, "If it's necessary, then I suppose."

"Then nothing, Bernie. This connection will be broken. I'll be gone and you'll sail your boat on your own."

Bernie paused, thought and smiled, "Alright, what about timing?"

"I will set it all up through Ms. Wallace, we will not speak again."

"What should I do now?"

"I will email you a few instructions. Follow them."

"When should I authorize her to ..."

"Immediately."

The line went dead, and Bernie stopped the recorder.

*　　*　　*

Metropolitan Police Department, Washington, DC

The only common thread for the Washington based investigation seemed to be Temple Enterprise. Jason and Ross both did part-time work in the warehouse, the two California thugs murdered in the desert had recently been in the Washington area when Lake and Kat were shot and two days later they had left town and were dead in the desert.

Robins and Leonard had returned from their visit to Flagstaff with very little additional input for their investigation. They called for a meeting at the first district building to put everything on the table and see what might happen. Stan Reed, Mike Farley, Dan Carney, Ian McLarry and Freddy Knolls were all in attendance with Bob Leonard and Craig Robins. The discussion began with Robins reporting on the trip to Flagstaff and the few new pieces they obtained. Freddy Knolls said the blood types found at the deserted building and in the alley, matched the two thugs buried in the desert. "DNA results should be available in a few days," he added.

Dan said he was at the hospital when Kat said that the vehicle in the alley was a white van, "A white van similar to the ones used by Temple Enterprise and she said one of the men called the other Tomas."

"We have to talk to Kat Murano," said Ian. "She may be able to pull a few more pieces of this puzzle together and get this investigation moving in the right direction."

*   *   *

Washington Hospital Center, Washington, DC

Dan drove over to the hospital after his shift and went to the surgical recovery area. "She's been moved to a private room," said the nurse as she punched a few keys on the computer and gave Dan the new room number. He hurried to Kat's room, found her sitting up in bed, her father next to her and two people he had never seen before.

She looked at Dan as he came in the door, "Hi," she said with a hint of exhaustion, "tell me, what happened to Lake? I remember seeing him down."

He looked at Kat, "Listen, you have to get better, that's all we should be thinking about now."

"Dan, I have to know, is he ...?"

He stepped closer to the bed, held her hand and said, "Yeah, he's gone. They shot him four times. He was probably gone before the last bullet was fired." He looked at Kat and saw she was reliving the event.

"I was there," she said, "I saw that man shoot Lake ... Tomas, the other one called him Tomas."

"We're trying to figure out how this went down. It looks like Lake hit one guy over the head and was shot by another. What do you know about this Tomas character?"

Kat was trying to keep her eyes open and not doing well. The nurse came in and said, "She needs to rest. That means peace, quiet and no more questions. Y'all understand?"

Dan was about to explain how important the information was, and the nurse cut him off, "Look officer, we took a bullet out of her chest, and she needs to heal. So, you sit quietly, and you can stay. Ask her one more question and I will ask you to leave."

"Yeah, I'm just …" started Dan.

The little nurse walked up to Dan, looked up at him and said, "You will wait until I say she's ready to answer questions, then you can do your job. Right now, I am doing mine." She put her hands on her hips and didn't move.

Dan looked around the room, then down at the nurse, "Okay, I'll wait," he backed away and sat in a chair.

*   *   *

Washington Hospital Center, Washington, DC

Kat was awake at 6:30 the next morning and Dan was asleep in the chair. The day shift nurse came in, looked at Dan, smiled and went to Kat's side, "Your boyfriend?"

Kat liked the sound of the question, "We work together," she paused, smiled and continued, "I like him very much."

"Yes, and he likes you. He has been here every day since you were brought in. I talked to the other nurses in the ER, recovery and the ICU. They all remember him."

Kat looked at Dan, "Well he's kinda' hard to miss."

He began to stir, and the nurse said jokingly, "Any more like him at home?"

Dan stood, shook his head and stretched. Kat replied, "As a matter of fact, there's a bunch of them. A whole Clann."

He walked over to the bed, "Good morning, how you doin' today?"

"I feel pretty good, tired, but good," she replied. "Now, tell me about Lake. I don't remember much about last night."

Dan smiled, "Kat, it's been two weeks."

"Two weeks, what day is it?" she sputtered.

"It's Thursday," said Dan.

"Oh my God, two weeks," she relaxed back on her pillows. "My dad, he must be …"

Dan smiled, as he cut her off, "He's usually here first thing in the morning," he said as he looked at the clock on the wall.

Kat closed her eyes, then opened them. "How is Lake, I saw him take one," she paused, thought and continued, "Two, no three shots," her eyes widened, and she tried to sit up, "Dan, tell me he's okay."

"You don't remember Kat? He's gone," said Dan as he touched her hand, "gone."

She laid back down and the color seemed to drain from her face, she closed her eyes and a tear appeared, "Lake, oh, Lake." Her chest rose and fell with each sob.

Kat's dad arrived shortly after she learned about Lake, and as sad as he was to see her cry and feel the pain of the loss of someone that close, he was happy to see her awake and alive.

Dan stepped out of the room and called Ian, "She's awake and starting to talk."

*   *   *

25

Bernie Temple was having his morning coffee, casually thinking about Franklin's instructions. Both Dave and Myra were to be eliminated. He understood and accepted the loss of both and even derived some satisfaction in the knowledge that he would now be less vulnerable. As he was envisioning attending Myra's funeral and how he would be appropriately saddened and lost without her, his computer pinged, announcing a new email.

"Bernie, Dave Saunders presence is required in Los Angeles next Monday morning. Details will be provided at the LA warehouse upon arrival.   F."

It was not unusual for Dave to make such trips to the various warehouse sites. He was well versed in procedures and particularly where sensitive materials were involved.

A second ping announced the arrival of another email.

"Bernard, A file transfer to the London office will be necessary this coming Monday. Ms. Wallace should carry the materials, make the delivery and be prepared to remain for at least four business days in the event a return file transfer will be required.   F."

Bernie thought about the two remaining terminations and wondered about the resulting investigations. The killing of Jim Millington, George Klemper, the two part-time laborers, the cop and the two thugs from Los Angeles was stirring up too much interest in his operation. He understood the need to cut his losses and giving up Dave and Myra at this point was probably not necessary, but wise. He would now be the only one who knew any of the details of the several killings and he could trust himself. Of course, all this activity was sure to bring the authorities to his door again, and the noose was getting tighter around his neck. He buzzed Myra.

She entered his office with note pad in hand, "Yes, Mr. Temple?"

"Myra, would you please authorize the next two payments to Sandway Security as soon as they come in? And I need to talk to Franklin, could you post another notice?"

"Of course, Mr. Temple, I'll do it immediately," she said turning and walking out of his office.

Bernie watched her walk away, "What a waste," he mumbled. "But better safe than sorry."

*   *   *

Temple Enterprise Office, Washington, DC

Bernie's cellphone buzzed, "Hello."

"Bernard, this is Franklin. What is the problem?" asked the mechanical voice.

Bernie pushed the record button and replied, "This is getting too dicey. The feds will be all over me as will the locals, I am concerned."

"Things are too far downstream. The Millington and Klemper incidents were manageable, the elimination of the two warehouse workers was even manageable, but the two men from LA killing the cop was a gateway we cannot back through. What's done is done and now you have to cut your losses and save yourself."

"I'm not sure I can continue under these conditions. The legal mess will smother me."

"I understand you have had offers from several competitors to buy you out. Perhaps now is a time to accept an offer, sail off into the sunset, and allow the dust to settle as it may."

"Sell? I don't want to sell. This is a very profitable business and I still have several good years left."

"You're not listening, Bernie. The mess your people made killing the cop is too much. Sell the firm, sail to Bermuda, trade in the yacht for something smaller, and blend in with the other wealthy retirees. You do have a condo there, don't you?"

"Yes, I do," said Bernie, "but this business is far too profitable to let go."

"Sell, Bernie. Sell, retire and spend the rest of your life playing golf and fishing. It's far better than doing twenty to life making license plates."

Bernie was about to comment further when the line went dead, and he stopped the recorder.

*   *   *

Myra booked Dave on a round trip flight to Los Angeles and allowed three nights in a hotel near the LA warehouse. Dave would catch an afternoon flight on Sunday and arrive that evening in LA She arranged a car rental and a hotel for the three days. She checked her incoming mail and found an invoice from Sandway. She opened the invoice studied it for a moment, stamped it approved, added Bernie's initials and put it in the inter-office mail to accounting.

*   *   *

Temple Enterprise Offices, Washington, DC

Bernie assembled several files, made copies and put the copies in three large envelopes. He asked Myra to join him in his office and began by telling her she would be going to London to deliver the files and wait for the return packages. She had made similar trips several times in the last four years and each time took an extra few days to visit the museums or enjoy live theater in London.

"I'd like these to get there tomorrow, and they could be finished by end of Monday. Let's assume you can pick up the return files Tuesday morning and be back here Tuesday night." He thought for a second, "Perhaps we should allow them an extra day or two, to be sure all the i's are dotted, yes, schedule a pick-up at the office in London on Tuesday and fly back here on Wednesday."

As Myra took the envelopes, she said, "I'll get online and book the flights immediately." She turned and walked out of Bernie's office.

Bernie watched her walk away, thinking, soon she would be a memory. He sighed and returned to the papers on his desk.

Myra sat at her desk and planned an itinerary for her trip then booked her flights. She reserved a hotel room in London for the days she'd be there and also made arrangements for two evening performances at London theaters. She then walked into the personnel office, pulled several files, copied a few items, put the copies in an envelope, returned the files and left the personnel office.

Bernie was pleased with himself. He had successfully arranged the end of the two prime possible leaks. His phone beeped, "Yes, Myra."

"Mr. Temple, I've booked a flight leaving at 7:30 this evening, so I will be leaving here very soon."

Bernie didn't hesitate, "Not a problem, Myra. Have a good flight and enjoy the trip. I'll see when you get back."

She packed her briefcase, took a few items out of her desk, wiped off her desk and keyboard, and walked out the front door.

*   *   *

Heathrow Airport, Langford, UK

Myra Wallace arrived at Heathrow at 7:14 Friday morning. She took the train into London and a cab to her hotel. She showered, dressed for the business world and arrived at the London office of Temple Enterprise at 9:45 a.m. She had a short day and nothing else on her plate until the return pouch would be prepared. In that it was due to be ready the following Tuesday, all the time in between was hers to spend as she wished. She returned to the hotel, changed into a more comfortable outfit, filled a backpack with essentials and walked out of the hotel. Myra Wallace walked toward the business district and disappeared into the crowd. She did not return to the hotel that night or the following day.

*   *   *

Temple Enterprise Offices, Washington, DC

Friday afternoon Bernie's computer pinged. The note stated, *the bridge is clear*, and Bernie knew Myra was no longer a problem. He leaned back in his chair and thought about Franklin's recommendation to sell and retire, "It's probably the wisest thing to do," he said softly. Myra was no longer in his thoughts.

*   *   *

LAX International Airport, Los Angeles, CA

Dave Saunders arrived in Los Angeles Monday afternoon. The rental car was ready when he arrived. He drove immediately to the hotel, dumped his bags in the room and went down to the bar for a late dinner and a drink.

She was blond, tall and well proportioned. She wore a close fitting, dark blue dress that showed more than it covered. Her skin was a light tan, her eyes, big and dark with long lashes, her lips brilliant red. She walked with authority up to the bar and ordered a drink. Dave saw her come in and watched her cross the floor, wondering if she was natural or did some plastic surgeon contribute to her body. He listened to her voice as she ordered her martini and caught her eye as she took her first sip.

She smiled, took the three steps between them and said, "Hi, I'm Denise. Is this seat taken?"

They sat at the bar, talking and drinking for a few minutes and Dave forgot about dinner. Denise suggested they find a more private place to continue, so Dave bought a bottle of wine and led her to his room.

Less than an hour later, Denise stood and surveyed Dave's room. She had been careful to touch very little in the room, including Dave. When they entered, she excused herself and went into the bathroom. She came out a few minutes later with a towel wrapped around her, held with her right hand, her left hand behind her back. She teased him with what he thought was going to be a lap dance and after allowing the towel to fall away, Dave hardly noticed her left hand wearing a latex glove coming from behind her back holding a small pistol.

"This is going to be the best part," Denise said as she draped the towel over her gloved hand. The gun was a .22 caliber, small and relatively quiet. The towel muffled the sound even more and the three shots fired into Dave's head coincided with the sounds of a football game on the television.

She used a damp washcloth to clean the blood spatter on her face, arms and legs. She checked her hair, dressed and wiped down the several places she might have left her fingerprints with another cloth. Then she removed two plastic bags from her purse. One contained several tissues and the other a glass with someone else's finger and lip prints. She left two of the tissues in the bathroom and another on a nightstand next to the bed. She poured some of the remaining wine in the glass, swirled it around, placed it on the nightstand next to the tissue. She wiped down the glass she had used and placed it in one of the plastic bags. Then put the two small washcloths and the latex glove in the other bag.

Finished checking, Denise walked out of Dave's room, took the elevator to the first floor, checked the time on a clock in the lobby. She discretely left the glass in the lobby on a table and walked out the main door with her head tilted down. She walked two blocks to another motel, went into the elevator and rode to the third floor. She went into a room, changed her dress, her wig and shoes. Leaving the motel, she walked a block away and deposited a bag containing the clothes she wore to Dave's motel in a Goodwill collection container. She returned to her motel, took a cab to LAX, boarded a flight to San Francisco and caught another flight to Dulles International, outside of Washington, DC.

She landed in Virginia, walked to a car in the North Parking Garage and drove out to Winchester and a townhouse. She opened a disposable phone, punched in a number, rigged the voice changer and left a message then removed the wig, let her long dark hair fall to her shoulders, undressed, removed the heavy make-up from her face and stood in a hot shower, rinsing away the rest of Dave Saunders' blood.

*   *   *

Temple Enterprise Offices, Washington, DC

Bernie's phone beeped and he answered. The receptionist occupying Myra's desk, "Sir, there is a call from the Los Angeles Police Department. Something has happened to Dave..." she said in a panic.

"I've got it," Bernie replied. He pushed another button on his phone, "This is Bernard Temple."

The voice on the other end said he was a detective with LAPD, "We are trying to contact the next of kin to a David Saunders."

"Dave? Is there something wrong? Is he alright?" asked Bernie.

"Is Mr. Saunders one of your employees?" asked the detective.

"Yes, yes he is," returned Bernie. Then in a slightly panicked voice, "Has something happened to him?"

"We would like to speak to his next of kin, can you tell me who that may be?"

Bernie smiled, the termination of Dave had been completed, "I don't think there is any immediate family. I suppose we are as close to family as you will get."

"Are you Mr. Saunders' direct supervisor?"

"I am," said Bernie. "Dave has been with me for over ten years."

The detective paused and continued, "I'm sorry to tell you Mr. Temple, David Saunders was the victim of a shooting here in Los Angeles. He was pronounced dead at the motel where he was found this morning."

"Are you sure this is our Dave Saunders?" asked Bernie.

"His Virginia driver's license identifies him, and he is in possession of a number of business cards indicating he is employed by Temple Enterprise. The people at your warehouse here in LA suggested we call you and ask about his family."

Bernie fell silent for a moment, then, "Detective, what happened?"

"We are just beginning our investigation," said the detective. "We will be asking a lot of questions of you or your people here in LA."

"I'll be there as soon as possible," said Bernie. "Where should I go to see Dave and meet with you?"

The detective left Bernie his cell number and said he should contact him when he arrived in LA.

Bernie hung up and leaned back in his chair, "Two down," he muttered. "That should be the end of it," he smiled as he buzzed the receptionist.

"Carol, could you book me on the first flight to LAX tomorrow morning out of Dulles."

"Certainly sir, will business class be acceptable?"

"Yes, and let's do a return on Thursday morning."

*   *   *

26

Kevin Shelton called Ian on his cellphone, "Ian, Kevin," he began, "I've got something for you."

"I'll take anything I can get," said Ian. "This puzzle is missing a bunch of pieces."

"You were looking into two characters from LA, Clint Marsh and Tomas Relatto, for a murder in DC," said Kevin, "now we have a murder on our turf involving someone from Virginia, his name is Saunders, David. His business card indicates he worked for Temple Enterprise."

Ian wrote the name and said, "I know the name, what happened?"

"We don't know yet, he was found in his motel room with three small caliber bullets to the head," said Kevin. "Timeline is a little fuzzy probably between 9:00 and midnight last night. The cleaning people found him this morning. He was naked, laying on the bed, no struggle, evidence collected includes a half-empty bottle of wine, a glass with lipstick and fingerprints, several tissues, and three shell casings."

"Any body fluids?" asked Ian.

"No, not yet," said Kevin, "we're still looking at stuff. I don't think our victim and his partner ever got around to swapping spit."

"Anything else?" asked Ian.

"His wallet was empty, no cash no credit cards."

"Robbery gone wild?" quizzed Ian.

"I don't know, he still had his watch on and a ring, didn't smell quite right," said Kevin.

"Got it," said Ian, "anything else?"

"Yeah, very preliminary, the wounds to his face angled like the shooter is left-handed. It ain't much, but every bit counts."

"Thanks, Kevin. Anything else on the timeline?" asked Ian.

Kevin flipped a page in his notes, "Yeah, our vic checked in at the front desk around six-thirty, went to his room and returned to the bar/restaurant around seven. Bartender says he was sitting at the bar looking at the menu when a female approached him, began a conversation and after a while, he bought a bottle of wine and the two left the bar. That was around eight," Kevin added, "bartender's not sure about the exact times, just rough guesses."

"So, they go to his room, he gets naked, lays on the bed and she pops him?" said Ian.

Kevin added, "Yeah, and there was a towel on the floor next to the bed. It had powder burns, probably used to muffle the sound."

"Do we have a description of this woman?"

"Sort of," said Kevin, "tall, maybe five-eight or more, long hair, blond. Barkeep thinks she had dark eyes, almost black. He said it was hard to tell, she wore funny colored glasses, blue or purple."

"Lenses?" said Ian.

"Maybe," said Kevin. He continued, "Well built, maybe around 140 pounds or more, healthy. Probably mid-thirties. Dressed to sell, tight fitting, short skirt, didn't see the shoes, so the height estimate could be off. She wore gloves and the glass she was using went through the washer, so, no prints."

"Was she staying at the motel?" asked Ian.

"Could be, like I said, we're still checking stuff here. Nate Candry is the lead detective on this one. He talked to the vic's boss at Temple Enterprise in DC this morning and apparently the guy is coming out here."

"When will that be?" asked Ian.

"I think tomorrow," Kevin paused then added, "Ian, I don't know but, do you think this may be related to my two guys in the desert?"

"It's pointing in that direction, so, we'll keep in touch," said Ian.

"When the CSI guys have something else, I'll give you a yell," said Kevin. "The glass and tissues collected could tell us something and the shell casings were not printed yet when I was downstairs. Talk to you soon."

They hung up and Ian called Dan on his cell, "Danny boy, we got some more pieces to our puzzle. When can you be here?"

When Dan arrived at the end of his shift, Ian was in a conference room with Stan Reed, Bob Leonard, Craig Robins and Mike Farley. He came in as Ian was about to inform the group about the developments in Los Angeles. "Dan, just about to start. The investigation into Lake's killing has stalled on a number of fronts. What I have here may help to clarify or help to muddy the waters, one way or the other, here's what I got this morning."

He opened a dry marker and wrote the date on the far right, then wrote the date of George Klemper's trip to New York City on the far left. Then he noted Georges questioning by the FBI, then the date of George's murder, the date of Lakes murder, the date of Jason and Ross' murders, the date of Tomas and Frank's murders and then he said, "These all are related to Temple Enterprise and this morning I got a call from my cousin with the LAPD, and we have another name for this hit list." He pointed at the last date on the whiteboard. "This morning at 9:20 Pacific Standard Time, the body of David Saunders was found in a hotel in LA." He looked at the assembled people, "He was the warehouse manager in Temple's Northern Virginia warehouse." He paused, "He was shot three times in the head."

"Was this our friend, Franklin?" asked Craig Robins.

"No," said Ian. "This was most likely a woman. She met him in the bar around eight last night, they left around nine and his body was discovered this morning." He looked around the room, "LAPD is still checking prints and DNA, that's gonna take a while to come in. We don't have a suspect yet, but this looks to me like a professional hit made to look like he was some hooker's latest victim."

Dan tapped his finger on the table, "So, does this babe work for Franklin?"

"I guess anything is possible," returned Ian. "At this point, not much would surprise me."

"Time for another talk with this Bernard Temple," said Leonard. "I think we should get him off his turf and onto ours."

Stan Reed said, "Bernie and his admin, Myra, both should be questioned."

"Temple is scheduled in LA tomorrow, according to my cousin out there," said Ian, "but I agree, let's get him in here—our house and our rules. There's got to be something we are not getting from him."

"Any idea how long he'll be out there?" asked Leonard.

"No idea, but I'd give it at least two days," said Ian.

"Yeah," said Robins, "we can do this on Thursday. He should be back by then, Friday at the latest."

Stan chimed in, "I've talked to the guy several times and never felt I had a complete story." He hesitated, "Then there's his admin, Myra Wallace. She's probably up on everything Bernie Temple does."

"Do you want to bring her in before we talk to Temple?" asked Ian.

"Sure," returned Stan, "we'll want to talk to her sooner or later, and with Bernie out of town for a few days, she may be the best game we can play. Let's get her in here tomorrow."

*　　　*　　　*

Temple Enterprise Office, Washington, DC

"Stan and Ian walked into the Temple Enterprise offices at 8:15 the next morning. The open office area was alive with activity and as they looked around, a woman came out of the corridor leading to Bernie's office.

"May I help you, gentlemen?" asked the woman as she placed a cup of coffee on the receptionist's desk.

"Yes," replied Stan, "we're here to see Myra Wallace."

Carol stepped behind the desk and said, "Ms. Wallace is not in right now. Can I help you?"

"When do you expect her?" asked Stan.

"May I ask what this is about?" asked Carol.

Stan produced his badge wallet, "We have several questions for her. When do you expect her?"

Carol looked at Stan's badge, "Excuse me Detective, Ms. Wallace is traveling out of the country. She is due back here next week. Friday—I believe."

"Where did she go?" asked Ian.

Carol hesitated, "She has taken something to our London office and will return when they have finished refining it."

"And Mr. Temple, when is he due back?" asked Stan.

"He'll be back in town late Thursday."

"And he'll be in here on Friday as well?" said Stan.

"That is the plan."

As Stan and Ian left the Temple offices, Stan said, "They'll both be back about the same time. Temple first and the lady second?"

Ian frowned, "This is dragging out, I want to kick this damn hornet's nest and see what happens."

*   *   *

27

Temple Enterprise Office, Washington, DC

Friday morning, Ian and Stan again went to the eighth floor occupied by Temple Enterprise and asked to speak to Bernard Temple. Carol buzzed Bernie's office and he immediately came to the lobby.

"Good morning, Detectives. Please give me a moment," he said as he turned to Carol. "See if you can reach Myra, I thought she might be back today. Please find out when she'll be back. She may wish to take another day or two."

Carol reached for the phone, "I'll ring her right now."

Bernie looked at Stan, "Now, how can I help you?"

Stan said, "We have several questions for you and would like you to come to the first district office to meet with several of our staff."

Bernie looked appropriately confused and asked, "Is this about Dave Saunders?"

"We have a number of areas we would like to cover, Mr. Temple," said Ian.

Bernie turned toward Carol, "I don't have anything important until two this afternoon. I'll call if the detectives need me to stay longer." He looked at Stan, "Is that alright with you, Detective?"

"That works," returned Stan, and they left the building.

*   *   *

Metropolitan Police Department, Washington, DC

The conference room was used to interview Bernard Temple. Each of the Federal agents had questions as did each of the detectives. Bob Leonard led with a battery of questions about Dave Saunders, his position in the company, his usual travel arrangements, the purpose of this specific trip and finally, who might want to kill him.

Bernie couldn't think of anyone who would wish Dave harm, "He is practically my right arm here in the Washington area, and he helped set up the other warehouses. Every one of those warehouses reports to him," Bernie paused, "or did." He paused again, took a deep breath and looked at Leonard, "What else can I tell you?"

"Did you carry keyman insurance on Mr. Saunders?" asked Ian.

Bernie looked slightly surprised, "No, no I never considered it." He bowed his head and added, "It sounds cold now, but perhaps I should have had that insurance. Dave will be very difficult to replace."

Craig Robins, Stan Reed and Ian all took a turn asking Bernie questions and he maintained his storyline through it all. Ian finished with, "Your admin, Myra Wallace, where is she?"

Bernie replied, "Myra took some files to our London office to be worked on and returned here. These things sometimes take several days, and she uses that extra time to visit art galleries and museums. She thoroughly enjoys these little visits to London. I expect her back in the office today or Monday at the latest. Would you like her to come in to talk to you at that time?"

"Yes, please have her contact us as soon as possible," said Ian.

Bernie nodded, shook Ian's hand and walked out of the conference room.

"You don't want to talk to Myra?" asked Robins.

"Oh, I definitely do," said Ian. "But I don't have to tell Bernie what I'm doing."

Stan said, "We should do this again next week, Friday with Myra, or Bernie or just us to see where we all are."

"Agreed," said Leonard, "how about Friday morning, here around ten?"

Ian stood, "Let's hope we have more to talk about in a week."

*   *   *

Bernie walked out of the first district office building before noon and took a cab back to his office. He was very pleased with his performance, but being a very cautious man, he did not celebrate his perceived victory. For all he knew, the cabbie could have been an undercover cop just waiting for Bernie to drop his guard.

When he arrived at his office, Carol looked frightened, "Mr. Temple, I can't locate Myra, she doesn't answer her phone and I checked with the hotel manager, she hasn't used her room, she seems to have disappeared."

Bernie felt a rush through his whole body, *Myra was gone.* "Not to worry, Carol. She often will take a little side trip to Stratford on Avon, or perhaps she took the train to Paris, these little side trips are not at all unusual." He smiled and looked at Carol, "Perhaps she met someone, and they are off somewhere."

Sitting behind his desk, Bernie wondered about Franklin. How did he manage to take care of both Dave and Myra in a one-week span, one in California and one in England? He scratched his head, smiled and muttered, "Not my problem, it's over and done with." He moved some papers on his desk and was reminded of his last conversation with Franklin, "Sell and retire." He called his CFO and asked him to join him in his office.

*   *   *

Temple Enterprise Offices, Washington, DC

The next morning, Bernie arrived at his office around eight and unlocked the front door. He walked to Myra's desk, touched her name plate and thought about her. *I wonder if she would have talked, no, this had to be done.* He went to his office and looked at his emails from several weeks prior. He found one that fit his curiosity. It was from one of his competitors, asking for a lunch meeting. He read and reread the letter, then picked up his phone.

It was difficult to casually guess the value of Temple Enterprise and Bernie had asked his CFO to pull together a number for him to consider. The evaluation included the warehouses in several cities, operating equipment, outstanding loans, personnel and revenue streams, among other factors. The thought of selling was not appealing to Bernie, but an avenue he should explore. He arranged a lunch meeting with Tim

Marchand, one of the several parties who had inquired about buying Temple Enterprise. Tim was almost as deeply into shady deals as Bernie, but he didn't have the history of completed transactions as Bernie did. His pitch to Tim would be his desire to retire while his health was still good.

"Tim, you know my father passed away in his sixties and my mother shortly after. I'm already in that range and want to slow down. It would be nice to still be here in ten or twenty years, so, I am thinking about your offer. We're not far apart and I think there may be an arrangement that could work for both of us."

They appeared to reach an unofficial agreement. Bernie invited Tim and his team to come and meet the Temple leadership in their offices, "Once you know a bit more about my operation, you may revise your offer and we can meet again."

Tim agreed to the meeting at Temple's office and it was arranged for a week out, the teams would meet and both sides would be ready to negotiate. When the meeting would occur, Bernie expected a revised offer that could be more tempting than the possible profit he may realize by remaining in the game.

Over the weekend, Bernie vacillated between selling and not selling. The money he could make over the next few years, the never-ending questioning by the police, the fun, the thrill of completing some of his shadier deals, he was torn.

*   *   *

Temple Enterprise Offices, Washington, DC

Monday morning, Carol came into Bernie's office in a frenzied state, "Mr. Temple, we still haven't heard from Myra. I called the hotel, and she hasn't returned to her room. Her bags are still there, and the room hasn't been used. I think something may have happened to her."

"Relax, Carol. I'm sure there's an explanation. Myra has always been very dependable, I'm sure she'll turn up."

"Sir, her flight has already left Heathrow, and she's not on it. What should we do?" asked Carol.

Bernie looked appropriately shocked and replied, "I'll call the London office, if they haven't heard from her, they can file a missing person's report." He hesitated, then, "Carol, schedule a conference call with the London office tomorrow."

Later that morning, Carol called Bernie, "A Mr. Comstock called and insisted I get you to contact him. He said it's very important."

Bernie checked the time and called the client.

"Bernie, since Jim Millington is no longer in the picture, you're the only one I trust to handle this shipment. It has to go to Columbia, but I am troubled, you lost your man, Dave. Killed in a hotel in LA."

"Yes, very unfortunate, but I have other people," said Bernie.

"And I hear you are considering a sale to Marchand."

"Also, true. I've been thinking about retiring," said Bernie.

"You retire, you'll be bored. You're too young to retire, Bernie." Comstock paused, "And I have other shipments wanting to be moved over the next year, nine of them."

Bernie hesitated, thought for a moment, *I got Jim Millington out of the way for this deal, hate to let it go now*, then he said, "Not to worry my friend, I will handle all of them, then maybe think of retirement."

The caller said he had the first of nine ready in a warehouse as soon as Bernie was ready to move it. They talked for another minute and hung up. Bernie leaned back in his chair, paused, grinned and said aloud, "Retire, I think not."

*　　*　　*

28

Temple Enterprise Office, Washington, DC

Bernie sat in the main conference room looking at a wide-screen monitor on the wall. Devon Hartly, the London office manager and Inspector Robert Avery, from Scotland Yard were on the screen. "She's a very dependable person, very organized, never late and this is totally out of character for her. We are very concerned."

"Understood, Mr. Temple," replied the police inspector, "she has been missing for five days now, correct?"

"Today will be the sixth day since anyone has had contact with her," returned Bernie.

"We have searched her room at the hotel, her bed has not been used, one suitcase is unopened, a purse with some cash, several debit cards, her return airline ticket and a number of personal items were on the writing desk," said the inspector.

Bernie could see there was something else the inspector was not saying, "What does that add up to?" he asked.

"In itself, not that much," said the inspector. "You say she is a very organized person, correct?"

"Yes, very," replied Bernie.

"Is she a very neat and clean person as well?" asked the policeman.

"I'd say yes," replied Bernie, "I often thought her a bit compulsive, the way she kept her desk so clean, and organized." He paused and thought for a moment, "I thought it was because she knew she was the first person people met as they came into our offices. She created a very positive atmosphere. Made a great first impression." Bernie still noticed a slight reservation on the part of the inspector, "What is it that you're not saying?"

"Very neat, very clean, compulsive, you say?" asked the inspector. "Well, Mr. Temple, she seems to have left no trace of her ever being in that room."

Bernie was now confused, "She checked in and her bags were in the room, correct?" He paused, "She was there on Friday."

"Yes, someone was there, but that someone left no trace of themselves. We found no fingerprints and we're still looking into any DNA on her bags, purse and credit cards," said the inspector. "As of this moment, we have no evidence that she was ever here. Someone checked in, that someone fits her description. Someone left her bags in the room, but after the initial check-in, nobody recalls seeing her."

"She went there, to the office," said Bernie.

Devon nodded, "Yes, she was here on Friday. I spoke to her. We discussed the status of the documents we were to review and the updates as they may occur." He looked at the inspector, "Then she left and said she'd call to check on progress and be back when the package was complete."

"According to your account, she was wearing a brown herringbone business suit, light blue blouse a tan raincoat and brown leather gloves," said the inspector.

"Yes, I believe so," said Devon.

"That was at 10:00 a.m.on Friday?" quizzed the inspector.

Devon looked shaken, "Yes, as I recall."

"Where does this take us?" asked Bernie, "I mean, she was there, she went to the office and now she's gone." He was as confused as the inspector.

"Her room key was used at 11:17, so she returned to the room about then," said the inspector. The security cameras in the lobby show her walking through about that time and leaving less than an hour later."

Bernie still noticed something not being said, "Inspector, what are you not saying this time?"

"We can see her arriving at the hotel Friday morning, leaving for her meeting, returning and leaving again," said Inspector Avery.

Bernie said, "Yes, we established that, what else is there?"

"She changed her clothes to come to this office, then changed again before leaving the hotel the second time," said Avery.

Bernie said, "Okay, so what?"

"So, the clothes she wore to this office are nowhere to be found," said Avery.

Bernie paused, "Why is that important?" he asked.

"I don't know," said Avery, "but her clothes could have been a source of her DNA."

The three men sat in rooms, several thousand miles apart quietly for several minutes and Inspector Avery said, "A missing person that may not want to be found."

Bernie was now concerned. Just how did Franklin dispose of Myra and why all the mystery? "You're suggesting that Myra may have orchestrated her own disappearance?"

"There are several possibilities," said Inspector Avery, "and we must consider them all until we have an answer."

"This is totally out of character for Myra," said Bernie, "I'm afraid she may have come to great harm and you're suggesting she may have run off. No, I can't believe she'd do that. I'm now even more concerned." The call ended and Bernie puzzled over the method Franklin had employed in terminating Myra.

*   *   *

Metropolitan Police Ddepartment, Washington, DC

Ian called Temple Enterprise's office. Carol buzzed Bernie and he answered the phone, "Good morning, Detective. What can I do for you today?"

"We're trying to locate your admin, Myra," said Ian, "is she in today?"

"No, Detective," Bernie had a shaken, nervous quality Ian had not noticed before. "Myra went to London over a week ago and has gone missing."

"Missing?" quizzed Ian.

"Yes, Detective. I'm very concerned about all this tragedy developing around my company. Dave Saunders was killed by a hooker in Los Angeles, my good friend Jim Millington shot dead in front of his home, George and those two laborers. Detective, I am very, very concerned."

"How did you hear about Ms. Wallace missing in England?" asked Ian.

"Carol was worried and called the hotel in London," said Bernie. "Myra hadn't been seen and hasn't contacted the office as scheduled. She missed her flight home, hasn't been seen in about a week."

"But no evidence of foul play?" quizzed Ian.

"No, Detective, no evidence," said Bernie, "but really, look at all that has happened over the last month. Is Myra next? Am I next?" He took a deep breath and sighed, "I called the London office this morning and spoke to our manager and a police official. No one knows where she is."

"What about her family? Has she contacted them?" asked Ian.

"She has worked for me for six years and I don't recall any conversations about her family," returned Bernie. "As a matter of fact, I've never heard her talk about a boyfriend or a girlfriend either."

"Okay, let's start with the basics," said Ian, "you may want to pull her employment records. I'll need her social security number, any references she cited when you hired her, date of birth, birth city, state, school records. I'll be there shortly."

*　　　*　　　*

Temple Enterprise Office, Washington, DC

Ian and Stan arrived at Temple's offices and met Bernie. "Detectives, I'm at a complete loss. Myra Wallace's personnel file is incomplete. Her resume, photograph and the list of professional and personal references are missing." He opened a file and continued, "These are her annual review forms and several notes praising her performance." He looked angry and rattled as neither detective had seen before, "I put some of these notes in here myself and I know her file was complete six months ago."

"Six months ago?" quizzed Stan.

"Yes," replied Bernie, "that's when I last reviewed her."

"Could the file be with someone else for review or updating?" asked Stan.

"No, I checked with the only other people who would have cause to touch these files," said Bernie. "Her resume and letters of recommendation from several people … missing. One was from her coach at Michigan."

"Coach?" puzzled Stan.

"Yes, she was a swimmer, long distance."

"Let's look at Dave Saunders' file," suggested Ian.

The same result, the file had been cleansed as was George Klemper's. Andrew Ross and Jason Barrett were lower level, part-time employees and the files on both had also been thinned out. Bernie was confused and visibly upset.

"Are you sure it was The University of Michigan in Ann Arbor?" asked Ian, "Or could it have been Michigan State in Lansing?"

"I'm sure it was in Ann Arbor," replied Bernie. "I was there on business several years ago and we talked about Canham Natatorium. She spent a lot of time there swimming. Said she tried out for the water polo team, but much preferred the long-distance swimming."

"Okay," said Ian. "I'll put in a call to the registrar's office at Michigan and get copies of her records. We'll go from there." He placed the call from his cellphone as he and Stan returned to his car and requested copies of records of one Myra Wallace any time between 2000 and 2010. The search of records would take a few days and after confidentiality hurdles were cleared, the information would be sent to Ian at MPD.

*   *   *

29

Bernie was feeling the pressure at last. His chance to make a final score with eight or nine shipments with Comstock was very tempting. If he completed the first of the nine projects and the air was still clear, he may be able to stay on course for the second project. If he sensed a deepening problem, he could accept Marchand's offer and sail off to Bermuda as Franklin suggested. He called Comstock and arranged the first of the nine shipments. Then he called Marchand and said he had to complete a few more tasks before the sale could be executed.

"I'm a bit shaken by the events of the last month and need a little time to work things out in my head," said Bernie. "So, I'll be taking the *Lanita*, my boat, to Bermuda this week. It's quiet and peaceful out there on the big water and I also want to see how the boat performs and determine if I want to keep her or get something a bit smaller."

"*Lanita?*" said Tim, "What kind of boat is it?"

"Named after my mother. She's an 86-foot Hatteras," replied Bernie. "I lived on it for a while after getting out of the Navy."

"When you return, we should talk," said Tim.

"Agreed," returned Bernie, "I should be back in DC in about a week."

*   *   *

Temple Enterprise Office, Washington, DC

Bernie called Carol into his office, "I'll be taking a little time this week and next," he said. He explained his intent to sail to Rudee Inlet at Virginia Beach, visit with a few friends, then sail to Bermuda and if selling the Lanita proves successful, fly back. "I should be back here late next week. Friday at the latest, so let's clear my schedule 'til Monday, the tenth and we'll stay in touch by phone."

"Yes sir, should I book your return flight now?" asked Carol.

"No, I don't know what will take place when I arrive in Hamilton. I'll play it by ear at first and see what the market for the *Lanita* might be. Everything is up in the air, all options are on the table," returned Bernie.

Carol made a note and looked at Bernie, "What about the police—if they call?"

"I'm completely available, just call any time. When I get to Hamilton, I'll check in with you and I'll only be a flight away."

*　　*　　*

Yacht Club, VA

Bernie checked with two other yacht club members to verify his route downstream on the Potomac to the Chesapeake. When he passed Colonial Beach, he relaxed and put the *Lanita* on automatic pilot. He set a course for Virginia Beach and Rudee Inlet where he planned to take on fuel and food for his trip to Bermuda. The trip would cover around 1,000 miles of open sea and take four days. The weather was almost perfect for the journey, afternoon high temperatures predicted in the 70's with little wind and calm seas.

He had reserved a docking space in the inlet and upon arrival, checked his fuel levels, topped off his tanks and called his office.

"Carol, I'll be having dinner with a few old friends this evening and may stay the night ashore. Please call Comstock's office and confirm my appointment on the 27th and see if you can arrange a meeting with Marchand for the end of that week, Friday would be best. Anything else, I'll be back aboard tomorrow afternoon and you can contact me there. I'll probably set out for Bermuda by mid-afternoon and get away from the local traffic before sunset."

Carol made a few notes, called Comstock's office then Marchand's and had a brief conversation with her counterparts in both offices.

*　　*　　*

I-95 South, VA

After an early breakfast and a hot shower, she left the motel west of Washington in Fairfax County, driving south on I-95 before 9:30 a.m. After a stop in Williamsburg for lunch and a little sightseeing, she arrived in Virginia Beach just before 4:00 p.m. and registered in a beachfront hotel. Dressed warmly, complete with a hoodie, she walked the boardwalk down to Rudee inlet, surveyed the docking area, and walked back to her hotel. After having dinner, she laid out her outfit for the morning, a wetsuit complete with boots, hood, and utility belt. A cellphone, a .22 caliber pistol, a diving knife, and an inflatable mattress placed in a shopping bag for the morning, she turned out the lights and went to sleep.

*　　*　　*

Rudee Inlet, Virginia Beach, VA

Bernie arrived at Rudee Inlet as planned, topped off his fuel tanks, tied up in his reserved space, made several calls from the *Lanita's* bridge, then met his old friends on shore and went to dinner. The talk and drinking went on 'til the late hours and Bernie stayed the night at a hotel. The following afternoon, he returned to his boat with two bags of groceries and several bottles of wine. He stowed the supplies in the galley, went to the bridge, powered up, and steered the *Lanita* out of Rudee Inlet.

The seas were as promised, very calm and the temperature warm. He set the automatic pilot east-southeast toward Bermuda and leaned back in his captain's chair looking out over the open sea. It was 3:35 p.m., the city of Virginia Beach was still in view, and he thought he would sample one of the bottles of wine. He left the bridge and went below to the galley, retrieved a bottle of wine, a glass, and a corkscrew and as he started back toward the bridge, he heard something. It came from the rear deck. He set the wine down and went down the ladder to investigate. The chair was secure, nothing appeared loose. A bungee strap casually bounced against a bulkhead, and he wondered how it had come loose. He reattached the loose end and went to the transom to look over at the wake. His back was to the hatch to the lower level and he neither saw nor heard her come up.

She quietly watched him for a moment then, "You didn't take my advice."

Bernie was startled, he turned and saw the woman in a wetsuit with a gun pointed at him. Before he could speak, she shot him in the chest, then as he stumbled and fell to his knees, she stepped closer and shot a second time, through his left eye. "I told you to retire," she said as he twitched twice before becoming still. She scanned the area and seeing nobody within hearing range, calmly dropped the gun over the side.

She went below again and returned with the four diving belts Bernie had left on the boat weeks before. She secured them firmly around him, opened the door on the transom, and pushed Bernie's lifeless body out and into the deep. He immediately sank out of sight. Very pleased with everything thus far she went to the bridge and modified the autopilot command, increasing speed to fifteen knots. On her way back to the rear deck she picked up the bottle of wine, popped the cork, poured some in the glass, and continued to the rear deck. A quick wash of water over the blood and the rear deck looked clean. She spilled some of the wine on the transom and dropped the bottle and glass on the deck. Then she checked her watch, took a disposable phone from her belt, punched in a few numbers, waited for an answer then tapped four times, paused and tapped four times again. On the other end, Tim Marchand returned the four taps and listened as the phone went silent.

She pulled the battery and dropped the phone in the ocean, blew air into the inflatable mattress, checked her boots and hood, threw the mattress over the side and dove in. The swim to shore was going to take time, she wanted to arrive as daylight was fading and casually laid on the mattress and slowly paddled toward the beach.

She came ashore near Neptune's Statue, let the air out of her mattress, dropped it in a pile of beach toys, and walked to her hotel a few blocks away. A hot shower and an early bedtime readied her for an early morning start.

*   *   *

30

Stan Reed handed Ian a printout from the fax machine, "You got answers from Michigan."

Ian looked at the letter, "They have no record of a Myra Wallace ever attending any classes at Michigan University during the first ten years of this century." He looked at Stan, "This lady has disappeared, and we don't have any idea who she really is. She didn't attend Michigan, much less graduate as she apparently claimed. Her personnel file has been cleaned out and all we have is a Social Security number Temple Enterprise had in their tax files. That's a legitimate number, I gave it to the feds, and they took it to the Social Security Administration. They only have five years of income records for that number and the return each year has been applied to the next year's tax."

"Wonderful," said Stan, "we now have a missing person with a mysterious past."

"I sent a request for information about our missing person to Wayne County in Michigan. They came back with a Myra Anne Wallace, born July 10, 1982."

"You got her," said Stan.

"Not exactly," returned Ian, "this Myra Anne Wallace died December 3rd, 1983."

"Is there another Myra Wallace?" asked Stan.

"Not that I can find," said Ian. "So, apparently our Myra took the deceased baby's number and established a new identity for herself."

"Any other employment records?" asked Stan, "Money paid into SSA from other sources?"

"Nope," replied Ian, "nothing."

"By the way, I checked with CSI this morning," said Stan, "they don't have any prints on our mysterious Myra, no DNA, no photos, nothing more than a description that could fit any great number of people."

As Ian thought through the information, scenarios began to take shape in his head. *Myra Wallace was not who she pretended to be. Was she someone with a dark past and she started anew with a different identity? Was she escaping from something dangerous? Was she a criminal herself operating with her new or real identity? The final question was, where was Myra? Others were killed and their bodies recovered, Myra on the other hand simply disappeared. Or did she?*

The equally mysterious Franklin also left a number of questions beginning with, *could he be someone Ian already knew? Or was he someone in a distant location, a puppeteer pushing buttons and pulling strings? Could Myra and Franklin be a team or were they one and the same?*

Myra's position in Bernie's company gave her the freedom to control the positioning of Dave Saunders and scope out Jim Millington prior to his demise. She could have also controlled the execution of the two LA thugs who killed Lake and wounded Kat. Ian wanted to talk to Myra.

"Questions to ponder over the weekend," Ian said to Stan.

*   *   *

Metropolitan Police Department, Washington, DC

Leonard and Robins arrived for a scheduled meeting to review the status of the several related investigations. "Our friend Bernie is taking his boat to Bermuda. He'll be back by the tenth at the latest," said Robins.

Ian raised an eyebrow, "Why now?"

"His office said he needed time to clear his head, needed to think things through," said Robins. "He may be selling his boat in Bermuda, according to the lady I talked to."

"Carol," said Ian, "she has stepped up to fill Myra's shoes 'til she returns."

"If she returns," said Stan.

"Yeah, there's a mystery in itself," said Ian. He relayed the information gained that morning from Michigan. "So, who is Myra Wallace? And where is she?"

"If she's not who she traveled to London as," said Stan, "she could have returned as someone else."

Ian stood, "Bernie is sailing to Bermuda, Myra is missing. Could she be with Bernie, could he be meeting her in Bermuda?" He looked around the room, "I want to talk to Bernie. Now!"

"Carol said he'd be available by phone at any time," said Robins. "He could be in Virginia Beach now or on his way across to Bermuda."

Ian looked at Leonard, "Can we call the Coast Guard down there, have them freeze the boat? Then we'll get a hard look at it."

"We'll need a warrant," said Robins. "I'll take care of that."

Leonard said, "I'll see if we can use the jet at Andrews, it'll get us there a lot quicker than driving."

The four men piled into the SUV and hurried to Andrews as Robins made a series of calls. When they arrived at Andrews, the jet was waiting. The pilot said, "I have clearance to land at Oceana Air Station and a car will be waiting for you. That's as close to Rudee Inlet as we can get."

*   *   *

Rudee Inlet, Virginia Beach, VA

By the time they landed it had been determined that the *Lanita* had left Rudee Inlet around noon on Thursday and could be 400 miles out to sea. "We've tried to hail her from here with no luck. All phone calls ring six times and go to message. Either he doesn't hear it or he's ignoring it," said Coast Guard Officer Ken Morris.

"What's the range of that model boat?" asked Ian.

"If she's carrying a full load in her tanks, she could go between 700 and 1400 miles, depending on speed and how rough the seas are."

"So, she could be 400 miles out?" asked Ian.

"If she's making for Bermuda, I'd say she'd be doing around 10 knots and would be less than 300 miles out," replied Ken.

"Can we do a search out that far toward Bermuda?" asked Ian.

"Does she have an AIS Transponder onboard?" asked Ken.

"A what?" asked Ian.

"It's a device that is used to locate boats at sea. I'll check it out."

Ken returned a few minutes later, "She's about 375 miles out and well north of where she should be."

"So, where's he going?" asked Ian.

Ken shook his head, "Nowhere, at that speed, he'll run out of fuel and be adrift in short order."

"It doesn't sound right," said Ian.

"Nope, it doesn't," said the officer. "We're going to have to go get him."

*   *   *

Little Creek, Virginia Beach, VA

The *Lanita* was sighted as predicted almost 400 miles north of Bermuda. She was hailed, there was no response. She was approached and no one was seen on board. She was boarded and searched. Nobody was aboard and the fuel gauge read empty. The only evidence that someone had been aboard was a little blood on the rear deck, spilled wine, a broken glass and a half empty wine bottle rolling about.

The Lanita was towed into the Little Creek Coast Guard Station and a forensic team was busily scanning everything. Ian approached the officer in charge, "Can I go aboard and look around?"

"Give my team another hour and you should be able to conduct your search," replied Ken.

"Have they found anything yet?" asked Ian.

"Yeah, the galley had fresh food stowed, and the boat's paperwork was on a table with a notepad and some sales figures. There was a blood stain on the rear deck, a broken wine glass, an empty bottle," said Ken.

"A wine bottle and only one glass?" asked Ian, "What about the cork?"

Ken looked at Ian, "The cork was in the trash with the foil and a protein bar wrapper. It's all right there," he said pointing to a table.

Ian casually walked over to the table and looked at several small items thus far removed from the *Lanita*. He looked at the wine bottle then he saw the protein bar wrapper. He waved Ken over, "Has this been printed?" he asked pointing to the wrapper.

"Not yet, why?" returned Ken.

"I'll bet you a nickel, it has our mysterious lady Myra's prints on it," said Ian.

Ken called one of the forensic team over, "Billy, see if there are any prints on this wrapper."

Billy took the wrapper into a building and returned as Ian was about to go aboard. "We have one print that's clear enough to be used as an identifier. Ran it, nothing in our database."

Ian did a walk-through and came up with nothing, "She was here, I'm sure of it," he said out loud, "and now they're both missing."

The DC team drove back to Washington and Ian sat quietly during the trip, running the several scenarios through his mind. The question of Bernie's involvement, and now his disappearance complicated things even more. His initial theory that Bernie was controlling everything was not holding up under this latest event.

*   *   *

Temple Enterprise Office, Washington, DC

"Good morning, Detective," said Carol as Ian walked through the door, "any further news about Mr. Temple?"

"No, I'm afraid not," returned Ian. "I'm here to ask you a few questions."

"I hope I can help," said Carol.

"First, who knew about Mr. Temple's trip to Bermuda?"

"I know Mr. Comstock and Mr. Marchand's offices were aware, I know because I told them."

"Anybody else?" quizzed Ian.

"Not that I'm aware of," said Carol, "but he could have told a dozen more people."

"Who is Comstock?"

"I've never met him, but he is one of our clients. He imports machine parts from Europe."

"And who is Marchand?" asked Ian.

"Mr. Marchand is interested in buying our firm and he and Mr. Temple have been negotiating. He even had a team of his people here a week or so ago, to look us over."

"Could you give me contact information for both of them?" asked Ian.

Carol tapped a few keys on the computer and said, "Shall I email it to you?"

"Perfect," said Ian.

*   *   *

Metropolitan Police Department, Washington, DC

Ian was informed a Clarence Comstock was there to see him and he went to the reception area, "Thanks for coming in, I have a few questions and you may be able to help us out," said Ian as he led his visitor to a small room.

"I'm looking into a number of situations with Temple Enterprise. You know Bernard Temple?"

"Yes, of course, we have used Temple Enterprise for several years, moving machine parts from Europe and from Asia. He's always been very reliable."

"Did you know Bernard Temple was taking his yacht to Bermuda this week?" asked Ian.

"Yes, his office called last week, Monday or Tuesday to let us know," said Comstock.

"Did that have an effect on any work he was doing for you?"

"No, not at all. Bernie travels frequently and can always be reached by phone," said Comstock.

"Even if he is out to sea?" asked Ian.

"I don't know, I haven't called. Should I try?"

"No, that's not necessary," returned Ian. "Are you aware of anyone who may wish to harm Mr. Temple?"

"No, but I heard he lost his warehouse manager, Dave Saunders," said Comstock, "shot dead in a motel in LA."

"Do you know his administrative assistant?"

Comstock thought for a second, "Yeah, Myra something. We've never met, but I've had short conversations on the phone with her."

The interview covered a few more unimportant topics and Comstock left.

*   *   *

Metropolitan Police Department, Washington, DC

Tim Marchand arrived at MPD as requested, "I'm here to see a Detective McLarry."

The receptionist called Ian and showed Marchand to an interview room.

Stan Reed joined the meeting and Ian began with, "We're looking into the killing of Mr. Temple's warehouse manager, Dave Saunders. At the same time the disappearance of Temple's administrative assistant, Myra Wallace, has given rise to other questions including possible connections between the two."

Marchand said, "I don't know how I can help you; I didn't really know either of those people well and as Bernie and I discussed the possible purchase of his firm, they were both part of the reason Temple Enterprise was desirable. Understand, they were not considered indispensable, but they both have been in their positions for a number of years, and I had no intention of replacing either of them." He leaned back in his chair and added, "The murder of Mr. Saunders was very upsetting and now the disappearance of Ms. Wallace is giving me pause. I may wish to back away from this purchase."

"You'll withdraw your offer to buy?" asked Stan.

"Yes, at least for the time being," said Marchand. "When Bernie returns from Bermuda, I'll talk to him and we'll determine if we'll continue, delay, or drop the matter."

"When did you last speak to Bernie?" asked Ian.

"Sometime early last week, as I recall," answered Marchand. As he spoke, his cellphone buzzed. "Excuse me, it's my office," he answered the phone, "please hold my calls 'til I finish here, this is important," he paused, "ask Mr. Franklin to call me later this afternoon." He ended the call and apologized for the interruption.

"Not a problem," said Ian. "When a client calls, you have to respond, right?"

"That wasn't a client, it was a security consultant," said Marchand.

"Security?" questioned Ian. "Bernie could have used a little more of that of late."

"Actually, this is one of the firms that Temple has used, and we began a dialogue a few weeks ago," said Marchand.

"And that Mr. Franklin is a point of contact?" quizzed Ian.

"He's the only one I have talked to," said Marchand. "Very brief conversations so far."

"I'd like to talk to him," said Ian. "If he's in the security business, perhaps he could help us in these investigations." He looked at Marchand, "Do you have his contact information?"

"Not on me, but probably back in my office," returned Marchand.

"Could you call your office and get that info?" asked Ian. "It would be a big help."

Marchand called his office and came back to Ian, "He has called us, and we don't seem to have a number to call him."

"What's the name of his firm?" asked Stan.

Marchand hesitated, "Sandway Security."

*   *   *

Temple Enterprise Office, Washington, DC

Carol greeted Ian and Stan as they arrived, "Good morning, Detectives."

"Carol, we'd like to talk to someone in your accounting department," said Ian.

"Certainly, Mr. Tyler should be in," said Carol, "I'll ring him."

A man emerged from the back office, "Good morning gentlemen," he said as he extended his hand, "Sean Tyler. How can I help you?"

"You have a security consultant, Sandway Security. We'd like to talk to them."

Tyler looked a little uncomfortable, "As would I," he said. "I've been trying to reach them for the last few days, and they seem to have evaporated."

"Is there a problem?" asked Ian.

"That's what I'm trying to understand," said Tyler. "There have been two very large payments to Sandway, and I can't find a proper invoice."

"How much is in question?" asked Ian.

"I'm not sure. The last two payments total over $350,000."

"Who authorized the payments?"

"Ms. Wallace issued the transfer orders and did so with Bernie's approval."

"Can I have any and all contact information on Sandway?" asked Ian.

"Of course, I'll dump everything I have on them if it will help," Tyler said as he headed to the back office. He returned a few minutes later with a single sheet of paper. "This is all that remains in our database. I'm not sure how much there was originally, but normally we have a lot more. They have only been a consultant for a few months and the initial payments were less than $5,000 each month."

"Exactly what did they do for you?" asked Stan.

"You'd have to ask Bernie," replied Tyler.

"Yeah, we'd like to," said Ian.

*   *   *

Metropolitan Police Department, Washington, DC

"Bernie is missing, Myra is missing, and about $350,000 dollars is missing," said Ian. "I've checked on this Sandway Security outfit. It's a P.O. box and a phone with an answering machine in the Cayman Islands. I called the bank where the payments to Sandway were sent, told them I had a check for $3,500 and wondered if it would be covered if I deposited it."

Mike raised an eyebrow, "Should I guess?"

"All money was transferred to a Swiss bank," said Ian, "and the account was closed on Friday, the 31st."

"The Swiss bank said the money was dispersed to several other banks and the remaining $2,000 could be frozen," said Leonard.

"So, where's the money? Where's Myra? And where's Bernie?" asked Mike.

"Working on that," said Ian. "Kinda hard to carry that much cash into the country, but if it were in another form, like jewelry, it would be easier."

"Like diamonds?" asked Stan. "It would only take three or four pieces and they could be wrapped around a lady's neck and wrist."

"A lady like Myra," said Ian as he stood and picked up a black dry marker. "Of course, whoever is controlling the money could easily have put it in another bank or two and used debit cards to move it around. Let's back-up and come forward again." He wrote on the white board, "Millington, Klemper, Ross, Lake, Kat, Barrett, Relatto, Marsh, Wallace, Saunders, Temple and Franklin. Twelve characters. First event is the killing of Jim Millington, a professional hit. Neat, clean, two shots and the perp leaves through a cornfield to a car on a dirt road. Nobody saw him or his car. Millington had a lunch meeting scheduled with Bernie Temple at noon that same day. Both were in the import/export business, and they were discussing a merger of sorts."

He put an X through Millington and pointed to Klemper, "George made a run to New York for Millington, talked to the FBI. A few days later, Temple's warehouse is raided, and George is tortured to death." He put an X through Klemper as he said, "Bernie Temple's warehouse."

Ian pointed at Ross' name, "Andy Ross was a guy in the wrong place at the wrong time. Best we can figure, Ross and Barrett both worked part-time at the Temple Enterprise warehouse. They picked up little bits of information regarding George Klemper or something related to the FBI raid and Lake was giving them money for that information." He put an X through Ross and another through Barrett, "Once again, Temple."

"We all know what happened to Lake and Kat. She has been able to clarify some of the events, like there were at least two men, one named Tomas, a white van and she's positive there was another man driving the van. Her very limited description of the driver points at Dave Saunders as a possible. The two bodies recovered in the Arizona Desert are Relatto and Marsh. Conversation with Dave Saunders confirmed they were at the warehouse, so there's a connection between them and Bernie."

"Myra Wallace goes to London on business and promptly walks out of the picture, she's been gone for two weeks without a trace. Then Dave Saunders takes a trip to LA, meets a lady of the evening and is killed in a supposed robbery. Finally, Bernie takes his boat to Virginia Beach, takes on fuel then heads for Bermuda and he goes missing. The boat is found drifting north of his supposed destination and there's a trace of blood on the rear deck. Lab still has it; we may get something yet from that."

"Okay," said Mike, "you broke it down, now build something from all these pieces."

Ian began, "Millington was probably going to be an equal partner, or close to it and I think Bernie wanted more than the share they talked about. Both companies were apparently on board with the idea of a merger and when Millington was killed, everything was in line for Bernie to pick up the pieces without sharing the top spot. He would still be number one with no number two."

"So, he'd have it all to himself," said Mike.

"Yep, and it was probably going to work. Bernie waited a respectful couple of weeks and was ready to make his move on Millington's operation when the FBI raided his warehouse. The raid was completely unrelated to George's interview with the feds, but Bernie didn't know that. The raid made his California client nervous, and he sent two guys to check on everything here. At the same time, Bernie wanted to know what George may have said to the feds and the questioning led to George being brutally beaten and dumped in the Potomac."

"Relation to Millington?" queried Mike.

"Only the suspicion that George had given the feds cause to raid the warehouse," said Ian. "George was not supposed to be found, but he floated."

"Okay so, what about the two laborers and the two characters from California?" asked Mike.

"Not part of the original equation," said Ian. "The nervous client wanted to be sure his machine parts, or whatever was really in those crates, was safe. So, the leg-breakers he sent to check on things over-reacted to the two sweepers talking to Lake and Kat. They wind up killing Ross and tried to make it look like Barrett was the only fox in the henhouse."

"So, you figure these two characters from California catch up to Ross and Barrett at McPherson and that led to the exchange in Burns Alley, leaving Lake dead and Kat wounded?" asked Mike.

"Yeah, they staged the scene to look like Lake popped Ross with a night stick and figured both Lake and Kat were dead," Ian surmised.

"That leaves the other sweeper, Barrett," said Mike.

"This didn't add up at first. The two California thugs didn't seem bright enough to orchestrate the scene at the alley or at Jason Barrett's digs and they both wound up dead in the desert. I think Dave Saunders was driving the van at Burns Alley and he supervised the rigging of the scene. According to Kat, she put a round into Relatto and he in turn shot her. When he shot Kat, Marsh was holding her and the bullet passed through Kat's cheek and hit Marsh, leaving both Relatto and Marsh wounded. They're now a liability, so Dave cleans them both up, well enough to travel and puts them on a plane to Vegas."

"You had someone in Vegas track these two out into the desert?" quizzed Mike.

"I didn't have anybody do anything," said Ian. "Somebody tracked those clowns and passed along information. How they got what they got, I don't know."

"Okay Ian," said Mike, "but you have to understand, all that information is tainted and will be problematic at trial."

"Right now, I'm trying to find Jim Millington's killer and all that desert activity is getting me answers. So, I'll give up the two desert rats if it takes me closer to Millington's shooter."

"Okay, let's move on," said Mike.

Ian picked up his notes and said, "Dave Saunders flies out to LA on business, not unusual, he's made that trip a number of times. He meets a woman in the bar, takes her to his room and winds up dead." He looked at Mike, "We have nothing on this woman. A few tissues, a glass with prints and it goes nowhere. She's not in the system. She shoots Saunders and walks away; we can't find her." He put several photos on the table, "Security camera caught these pictures. That's her, tall, blond probably 5'10" and 140 or a touch more. No idea on the eyes, bartender says they were dark, she was heavily made-up and best guess is mid-thirties."

"We knew that the other day, what do you have to add to that?"

"The blond hair may have been a wig, the eyes could be any color, the weight may be less than the assumed 140 and she could be as young as 25. If I describe Myra Wallace and match the two up, it could be her."

"But Wallace was in England," started Mike.

"Was she?" asked Ian. "She disappeared two days before Dave was shot and her identity is in question. Whoever she really is, she could have traveled back here under a different passport, gone to LA, shot Saunders and melted into the background."

Mike leaned forward, shuffled the photographs and looked at Ian, "That's a stretch, Ian."

"Not really, Myra Wallace made all the reservations for Dave's trip," said Ian. "She's probably the only one who could have pulled this off."

Mike scratched his head, "You have more?"

"Yeah, Bernie Temple hops on his boat, sails to Virginia Beach, spends the night in town and sets sail alone the next afternoon, making for Bermuda. A day later his yacht is found adrift a few hundred miles off course, no Bernie, spilled wine, a broken glass and a trace of blood on the rear deck and transom," said Ian. "I think someone else was on his boat, waited 'til he was out of earshot of land, shot him, tossed him overboard, adjusted the speed control and direction on the auto pilot so that it would run out of fuel and drift in the mid-Atlantic until it was found, then dove overboard and swam ashore."

Mike thought for a moment, "The end of October, water is cold, probably a mile swim, I don't know Ian."

"Wallace claimed to be a long-distance swimmer, according to Bernie," said Ian. "Yes, the water was getting colder in late October, but it was still warm enough if she wore a wet suit and had some kind of floatation device."

"Okay, maybe that all works, but why?" asked Mike. "What's her motive?"

"Money, plain and simple, money," returned Ian. "The Franklin character billed $350,000 in the last two months through Sandway Security and now the money is gone."

"Gone?" quizzed Mike. "Gone where?"

"Payments were made to Sandway Security in the Cayman Islands. As soon as the money hit the bank, it was dispersed to several other accounts in other banks. There were a couple of transfers to our favorite desert thugs over the last few months and similar transfers to another account in Detroit."

"Whose name is on the account in the Caymans?" asked Mike.

Ian smiled, "Franklin Smith."

"That brings us to the big question, who is Franklin?" asked Mike.

"Nobody ever sees Franklin," said Ian. "He communicates over the phone and his voice is disguised with a voice changer."

"Phone company records?" queried Mike.

"A few prepaid throwaway phones," answered Ian.

"So, what led you to Myra Wallace as a player in this mess?" asked Mike.

"A protein bar wrapper."

*   *   *

31

Ian sat in the conference room with Mike, Stan and the FBI agents, Leonard and Robins. "Bernie is gone, and I assume he's at the bottom of the Atlantic, food for deep-sea critters."

"The girl," said Leonard, "Myra Wallace, still missing and no sign of her leaving the UK. If she is back here in the USA, she did it with another name and another passport."

"Well, we've hit dead ends with our investigation into Lake's killer or killers," said Mike. "The two California thugs are dead, Bernie is missing and probably dead, Dave Saunders is dead, and Myra Wallace is missing." He looked at Ian, "So, you have a theory and Myra is the key."

"We had Tim Marchand in here on Monday and I overheard him reference a Mr. Franklin on a phone call. I asked a few questions and he indicated he may use Franklin's security firm for some smaller tasks."

"Sandway Security?" posed Mike.

"Yeah, according to Marchand," said Ian.

"What's your next step?"

"If I'm right about Myra and she is close to Franklin, she may be the point person, the one who gets in close to the victim and may even influence some of the decision making. With Bernie, she was his admin for six years. That may have been a comfortable platform for her to be out in the world and see things up close. She may have done other things for Bernie that we're not aware of or she could have engaged others, again that we don't know about. What I want to do is watch Marchand's operation for a while and see if she turns up."

"Won't someone recognize her?" asked Mike. "She did work with a lot of people in that arena."

"True, but a little change here and there and she could look totally different," said Ian. "Give herself a nice tan, black hair and dark eyes.

Use a little more make-up, dress in a different style and bingo, a whole new person."

$$* \qquad * \qquad *$$

Marchand's Office, Washington, DC

Ian sat in a coffee shop across the street from Marchand's office watching the main entrance. The early morning crush of office workers calmed, and Ian got up, walked around, and returned to his perch before the lunch hour threw hundreds of people back into the streets. He watched as closely as he could, and several times thought he may have seen someone who could be his target. "Maybe I have this all wrong," he muttered to himself. He left the coffee shop, crossed the street and entered Marchand's building. Their offices were on the third floor. The elevator doors opened to a reception area that nearly matched Temple's in plush furniture and museum quality statues and vases.

"May I help you?" asked the young woman at the front desk.

"Is Mr. Marchand in?" returned Ian.

"I believe he is, may I tell him who's asking?"

Ian opened his badge wallet and said, "Detective McLarry."

The woman lifted the phone and pushed a few buttons, "A Detective McLarry is here to see you."

A minute later Tim Marchand was in the reception area asking Ian to accompany him to the main conference room, "How can I help you, Detective?"

"I'm still working on Bernie Temple's disappearance. So, just a few things I'd like to clear up."

"Certainly, Detective."

"I understand you were interested in buying Temple Enterprise."

"Yes, I was," said Marchand. "One moment Bernie was in the mood to sell, the next—no. I was interested, but only if I could keep him on as a contact to all his current clients. That's where the value is—or was. The events of the last few months seemed to make Bernie just want to go south, or was it Bermuda? He seemed less and less inclined to want to be part of my vision, so I was ready to cancel all talks of a buyout or merger."

"Does that mean you won't try to pick up his business if Temple Enterprise falls apart?" asked Ian.

"I don't think that will happen. Jim Millington's group is still interested in merging with Temple, and they are both strong enough to continue. If they do merge and operate for a few years, that may be an interesting acquisition."

As they were talking, a woman entered the reception area, looked through the glass wall of the conference room, muttered a few words to the receptionist, then turned and left. Neither Tim nor Ian had seen her. When they had finished their conversation, they walked out into the reception area and the woman behind the desk said to Marchand, "Excuse me sir, a Ms. Hendly from Sandway Security was here to see you."

Ian looked at the receptionist, "When was she here?"

"About five minutes ago. She saw the two of you in the conference room and said she'd call later."

Ian looked at the elevators, "Which elevator did she take?"

"I… I didn't notice," replied the receptionist.

"Did she touch anything here at your desk?"

"No, just the top," she said pointing to the smooth marble surface."

"Where, exactly, did she touch the stone?" asked Ian.

The woman pointed, "Somewhere about here."

Ian covered the area with a few sheets of paper and took out his cellphone, "I need a print guy."

Twenty minutes later, the elevator door opened, and Freddy Knolls strode into the reception area, "When I heard it was you, I just had to take this call."

Ian showed Freddy where the prints should be, "Okay Detective, let me do my thing and we'll see what pops." He photographed the surface then started to dust at one end and when finished, he had over thirty prints, all tagged and photographically located. I'll get this back to the house and run the lot for you."

"Check these against the print we got off the protein bar wrapper on Bernie's boat," said Ian.

"Will do Detective I'll get back to you as soon as I have something."

Ian left the third-floor office and went to the security office on the first floor. They had a recording of traffic through the main lobby. Ian narrowed the time to a few minutes before and after the woman had come to Marchand's office and there she was. The third woman to pass through the lobby was initially observed walking toward the camera with her head tilted down. The same woman was observed minutes later walking away and Ian could hear himself and Lake weeks before as Ian said, "Not bad, eh cousin?" and Lake replied "What, the room or the dame?" It was definitely the same woman.

Ian checked outside the office building and found a few more cameras. The woman was tracked to a health club where she disappeared inside.

*   *   *

Metropolitan Police Department, Washington, DC

Sitting in the conference room with Mike and Stan, Ian went through the entire observation sequence. "I know that's her," he said.

"Could you be assuming too much?" asked Mike, "Are you absolutely sure?"

Before Ian could answer, Freddy opened the door, "Detective, I have three prints that match your candy wrapper."

Ian smiled as he said, "Protein bar, Freddy. Protein." He turned and looked at Mike, "Yeah Mike, I'm absolutely sure."

*   *   *

Ian and Stan returned to the health club and interviewed three members of the staff when they finally got another piece of the puzzle, "Yeah, sure that looks like Ms. Barclan—Tina, I think. Yeah, Tina Barclan."

"Do you have an address?" asked Stan.

The man entered a few things in his computer and said, "Yep, 10584 Raspberry Road, Fairfax."

The drive took 36 minutes, when they arrived a black Audi was parked in the driveway. Ian pulled his car in behind the Audi, and they got out. Stan went to the front door and Ian walked around toward the rear. Stan rang the doorbell and waited. Ian stood half-hidden by a bush watching the rear door.

She heard the doorbell, looked out and saw the car blocking the driveway. She opened a cellphone and made a brief call then pulled the sim card, crushed it and tossed it in the trash. The phone was left in a desk drawer, and she went to the rear door. As she exited the house and was about to cross the back lawn, Ian spoke, "Good afternoon, Myra— or should I say Tina?"

She turned to face him, and the color drained from her face. She glanced at the woods about 200 feet away as if she considered running.

"Please don't run," said Ian. "I really don't like shooting people, but I will if I have to."

She stood still as she seemed to regain composure, "Detective McLarry, as I recall."

"And what is your real name?" asked Ian.

"Does it matter?" she asked.

"No, not really, please turn around, hands over your head." He placed the cuffs on her wrists, read her her rights and led her to the front of the house. "Stan, give the Fairfax County Police a call, let 'em know we're here. Someone has to enter the house and clear it."

Ian opened the rear door to his vehicle and guided her in. He closed the door, got in the front seat, and turned to face his prisoner, "I can call you Myra, if you want, but we'll have your real name sooner or later." Ian looked again at the house, "Is anyone else in the house?"

"No, it's empty,." she looked at him, "the owners are in Europe for another month. I'm the house sitter."

"You're being arrested for your involvement in the murder of James Millington. There are eight other murders or missing persons in several jurisdictions in which you are a suspect. Do you understand what I have just said?"

She looked at Ian quizzically, "Eight?"

"Martin McLarry, a detective in the District of Columbia," said Ian.

"Martin was a relative?" she asked.

"My cousin," replied Ian.

"I had nothing to do with that," she said.

"I figured," said Ian.

"Andrew Ross and Jason Barrett?" Ian posed.

She shook her head.

"Relatto and Marsh?" He quizzed.

"Those two are dead," she continued.

"Yeah, you did do that," said Ian.

"No comment."

"My official involvement is with the Jim Millington killing," said Ian. "Care to say anything on that?"

"No comment," she again replied.

"Dave Saunders, that was also you?"

"No comment."

"George Klemper?"

"No, I had nothing to do with that either."

"Finally, Bernie?"

"No comment."

"Do you want to make any statement?"

"No."

"Okay, Myra or Tina or whatever your name is. Sooner or later, you will want to talk. I'd like to know why each of the killings had to occur and exactly who was involved. When you're ready to talk, I'll listen," he started to get out of the car.

"Angela," she said, "I will not lie to you and there are things I want to know."

Ian paused, "Fair enough, Angela, should we begin now?"

She looked at Ian and wondered what kind of man he was. If things were different, would he have been a friend, or more. She took a deep breath, exhaled and said, "That's enough for today."

Ian leaned forward, looked closely at her, "A lot of people will be asking you questions, including the FBI."

"Yes, I know," she replied.

Ian relaxed, "We will be talking again, soon."

She returned the relaxed look and said, "Yes, we will."

*   *   *

32

The interview room was small, just enough room for Angela, Ian, Ned Bowen and Craig Robins. Ian began the questioning with "What is your full name?"

"Angela Bentley," she replied.

"Any middle name?"

"Marie."

"Where were you on September fifth?" asked Ned Bowen.

"I don't remember exactly. If that was a weekday, I was most likely at work, Temple Enterprise, in the District."

"Do you know James Millington?" asked Ned.

"I know who he was, we met briefly a few times in the Temple offices."

"Do you know a Franklin Smith?" asked Ian.

She looked at Ian, and said, "I think I should consult an attorney at this point."

"If that is what you want, Angela," said Ian, "then this interview is over."

She looked at Ian and smiled.

*   *   *

"What's next?" asked Ned.

Craig Robins replied, "We'd like to have her in our house for an interview."

"Okay," said Ned, "she's already lawyered up and we want her to stand trial here for the Millington murder as soon as we can prep the case."

"It'll take months to get all our ducks in a row, be ready for trial," said Ian, "and who knows how much interference her attorney will put in our way. I'd let her rot in a federal facility while the several jurisdictions prep their cases."

"Agreed," said Ned Bowen, looking at Craig Robins, "how do we go about transferring her to you?"

"I'll get the paperwork started right away," said Robins, "it could be today or more likely, tomorrow at the latest." He left with cellphone in hand calling his office in the District.

Angela quietly asked Chief Bowen if she were allowed a phone call, "My lawyer," she said. She dialed a number, waited, muttered something about after hours and left a message, "They're going to move me to the federal detention facility in the District, I may be there in the morning."

Ned Bowen told a deputy to move Angela to a holding cell and schedule a 24-hour watch on her until she was picked up by the feds. "What about you, Ian? This has been a busy time for you. You wanna take a few days before we attack the prosecution phase of this case?"

"Actually chief, I have an invite to visit some family in Ireland. Maybe I'll disappear for a week or two. I'll make a few calls and see if the invite is still open." He made the first call from his desk and rushed into Ned's office, "They've got me on a flight out of Dulles tomorrow morning."

"Well, get outta' here, go home and pack," said Ned. "We'll keep the peace 'til you're back."

Ian hurried out the door thinking, *sure as all hell, if I don't get moving, someone will shoot someone else, and I'll be back in it.*

*   *   *

Chief Bowen stopped at the reception desk as he was leaving for the day. Pulling on his overcoat he said, "It should be a quiet night, the US Marshall will be picking up the prisoner tonight or tomorrow and Detective McLarry will be out for the next three weeks on vacation. I'm going home, pour myself a stiff drink, sit in front of the fireplace with my wife and relax. Anything exciting happens, call me at home."

"Will do, Chief," returned the officer at the reception desk, "enjoy the evening, we'll see you tomorrow."

"Goodnight," said Chief Bowen as he walked out the door into the cool evening air and his car.

Vaneksburg is a peaceful community thirty miles west of the District and the main office of the Police Department had cleared for the day leaving the evening/night shift on duty. An hour after Bowen left, two men entered the station and approached the officer at the reception desk. "Excuse me miss," said one of the men, as he opened a badge wallet identifying himself as US Marshal Steve Wilson. He handed her an envelope and said, "We're here to transfer a prisoner."

She read the label on the envelope: *Transfer Authorization: Bentley, Angela Marie, From: Vaneksburg Police Custody, To: Federal Detention Center, Washington, DC.*

She looked at Wilsons badge wallet again and turned to his partner with a quizzical look.

He opened his badge wallet identifying himself as Marshal Dave Bender.

"Yes," she said turning back to Wilson, "we've been expecting you." She picked up the phone, pushed a button, "Sergeant, there are two gentlemen here to transfer the prisoner to the Federal Detention Center in DC, U.S. Marshals Wilson and Bender."

"That was quick," returned the sergeant. "I'll be right out, and we can do the paperwork. It'll take a few minutes to get her ready for travel … jumpsuit and leg irons … I'm on my way." As he opened his office door, he told another officer to be sure Angela had her orange suit and he took a set of leg irons off a hook, handed them to the officer and walked out to the reception area.

The reception desk officer had shown the two agents to the conference room, offered them coffee, and placed the transfer authorization envelope on the table.

"No, but thanks," said Bender, "we get this Bentley woman downtown and we're both off duty and I'm going home to watch a movie on the tube with my wife … and I don't want to stay awake."

Wilson nodded and smiled.

Sergeant Markus joined the agents in the conference room, "They'll bring her out in a few minutes. You have some paperwork for me to check out and sign?"

Wilson slid the envelope across the table to the sergeant, "There are two copies, I signed the third page and I need your signature on page four."

As Sergeant Markus was reading the paperwork, Angela was brought into the conference room in leg irons and handcuffs. He turned to page four, printed his name and signed on the noted line on both copies.

"Has she been any problem?" asked Bender.

"No," returned Markus, "she's been very cooperative."

"Well, these irons are required — I hope you understand," said Wilson as he glanced at the prisoner and accepted his copy of the paperwork. "They'll remove the restraints after we've passed security at the center."

Angela said nothing, kept her head down and looked defeated.

The prisoner, ready and the paperwork signed, Wilson said, "If there's nothing else, we'd like to get going."

"Of course," said Markus. "Where are you parked?"

"Out front," replied Wilson. "Should I go to another door?"

Markus looked out through the window, noted the parking lot was well lit and said, "No, we can do it out the front." He then asked the reception officer to get two more officers to come out front for the transfer to the black SUV.

Angela was guided out the front door to the awaiting vehicle, placed in the backseat, secured and wrapped in a warming blanket. The two marshals shook hands with Markus, wished him a quiet night and got in the SUV. They drove out of the parking lot and turned north toward Route 66.

Markus went back inside the station, rubbing the chill out of his hands and placed a call to Ned Bowen. "Chief, two U.S. Marshals, Steve Wilson and Dave Bender have picked up the Bentley woman and are on their way into town."

"Great timing, Sarge," he said, "we just finished dinner and I think I'll have another large bourbon to celebrate." He paused, then he said, "They signed off on her, right?"

"Yeah, got the paperwork right here," said Markus.

"Great, I'll give Craig Robins a call and let 'em know she's on her way."

Ned poured a second drink and dialed Robins' cellphone. It went to voicemail and as he listened to the greeting, he took a sip of his bourbon, left a brief message and returned to the dinner table taking another taste of his drink and asking his wife, "So, what's for dessert?"

*   *   *

An hour later, Ned called Craig Robins again to confirm the transfer was complete and the prisoner was secure. Robins said the paperwork was still in the works and he'd be ready to effect the transfer about noon Friday.

Ned cursed, put his drink down hard and said, "Two U.S. Marshals picked her up this evening, about two hours ago."

"Nobody was sent to get her," said Robins. "What two men?"

"Two U.S. Marshals, a Steve Wilson and Dave Bender, we have their transfer paperwork at the station."

"I don't know any Marshals named Wilson or Bender attached to the DC office," shouted Robins. "I'll check and get back to you as soon as I can." He called back in less than three minutes, "Nobody was sent to pick up a prisoner yet. They're still getting the paperwork in order."

Ned angrily spat into the phone, "I'm going in there now to see what the hell's going on." He punched in another number on his cellphone, "Ian, we have a problem."

*   *   *

VPD, Vaneksburg, VA

The FBI paperwork provided by the two fake agents was as genuine as a three-dollar bill. The agents looked, sounded and acted real and the staff on duty suspected nothing.

"Who were those guys?" asked Ned.

"My guess is they work for her," said Ian. "She must have had a plan in place to address this kind of an event. Probably has one for several possible scenarios."

"Yeah," said Ned, "and what do we have?"

"We know her name, we have her prints and could probably get her DNA," said Ian.

"We searched the house in Fairfax," said Robins. "She's lived there for the last five months. Owners were easy to locate."

Robins shrugged his shoulders, "She left very little in the house, a few outfits, some personal grooming items and that's it. She obviously has another site where she has more."

"The two fake feds who picked her up?" quizzed Ned.

"Just like the two thugs in Vegas," returned Ian, "they probably work for her."

"They said they worked for Franklin," said Robins, "maybe she does too."

"More than likely, she is Franklin," said Ian.

"So, we find her lackies, and we find her," Ned mumbled.

"I'd bet the two who picked her up had no idea who she is," said Ian. "They were probably directed by Franklin to pick up a woman and take her wherever she directed them, and they were done, no further contact. Finding them may bring us nothing."

"So, where is she?" asked Robins.

"Gone, in the wind," said Ian. "She has a three-hour lead, could be a hundred miles in any direction, north, south, east or west. We have no way of knowing. She could be that far away or hiding right in plain sight. This girl has used at least two false identities and probably more. And, she has a stockpile of cash, at least \$350,000, probably more, stashed in several banks somewhere and access to it with credit or debit cards in some other name. We have more work to do."

Ned looked at Ian, "Best guess?"

"Gone," said Ian, "gone and we'll probably never find her."

*　　*　　*

33

At some point in Loudoun County, the black SUV carrying Angela Bentley into the District, exited Route 66 and pulled into a vacant parking lot. The driver parked in a dark corner, away from curious eyes where the leg irons and cuffs binding Angela were removed and her orange jumpsuit was exchanged for blue jeans and a warm hoodie. As the Suburban's plates were being changed a woman matching Angela's description, driving a dark blue Ford Explorer entered another parking lot two hundred feet away. She hurried across the grassed area between parking lots as the bogus U.S. Marshalls finished changing the SUV's plates. She helped gather up the leg irons, cuffs, and Angela's orange jumpsuit, placed them all in a duffel bag, and put the bag in the SUV.

Steve Wilson handed Angela the keys to the Explorer and said, "You get that dark blue Explorer in the next lot. Take a few backroads and get back on 66 heading west and we'll take the SUV."

Angela then said in a nervous voice, "Did he say where I was to go?"

"Yeah, he said you should get on 66 West and go north on route 15 to the green building," said Wilson.

"Okay, thanks. I know where that is. I'll tell the man you gents did a great job," she said and the two vehicles left the parking lots in different directions, Angela going through a few back roads and to Route 66 West in the Explorer and the two bogus agents with the woman, driving east on 66 to the New Carrollton Metro Station where they parked the SUV, locked it, leaving the keys in the glove compartment and hurried to the train heading back west.

By the time Ned Bowen was arriving at the VPD, Angela had already driven back west on Route 66 passing both the exit to 15 north and the Vaneksburg exit. She was heading for Winchester and an apartment she had registered under another name.

*   *   *

Winchester, Virginia

Angela finished packing her third suitcase and wiped down the entire apartment. She stood in the middle of her living room, running through her mental checklist then checked her bank account dedicated to this address and added enough money to cover the automatic rent and utility payments for the three months remaining on her lease. She went to the garage, loaded her suitcases in the Explorer, covered her dark brown hair with a blond wig, checked her new ID and drove out to Route 81 heading south. She was now Caroline Brady heading home to Austin, Texas. *It's a long way away,* she thought, *almost fifteen-hundred miles. I'll probably make three or four stops before getting to Austin.*

*   *   *

Route 81 south of Front Royal, Virginia

She was heading for Austin, Texas and another address she had established several years ago. Her first stop was after four hours, in Bristol, Tennessee for food and a fill-up, all with cash. She logged another five hours getting through Nashville and turned southwest toward Memphis. A rest area, a nap and a quick restroom stop followed by an inexpensive breakfast had her through Memphis and on her last leg toward Austin.

She reached her apartment in North Austin at 3:30 in the morning, left most of her luggage in the Explorer, opened her apartment door, dropped the single suitcase she was carrying, slowly walked to the bedroom and stretched out on her bed. "Sleep …"

*   *   *

34

Helmand Province, Afghanistan

A small, deserted village in southern Helmand, about 100 kilometers from the Pakistan border had twice served as a night-time stopover for a man making a journey to the north. He had made the trip successfully twice in the last year and this was to be no different. Very few knew of this planned journey, but one man had talked to a friend and word was unknowingly passed along to an Afghan translator working for the American force.

Intel gathered from several other sources corroborated the information indicating the Taliban leader would soon make this trip north through the little village. The information further indicated the journey would happen in the next two or three weeks. Then further intel showed the trip would begin within a three-day window starting in eight days.

The man had stopped at this deserted village the last two times he made the trip and as the days grew shorter and travel at night grew ever more dangerous it was assumed he would stop there again.

Jake Brennan walked into the command tent at the American base in Afghanistan. He spotted the strike team at a conference table and joined them.

"We need definite proof of the kill," said Jake.

"DNA will do?" asked Colin, the strike team leader.

"That it will," returned Jake.

"Good," returned Colin, "then we're ready to move out as soon as the intel is cleared."

"Keep me updated and I'll see you back in Langley when it's done," said Jake, "now I gotta run, we have that other file to address when you're done here." He left the team to continue their discussion and practice runs and he was on a flight back to Virginia within an hour.

The potential time frame and route to the north was defined and satellite observation of the small village as well as the surrounding terrain had been ordered. Assuming the target would be spending the night in the village again, it was determined the strike team could be dropped near the village and approach under the cover of darkness, enter the village, eliminate the target, gather the required proof of the kill and get away with a minimum of opposition.

The team tasked with the strike had been given little time to prepare so, a basic plywood mock-up of the village was set up and practice runs were done in the dark each night. A drone was flown over the site, capturing as much detail as they could on short notice and from a fair distance. The probable location of their target within the village was narrowed to one of three stone and mud huts. There were twelve structures in the village, most damaged in some way. Doors broken or missing, roofs gone or collapsed in, walls crumbling. It was a warzone and the population had fled four months ago for safer ground.

The practice runs were hurried and left several questions unanswered. Satellite scans would answer some of the unknowns in real time and thus several variations had to be addressed. Which hut, how many people would be there, were there any civilians in the village or near it.

The night-time op was planned assuming there would be little if any cloud cover, temperature 10°c to 12°c, (50°f to 53°f) a gentle wind out of the south and dry. There had been little to no human activity in the immediate area in the last two months and the latest scans still showed no signs of life.

Not wanting to draw attention to the man, a small convoy of five vehicles and a security detail of thirteen seasoned fighters was considered sufficient for his safety. They would leave their base late in the afternoon and arrive at the village as the sun set in the west a few minutes after 1800 local time (1430 Zulu).

Sunrise was going to be around 0600 (0230 Zulu) and the team had a twelve-hour window to effect a strike and return to base.

Notice arrived that the five-vehicle convoy had left the city and was traveling north. "That has to be him," said Colin. "It all fits, five vehicles, only thirteen men. Check our sources and let's be ready to move."

Word came in within the hour, "He's on the move, going north with a small protective force, twelve guards and himself."

The little convoy drove north for three hours, arriving at the village shortly after dusk. Satellite imagery showed the vehicles were aligned in front of the largest of the three habitable huts.

"That's our target," said Colin, "saddle up, we're on the clock."

The helicopter to transport the team was fueled, the flight plan determined, and the crew rested and ready to take off. The flight to their drop-off point would take about forty-five minutes and the final leg on foot, another forty-five.

At 2030 Zulu the chopper lifted off and headed south. Ten minutes into the flight, the pilot turned east and dropped to a still safe altitude, flying as close to the ground as he could at night. The flight was timed to coincide with the next satellite pass over.

The team was silent, each thinking through their part of the planned operation and any variation that may be required, each armed and equipped with enough to complete the mission, not over-loaded. Speed would be critical on the exit and any ordinance would be expended as part of the mission. Baines carried seven explosive devices with remote detonation capability intended to disable transportation vehicles.

Less than an hour into the flight, the pilot turned to the team leader, "We're four clicks out Colin, are you ready?"

"As ever was, Lieutenant," returned Colin as he looked out at a rare cloud, about to hide the moon in the night sky. The terrain below was nearly barren, small rolling hills covered with stretches of dirt and stones briefly interrupted with small clusters of grass and smaller gatherings of trees. He again looked at the clouds *Stay with me*, he thought, *we need all the cover we can get.*

Two minutes later as the chopper slowly set down, all five of the team members put their hands in a small circle and did a fist bump. The chopper stirred up a cloud of dry dirt as five dark figures, clad in local garb, dropped to the ground. The chopper lifted off and moved a kilometer west, staying low, the team continued east.

They were still two clicks from their target, the small, abandoned village and they moved quickly and quietly over low rolling hills. They covered about half the distance when Colin stopped, looked around and turned to Baines. "Set the beacon back there between these last two rises."

"Aye sir," she responded and rushed down the slope to the low point, stabbed the beacon into the ground, flipped a switch and returned to Colin, "done."

Colin looked at the team, pointed at the beacon and said, "Pick-up location." They all looked around at the area, low between hills that would provide cover during pick-up and nodded. Each carried a sensor that would lead them to that beacon and the chopper pilot had a similar sensor.

They continued over the few remaining low hills toward the little village where their target was known to be spending the night. As they approached the final low rise, they could see the outline of the hills behind the village against a pre-dawn sky. Sunrise was still more than an hour away and that allowed them more than enough time to complete the mission and return to the pickup point. A few flickering lights from sentry fires and more within a few of the huts defined the village. They silently crept closer then at a distance of two hundred meters west of the village, they spread out and surveyed the perimeter. Colin tapped his comm link and said, "Clearance?"

"Seven perimeter positions identified," came the reply through their comm links. "You're on the 9:00 o'clock hour. One directly ahead, another at six on the clock. One at 10:00, another at 2:00, one at 5:00 and one at 7:00. Three in the large hut, sleeping with two outside standing and walking. That's your prime location. Two more in the other huts, sleeping. Three trucks and two hummers lined up in front of the hut."

Colin looked at Baines, "Five vehicles, do we have enough?"

"I brought seven party favors," returned Baines.

Colin grinned, nodded and he said into his link, "Outside the village?"

"Clear west over ten clicks, six north and four south," returned the satellite controller, "all lights green."

Colin tapped his link three times, and the link showed a green light. He looked at his team and tapped twice. The team spread out slowly moving closer to the perimeter and stopped.

Davis sighted a sentry and tapped his link, "I have 10 o'clock."

"I have 8 locked in," said Carone.

"I'm on number 9," said Fallon as all three tapped their links.

Baines added, "All charges set for remote det."

Fallon looked at Colin, "As soon as you're clear," he said holding the remote.

Colin and Baines scanned the area directly ahead and Colin tapped his link three times sending a green light to his team.

Almost in unison, three suppressed shots were fired, and three sentries were taken out. The team heard the "Clear" from the satellite observer signaling Colin, Baines and Fallon to move forward. Davis and Carone remained in their positions to cover the retreat as they watched for the remaining sentries to react to the downed guards. As they passed the vehicles, Baines set a charge under the driver's seat of each vehicle.

Satellite surveillance monitored each heat signature in the village and conveyed movement to the team as they moved to their target. Any signatures identified as threats would be targeted and neutralized.

The strike team approached a larger mud hut spotting two armed men outside, at the entrance. The satellite senser had also indicated three individuals inside. Both guards were shot, and the team quickly approached the hut, kicked the door, burst through, shot the three men inside and checked each.

They found their target. He had been sleeping on a filthy mattress on the dirt floor and appeared to be dead. Colin rolled him over on his back, put his weapon in the man's mouth and fired one more time. He wiped a gauze pad in the man's blood, placed it in a plastic bag and photographed the dead man. Baines set the last two charges inside the hut and the team quickly left and made their way back to their village entry point. Colin tapped his link three times, waited for a return tapping and the team ran from the village as the remaining sentries, hearing the gunfire, had gathered near the large hut to see what had happened. The team was about fifty meters past the parked vehicles when Fallon used the remote. All seven devices detonated at the same time, destroying the hut, killing two more guards and destroying all five vehicles.

*   *   *

The strike team had the one objective and once accomplished, they had to hurry back to the pick-up zone. "Eleven down including prime," said Colin into his comm, "less than a click from pick-up."

"Copy that," returned the chopper pilot, "ready and waiting."

The team began their run toward the pick-up point with the three remaining Taliban fighters in pursuit on foot. As they were crossing the second hill, Baines seemed to stumble and fall to the ground, her left leg bleeding. "I'm hit," she blurted out.

Davis and Carone quickly shouldered their weapons and lifted Baines onto Carone's back as Colin and Nick turned, knelt and returned fire. The pursuing Taliban fighters were at least two hundred meters behind the team and continued to fire as they ran. As the team was crossing the last hill, Davis was hit in his left shoulder but kept moving. The last stretch to the chopper was downhill for the team but out of sight for the pursuers. Carone lifted Baines into the chopper and Davis stumbled aboard. Fallon grabbed the beacon and was the last aboard. Colin nodded to the pilot and the chopper lifted off. Baines was strapped in and Carone started to apply a tourniquet to her leg. Davis fell into a seat and tried to belt himself in as Colin and Fallon watched for movement at the last hill.

As the chopper moved quickly west, staying low, Colin turned to check on Baines and realized Davis was also bleeding.

Landing at their base, Sarah Baines and Mark Davis were taken immediately to the medical tent. "Doesn't look good for Baines," said the doctor. "Really tore up her vastus lateralis and hit the femur."

"And Davis?" asked Colin.

"He'll be okay, but his shoulder is a mess. We'll fix it but he's done with these type ops at least for a few months."

"What's that mean for Sarah?" asked Nick.

"She'll be okay," returned the doctor, "but it means she won't be running any marathons or lifting and heavy loads for quite a while … maybe never."

Colin was immediately on a call to Langley, "Jake, this one is done. The sample is on its way to the lab. Sarah and Mark both took a hit and will be out of action for a while. We'll talk when I get there."

"We have another project for you," said Jake.

"I'm ready," said Colin, should we start now?"

"A few details are being worked out including rebuilding your team so, take a few days, relax and I'll call you.

*　　*　　*

Langley, Virginia

A week later, Colin was having breakfast with friends at a small café on M Street in Georgetown when his phone chirped. "Jake, I can be there in thirty …" He took a final sip of his coffee, excused himself and hurried to his car. He drove across the Key Bridge to the Virginia side, got on the George Washington Memorial Parkway north and headed for Route 123 and the George Bush Center for Intelligence.

Wearing a black knit shirt, blue jeans and western boots, Colin sat in Jake Brennan's office at Langley, "We were lucky, none of our people were killed, but two are now relegated to desk-type jobs."

Jake nodded as he picked up a file folder on his desk.

Colin continued, "Has the DNA confirmation come through yet?"

"Just got it, a perfect match," said Jake, as he handed Colin the file still in his hand.

Colin smiled, feeling good about another operation being completed, "So, what's next on the agenda?" he asked as he browsed the file.

Jake shuffled a few papers on his crowded desk and pulled out a second file, "You're back on the quiet side with this one, the weapons that came out of Germany or Austria and evaporated somewhere on our side of the pond."

Colin exchanged folders with Jake, "Any further leads?" he asked.

"A few points," returned Jake. "Everything we have points toward a group of drug outfits in Tangenillo, Mexico, but nothing sufficiently concrete yet. We're holding this one close, so read the file and put it back in the secured bin."

Colin leafed through the paperwork and said, "How about I take point, go down there and look around meantime we rebuild the team."

"Agreed," said Jake, "I have a list of possible candidates for you to consider, included in the file. People who have looked real good in training or in other field ops. My list also includes a couple of former SEALs and MARSOC personnel and a few current law enforcement people. Recognize anyone?"

Colin found a list of forty names and as he read down the page he said, "I want to have lunch at Chloez, sit down with Joe, talk about these characters and his impression of who will fit in."

"I spoke with him, yesterday, gave him a little background and he's checking several sources. He's no longer active," said Jake, "and he won't be making the trip."

"I figured," returned Colin, "but he did prep for several possible missions over the last few years and probably knows some or most of these guys on the list … so, his input will be very useful." He leafed through the file again and said, "I was hoping to find one man and one woman." He reached the second last name on the list, "Cousin Ian, the Virginia cop?"

"Yep, you know he did six years in the Corps with two tours in Afghanistan and 12 years as a street cop in Pittsburgh and … What missions?"

Colin grinned, "Ask me no questions … Look, I asked him to keep us in mind when he changes jobs, but he may not be up for this kind of mission. And he's old, isn't he like 45?" objected Colin.

"39 but still in great shape," returned Jake.

Colin laughed, "Yeah, for an old fat guy."

Jake lowered his glasses, peered over the rims and said, "Younger than me and I'll wager it's more muscle than fat. Plus, he has background with Temple Enterprise."

"Our favorite gun import/export runner," said Colin, "Bernie Temple. What's the latest on him?"

"Bernie's gone," returned Jake, "he went missing in the middle of the Atlantic Ocean and he may be dead, so we continue to follow the leads we have. The latest info indicates the weapons are still in route most likely to that drug outfit in Tangenillo."

"What do we know about this Mexican outfit?" asked Colin.

"Preliminary, enough to start our op and still refining," said Jake. "I had a brief conversation with Joe about the three families that we think are looking at the possibility of working together: Hernandez, Rodriguez and Perez," said Jake. "The biggest of the three is run by Ricardo Hernandez. We think he's arming his own people first with these new European weapons and will use the rest to arm the other families as they join his little cartel."

"Joe may have some more info on these three families," said Colin.

"Does Ian have any background on any of these three families?" wondered Colin.

"Not that I'm aware of," returned Jake, "Ian was working on a few murders around Bernie Temple and an assassin by the name of Franklin."

"Okay," said Colin, "I heard some rumblings about this Franklin character before I had to prep for the Afghanistan op so, bring me up to speed on him."

"He's suspected in several missing person and murder cases all surrounding Bernie Temple and his business," said Jake. "We know Bernie had a connection to one of the families in the Tangenillo group and the assassin Franklin may have been part of the mix."

"What do we know about this Franklin?" asked Colin.

"I've gotten hints that this guy is known here within the agency but not talked about much."

"You mean he's one of our assets?" questioned Colin.

Jake raised his eyebrows, "Whenever his name has been mentioned, someone changes the subject," he said. "I've heard the name come up several times over the last six years, but not much more," then he added, "Ian has arrested a woman, Angela Bentley, she worked for Bernie as an admin and she's somehow connected to Franklin, so she may be able to shed light in some of the dark corners. Anyway, she's scheduled to be transferred to the federal detention center in the district and we can all have a go at her."

"Good for him but he may be too old," said Colin.

"All the same, get him in and run him through a few courses, see how he does."

"Obstacle, rifle, pistol …?" questioned Colin.

"Yep," returned Jake, "and anything else you can arrange."

"Three weeks, if he needs more …?"

"He's gonna make a choice … the VPD or our little SOG."

"Okay Jake," said Colin as he stood, grabbed his leather jacket and turned toward the door, "but don't get your hopes up. I'll look at all forty you have listed here and then we'll talk."

*   *   *

Colin left Jake's office and walking to the parking lot, he made the call to Ian, "Hey cousin, I've been talking to Jake Brennan, he suggested we get you out to Quantico and see if you can still make it around the quarter mile track in under an hour."

Ian laughed, "I was planning on a little vacation in a week or two, how soon do you want to do this?"

"I have a training session set for this coming week. We're checking out a few people for different assignments, so the sooner, the better," said Colin.

"Monday?" returned Ian.

"Monday will be great," said Colin, "but breakfast first."

"Where and when?" asked Ian.

"A little place on Ox Road, Route 123, called Chloez Café, a mile or so south of Braddock Road. They open at 9:00 a.m. and I have a few questions for an old friend."

"How long will this take?" asked Ian.

"Not long, Joe and I go way back, and he may add a little to the info pool that may answer a few questions."

"How much time should I set aside for this little vacation?"

"Pack for a week, we have a few other courses to run you through and maybe a couple of other challenges," said Colin.

"And where will all this lead to?" asked Ian.

"Everything is a maybe at this point, but we have a few immediate openings and you've made the first few cuts."

As Colin started his car his phone beeped again, "Jake, what's happened in the last twenty minutes?"

Jake cleared his throat, "I just got word, this Angela Bentley has escaped."

*　　*　　*

35

Vaneksburg, Virginia

The investigation into Angela's escape led to a review of the cameras located on the face of the Vaneksburg PD building. They showed the two bogus U.S. Marshals arriving and leaving the immediate area. The plates on their black Suburban were found to be fake and other cameras on nearby gas stations and banks showed their vehicle coming from the east on Route 66 and returning the same way. The cameras also unknowingly caught Angela driving west on 66 in the Explorer and she was not recognized. The Suburban was seen turning off the highway and disappeared for 25 minutes, then it appeared to be the same vehicle returned to 66 where it made its way to the Capital Beltway and turned north. Several vehicles all looking like the suspect SUV were tracked on the beltway. One SUV exited at the New Carrollton Metro station and was left in the parking lot. Two men and a woman exited the vehicle and entered the station where they blended in with the general population and disappeared. The SUV was located, searched and the duffel bag found. The vehicle had been stolen and the plates were registered to another SUV.

*   *   *

Ian compiled all the information on Angela he had and shared it with the FBI, ATF and after a call from Jake Brennan, the CIA, "She's been a very clever individual," he said to Craig Robins. "This woman managed to orchestrate her supposed disappearance in London, England, the killing of Dave Saunders in California, and the disappearance of Bernie Temple while on his boat heading for Bermuda. All within a few days and now … she's escaped our custody."

"Embarrassing," said Robins, "for both of us. Where do you think she may have gone?"

"She was headed in toward the District on 66 but there's no way to know if when they got off the highway and went missing for half an hour, she could have switched vehicles and gone who knows where … She could have flown out of Reagan Airport or gone into Union Station, caught a train to New York or Miami."

"So, we have nothing to point us in any specific direction," returned Robins.

"Nope, the SUV was recovered at the New Carrollton station. CCTV caught two men and a woman exiting the vehicle and going into the station. She may have been the woman, but for all we know she could be in a motel somewhere around here," said Ian, "just waiting for the dust to settle and she'd be off and running."

"We'll put her on a nationwide search and hope for a lead," said Robins.

"Yeah, so will I," said Ian.

"You will?" questioned Robins.

"Yeah," said Ian, "I have more cousins than I can count, first, second, third … it all adds up and many of us are in law enforcement so, maybe one of them will come across something." He posted a note and picture of Angela on the family's web site thinking *it's an outside chance, but a chance none the less.*

"So, can we touch base Monday morning?" asked Robins.

"I'm going to be pretty busy for a few days," said Ian, "but if anything pops on my end, I'll let you know."

"Yeah, Chief Bowen said you were going on a vacation … to Ireland … check on your roots."

"That was the plan, but some family business has popped up and plans have changed."

*   *   *

36

Fairfax, Virginia

They were quiet, very quiet but the dog heard them, and Jorge quickly silenced him with a bullet. Bryan sat up in bed, "What was that?"

"I heard it too," said Jennifer. "Is the TV still on?"

"Yeah, must be," returned Bryan as he glanced at the alarm clock. "It's 1:34," he said as he stood and reached for his robe.

Suddenly, the bedroom door opened, and Jorge, a large dark figure holding a pistol with a long barrel, stood staring at Bryan and Jennifer, "Bryan Carson?" questioned the figure.

"Who the hell are you?" returned Bryan.

"I ask you again, are you Bryan Carson?" demanded Jorge.

"I am," said Bryan. "What the hell is this?"

Jorge stepped into the room and was followed by two others. They were all wearing dark, hooded outfits and face masks. "We have some questions for you," said Jorge with a slight Hispanic accent, "now sit down and listen." One of the others pointed his weapon at Jennifer as Jorge continued, "Answer the questions and nobody gets hurt, understand?"

Bryan was a hard man, a concrete contractor who had dealt with all sorts of characters in his line of work, but these men were in his home with weapons and the threat extended to his wife, "What the …?"

"Shut up," said Jorge, "I'll ask the questions and you answer them."

Bryan had no choice, and the threat was all too real, "Yeah, understood."

"Good. Your kid, Declan was killed a few weeks ago. An accident, right?"

"Yeah," said Bryan, "it was an accident."

"He got hit 'cause he was snortin' some coke and he stepped offa the curb and in front of a truck," said Jorge.

Jennifer was in tears, scared out of her mind, "It was an accident," she sobbed.

"So, you went after the dealer, right?" asked Jorge.

"Whatta ya mean, I went after the dealer?" asked Bryan.

"The dealer, a guy named Trammo," said Jorge, "you went after him and his buddy, right?"

"Trammo, they arrested someone by that name for a murder at the university," said Bryan. "Some campus drug dealer named Tyler."

"Yeah, then you went after Victor, right?"

"I didn't go after anyone," said Bryan. "I didn't even know their names until the police told me about them. And that Victor, wasn't he killed too?"

"Right," said Jorge, "so who did you send to screw with our operation?"

"I didn't send anyone. My son was killed, and we just buried him," said Bryan. "We didn't go after anyone; the police did all that crap."

"No, the cops didn't find Tyler and they didn't hit our man downtown and take our money," said Jorge. "You wanna tell me who did?"

"I don't know what you're talking about," said Bryan, "I didn't go after anyone."

One of Jorge's minions grabbed a fist full of Jennifer's hair, pulled her down to her knees, again pointed his weapon at her, and looked to Jorge, "Should I kill her, or just mess up that pretty face?"

Bryan was beginning to panic and yelled, "We didn't do anything, what can I say or do?"

The minion then hit Jennifer across her face with the back of his hand and she screamed.

Bryan started toward him, and Jorge shot Bryan in his leg, "You're starting to piss me off, Bryan. We're asking simple questions and need simple answers."

Bryan screamed, fell to the floor and grabbed his leg. The bleeding began to soak the carpet and Jorge said to one of his thugs, "Tie that thing off, Senor Hernandez don't want him dead, he wants him talkin'."

Bryan watched in pain as a belt was placed around his leg and pulled it tight. "Hold onto that," said Jorge, "Keep it tight."

The bleeding slowed and Jorge asked, "Who went after our people?"

Bryan was feeling dizzy and the pain in his leg increased, "I really don't know …"

"Let's get outta here," said Jorge. "These fools don't know shit." He put his gun close to Jennifer's head, "I find out different and I'll come back and fuckin kill both of you." He then hit Jennifer across her face, with the barrel of his pistol.

Jennifer screamed as she fell backward. Her face was bleeding and she moved to Bryan's side.

Jorge tossed a phone to her, "Make the call …"

As the three men left, Jennifer grabbed the phone and called 911.

*   *   *

She was holding a few folded paper towels against her cheek, still bleeding when the paramedics arrived and both she and Bryan were transported to the hospital. During his treatment and under the influence of some painkillers, Bryan muttered something about contacting someone to take care of "those damn thugs … and Hernandez."

"Someone like who?" asked Detective Dave Garrett.

Bryan drifted off saying, "Franklin, he'll get 'em … all."

Garrett knew Ian McLarry was related to Jessica O'Leary and he contacted him in Vaneksburg. "Ian, I thought you might be interested. Your cousins, the O'Leary's may be in for some trouble with the drug dealers that got Jessica and Declan Carson killed. A couple of thugs broke into the Carson's home, asked a bunch of questions and shot

Bryan. They were looking for information like, who was screwing with their drug operation. They didn't get what they wanted, so they're probably going to ask the same questions of the O'Learys."

"Tell me more," returned Ian.

"I've already sent a couple of units to the O'Leary's place."

"What about the Carsons, can they identify their attackers?" asked Ian.

"Bryan's not in any condition to talk right now, but he mumbled a few things that are interesting," said Garrett.

"Such as?" quizzed Ian.

"He mentioned a character by the name of Franklin. Something like Franklin will get them all," said Garrett. "He also used the name Hernandez … I think he was suggesting the thugs came from a drug outfit in Mexico run by a Ricardo Hernandez. I don't think he should mess with these people or their friends. They are very dangerous people."

"Thanks Dave, I'll come in, are you at Fairfax Hospital?"

"Yeah, I'm about to talk to Jennifer Carson, see what she knows."

Ian arrived at Fairfax Hospital, checked in at the nurse's station, learned Bryan was still in surgery and Jennifer was in a treatment room being taken care of. He noticed an EMT team restocking their supplies and asked if they were the ones who brought the Carsons in.

"Yeah, and we're in a hurry to get back out there so, all I can tell you is it was a little messy and it'll take a while to get the bullet and stitch him up," said one of the techs, "but everything's looking good. He'll be fine in a few weeks and the woman took a beating, got a nasty cut across her cheek, but she'll be okay … physically."

Ian went back to the nurses' station and was shown to the treatment room where a doctor had finished stitching Jennifer's face.

Dave Garrett was sitting off to one side, waiting for the doctor to say he could talk to her when Ian tapped on the door. Dave waved him in, and the doctor turned to both detectives, nodded and moved toward the door.

"Easy, gentlemen," said the doctor, "she's had a rough day already."

Jennifer was sitting on a treatment table, her face bruised, stitched and bandaged. Garrett started, "Jennifer, this is Detective Ian McLarry, he has a few questions for you."

"Jennifer, I checked in at the nurse's station and they said Bryan is doing better than expected. The procedures are going to take a little longer," said Ian. "Apparently the bullet didn't do too much damage and he'll be back to normal in a few weeks."

Jennifer's left eye was half closed, "They asked if we went after them after Declan died … why would they think that?" she wondered aloud.

"Somebody obviously did," said Ian, "and now they're down a few people and a pile of money short. These people don't care who they hurt. They don't want people interrupting their business and they want their money."

"Their money?" said Jennifer angrily.

"That's how they see it," said Ian. "Do you know anyone who may have stepped into this mess, for any reason? Bryan apparently mentioned someone named Franklin, do you know who he's talking about?"

"No," returned Jennifer, "Bryan works with some very rough people and has a lot of friends. Maybe one of them … but I wouldn't know. You'd have to ask him."

"He probably won't be in any condition to talk until much later today or tomorrow so, I'll come back in a few hours," said Ian. "Maybe then we can develop some possibilities."

Jennifer said, "What about the girl's family?"

"Yeah, we thought about that," said Garrett. "They're here in Fairfax County and we sent a separate team to check on them so, we'll be keeping an eye on both houses."

*   *   *

Vaneksburg, Virginia

Ian returned to Vaneksburg PD and was going over his notes concerning the arrest of Angela Bently when his phone rang, "Jake, what can I do for you?"

"More like what I can do for you, cousin," returned Jake.

"I'm all ears, whatcha got?"

"Jessica O'Leary and the Carson boy," said Jake, "both drug related deaths and someone stirred the pot. Whoever it was got a couple of drug dealers killed and made a bunch of money disappear."

"I know Jess was family, Jake. Are you telling me we caused this situation?" asked Ian. "Was that one of us who kicked the hornet's nest?"

"Ian, you know the deal … ask me no questions and I'll tell you no lies."

"So, you know," said Ian, "but you're not saying?"

"Again, no questions," said Jake, "and I have no control."

"You know the drug dealer's organization probably sent that crew to question the Carsons," said Ian, "and next they'll want to talk to the O'Learys. These bogeys are down a few people and out a pile of cash … people are cheap, so they've probably already replaced them and now they want their money."

"Yeah, and now you want to talk to Bryan Carson. I heard he mentioned your friend Franklin, and he used the name Hernandez," said Jake.

"Hernandez, that's a very common name. How did you …?"

"No questions …" returned Jake, "but know this, we have an interest in Hernandez and their relationship with Temple Enterprise."

"Bernie Temple," returned Ian, "he went missing in the middle of the Atlantic and I think Franklin was involved."

"Our interest initially was just the movement of new weapons out of Europe to somewhere here in the western hemisphere," said Jake. "We're sure Bernie was involved and now see the weapons and the drugs may be connected. We should talk."

*   *   *

37

Jessica O'Leary was with Declan Carson when he purchased the drugs that led to both of their deaths. They sat in her car outside her house after buying the two little bags of drugs and sampled the cocaine. When they went their separate ways for the night, each held a portion of their buy, intending to bring it all to a party that Friday evening. Both fell victim to curiosity and "just a little more". As Declan walked back toward his dormitory, he casually tried to snort the remaining powder off his fingers, and he stumbled in front of a speeding pickup truck.

Jessica had handled the cache of designer drugs, little squares of paper saturated with a drug. She was excited and giggling as she shuffled them about on the desk in her bedroom. She absorbed a bit from each square she touched sending her deeper into a blurry world from which she would never return.

Her little sister found her the following morning, dead.

The two bodies were brought together the following day in the medical examiner's office where the police learned of the connection and began their investigation.

*   *   *

Jorge and his companion thugs found Jessica's house and watched through the evening from a safe distance as the police arrived and left, leaving one officer to keep watch. It was past 5:00 in the morning when the three decided to make their move. They approached the house and Jorge gently tapped on the door saying he was the officer's relief. As the door opened, he shot the officer in his throat and all three rushed in the house.

Jessica's mother, Margaret, was up early and on her way to the kitchen for her first cup of coffee. She rounded the stairs just in time to see the officer shot and the thugs rush in. She screamed, startled the thugs and Jorge immediately shot her. Margaret's body tumbled down the last flight of stairs and the three intruders hesitated, then dispersed, two started up the stairs and encountered Tom O'Leary and his handgun. Tom fired twice striking Jorge in the neck and hitting Francisco in his shoulder. Jorge was four steps up the stairs and fell backward into Francisco, two steps behind him. Juan came around from the kitchen, saw Tom and fired once, striking him in the chest. Tom fell backward on the stairs and Juan helped Francisco out the front door.

The noise of gunfire woke the nearby neighbors who immediately called 911. Barbara O'Leary Jessica's little sister, saw her father bleeding on the stairs and her mother lying dead at the bottom of the stairs with a strange man's body at her feet. She screamed and ran to her cellphone and called 911.

Francisco and Juan made it to their car, got in and sped away, leaving Jorge dead in the O'Leary's house.

*   *   *

Bryan Carson had contacts in the dark world, including a mysterious assassin by the name of Franklin. Three years prior, he had a problem with another concrete contractor and considered an extreme option, assassination. Time passed, tempers cooled, and Bryan withdrew the contract. Franklin, the hired assassin, was paid for his consideration and Bryan held on to Franklin's contact information. Now, his son was dead, he and his wife had been threatened and his home invaded, he wanted the last two of the three-man crew of bandits, found and punished-severely, "This time I will not back down."

As he had done previously with Franklin, Bryan made a subtle change to his company's web page and waited. Two weeks passed before a package arrived with a throw away cellphone and a note. Bryan turned on the cellphone and dialed the number in the note.

*   *   *

Austin, Texas

Angela had settled into her apartment in Austin and her interest was piqued after several months of inactivity and the loss of one of her bank accounts. She answered Bryan's call through her voice changer, "This is Franklin, what is your situation?"

Bryan explained the series of events and said he had very little confidence in law enforcement resolving the situation. "They attacked our home and the O'Leary's home. Killed Margaret and left Tom for dead … I want them all dead," he stated, "that's why I contacted you."

"There were three of them?" she quizzed.

"Yeah, Tom O'Leary managed to kill one of them and wound another. The third bogey got away with the wounded guy and the cops are still trying to ID them. They're narrowing in on the name Hernandez."

"I can't guarantee anything, only that I will try to find them," Angela said into the voice changer, "and then we can determine if they should be handed over to the law or terminated."

Bryan agreed and was told he'd receive an invoice from a security company for a basic retainer. "Pay the retainer and I'll begin the process. Keep the phone but don't use it for anything. Only answer it when the display shows an 'F'. All other calls would be spam or robo calls. I will contact you again."

The first invoice was paid, and Angela started with several old contacts learning a small gang dealing in the area where Declan and Jess bought their drugs matched up with the name Hernandez. It was based in Tangenillo, Mexico and run by one Ricardo Hernandez. At the same time, Fairfax County Police had identified the killed intruder as Jorge Hernandez, the third son of Ricardo.

Angela realized the two targets were probably in Mexico and the different conditions there may require a long-range hit. She found a shooting range in the Austin area and began practicing with a rifle. She preferred an easily concealed handgun rather than a bulky rifle, but the weapon of choice would be based on conditions at the appropriate time.

Another two weeks passed, and Bryan wanted an update. He called Franklin, "The two who got away, have you identified them?"

"Still working on that, but getting close," returned Angela through the voice changer. "Don't call me again. I will contact you when there is something to report. Remember, the less we talk, the better. Be patient."

*   *   *

Tangenillo, Mexico

Tangenillo is a pleasant sea-side community and Angela booked a three-week vacation at a sea-side hotel under another alias, Maria Lopez. She drove to San Antonio, flew from there to Mexico City where she made contact with a dealer who could get her any weapon she wanted. A purchase of a small, .22 caliber pistol fit her immediate need and she caught another flight to Tangenillo. She registered at the beachfront hotel and began her search for the two miscreants.

Angela visited the local hospital and learned a man, recovering from a gunshot wound made weekly visits to the outpatient clinic to track his progress. Francisco was healing but still could not drive. His brother Juan drove him to and from the clinic and Angela was able to follow the brothers from the hospital to an apartment building.

As she was watching the apartment building, trying to plan her next move, she saw a chauffeured limo pull up and an elderly gentleman get out and walk into the building. She approached and walked into the main lobby where she heard the older man being referred to as Senor Hernandez and twenty minutes later, she noted his grim expression as he left the building.

The next day Ricardo's son's body was returned to Tangenillo from the Commonwealth of Virginia. A two-day vigil was arranged at the Hernandez Hacienda the coming weekend to mourn the loss of Jorge and see him buried. It began with Ricardo giving a short eulogy followed by several relatives adding a few words in praise of Jorge. The burial occurred on Saturday in a family plot on the Hacienda grounds and the celebration of his life ran through the day Sunday. Food, drink and music were the order of the day and Angela found easy access to the grounds. The vigil was well attended, the main gate was open to all the local residents and Angela, dressed in local garb with wig and sunglasses attended, pretended to offer a prayer and offered condolences to Ricardo and the Montoya brothers as well as a number of other family members.

In the course of her wandering the grounds, she heard several references to the three-man team that went to Northern Virginia and reinforced her suspicion that the Montoya brothers were Jorge's accomplices.

The brothers waited a few days after Jorge's vigil to approach Ricardo and ask to be allowed to go back to Virginia and avenge the killing of their cousin. Ricardo rejected their offer, "You are probably identified by the police in Virginia, I will make other arrangements."

The operation in Virginia was a disaster and Ricardo was angry with the brothers for leaving Jorge behind, but they were his nephews and he resisted punishing them. Realizing they had dodged a bullet they went out to a bar to celebrate their good fortune. Angela followed them and remained close as they drank and said too much. Knowing where they lived, Angela found a safe spot to observe them coming home late at night. They walked to and from the bar so they wouldn't get picked up for driving drunk. Their trek home took them through a remote grove of trees away from traffic in the wee hours of the morning.

A quiet night, rain was predicted with the probability of lightning and Angela hid herself in the grove and waited. She was armed with her .22 caliber pistol and dressed in a dark raincoat and wide-brimmed hat. As the brothers were staggering home, she readied herself and eased out of the shadows, making her way toward them, gauging her point of meeting them in a very dark stretch of the grove. They were talking and laughing as they passed Angela. She took two steps beyond them, turned and stayed a few steps behind. A flash of lightning and Angela raised her pistol, then as thunder rumbled, she fired twice, striking each of the brothers in the back of the head. She stepped closer, waited for another flash and shot each a second time then quickly ripped their wallets from their pockets and hurried back through the grove, taking the cash and scattering the other contents of their wallets.

The two thugs were down, and her contract was complete. She returned to her hotel, stopping once near a dumpster to dispose of their hat and coat. She still had three days left on her scheduled vacation and spent the next day on the beach, tanning and swimming in the surf.

The police found the bodies of the brothers in the morning and knew this was not a typical robbery. Ricardo wasn't sure if it was a revenge hit from the Americans or possibly someone trying to impress him by punishing the brothers for not protecting Jorge.

Either way, he was not pleased.

*   *   *

38

Tangenillo, Mexico

The warm air coming in off the Pacific was carried by a gentle breeze. The sky was free of all but an occasional small cloud and the surf casually lapped on the sandy beach as people began to populate both surf and sand. A pleasant day to walk in the shallow water or along the boardwalk or relax on the beach soaking up the sunshine.

Colin walked by at a distance, and Angela didn't notice. As the sun drifted higher in the sky, she shifted her hat and continued to read. He kept moving, walking closer to the water's edge about sixty feet away. He turned his head toward the water and raised his phone to his ear, "Yes, I'm sure, it's her." He continued down the beach several hundred feet, returned to the boardwalk and headed back to the hotel.

An hour later she walked into the restaurant's outdoor dining area, found a table and began looking at the menu as Colin approached, "May I join you?"

She smiled, "I don't believe we have met."

"True," returned Colin, "but I know who you are, Miss Lopez … or should I say Miss Bentley?"

She looked casually about the restaurant, "You have me at a disadvantage."

Colin smiled, "Not at all. We simply want to talk."

"We?" she quizzed.

"Yes, we," he replied, "for now, it's just me. My friend may join us tomorrow."

"Talk about … ?"

"You have a very specific skillset that we are interested in."

"Which is?"

"Terminations."

"I'm retired …"

"Yes, we know."

"Are you going to arrest me, take me back to … what, Virginia or California?"

"No, as I said, you have a skillset we could use. Your prior activities may merit you a life-long membership in the federal housing club or an unpleasant injection, but I'm not interested in your history, just what we can arrange going forward."

"I'm not sure I understand."

"Why are you here in Tangenillo?" asked Colin.

"A vacation."

"And a little business?" he quizzed.

"Business?" she returned with a question.

"Yes, the Montoya brothers," returned Colin. "Let's take a walk along the beach, get our toes wet."

"Are we being watched?"

"I'm not sure, but I think not," said Colin. He smiled, "An ounce of caution is better than a pound of cure."

They walked to the water's edge and started going north with the surf splashing around their ankles. Angela reached over and took Colin's hand, "We should look like a couple."

Twenty minutes up the beach and back, they talked about the tragic deaths of Declan and Jessica. "I'm related to Jess," said Colin, "and several other characters you may know."

Angela was confused, "Who may that be?"

"Ian and Lake McLarry, both detectives."

"Lake was killed … I had nothing to do with that," she replied as she pulled her hand away from Colin.

"Yes, we know. We also know you orchestrated the termination of the two who did kill Lake."

"I think this conversation is over," said Angela.

"For now, yes," said Colin, "but we will talk again."

"How did you find me?"

"Find? Angela, we have been casually watching your former employer, Temple Enterprise for a few years. Their suspected activity in the transport of various weapons has been one of our main interests over that time. Now we have a connection between Temple Enterprise and the Hernandez family here in Tangenillo."

"What does that have to do with me?" she asked.

"The Montoya brothers were with Jorge Hernandez in Fairfax, Virginia a few weeks ago," said Colin. "They killed Margaret O'Leary, wounded Tom O'Leary and assaulted the Carsons."

"And …?" quizzed Angela.

"And Bryan Carson put out a contract on the Montoyas which you filled," said Colin. "We have been in the process of collecting as much evidence as we can when people started dying. A few of Temple's low-level workers then Lake, and the list goes on. I'm sure you know all the names including Bernie Temple. You were even on the list … as Myra Wallace."

"So, you know everything since London?" asked Angela.

"No, not everything. First, we had to find you, Myra Wallace and Franklin, also you. Actually, Ian found you. That happened after Dave Saunders was killed in California and Bernie Temple went missing in the middle of the Atlantic. When Ian found the candy wrapper on board the Lanita, it pointed more directly at you as a closer connection to the mysterious Franklin."

"Candy wrapper?"

"A protein bar wrapper, tied in a knot and found in a trash can," said Colin, "along with a cork and foil from a wine bottle."

Angela thought for a moment, then remembered being on board the Lanita when Bernie was dropping off a few diving belts. She nodded knowingly, "How careless of me."

"Ian had put most of the pieces together, found you somewhere out in Virginia and arrested you." He paused, "Then you quietly slipped away. Very nicely done, by the way."

"For all the good that did me," said Angela, "and you followed me here?"

"No, we knew Bryan Carson contacted this Franklin character and he wanted the two bogeys who got away, found and killed. We also have been here watching a small criminal organization, run by Ricardo Hernandez. As it turns out, Ricardo deals in weapons and drugs. The drugs that killed my cousin and her friend were supplied by this little drug cartel. So, when we heard Franklin may also be coming here to address the Montoya brothers, we kept an extra eye open, and we found you."

"So, what exactly do you want of me?"

"Let's save that for tomorrow when the three of us can meet."

"Three?"

"Maybe four, we're still evaluating our options. Your activity here has stirred the pot and we want to make the most of it. Franklin was not a priority for us, but, we have had to make some personnel adjustments and these recent events have placed you in the mix."

Angela thought for a moment and asked, "Exactly how does that affect me?"

"We'll continue this tomorrow so, don't wander away," said Colin.

Angela puzzled, "You're not arresting me?"

"Nope, we don't have jurisdiction here in Mexico … and … I'm not a cop."

Angela looked puzzled, "FBI?"

"Nope, we'll talk tomorrow," said Colin.

"What's your name? McLarry?"

"No, O'Leary," returned Colin, "more tomorrow."

"Who do you work for?" she puzzled.

"Ask me no questions and I'll tell you no lies," returned Colin with a wink and a smile.

*   *   *

39

Langley, Virginia

Jake Brennan walked into a small conference room and was joined by three other men including the CIA Director, Barry Albright.

"Jake, you know everybody?" asked Albright.

Jake extended his hand to the one of the unknown men, "Jake Brennan."

The man returned the gesture, "Paul Danvers, FBI."

The other unknown man offered his hand, "Craig Robins, ATF."

Albright began, "Jake, this is a quiet room so, tell us what we have."

Jake looked at the group and passed out a printed summary, "One of our field teams has been hurt with the injuries to two people. Sarah Baines and Mark Davis will not be returning to full field operations any time soon, if ever so, I've been looking at replacements and have a recommendation and a suggestion. First is Ian McLarry. Background: USMC, Pittsburgh PD, currently Detective with Vaneksburg, VA PD and he's been on our radar for some time."

Robins quickly leafed through the handout, "Age?"

"Thirty-nine," returned Jake,

"Married?" quizzed Albright.

"No," replied Jake.

General Cunninghan cleared his throat and asked, "Is he physically fit? I mean thirty-nine is getting up there."

Jake grinned, "General, he was just run through several of the courses at Quantico, didn't knock anybody's socks off but he made some of the younger trainees look bad. So, yes General, he's good."

"No argument there Jake, but isn't he more of a foot soldier?" asked Cunningham.

"We all know he's a bit rough around the edges but he's smarter than the average grizzly and physical is exactly what we need in so many cases," returned Jake.

Director Albright closed his copy of the file and asked, "How well do you know him?"

"He's my cousin," returned Jake. "Actually, my third cousin. Known him all his life."

"Do we have any concurring recommendations?" asked Albright.

Jake nodded, "Yes sir, several, including both the team leader, Colin O'Leary, and Lucas McLarry."

"Gunnery Sergeant Lucas McLarry," said Cunningham with an approving nod.

"You know him, sir?" quizzed Jake. "He retired a few years ago."

"I'm aware," returned Cunningham. "Lucas is a good man. I'd trust his judgment."

Albright slowly scanned the file and said, "This McLarry and O'Leary look like a pair of linebackers, I wouldn't want to be on their bad side." He put the file down, "Okay, let's hear about the other one."

"Second is Angela Bentley," said Jake.

Robins looked surprised, "The one that escaped our custody a few weeks ago?"

"I know the Bentley woman walked out of his jail," said Whitley, "so, how do you think McLarry will react to her also joining us?"

"Ian may lack a little polish, true enough but he's a damn good cop," said Jake, "and he's also reasonable. He may well see the advantage of working with her without our pushing her case. Let's back up a little. Our initial interest was the firearms being moved to someone in our half of the world. We now have information indicating the Hernandez group out of Tangenillo, Mexico is our target. This is the same group that has been supplying drugs in the U.S. including the DC area. Drugs that killed two college-aged kids here in the DC metro area a few months ago."

Albright chimed in, "We stepped into the shadows and allowed someone to look into the drug ring that supplied those two kids, and he kicked a hornet's nest. He dropped a few hints, pointing the finger at a few of the organization's people as he walked off with a pile of their money and they, in turn, tried to tie up a few loose ends, killing a couple of their own people. Now they want their lost pile of cash."

Jake leaned forward, "So, like it or not, we're in this mess up to our earlobes. The drug kingpin in Mexico sent a three-man crew to find out who took their money and wound up wounding the Carsons and Tom O'Leary ... and killing Margaret O'Leary."

Albright added, "They lost one of their people, Tom O'Leary managed to kill one of the attackers, wound a second one, and one of them shot him."

"They still don't have the answers they wanted," said Jake, "and we're sure they'll be back to mount another attack, soon."

"Now let's add to the mix an assassin by the name of Franklin," said Albright. "This guy has been on the fringe of our investigation into Temple Enterprise for several years. He has managed to stay in the shadows, no real name, no photos, no fingerprints and no DNA."

"That is until now," added Jake. "Ian McLarry arrested Angela Bentley, AKA Myra Wallace, former administrative assistant at Temple Enterprise. She is either a close associate of Franklin—or, as Ian has theorized, she is Franklin."

"And we believe this 'Franklin' has been contracted by Bryan Carson to nail the two who got away," said Albright.

Jake continued, "When the Vaneksburg cop finally arrested Bentley and let it be known he believed she was either working directly for this Franklin character or might actually be Franklin, our interest in her was aroused. When she did her Houdini act and walked away from the VPD and the USMS, we were even more interested."

"Then word came down that Bryan Carson had a connection with this Franklin", said Jake, "and was going to hire him to take out the two remaining rats from the drug dealing group who threatened him and his wife."

Albright added, "We're sure they're the same crew that attacked the O'Learys, killed Margaret and left Tom O'Leary for dead. Now we have a strong probable connection to the group in Tangenillo run by Ricardo Hernandez."

"Our man, Colin O'Leary is in Tangenillo," said Jake. "He's been gathering intel on this cartel and learned two low levelers had been killed in an apparent robbery. The two who we suspected had been in Virginia a few months ago when the Carsons and O'Learys were attacked."

"Carson's hit list," said Albright.

"So it seems," said Jake, "we sent Colin a brief on the Bentley woman, he looked around and was able to verify she was also there."

"Where does all this leave us?" asked Danvers.

Jake leaned forward, "We're developing a clandestine plan that may take advantage of the hits on the two losers from the Hernandez clan. It will involve several additional selected hits on members of two other families possibly coming together forming a small cartel. We may make it seem as though these families are killing each other, each trying to put their own people at the top of the heap."

"You're talking about starting a war," said Danvers.

"Yes, a small, limited internal war,' returned Jake. "We'll be taking out the key players as high up as we can in each family and leave the finger pointing to the other families."

"Like one of the families is trying to take over everything?" asked Albright.

"Yes, only we're controlling the action and getting rid of the key players," said Jake.

"Can we keep the civilian population out of harm's way?" asked Cunningham.

"That's the idea," said Jake. "The activity will take place in or near the several plantations controlled by the three prime families. The two killed the other day were in the city, but the next hit will occur away from the population."

Whitley tapped the table, "Okay, now how do you want to proceed?"

"First we get McLarry on board," said Jake. "I'll have a conversation with him tonight at dinner."

"Where and when will you two meet?" asked Whitley.

"Probably at the Auld Shebeen in Fairfax, around seven," said Jake, "and the door's wide open if you'd like to join us."

"I'll get there around eight, after you've had your talk."

"Are you sure this new team can work on the dark side?" asked Whitley.

"I'm sure they can," said Jake, "the Bentley woman has been there for several years, and Ian has dealt with these types even longer. We'll talk and he will either buy in 100% or we go down the road to someone else."

"That works," returned Jake. As he was leaving the meeting, he punched in a few numbers on his cellphone. "Ian, dinner tonight around seven?"

*   *   *

40

Fairfax, Virginia

Fairfax City, located in the center of Fairfax County, is about six square miles of narrow streets, older buildings and limited parking. The Auld Shebeen is an Irish Pub in the heart of the city and a regular meeting place for Ian, Jake, friends and other members of the family. Ian pulled into a parking garage a block away from the restaurant and ran into Jake as he exited his car. "What's the occasion?"

"Let's have a pint first and then we talk," said Jake as they crossed the street and walked up the steps of the Auld Shebeen.

They found a table in the library by the fireplace and ordered a round of drinks and dinner. Discussion was initially about baseball and the upcoming season. Then as dinner arrived, Jake said, "You've been running through the paces at Quantico with Colin for more than a week, how are you holding up?"

"I'm not a teenager anymore but I think I did fairly well," replied Ian as he pretended to rub an aching shoulder.

"At one time you were interested in our Special Ops group?"

Ian looked a little tentative, "Yeah, still am."

"Are you willing to work in the shadows, our projects often involve non-sanctioned activities," said Jake. "We work quietly and frequently off the books. Some of our work requires a harder approach than our colleagues in other agencies can't—or won't—touch."

"I was aware of some of your activities while stationed in Afghanistan. I know what you do or can do and I'm ready to join in."

"We lost two people in an Op a few weeks ago and the door is open," offered Jake.

"Two?" quizzed Ian.

"You've met them both, Mark Davis and Sarah Baines," said Jake.

Ian looked startled, "Are they …?"

"They'll both be on light duty for a while," said Jake, "possibly forever."

"And the others, Colin …?"

"They're good and busy prepping for another op," returned Jake.

"Who else are you looking at?" asked Ian.

"Well, there's the problem. A problem that you may be able to settle."

"You're losing me."

"One step at a time, if you're in, then we talk about the other new team member."

As the two were finishing dinner, Whitley walked into the Library, "Gentlemen, may I join you?"

Jake tapped a chair and Whitley sat down, "Ian, you remember Director Whitley?"

"I do," said Ian and he shook his hand.

"Are you interested in our proposal?" asked Whitley.

Ian looked at both men, then said, "Who's buying dinner?"

Jake grinned, "Are you in?"

Ian nodded, "Yes."

"Then dinners on me," said Whitley. "Welcome to our team."

Ian sat up straight, "Now, what's the problem that I have to settle?"

"Sarah's replacement," said Whitley, "she didn't follow the traditional path to this position and is still a large question."

Ian looked puzzled, "Do I know this person?"

"Probably better than anyone else," said Jake. "Ian, we're in a unique position. The op we're planning will hopefully take down or at least reduce the threat of an organization operating out of Tangenillo, Mexico. Three crime-oriented families are coming together to form an organization that could be very difficult to deal with. They're into drugs, arms, and human trafficking. Each comprised of a nasty bunch of individuals that would be much worse as a single cartel. Now, they've already been kicked in the shorts with the elimination of a few low-level players by a couple of their victims both here in Virginia and in Tangenillo."

"Are you referring to the Tom O'Leary shooting Jorge Hernandez here in Virginia?"

"Yes, and Bryan Carson's contracting two more killings in Mexico."

"I know the name 'Franklin' was mentioned," said Ian.

"Yes, we believe he may have taken out the two in Tangenillo," said Jake.

Ian nodded and said, "You mean 'her'?"

"Yes, if it is a 'her'," returned Whitley, "she's in Tangenillo and we've already made contact with her."

"We have every reason to believe she took out two low-level cartel soldiers," said Whitley.

Ian nodded, "Took out …" he looked slightly puzzled, "you are talking about Angela Bentley."

"Very good, Ian," said Jake. "This is in some measure based on your analysis that she is the assassin, Franklin."

"And you want her on our team?" asked Ian.

"She's there, she's already taken out two cartel members and Colin has opened the door with her," said Whitley. "I want you in Tangenillo ASAP and help to make this arrangement work."

"That's a lot of effort over a few murders," said Ian.

"Our interest is and has been the movement of firearms from Europe to an organization in Mexico," said Whitley, "weapons they may be planning on using both here in the US and in building a more dangerous cartel in Tangenillo."

"Now," added Jake, "with the drug connection and a possible human trafficking element added to the mix, we have a three-pronged operation to deal with. She could well fit in perfectly with our objectives."

"She's a murderer," said Ian.

"True enough, Ian," said Whitley, "but understand we have objectives that require drastic measures and that includes having someone with her talents. Someone who can work on the dark side, completely off the books."

"It's not like we haven't used operatives from the dark side before," said Jake.

Whitley lowered his head as he watched Ian and nodded in agreement with Jake.

*   *   *

41

"We'll need a cover and a base of operations," said Whitley, "Tangenillo has a nice harbor so, I can send the Miriam C down."

"The Miriam C?" questioned Ian.

"It's a yacht," returned Jake. "Renamed after some bigshot's wife after it was seized a few years ago. She's a 86-foot Hatteras, fitted out with the main salon as a meeting room. Sleeps eight including the captain and a two-man crew."

"A government yacht? Won't that draw attention?" asked Ian.

"Yeah," said Whitley. "We're a government agency on a special assignment developing a series of sensitivity seminar presentations for various other agencies and to do this we had to get away from the center of activity."

"But the boat?" quizzed Ian.

"Yep," said Whitley, "it may not be cheaper than renting eight rooms at a hotel, but it includes a large meeting room that we control and can keep secure. And as I said, the boat was seized in a take-down of a criminal enterprise in Oregon. It's our boat until they auction it off … and there's no connection to any Mexican organization."

"And we're all government employees?" puzzled Ian.

"Or consultants," said Whitley, "so, you and Jake get down there ASAP and firm this arrangement up with the team and we'll be along in a few days."

"We?" quizzed Ian. "Do you have a crew?"

"We have one with Fallon and Carone. Mark Davis is a registered captain and he's well enough to travel. He'll of course, be unable to lift and carry and will have to stay with the boat, so, no running around."

"Mark is good," said Jake, "and we don't want any surplus people. We have a complete team, and we'll handle all the onboard chores."

"Got it," said Whitley. "The main salon is a working space. It's rigged with three wide screens, and we'll load some bogus corporate training stuff in case you have visitors. You've seen a number of the training videos we have. We'll do a checkout, fuel up and stock the fridge. How many will be sleeping on board?"

Angela and Colin both have hotel rooms booked," said Jake, "so, the rest of us will be on board after the boat has arrived."

"Okay, I ran a quick calc," said Whitley, "if we leave San Diego tomorrow morning, we could be there in three days."

*   *   *

Tangenillo, Mexico

Jake and Ian landed at Tangenillo airport at 11:34 a.m. and were met by Colin. He looked his cousin up and down and said, "Ian, all that running around at Quantico was directed at this little adventure. Are you ready for it?"

"I'm good," returned Ian, "still a little fuzzy on the details of this plan you and your team have been hatching."

"He means, in part, why are we tying a knot with the Bentley woman?" said Jake. "By the way, Mark is driving the Miriam C down with Whitley."

"Mark doesn't like missing out on anything," said Colin, "somehow, I knew he'd find a way to be involved. We'll see about this whole deal after we talk," said Colin.

Ian shook his head, "So, where is our new-found friend, Angela?"

Colin checked his watch, "Probably about halfway through her morning swim."

"So, you don't have her in chains, behind bars, locked up with four or five guys watching her?" quizzed Ian with a grin.

"No, actually she seems to be fully on board with us," returned Colin.

"Well, we had her in jail, behind bars, with locks, keys, guns and guards … and she walked away. No guns, no threats, she just walked away. So, you think she'll still be there when we arrive?"

"We'll know soon enough," said Colin, as he stopped the car in front of the hotel entrance. He handed the keys to a valet and said, "You guys check in and I'll meet you out back in the restaurant."

Twenty minutes later the three were seated at a table in a small cabana away from other diners and Ian asked, "So, where is she?"

Colin scanned the immediate area and looked toward the water, "I think that's her coming now."

Ian looked toward the ocean and saw a tall, tanned, athletic brunette in a navy-blue swimsuit walking toward the hotel. She looked at the cabana and paused as she seemed to recognize the man sitting left of Colin. She smiled, then continued toward the three men and stopped at their table. She looked at Colin, "Am I invited?"

"You are," returned Colin.

She extended her hand toward Jake, "I don't believe we've met, I'm Angela Bentley."

Jake shook her hand and said, "Pleasure, I'm Jake Brennan."

She looked at Ian, "Detective, you're looking well."

Ian stood and as he shook her hand he said, "I have a pair of hand cuffs in my suitcase. I don't suppose you'd like to accompany me back to Washington for a conversation with the ATF."

"I'd really rather not," she replied, "now, if you gentlemen will excuse me, I'd like to dry off and get dressed." She looked at Colin, gently touched his shoulder and said, "Please order me an iced tea, unsweetened and I'll be right back."

Colin nodded and watched her as she walked away, "An interesting young lady."

"Interesting? Colin she's an assassin," said Ian.

"Yep," returned Colin with a smile, "an attractive assassin."

Jake rolled his eyes, "Come on you guys, business first."

Angela returned within twenty minutes wearing a wide-brimmed hat paired with a sundress. She turned heads as she walked across the patio to their cabana and took the seat between Colin and Ian and said, "Have you ordered lunch?"

Ian handed her a menu. She placed it on the table, folded her hands over it and said, "You gentlemen wanted to talk. I'm not here by choice and you have the floor so, why are we here?"

Colin looked at Jake, "You're drivin' the bus, Jake."

Jake leaned in and began, "Angela, we are a special operations group who sometimes operate outside the parameters that constrict our fellow federal agencies. We act in ways others cannot and we're here in Tangenillo because we're targeting three small organized crime families that may be trying to come together as one cartel. They're individually into drugs, human trafficking and firearms and as separate entities they are limited in a number of activities. Together they would have greater buying power, greater distribution capability and more access to people of influence in their target areas. Our objective is to keep them separate and cripple them as much as possible."

"You want to kill them all?" quizzed Angela.

"No, our objective is to discourage the union of these three groups by killing off the top players from each group," said Jake, "and leave the leftovers thinking it was one of the other groups responsible and thus not trusting each other."

"If we can terminate several key players from each group," began Jake, "and there will be some collateral damage … as in some of their soldiers, we will have crippled the 'cartel'."

"Maybe enough to keep it from forming up for a few years," added Jake, "then we will have saved a lot of lives both here and in the USA."

The group sat quietly for a moment, allowing it all to sink in and Jake added, "Remember, the prime objective is to prevent the union of the three families and keep them scattered. We're fully aware another group will try to form up eventually, but the longer we keep them small and not trusting each other, the easier it is to deal with them stateside." He paused as a waiter came to the cabana delivering another round of drinks, then he continued, "A secondary objective is the recovery or destruction of the arms being shipped to this group by Temple

Enterprise." He looked at Angela and continued, "You're here to close a contract with Bryan Carson to avenge the attack on his home by the people who come from one of those families. Specifically, the family that made drugs available to his son, Declan, and invaded the Carson's home in Virginia threatening Bryan and his wife. They were the same group that entered the O'Leary's home killing Margaret and seriously wounding Tom O'Leary. You took out the last two from the Virginia attacks so, now our paths cross in a most advantageous way." He looked to Colin, "Please relay the condition of your team."

"My team normally consists of five people including me," said Colin. "On our last op we took two casualties, Mark and Sarah. They're both recovering from injuries and may not be returning to full field operations any time soon." He looked at Ian, "Ian is Mark's replacement and you," as he turned toward Angela, "have been proposed for Sarah's slot."

Angela looked at each man and said, "I am not a soldier. You want me to wear combat boots and crawl through barbed wire and mud puddles?" She looked at Colin, "Really?"

"No barbed wire and mud puddles, Angela," said Jake. "Your assets are your intelligence, ability to act under pressure and of course you know how to pull a trigger."

"Do I look like a soldier," argued Angela.

"She's never met Sarah," said Colin. "Sarah looks more like a fashion model than a soldier."

"I'm retired," said Angela.

"You're here," noted Jake.

"Your people confiscated my bank account," she complained.

"You had more than one," said Jake.

"It was one of the larger accounts," she returned.

Jake held up his hand, "Listen, you have operated around the world under different identities, avoided detection for years and we're sure you have already terminated two of the low-level thugs employed by this little developing cartel. Most likely the two that got away from the O'Leary's house several weeks ago."

"You're assuming …," said Angela.

"As far as anyone here in Tangenillo knows, you're a tourist, staying at a beachfront hotel soaking up the sunshine and enjoying the surf," said Jake. "If you're working with us, your cover will be that you're a part-time actress, you'll be narrating and presenting the seminar information. You've come down a few weeks early to enjoy the surf … you're a swimmer, you do a mile or two every day and nobody knows or cares who you are, to them, you're just a tourist who likes to swim." He paused, looked around the table, "For this operation at this time you're the best game in town. You work with us here and now and maybe we owe you a favor."

Angela leaned back in her chair, picked up the menu and said, "Like what kind of favor?"

"We can't give you a 'get outta jail free card' but we don't have to announce your presence or detain you when this operation is complete," said Jake.

"Do the locals know it was her on those two hits?" asked Ian.

"Our source says they don't have a clue," said Colin. "The local police have it down as a robbery."

"You have someone inside the Federales office?" quizzed Angela as she looked at each of the men at the table.

Jake smiled, "Ask me no questions and I'll tell you no lies."

Angela looked at Colin, "So, I've heard."

Jake smiled and nodded, Colin shrugged, and Ian looked straight at her and said, "Trust."

She sighed and opened her menu, "Lunch first."

The others glanced at the menu and Jake flagged a waiter. They placed their orders and as the waiter walked away, Jake quietly said, "This only works one way … we have to trust each other completely. We will not lie to you and if I say you're free to walk away, that's exactly what I mean. Any one of us could blow the cover for the rest of us and get us all killed—so, we don't make promises lightly."

Angela leaned back in her chair and looked at the surf then turned to Colin, "Ask them to put my salad in a box, I'm going for a walk." She stood and walked away toward the beach.

The three men watched her take off her sandals and carry them as she walked farther away south on the beach. Her head slightly bowed, she paused, watched the water covering her toes and the waves gently splashing against her ankles. Then, slowly, she began to walk again and was soon out of sight.

Ian stood, looked down the beach and said, "Is she coming back?"

All three laughed at the thought, then strained to see if she was still in sight. An hour later she came out of the hotel again and rejoined the table.

"Conditions," she said. "First, nothing I say or do will ever be used against me in any court of law."

Jake nodded, "Done."

"Second, I will be included in all planning sessions."

"Agreed."

"Third, if I say no to an idea, it's a no for me and I walk away."

"Any objection to an idea is always up for discussion," said Colin, "and we all have to agree for any plan to work."

"Finally, when this operation is over, I blend into the background and none of you come after me or help anyone else pursue me."

Jake nodded in approval and both Colin and Ian did the same.

She looked at Ian, "Promise?"

Ian thought for a second or two and said, "Promise."

"Okay, you agree with what I have said, and you know what I mean. No funny lawyer tricks and we may have an accord."

Colin reached over and shook her hand. She smiled and looked at Jake. He shook her hand and she looked at Ian.

"Okay, I don't get to arrest you," he said with a smile. "It's going to be interesting working with you," and he shook her hand.

*   *   *

42

Tangenillo, Mexico

Sitting in the cabana, away from prying eyes and ears, the group of four began a discussion that needed a secured channel opened to Langley. Then as Dennis Whitley and three others joined the meeting online, Whitley opened the conversation, "Jake, I assume the young lady at your table is our Miss Bentley."

Angela responded, "I am, and I don't know any of you."

Whitley held up his hand and said, "Dennis Whitley."

Mark, Ben, Sarah and Nick followed suit, each with a raised hand.

Whitley continued, "Okay folks, time to get serious. Standard op procedure: define objectives, gather intel, begin surveillance, refine objectives, develop plans, refine and solidify plans." He looked at the screen, "And remember, we're dark on this one. Any questions or comments."

"We have some very basic info on a number of the potential targets," said Jake. "This list of targets needs to be shortened to one we can address in an intelligent timeframe."

"Nick Fallon and Ben Carone will be joining the team in Tangenillo," said Whitley. "Davis and I will be staying with the boat primarily, I don't want to leave it unattended, and Mark is still on the mend."

"What about you, Sarah," asked Colin, "how are you doing?"

"Coming along," she replied. "I'm stuck in this wheelchair for a few more weeks and wouldn't be any good down there, so I'll be here, doing whatever I can to support y'all."

"She's tough," said Whitley, as he put his hand on her shoulder, "and she wants to be involved so, she'll be our contact here in Langley."

Mark spoke up, "My arm is still in a sling so, I'm not able to lift and carry but I have a license and I can drive the boat."

Whitley looked at each member of the team in Langley then he nodded as Sarah held out her arm with her hand in a fist. Mark put his fist next to hers as did Whitley, Nick and Ben. Colin held out his arm toward the screen and Jake did the same. Their heads turned to Ian and Angela. Both smiled, raised their hands toward the screen and the virtual fist bump was completed.

"Okay folks time to get serious," said Whitley. "If the Hernandez led organization is importing weapons through Temple Enterprise, we should be seeing some activity soon and a shipment of whoopie powder should soon be trying to make its way north."

"So, let's list as many of the players on the other side as we can," said Jake.

"We'll have several candidates from each of the three families," said Colin, "and each will have to be evaluated."

Starting with the Hernandez group," said Whitley, "Ricardo Hernandez leads the list."

"The two that were hit recently were low-level soldiers, they may not have made the final cut. We want to emphasize the current and possible future leaders."

"I don't know where Jorge Hernandez would have fit in the mix," said Jake, "but he's gone along with the Montoya brothers."

"There is a character by the name of Manny Hernandez," said Colin. "He seems to be the main security guy in the Hernandez organization and the two bodyguards that stick to Ricardo also work for him."

"Do these two watchdogs have names?" asked Ian.

"Yeah," returned Colin, "Fernando Cortez and Julio Martinez. Both mean, as in a junkyard dog sense."

"Okay let's give the list some thought," said Whitley, "and we'll gather again when we arrive in Tangenillo to put as many names on the table as we can. These characters will each be labeled as primary, maybe, and no problem."

The team both at Langley and in Tangenillo set about collecting names and assigning a value to each. Every person who seemed to have a connection to any of the three families was subject to scrutiny.

*   *   *

Aboard the Miriam C. In Tangenillo Harbor

After clearing through the harbor master, the yacht was assigned a mooring buoy and the team assembled on board. "Let's give them each a ranking," said Colin, "like Ricardo being a primary and the Montoya brothers as collateral or no problem."

"I have Ricardo's main security man as a primary," said Jake, "and the rest of the security force as maybes. These lower-level characters could be problematic when the lead begins to fly so, the more of them we neutralize, the better."

"You may have to take them all out before getting to the primary targets," said Angela.

"So, what do we know for sure," posed Whitley.

"On Sundays, Ricardo often goes to the marketplace in town, mingles with the crowd and passes out candy and trinkets to little kids," said Colin. "He's a cautious S.O.B., and doesn't go into anywhere without a protection detail."

"Some of them get there before him, mix with the crowd and are ready to come to his aid if needed. The rest arrive with Ricardo and join the crowd."

"Hitting anybody in the plaza is a non-starter," said Jake "so, we concentrate on nailing them after they leave the plaza and are returning to the ranch."

Angela offered, "I did notice the Sunday parade of security people coming back from town after the old man had made one of those visits to the plaza. They don't use the main entrance. They use a dirt road about a quarter mile down the main road that leads to the bunk house."

The security detail staggers the vehicles, leaving the bunk house about two minutes apart. As the first two security vehicles pass the main entrance, Ricardo's limo joins the parade. The last one or two follow Ricardo.

"Okay, if we assume four vehicles and four men in each," said Colin. "That's sixteen people we would have to deal with."

"The last time I saw the vehicles returning to the ranch, there were only two in one car, three in another and I'm not sure about the last two cars," said Angela.

She sat quietly for a minute before speaking again, "Gentlemen, please, if you're going to take out that many people, I would suggest you keep them in those small manageable groups and have several shooters ready to address each group as they move up the dirt road. Short of having fifteen to twenty-five people ready to act at once, we should perhaps plan several hits on those groups. Say four or five groups each with up to four targets and these must be done quietly and close together."

Ian looked slightly surprised, "Have you done one of these types of hits before?"

Angela looked at Ian, "No, but such scenarios have been considered and partially planned."

"You've planned multiple hit operations?" quizzed Colin.

Angela sat up straight in her chair, "One never knows when a client may call and make such a request. Best to be prepared."

"Just what kind of client would want that kind of hit?" asked Ian.

Angela paused, "Most likely the government."

"You've worked for the government?" posed Ian.

Angela leaned back in her chair, "Ask me no questions …"

Whitley quickly shuffled some papers and abruptly said, "Let's continue."

"So, if you have been involved in the planning of these kinds of hits," said Ian, "what would you recommend we do here?"

The room went silent, and Whitley looked at Angela, "Go ahead, tell them."

Everybody looked at Whitley and he repeated, "Ask me no questions …" He looked at Angela and nodded.

*   *   *

"Continue as you have already begun," said Angela, "we have defined a situation wherein there are several manageable targets and a location somewhere out of sight, the dirt road leading to the bunkhouse."

Colin added, "Going into town, Ricardo's limo follows the first two or three vehicles with his security people as they pass the main entrance to the hacienda, and he is usually followed by at least one other vehicle. The first car or two drop off several security guys at the market before Ricardo arrives. They wander about the plaza keeping an eye open for any trouble before Ricardo arrives."

"The old man waits 'til he is given clearance from his security guys," said Angela, "and walks around to the various merchants talking to people and buying little things."

Whitley brought up a video of the hacienda taken by Nick's drone. "When he returns to his hacienda in the late afternoon, he is usually visited by the heads of the other two families. They sit around the patio next to the pool and talk about the business of drugs and guns."

"Getting back to the security detail," Angela continued, "we should allow that a shooter may be able to take out two targets at the most," she paused, "as the first vic falls, the others will begin to react, move, maybe run. You have very little time to resight and find your second target. So, we assume multiple targets and we thus need multiple shooters … we must be coordinated, all fire at the same time …from different locations."

"What weapons do we have?" asked Ian.

Whitley walked over to a panel in the wall, pushed a button and slid the panel to one side revealing a small armory with rifles and handguns, "You'll find the ammunition on the lower shelves."

Colin said, "Pick out whatever works for you and enough ammunition to get comfortable with the weapons and we'll take a ride out to the desert for a little target practice."

*   *   *

Back on board the Miriam C, the team sat around a conference table discussing the plan of attack.

"The road leading to the bunkhouse is about a half-mile from the main house," said Colin. "The Sunday visit to town may provide an easy approach. As the security guys return from town, they leave in several vehicles a few minutes apart. If we meet them on that dirt road and take them out, one vehicle at a time …"

"You'll have to be quick," said Whitley, "we can not allow anyone to get away."

Angela added, "I would further suggest we make them disappear. That is, we dispose of the bodies immediately, leaving their actual whereabouts and condition unknown."

Colin nodded and added, "We won't be able to make them disappear forever, but long enough to finish our task. Hit them, hide them and get outta town before they're found."

"Shallow graves or feed 'em to the fish?" asked Ian.

"Or drop them in a well," added Colin.

Ian nodded, "I have an idea … it will leave the world wondering who did what …"

Angela looked at Ian, "You going to tell us?"

"You'll see," said Ian, "when the job is done."

"I know this all sounds cold and murderous … and it is," said Whitley. "Very cold—inhumane even. But these people are guilty of far worse and if not stopped they will do much more harm here as well as in our country."

Ian added, "And we want the weapons, right?"

Colin and Whitley both answered, "Yes, or see them destroyed."

*   *   *

43

Tangenillo, Mexico

"Surveillance," said Whitley as he brought up a series of aerial photos. "Our internet friends have fairly detailed photos of most of the world and the area around the Hernandez ranch as you see on the large screen, is no exception. We can zoom in on the several roads and structures in the area of the hacienda and gain limited info on the various structures."

Colin stepped closer to the screen and pointed at a faint line through a wooded area, "This is the road Ricardo's security team uses to go to and from the marketplace on Sundays." He traced the road with his finger and noted it was over a half-mile from the main road to a bunkhouse near the main house, "Some of the security team stays in this building, others only when they're on duty. There's always at least five awake and alert, walking the grounds wherever Ricardo is."

"This road from the main road to the bunkhouse," said Colin as he touched the map, "has three bends in it that we may use. If the first returning vehicle is stopped at the last of the bends, we'd have a few minutes to prep for the next vehicle at the second last bend."

"So, they don't travel as a tight convoy to and from the marketplace?" quizzed Ian.

"No," returned Colin, "at least two of them go before and position themselves in the square before he arrives with his two main bodyguards. Then Ricardo arrives and is followed by one or two more vehicles."

"So, he has only one or two cars watching over him on the road to and from the marketplace," stated Ian.

"Yeah, but on open road with a lot of traffic, not a lot of places to make a hit without involving a lot of civilians."

What about the security team, are they all away from the hacienda when he's on the road?"

"No, there's a small team of at least eight men at the Hacienda at all times," said Whitley, "and Ricardo often has the heads of the other two families join him on Sunday evenings an hour or two after he returns from the market."

"So, an additional two or three from each family?" quizzed Ian.

"Maybe as many as three or four people with each guest."

"Colin, as you said the security team uses this dirt access road going to and returning from the marketplace," said Ian. "It's in the woods, far enough away from the main buildings … could we take them out first and then move to the hacienda and deal with the rest of them?"

"Yes," said Colin. "I think we should hit them in the woods on their return trip."

"I would," returned Angela. "We have a few minutes between each arrival. Maybe enough time to move them off the road and hide them in the bushes."

Colin looked at the aerial photo again and said, "This narrow side road looks good to me, and the small structures scattered around could be used to hide them."

"I can fly a drone from the boat and get some better detail," said Nick, "but the thing has a limited range. The closer to the target area and the higher we are, the better info we'll gather."

"Sounds like a little night-time recon," said Ian.

"Okay," said Whitley. "You two study these photos, figure out where you want to be and which areas you want to survey."

The side road used by Ricardo's security team was seen on the aerial photos. The smaller branch roads or paths were not easily seen, and the condition of these dirt roads was not obvious. Nick noted a small hill rising up less than a quarter mile off the Hernandez property. "That will make a good base. The drone has a two-mile range, but I'd like to keep it under a mile and a half."

"That looks like it covers most of the side road," said Ian.

"Tonight is as good as we could have hoped," said Nick, "practically no wind, clear sky, no rain, and decent moonlight."

Ian gave a thumbs up and said, "We go around midnight and we're back here by two-thirty."

*   *   *

The sky was clear, a few drifting clouds that didn't block the light from the moon and Colin drove out the main paved road north and east. No other traffic in either direction was encountered and as they passed the dirt side road used by the security team, he slowed then pulled over to the shoulder, turned to Nick, touched his commlink and said, "Pick up here will be 1 – 1. 1 — 2 is a quarter mile down the road and the 2s are across the road."

"Got it," returned Nick. "Give us about an hour, then five-minute pauses. I'll use a three-burst when we're ready."

Ian and Nick dressed in all black, Ian with a side arm, Ka-Bar, and flashlight, Nick with a drone in his backpack. The two exited the car, moved cautiously across an open field, and melted into the brush, sixty feet from the road. Colin watched them disappear, checked the immediate area, pulled out onto the road, and continued driving north.

Ian led the way through the heavily wooded countryside and up the small hill the team had identified in the aerial photos. "You pick your spot," said Ian, "and I'll recon the rest of the area."

"A little higher would be good and I'll have a decent view of the sky over the target."

The two men climbed another hundred feet up the hillside and Nick said, "Here, this little clearing is as good as it'll get." He sat on the ground and opened his backpack. The drone was small, fully assembled, only about two feet square to the four propeller centers and another six inches for each prop. The drone was silent and showed no lights. Nick activated the propellers and looked at Ian, "I'm good, stay low and check-in every ten to fifteen minutes."

"Good luck, see ya," said Ian and he was gone. Nick launched the drone and flew it around the immediate area to check the controls and the camera. He tried to spot Ian, but he was well hidden in the brush. He flew the drone over the target area, pausing periodically to focus on several interesting subjects. After forty minutes of flight, Nick returned the drone to his location and landed it. He tapped his commlink four times and within a few seconds the signal was returned. Three minutes later, Ian appeared out of the brush and together the two men made their way back to the main roadside where they had been dropped off. They stayed low and lay quiet for a few minutes as Ian tapped his commlink three times, then sent the 1 − 1 signal and waited.

A return signal of three taps said Colin was within seconds of their location. The two men moved closer to the road, Colin arrived, and the two men leapt into the car, "Smooth as silk," said Nick as they drove back to the Marina and the Miriam C.

"Any problems?" quizzed Whitley as he looked at his watch, "Two-twenty-five a.m., good timing."

"No problems," returned Nick. "I got some decent footage that I'd like to clean up a bit and we can all have a look."

The images were much better than the aerial photos downloaded from the internet and showed much greater detail including a few smaller buildings and lesser-used paths.

*   *   *

"There," said Nick, "there's an old hay wagon with large wooden wheels parked near a small shed. Thing must be a hundred years old, meant to be pulled by a horse, but I wonder if it could be moved by hand out to the dirt access road."

'I'm sure the two of us could make that happen," returned Ian. "We pull this wagon out to the side road and block the first vehicle. Take out the two or three characters on board, move their car to the little shack, out of sight of the road, and do the same to each vehicle as it comes along."

"We'd need about five or six minutes to clear the first carload, like three guys, and get back in position for the next group," said Colin. "How much delay between carloads?"

Angela said, "Gentlemen, maximum three passengers or four in a vehicle?"

"Assuming the worst case, I'd say four," returned Colin, "so, we have three shooters, Ben, Angela and me. Let's make backseat right side, Angela's prime target, left side, secondary. I'll take the driver as primary and backseat left as secondary. Ben, you take shotgun as primary and scan the others."

The two nodded, and he continued, "Ian and Jake you move the bodies, throw them back in the vehicle and take them directly to the shed, hide their car, and be ready for the next batch. Angela, Ben, and I have to stay in place and be ready for the next bunch."

"Are we good?" asked Whitley.

All nodded and Colin added, "Then we take the cars back into town and leave them parked near to where they were during the day."

"And the bodies?" said Ian, "Do we just leave them lying about?"

"We'll put them in the shed," said Colin, "we only need to have them missing for a few days."

"Okay," said Whitley, "let's figure next Sunday if the weather cooperates. Until then we'll review the process and look for flaws."

Colin stood and said, "Time out, I suggest we go into town, have dinner, and enjoy the local music."

"Sounds good to me," returned Ian.

Angela grinned and said, "Am I invited?"

"We're a team, Angela," said Colin, "of course you're invited. You've been here longer than us, so where would you suggest we go?"

"I followed the Montoya brothers to a place a few blocks from the hotel, Eduardo's, I believe, and stayed for dinner a few weeks ago. The food was good and evening show looked promising," said Angela, "but the crowd was getting rougher as the evening progressed and I decided to leave."

Ian looked at Colin, "Are you game?"

"As ever was," replied Colin.

Jake nodded in favor as Whitley said he and Mark would remain with the boat. Nick and Ben wanted to try a different night spot.

Colin and Angela arrived at the restaurant and asked for a table for four. Ian stood outside answering his phone and Jake parked the car.

"A twenty-minute wait," said the hostess, "you may wait in the bar if you'd like."

Colin said he had to use the restroom and Angela went to the bar area, found a seat at the bar and ordered a glass of wine. A man approached her and said something in Spanish. She understood enough to know what he was suggesting, and she answered in English, "No Spanish," she smiled and added, "I'm waiting for my friends."

The man nodded, "Sure, I speak English." He moved closer to Angela and put his hand on her thigh.

She lost her smile and said, "No thank you," as she pushed his hand away.

He raised his voice as two more men came closer and stood behind the man, "You don't say 'no' to me senorita, I am Pablo and if I want to touch you, then I will touch you."

He reached for her upper arm, and Angela again said "No!" As he was about to use both hands, a deep voice behind him calmly said, "I believe the lady said 'no'.

All three men turned to face Ian and he looked at Angela, then back at Pablo, "She did say 'no'?"

Angela looked concerned as the other two men moved closer behind Pablo looking more threatening. Pablo looked at Ian and said, "I am here before you—you leave now, and we won't hurt you."

Ian again looked at Angela, tilted his head, turned toward the three men and said, "The lady said 'no', now walk away and there will be no trouble."

Pablo angrily thrusted his hand at Ian's chest and said, "You don't know who you are messing with." He raised his hand again as if he intended to strike Ian and another voice behind them said, "I wouldn't do that, Pablo." Colin stepped closer and Pablo backed off. He and his friends looked at the two hulking gringos and as Jake approached, they turned away and went to the far end of the bar.

"Well, that was exciting," said Angela, "may I buy you each a drink?"

After dinner, Ian stood and excused himself. He walked down the corridor toward the restrooms and the three men from the bar discretely followed him. As Ian was coming out of the restroom, Pablo waved a pistol in Ian's face, "Now you don't have your friends to help you. Senor Ricardo said you might be a problem—I have my friends, and I think we take a ride on the elevator to the roof."

Ian was forced into the elevator with the three men. Jose, the bigger of the three stood behind Ian and to the right. Pedro, the smaller and better dressed of the three, stood behind and to the left, brushing lint or dust off his sleeve. Ian stood in the middle of the elevator, looking at Pablo as he stepped into the elevator cab.

"You be a nice boy and maybe we don't hurt you," said Pablo.

Ian noticed Pablo was the only one displaying a gun in his hand. The other two didn't show any weapons, though he was sure they were both armed. He scanned the small elevator, noticing the size of the cab and mentally counting possible movements as he did, *one ... two ... three ... four ... five ... no ... four ...* Then as the doors closed and Pablo reached to press the up button, Ian massed a ball of spit in his mouth, turned to his left and pretended to sneeze and cough, spraying his saliva all over Pedro, causing him to react as if a flight of pigeons had divebombed him. Ian then swung his right hand in a balled fist back to his right striking Jose as hard as he could in mid-chest leaving him gasping for air and immediately brought his right hand forward, smashing his open palm into the back of Pablo's neck, driving his head into the stainless-steel elevator door.

Pedro was starting to pull a gun from under his shirt and Ian grabbed him with his left hand and yanked him across the cab into Pablo's slumping figure as he slid down the door to the floor. A hard punch to Jose knocked him out and a similar hit to Pedro turned his lights out as well.

All three bogies were down and blood from both Pablo and Pedro was smeared on the door and floor. Ian wasn't sure but Pedro did not seem to be breathing and Jose was turning blue. He took out his phone and called Colin, "We have a little problem ... I'm taking the elevator to the roof." He pushed the 'Up' button.

Colin hurried to the stairs to the roof and Jake paid the tab then he and Angela went to the lobby to wait.

Colin reached the roof level, looked at the elevator and saw the three men. He opened the door to the roof and found Ian looking around behind the air conditioning units and exhaust fans. He looked at Ian, "What happened?"

Ian pointed at the three men lying on the elevator floor, "They wanted to go up and I didn't."

"Up?" quizzed Colin.

"Yeah, that one waved a gun in my face and said Senor Ricardo thought we may be a problem. So, he wanted to come up here, maybe to give me a flying lesson … I didn't ask and I don't like trying to fly on my own."

"So, you killed them?"

"Yeah, well shit happens. I didn't set out to kill them and I wasn't about to go slow and easy so, now what do we do?"

Colin looked at the three bodies, "Are they all dead?" He checked each for a pulse and said, "Yep."

"We could leave them up here," said Colin, "but someone will find them probably sooner than later."

"Yeah," returned Ian, "and there's blood on the elevator door and floor."

"Okay, clean up time," said Colin. He took out his phone and called Jake. A brief conversation and Jake called Nick and Ben.

"Help is on the way," said Colin. "Let's figure out how to get these guys outta here," as he looked over the parapet and down eight floors to the alley behind the restaurant, "I see a dumpster." He called Jake again and said to Ian, "Let's get these three guys over here to the alley side."

Nick and Ben arrived after the restaurant had closed and the alley was deserted and quiet. They backed their truck in the alley near the dumpster and signaled Colin, "Ready when you are."

Colin checked each one, removing wallets, watches and other jewelry, then Pablo was the first to unceremoniously go over the edge and into the dumpster, landing with a '*whump*' in the bags of trash. Ben immediately opened a body bag and the two men dragged Pablo out of the garbage and bagged him. Pedro and Jose followed suit and all three were bagged and in the truck. Nick and Ben drove out to a quiet deserted beach, south of the city where Mark brought the Miriam C's launch up to the shallows.

The crescent moon was almost at a new moon stage and the water was calm. Mark had brought some chain from the Miriam C and the three men gathered a few rocks as more ballast.

Ben opened the body bags and distributed the rocks then added a little sand to each, closed the bags and wrapped them in chain, "Ready when you are," he said.

The bodies were transferred to the launch and Ben stayed with Mark as they pushed the launch off the sandy bottom and out to deeper waters.

"We'll go about a mile out and we can off load these guys," said Mark, "then it's back to the Miriam and we're done for the night."

Nick took the truck and headed back north toward the marina as Mark steered the launch out to deeper water.

At the restaurant, Ian and Colin had one more task, "Now, to clean the elevator," said Ian.

"Your mess, you get the floor, I'll do the door," said Colin.

*   *   *

44

"No time to waste, we have to move soon," said Whitley as he joined the group for breakfast. "We don't know when these three characters you took swimming will be missed and we can't take any unnecessary chances."

Ian said, "It's Sunday, time for our favorite friend Ricardo to make his visit to the marketplace. Are we ready to move on the hacienda?"

"I don't see that we have much choice," said Colin, "those three will soon be missed and Ricardo's people will then be on a higher alert status. We should hit them before they even suspect something is about to happen."

"I think a little recon is in order," returned Angela, "I believe you took the wallets, watches and keys off the three in the water."

"I did," said Colin, "gonna spread their crap around town to mislead any search party."

"Hold off on that and give me one of their wallets and keys," said Angela. She looked at Colin, "Let's take a ride out to the Hacienda and return this poor man's wallet." She opened the wallet, "Pedro's wallet."

Colin grinned, "And his keys?"

"Nope, we save them for a second visit. We want to count noses inside and may need a second visit."

Colin looked at Whitley, "What kind of weapons do we have?"

"Pistols and long guns," returned Whitley. "Behind that door."

Colin opened the door and stepped inside a small closet. He selected a nine mm pistol and a rifle with a suppressor. "I'd like to test these, maybe a little target practice."

Ian also took a 9mm and a rifle with suppressor as did each member of the team. What type of ammunition do we have," he asked.

"Choices," said Colin. "Since all the activity on the dirt access road will be close in, we can use the sub sonic rounds and suppressors. That should keep the noise down to an acceptable level. Then after we have taken out the security returning from town, we can fully engage the remainder of the bogies at the hacienda. r

"It's about a half mile to the hacienda, we have to hurry to get in position for that assault," said Ian.

We'll drive as close as we can and move in on foot through the woods. As soon as everyone is in place, we start taking out the outer guards."

"Nick, another flight over the grounds to get a better idea of how many bogies we'll have to deal with," added Colin.

Ian said, "I'll go with Nick and his drone and count the outside crew."

"Okay," said Jake. "let's assume there will be ten to twelve bogies in town. In the past, they travel in three or four vehicles, leaving a few minutes apart and Ricardo travels after at least two of them, giving a few of his men time to get into the square and spread out. The driver drops off a few guys in the square and goes to park the car or truck then walks back to the square.

They use a separate road from the Hacienda to the highway and Ricardo leaves through the main gate.

"After we hit the security teams coming back from town, they'll be down about a dozen bogies. That may still leave a bunch for us to deal with when we attack the hacienda."

"We estimate maybe twelve more soldier types around the grounds," said Whitley, "and then the three or four real targets."

*   *   *

45

Early Sunday afternoon, Whitley positioned himself with a good view of the marketplace and as Ricardo was dropped off at a restaurant, he called Colin on his cell, "Time in, I'll let you know when the first quarter starts." He clicked off.

Colin drove up to the main gate of Ricardo's hacienda, Angela smiled at the guard and in her high school Spanish said, "Excuse me, I found this wallet and a man at the gas station said I should look here for ..." She paused and opened the wallet, "for Pedro." She showed the wallet to the guard and said, "Did I come to the right place?"

The guard eased his grip on his sidearm, looked at Colin, and back at Angela, "Maybe he is at the house, you can go up and ask."

Angela smiled, said "Thank you," and nodded to Colin. The road took them to a second gate and then to the main house passing through a lightly wooded area. The land opened to two fenced pastures, one on either side of the access road. There were four horses in the right pasture, grazing on the thick green grass and one horse on the left side. Angela looked at the horse on the left and said, "Stallion."

"I'd guess," said Colin, "apparently Senor Hernandez raced that horse in the past, now he is used for breeding."

The road passed another checkpoint with two more armed men but no gate and two more fenced areas. The one on the right had several show jumps arranged in a course and three plastic barrels moved off to the side. The other was a round configuration and a man was urging a horse to casually lope around the perimeter at the end of a tether.

One of the guards lowered a cellphone from his left ear and waved them through. Colin nodded and as they passed the guards, he smiled and said, "Thank you."

They stopped in front of a large three-story house, "Nice digs," said Colin, "start counting noses. I got two at the first gate and two more at the second." He looked around the immediate area and added, "This guy holding a cellphone, coming out the door is number five."

Angela nodded, opened her door, and got out of the car as the man approached and said, "You are here for Pedro, he's not here and he doesn't answer his phone. I am told you found his wallet, show it to me."

Angela said, "It was in a parking lot at a restaurant where we were taken for dinner last night and there seems to be a lot of money."

"What restaurant?"

Angela looked confused, "I don't know, it began with an 'E', Ed something."

"Maybe it was Eduardo's," said a second man coming out of the house. He took the wallet and checked the identification and the money. I will make sure this gets back to Pedro."

"That's very kind of you,' said Angela. She turned toward the car then looked back at the man with the wallet and said, "Could I please use the restroom before we leave? I'm pregnant and I drank too much coffee this morning."

He seemed to soften and said, "Of course and led both Colin and Angela into the house. He pointed to a hallway and said, "Down that hall to the right."

Angela hurried as if she needed to. The man looked at Colin and said in English, "Your wife is a very attractive woman."

Colin nodded, "I agree, but we're not married … yet."

Angela didn't take long and as she returned to the main room, she looked at Colin, "We should be going."

She looked at the man and said, "You have a beautiful house."

This is the home of Ricardo Hernandez, I am Rafael Sanchez, one of his employees."

"Well, it is a beautiful house," said Angela. She looked at Colin, "We should be going, my uncle will be wondering where we are."

They left the hacienda and as they were driving out to the highway, Colin put a finger up to his mouth and said, "We'll be back at the hotel shortly and you can lay down if you'd like." He pointed at the underside of the dashboard and touched his ear.

Angela understood and said, "I think I'll be okay, it's a short drive, but still, I'm going to lean back and close my eyes."

As they were driving, Rafael and two other men were listening to their conversation."

At the hotel, Colin left the bug in place and gave the car keys to a valet.

*   *   *

The group assembled aboard the Miriam C to finalize the plan for the day. Whitley would take up position at the marketplace, watch for Ricardo, and track his activity. He'd also spot the security teams and keep Jake informed. Mark would remain with the Miriam C and be ready to leave the harbor when all the team members were back aboard. Whitley had already notified the harbormaster's office that they may be leaving sometime in the next two or three days.

Nick would take up a position where he could watch traffic coming from town to both entrances to the Hernandez ranch and keep the strike team apprised. Jake would take the rest of the crew to the access road the security people would use and set the scene for an ambush.

Whitley left for the marketplace, dropping off Nick on the way, Colin and Angela took the rental car they used earlier and talked about going to the beach for the afternoon, and Jake took Ian and Ben to the access road. Their conversation was listened to by three of the people at the Hacienda .

As soon as Whitley arrived at the marketplace, he found a table in a shady spot where he could observe most of the plaza. He ordered a tall iced tea, sent Jake a quick note, opened a book and waited. Mark stayed with the boat and Colin led the rest of the team to the dirt access road used by the security teams.

"We counted fifteen men at the hacienda," said Colin.

"I saw two at the main gate," said Angela, "two more at the second gate, the two that came out to meet us and once inside, four in the great room and two more down the hallway toward the bathroom."

"I agree," said Colin, "plus three more that I noticed in a game room. That makes fifteen."

Whitley reported Ricardo was still in town, wandering about the various vendors with his head of security, Manny Hernandez. He paused at several vendors, buying a little something here and there. After an hour of browsing the market and greeting people, he nodded to Manny, it was time to leave and his driver was called, "Antonio, we are ready to leave. Bring the car."

As Ricardo got into his car, Whitley saw Manny nod to one of the security teams. A light blue pickup truck stopped at the edge of the vendor area and the first of the security teams began to leave. Whitley tapped a number on his cellphone, "First quarter beginning, three in a blue pickup truck. This one may go to the barrio with Ricardo, so the next one to leave may be the first to get to you." As they were waiting Colin got another call, "Second quarter getting ready to start," reported Whitley, "this one is a red sedan. Two on board."

*   *   *

Ricardo's limo drove to the southern barrio where he waved at the people and stopped every few minutes to pass out little gifts to the children. The blue pickup with the three men on board was close behind.

As Ricardo was handing out candy and trinkets to the children, his other three security teams were leaving the market and heading back to the hacienda.

Whitley tapped his phone as a brown Honda with three men on board left the market area and again as a grey Chevy Blazer was picking up the last three of the security people. When all four vehicles were gone, he headed back to the Miriam C where he and Mark would prep the boat for departure, back to San Diego.

At the access road, Jake and Ian wrestled the hay wagon out to block the road while Colin, Angela, Ben and Nick found hiding positions along the road the security men would use.

"We may have the blue pickup with three on board or a red sedan with two. Be ready for either. I'll take the driver, Ben you have shotgun, Angela, take the right-side backseat and Nick you have the left side."

They all faded into the brush and waited, the drive from town would take about ten more minutes.

The red sedan was the first to come around the curve on the access road. As it appeared, Colin took careful aim and waited for the car to stop. The driver cussed at the hay wagon and stepped out of the car, Colin fired, striking him high in his chest just below the throat. He fell forward and Ben shot the second man immediately, striking him next to his right ear.

Ian and Jake quickly moved the two bodies back into the car and then Jake got behind the wheel and steered it down the path toward the shed. Colin signaled everyone else back into position as Ian and Jake moved the bodies into the shed.

"One down, three to go," said Jake.

Ian moved the bodies to sitting positions at opposite sides of the shed, then the two men hurried back to their hiding places and waited to hear about the next car.

"Took that buggy about fifteen minutes to get here," said Colin, "so, the next one should be here in less than five from now." He checked his rifle and his phone buzzed again, "Third car, a brown Honda just left, three on board. These last two are going to be close."

The next vehicle to come down the road was the brown Honda. A stifled curse in Spanish and the driver came to a stop. All three men got out of the car and as they were about to move the hay wagon, Colin shot the driver through his head and put another slug in his chest. Nick and Ben fired suppressed shots into their targets and Angela moved her sights from body to body but there was no movement. Ian and Jake suddenly appeared out of their hiding places and began to move the cars and bodies to the shed where Ian arranged them around the perimeter.

The third vehicle to appear was the grey Chevy Blazer. It appeared suddenly and again the driver came to a stop, cursing and yelling at his two passengers to get out and move the wagon. Their feet hit the ground and Colin fired, taking the driver down and immediately the other two men were cut down.

As Jake and Ian were moving the Blazer and bodies another vehicle was heard coming down the access road. "Everybody down," yelled Colin as the sound of the approaching vehicle increased.

The blue pickup came around a bend and the driver saw the Chevy Blazer, the wagon and three bodies on the ground. Confused, he reacted by slamming the car into reverse. Colin fired immediately and Angela took out the passenger in the back. The truck veered off the dirt road and the left rear tire slid into a shallow ditch. The passenger in the front seat had a pistol which proved useless against three rifle shots to his chest and head before he could push a button on his phone.

The last three bodies were loaded into the pickup and taken to the shed. The bodies were arranged with the others around the inside perimeter of the shed and each man's gun was fired from his position into the other eleven people. The guns were left with the bodies and four bottles of tequila found in the vehicles were opened, poured on each of the men and the bottles smashed in the middle of the shed.

"Looks like they had a drunken gunfight … no winners," said Colin.

"We'll leave the vehicles outside the shed and let them be found like this. It may take all week to figure out what happened here," said Jake.

Whitley called Colin, "Ricardo should be back at the hacienda by now. Time for phase two."

*   *   *

46

Tangenillo, Mexico, Hernandez Hacienda

A black Toyota Tacoma with four men turned off the highway onto the paved entrance to the Hernandez Hacienda. The road stopped at a closed gate that was guarded by two men each with a holstered sidearm.

"We are here with Carlos Perez," said the driver, "Senor Hernandez is expecting us."

One of the guards checked his cellphone, nodded to his partner and waved the truck through. Less than a minute passed and a second vehicle, a black Audi limousine with tinted windows approached. The driver opened his window and said, "Senor Carlos Perez to see Senor Hernandez."

The guard looked in the window and allowed the limo to enter the grounds. As the limo approached the second checkpoint, the pickup was parking in front of the main house.

Within the next twenty minutes Diego Rodriguez arrived in similar fashion, preceded by a vehicle with four of his guards then his limo with his security lead.

As Rodriguez was being let through the second gate, Ricardo with his head of security, Manny was greeting the first of his guests at the main entrance to the house.

*   *   *

Colin and Nick were well-hidden in the wooded area near the main entrance. Colin placed a call to Whitley, "Looks like the three big fish are in the barrel and the gunshots from the access road had not been heard. All is quiet at the main gate."

"We can start the music," said Colin.

The team set up at four points around the two main entrance check points and sighted the guards, "All targets sighted, give me green when ready."

Nick was first, "Green." Then Ben, "Green." Ian, "Green."

Colin said, "All green … on my count … three, two, one, zip."

Four suppressed shots fired at "zip" and four guards fell. The team rushed to their secondary positions in the wooded area around the house. The three prime targets were on a patio behind the main house each with a bodyguard, drinking ice-tea and engaged in conversation.

The strike team sighted the four guards stationed on the roof and spotted a secondary target walking the grounds. Again, Colin spoke into his mic, "Roof … one is green," Nick spoke, "two is green," Ben added, "three is green." And Ian finished the set, "four is green."

Again, Colin counted down—"Three, two, one, zip."

The four roof guards were taken out and the team resighted to the guards walking the grounds.

Angela was watching the four prime targets and as the ground-based guards were fired upon, she had Ricardo in her sights and fired. He fell but she was not sure he was dead. She resighted on Manny as he moved quickly toward the house and fired again. Manny fell but again she was not sure he was dead.

The other team members all had prime targets and had opened fire. Two of the walking guards were sighted and shot. Three other guards began to return fire and Nick was hit in his chest near his neck. Angela, nearest to Nick, said "Give me cover," into her commlink and moved quickly to Nick. He was still breathing as she rolled him onto her back and began to crawl toward the cover of a grove of trees.

"I think I hit the prime target," she said into her comm, "but he may still be mobile."

Ian returned, "I have eyes on him. I'll check it out," he said as he sighted Ricardo. He placed the crosshairs on Ricardo's head and fired, "Done."

The other prime targets were dispatched, and the team made a quick check of the grounds looking for any evidence of a shipment from Temple Enterprise.

Colin made his way to Angela and Nick, "Let's get him to a vehicle," he said as Angela tried to stop the bleeding from Nick's wound. She looked at Colin and slowly shook her head and Colin called for a vehicle, "Let's get him to the boat ASAP."

Ian rushed into the house, looked around, and saw a large desk in a room off the main room. He quickly rummaged through the papers on the desk and checked the drawers. In the third drawer, he found a few papers with a Temple Enterprise heading, gathered them and several other papers in a shopping bag, and ran to the main door. Ben was waiting for him with a vehicle, and they hurried to catch the other team members as they left the property heading for the Miriam C.

*   *   *

At the Tangenillo Harbor

Mark piloted the Miriam's launch to the dock and steadied it as Colin and Angela carried Nick aboard. He was still breathing as they placed him in the conference area to address his wounds. He had lost a great deal of blood and continued to fade, in spite of the team's efforts.

The rest of the team arrived, the launch was secured, and the Miriam raised anchor and moved toward the Harbor Master's checkpoint. Whitley stood on the bridge, lifted the phone, and told the harbormaster they would be back in a few hours unless the fishing was too good … then it may be morning when they returned.

The Miriam C cleared the harbor and moved to open waters, turning north as soon as possible and increased speed.

*   *   *

Meeting in the conference room, the papers Ian had taken were spread out and Angela began to organize them by dates and started to read. "I can't make out everything but the little I have been able to read indicates our friend Ricardo has received two shipments and is waiting on a third sometime this week."

"Where are the first two?" wondered Colin.

Angela perused the rest of the papers and found a note from a warehouse in the city, "If I had to guess, this looks very good as a place the shipments could be stored."

Ian looked at Colin, "A little night raid?"

"You and me, old man," returned Colin.

"Neither one of you two can read a word of Spanish," said Angela, "I'm in."

"We're talkin' mud puddles and barbed wire," said Colin.

"I said, I'm in," said Angela gruffly.

"But you said …" started Colin.

"Do it right or don't do it at all," she said firmly, "and we aren't done yet."

*   *   *

Mark slowed the Miriam C and the team members cast a few fishing lines as Angela, Colin and Ian took the launch ashore. They were close to the Hernandez Hacienda and Ian said, "Let's take one of the cars from the shed, drive into town, to the warehouse."

Jake said, "You have very little time to get this done and Nick has no time to hang around waiting for you three."

Colin responded, "Get him to SD as soon as you can, we'll figure out a route home when our work is done."

Jake looked at Colin, nodded and turned to Angela. She didn't hesitate, "Get him home," and she grabbed a homing beacon as she followed Ian.

Ian was already moving toward the launch, leaving no doubt where he stood. The three lowered the launch, climbed aboard, and headed for shore. The cars were exactly where they left them and they arrived at the warehouse after sunset, no one was around. No guards, no night watch … nobody.

The door was an easy pick and the three found the two crates marked with Temple's logo. Angela checked the paperwork and said, "Machine parts … is this what you expected?"

Ian found a crowbar and pried open one of the crates, "Machine parts, eh? He said these machines fire bullets."

"It's too much to lift and carry away," said Angela and burning them may bring down the entire warehouse and some of the neighbors."

Colin scrounged around and found a welding torch.

Ian found a workbench with a vice and various tools.

"Colin, you heat 'em up," said Ian, "and I'll bend 'em out of shape."

Angela had a hammer, "I'll have a crack at 'em as well."

They spent the next three hours heating, bending and smashing the weapons and as the sun was about to rise, they made their way back to the launch and headed out to sea.

"What's the plan?" asked Ian.

"Well, I hope they send someone to pick us up," returned Colin.

Angela raised her phone to her ear and answered a buzz, "We're a few miles out and heading north, Director. How's our man doing?"

"Nick is gone," said Whitley. "A damn good man and no one will ever know what he did for the world these last few years."

The Miriam C was still sailing north and would reach San Diego a few days later, "We'll turn this bucket around and pick you all up."

"Copy that," said Angela, "We'll turn on our beacon."

*   *   *

After Nick was buried, the team met at Langley with Whitley and Jake, "Let's take a few days and we'll get back on those last three shipments. We now know how they crossed the pond and then crossed the country. We have eyes on those routes, and we'll know soon enough when we have to move forward.

Whitley entered the room, "Angela, we have to talk."

"You promised," she said.

"Yes, we did," returned Jake, "and we meant it. You're free to go any time you choose, but … we want to make you an offer."

"Mud puddles and barbed wire?" wondered Angela aloud.

"No more than necessary," said Whitley.

"You have proven yourself an ideal team member and we'd like you to stay on. You can remain as Angela Bentley, live somewhere close by and be ready for … whatever."

"And my time is mine … no arrests from past?"

"All charges will be dropped, you're clean as a whistle," said Whitley.

Colin touched her shoulder and said, "The team is going to meet for dinner at the Auld Shebeen.

She sat quietly for a second and Colin held out his hand. She looked at him, smiled and took it in her own.

* * *

www.ingramcontent.com/pod-product-compliance
Lightning Source LLC
Chambersburg PA
CBHW020648120726
47906CB00001B/179